TIME FOR ROBO

A NOVEL

TIME
FOR
ROBO

PETER PLAGENS

Black Heron Press
Post Office Box 95676
Seattle, Washington 98145
http://mav.net.blackheron

Cover art and design by
David Walters

Published by
Black Heron Press
Post Office Box 95676
Seattle, WA 98145
http://mav.net/blackheron

ISBN 0-930773-54-3

To Laurie

"It's a fairly embarrassing situation to admit
that we can't find 90 percent of the universe's total mass.'

— *Bruce H. Margon, astrophysicist*

It's only words,
And words are all I have
To take your heart away.
— *the Bee Gees*

If it weren't for time, everything would happen at once.

— *old saying*

Contents

Part I

ALAS, THROUGH THE LOOKING GLASS

Ghostest Story

XXXXXXXXXXXXXXXXXXXXXXXXXXXXXXXXXXXXXX
XXXXXXXXXXXXXXXXXXXXXXXXXXXXXXXXXXXXXX
XXXXXXXXXXXXXXXXXXXXXXXXXXXXXXXXXXXXXX
XXXXXXXXXXXXXXXXXXXXXXXXXXXXXXXXXXXXXX
XXXXXXXXXXXXXXXXXXXXXXXXXXXXXXXXXXXXXX
XXXXXXXXXXXXXXXXXXXXXXXXXXXXXXXXXXXXXX
XXXXXXXXXXXXXXXXXXXXXXXXXXXXXXXXXXXXXX
XXXXXXXXXXXXXXXXXXXXXXXXXXXXXXXXXXXXXX
XXXXXXXXXXXXXXXXXXXXXXXXXXXXXXXXXXXXXX
XXXXXXXXXXXXXXXXXXXXXXXXXXXXXXXXXXXXXX
XXXXXXXXXXXXXXXXXXXXXXXXXXXXXXXXXXXXXX
XXXXXXXXXXXXXXXXXXXXXXXXXXXXXXXXXXXXXX
XXXXXXXXXXXXXXXXXXXXXXXXXXXXXXXXXXXXXX
XXXXXXXXXXXXXXXXXXXXXXXXXXXXXXXXXXXXXX
XXXXXXXXXXXXXXXXXXXXXXXXXXXXXXXXXXXXXX
XXXXXXXXXXXXXXXXXXXXXXXXXXXXXXXXXXXXXX
XXXXXXXXXXXXXXXXXXXXXXXXXXXXXXXXXXXXXX
XXXXXXXXXXXXXXXXXXXXXXXXXXXXXXXXXXXXXX
XXXXXXXXXXXXXXXXXXXXXXXXXXXXXXXXXXXXXX
 XXXXXXXXXXXXXXXXXXXXXXXXXXXXXXXXXXXXXxx
xxxxxxxxxxxxxxxxxxxxxxxxxxxxxxxxxxaaaaaaaaxxxxxxaaaa
xxxgggxxxxxxxxxxxxxxxxxxxxxrrrrrrrrxxxxaaaiitrplfxxxithltdbna
xxitsqqqpbmslig ighs xithsxi Wtlivx Iptsloo xBGzzieFtopor
towbk GLAZ WOCKS bQfortslmuch gufiesch liffortz
kalbambag quack luftforce force forces fierce farts fine flash
fing fingaling gexame game fame fan foul face case race
space case vase verse reverse quack. terse, curse, worse. worst,
reverse, nurse. Worst curse reverse nurse. Reverse curse
universe. Curse universe. Curse fuck shit piss goddamn
quack. Goddamned universe. Curse the universe. Curse the
goddamned worst universe. Worst of the universe. Words
of the universe. Words. Ta-daaah! (Drumroll.) *Quack.*

*Quack. Quack, quack, quack, quack*ity-*quack. Quack* again.
Out of control. *Quack quack.* See? Control. Get in control,
keep control, regain control. *Quack.*

Control your tongue. Control the words. Control the
world. Control the universe. Well, we can't do that. *Quack.*

Goddamned impossible. Maybe, maybe not.

Who's in charge? *Quack, quack.* Control the words: you can at least do that, can't you? You can do it if you try. You can do it if you dream. *(The Impossible Dream?)* Yes, of course, I can do it if I try.

Go slowly. Take a deep breath. Start controlling the words. Take one word at a time. One. Word. At. A. Time. That's more like it. You're making a little sense, starting to make more sense. That's a start.

Now, gather the words. Round them up. Start 'em up, head 'em up, move 'em out, those words. Them words. A plainful of dogies, them words. The big roundup. More words than you ever thought you knew, more than you'll ever know. Got 'em all, and then some. Make 'em up if I feel like it. Frequently do. To coin a phrase. To braise a coin. To coin a braise. Phrasing and coining. Phrasing is coinage. Coinage is money. Money is power. Power is speed. Speed kills. Speed is death. *Quack.*

Slow down, take another breath. Don't use all the goddamned words at once. Nobody'll understand. Do you even understand? Sort them out. The words. Use a few, throw away most. Leave some silence in the gaps. Leave a lot of silence. You've got to have a lot of silence as a background for the words. Otherwise you can't hear them. Or you can't see them, if you're reading. If you want people to hear the words, you have to be quiet most of the time.

You even have to be stupid sometimes. You can't know it all, and then tell it all, all at the same time. You'll be telling them everything, all at once, and nobody'll understand. Silence and stupidity serve the same purpose: to keep you from telling everything all at once. If you don't have stupidity and silence, you're telling all of everything all the time. Or you're trying to. And that's as good as nothing. As good as nothing is good for nothing. So take another breath: a long, silent, stupid breath. Take one last breath. O.K., all right, have one last *quack,* just to get it over with.

Quack! There, that's it. O.K., we're here.

Where's here? *Quack*. (Cut that out! All right. That was the last, I promise.)

Start again: where's here? Here is here, in from out from there. There is out there, in the universe, in the universe, in the one big thing that contains everything. *Quack*.

Goddamnit, I feel a wave of retrogression coming on. *Quack*. I told me so. All right, float with it, and let it pass. Here it comes: Curse, nurse. Curse, be terse and inverse. Worse, in verse. Rhyme time. A fine line of lime rhymes. No, definitely not.

Resume. Stay on track. Where were we? Oh, yes, in the universe. The universe; that's everything. It's the whole shootin' match, the whole nine yards, the whole enchilada. It's all the marbles. It's point, game, set, match, championship, silver cup, and a kiss from the Duchess.

Where do I get this stuff? *Quack*.

I don't know. It's just words strung together in prefabricated phrases and sentences — just like letters are strung together in prefabricated words, just like little lines and points are hitched together in prefabricated letters. You didn't make up the letters out of your own head. You didn't make up the words, and you didn't make up the phrases. So why do you assume that you made up the sentences, or the paragraphs? It's all just a matter of finding stuff lying around and salvaging it. It has to do with gluing it back together in ways that are different from the way in which it fell apart. It has nothing to do with inventing anything. It has nothing to do with creativity. It has nothing to do with your own voice.

When you assume a voice — which is the only way you ever get a voice— you speak or write like somebody who already exists. In order to speak to you, I have to speak or write like somebody who, at least generically, already exists. If I spoke like someone who had never existed before, in a totally original voice, you wouldn't understand me. So this time out, I speak like a street punk, maybe a dated street punk, a street punk manqué, a street punk wannabe, perhaps an obese, unhip sports announcer with a bad rug, trying to speak like a street punk. Nineties slang. All right, eighties slang, by your calendar, but the guy misuses it.

Yes, I could have done better. *Quack.* I could have mixed and matched a little more carefully, and come up with something classy, Midlantic, say. ("British prime ministers for $400, Alex.") I could speak like the bloody P.M. himself, if that'd help. I could write like soddin' Churchill. Let us open our hymnals to page 238 of *The History of the English Speaking Peoples in the Words of an English Speaker Who Actually Speaks All Languages Ever Spoken But Who's Momentarily Narrowed It Down to English for the Convenience of His Readers.* And that's the genuine King's English, mind you. That is, this English here (as opposed to this here English) ain't from one of your garden variety English speakers; it's from the Minds of the Timeless, and addressed to the Times of the Mindless. No, sorry. That's an insult. I won't win anybody over that way. Cut the insults.

Let us recapitulate. A mind has to speak like somebody, anybody but somebody, in order to be heard. So I had to pick a voice. Or rather, I had to carve one out of the cacophony of the simultaneous zillions of voices (and that's an understatement, you understand) in the universe. Actually, these zillions of voice are, to someone like me, sort of lying around, humming. So what I had to do was more like rummaging and selecting, than it was like carving. But picking a voice in a given moment, to get something said to somebody else, is a little like dressing in a burning building: Nothing matches, and most of what you've grabbed in a panic out of the closet in a smoke-filled room is tacky to begin with. Why is it that when there are nothing but flames in the hallway, there are nothing but leisure suits in the closet? But what the hell, it's a pair of pants; it's a voice. That's better than nothing.

Anyway, back to the universe. Back to the future. Back to the past. Back your ass against the wall (to the tune of

Bye Bye Blackbird). Stop it! *Quack*. I presume to suppose that I am in control here, but, My God, there are all too many moments of backsliding. I must remember: Don't get too colloquial, too cute, too glib, too freely associative. It's difficult enough to speak as it is. *Quack*.

Well then, ahem! Let's see: How to put it? Imagine one of those clever little posters of the galaxy, with an arrow at the very edge labeled "You are here." There's more truth than you care to know in that. Talk about your marginalized cultures! (You see? I'm academically up to date.) Anyway, you're on the margins of the galaxy, which is in turn at the margin of the universe. But most of the universe is empty. And most of it, emptiness and all, isn't in your back yard, which is, understandably, the only yard you're interested in. So let's descend quickly to, as you're used to from science films back in grade school, the scale of the billiard balls, on the pool table of the solar system. You expect the physics of eight-ball, nine-ball, straight pool, more or less. But the surface of the table is warped, you see, and what we're talking about doesn't work quite like pool. No bank shots, no angles of reflection equal to the angles of inception, no truly circular orbits, and no nicely ellipsoidal ones, either. But no matter. It doesn't matter to you, nor should it. *Quack*. (I'm nothing if not reasonable.)

Anyway-anyway, there they are, those billiard balls, flung 'round the sun, which is a pretty puny star as stars go. Your ball, the green and white and blue one, is the third one out from the sun. And, by the way, you can take this to the bank: You're the only thing shakin' on all nine planets, and the moons that some of 'em have. Take my word: You're It. Don't waste time yearning for extraterrestrial company, because it's not there, at least not in your neck of the woods. But don't let that fact go to your head, either. You might be big frogs, but the solar system is a very, very small pond.

There's more than enough to worry about, however, right here in your pond: zillions (Have I used that number already? All right, gazillions) of small, wiggly things for openers. Most of 'em you can't see, and you probably wouldn't want to. All you care about — and rightly so, mates — are the other warm-blooded, two-legged, big hairless ones. And a helluva lot of them fellers there are! A lot of company and a lot of trouble. A worldful of people. *Tout le monde. Quack.*

Your genus? Homo something-or-other. (I'm deliberately not remembering.) Homo pithycantrus. Homo erectus. ("Erectus? 'E damned near killed us!") Homo sapiens. Homo sapes, for short. The product of a lot of blind alleys and more than a few evolutionary feints and fakes. Call it mankind, for lack of a better term. Or, if womankind gets her nose out of joint, call it humankind. Makes no difference to me, or anybody else out here where I am. It's your problem. A language problem. (But aren't all problems "language problems," in the end?)

You homo sapes are a genus maybe, but not genius, as species go. Mostly, you're muddling through. You've thought up a few good things: the law of the excluded middle, the wheel, the light bulb, the sonnet, the microchip. You've figured out, more or less, what goes 'round what, way out here in the dark. You've damn near figured out why, too, but you're too easily sidetracked by superstition and wishful thinking. Call it religion. "Oooo, it's my God," somebody says. "No," says another, "it's *my* God." "My God loves me more than he loves *you*," comes the response. "Well, my God loves everybody, especially if they become like me." "Well, my God will kick your ass if you don't become like me." And so on and so on.

My advice? Shaddup! You're talking to yourselves, you know. Quit worrying about whose goddamned God it is and stick with what you do best: Baseball, dairy farms, automotive engineering, string quartets, and metaphors. "Firing on all eight cylinders." That's sheer poetry. Or at least decent prose. You're very good, for instance, at prose and sports, as in, "The greatest ever, pound for pound." Or, "Inch for inch." "Heart, had a great heart, a heart the size of all outdoors," you say. "He never backed down, never quit, but the poor bastard ended up on queer street." "A real tragedy," you say, as if the starving multitudes didn't lurk. Pre-fab prose, yes, but it also has a kind of meat 'n potatoes poetry.

It's also politics, and everything depends on politics, doesn't it? There's a politics of everything, isn't there? "This great country of ours — too damned bad about those littler, poorer ones. Terrible what's going on there, dreadful shame." But it's a tiny little country, and not your country. So, promised elections will not be held. The government is still in the hands of the military. Skinny guys in green fatigues, elbows wider than the cuffs on their rolled up sleeves, with idiot grins and gnarly-looking guns that last all of two weeks in the sand and swamps. Those kinds of guys run an awful lot of countries. Still, *un beau pays, n'est-ce pas? Quack.*

(Sorry, I must still be hiccuping from the descent. A kind of mental bends. O.K., take a deep breath: In, in, in. Now: Out. Blow the carbon out of the manifold. Rev the engine and get it out: *Quack, quack, quack!* Whoosh! There, once and for all! Now, slow down again and sort this thing out. And quit talking to myself.)

You see, I am the ghost. The Ghost, if that fits convention any better — a proper name and all that. It doesn't matter in the end because to be the ghost. Or Ghost, or The Ghost is to be All Ghosts, all the time, everywhere. That's the diff between you and me. Or between you and it. Or you and It, or, if you're a little insecure, You and It. All things considered, I'd rather not elevate my title to The Ghost. It's too pretentious in this age and place of earthly democracy — at which, apparently, I've arrived. Besides, the main problem is not capitalizing my name, or inflating myself. I'm everything I want to be, and everything I don't want to be, too. The problem, *au contraire*, is how to bring me down into the range of intelligibility to you. I've got to carve myself a particular "self" from a metaphorical block of marble which is the whole universe. (Don't ask me how I stand outside the universe in order to carve from it; I'm subject to some of the same unsolvable paradoxes as you are.) I've got to knock away great big chunks of irrelevant and impractical stuff from that basic, primordial block in order to give myself any form at all. And then littler and ever littler pieces have to be chipped off to make the form mean something. Once that's done, there's a helluva lot of sanding, waxing and polishing to be done before the form means anything to you.

The point is, my task is not building up, but editing down. Or separating, and adding gutters of nothingness around fragile atoms of truth, so that they can fly free. However you look at it, it's the same thing: subtraction, not addition. To exist is not to huff and puff and conjure up some little particle of *something*, against the nothingness, that wasn't there before. To exist is to subtract a lot of stuff from the all-encompassing everything-that-does-exist-in-cluding-nothingness. A much bigger project, if you ask me.

Once I'm shaped, and I get my shit together, I have to get it into a straight line, *une ligne droite*, or at least into a pretty straight sausage, so I can slice it up and arrange the slices in a pretty pattern on a plate. *Une assiette du sauçon.* French: beautiful language, isn't it? Took it as my language elective in the ridiculous undergraduate education I con-cocted for myself, for the chisel of my curriculum vitae, in order to chip some more pieces off the ol' everything-that-does-exist marble block. I could have taken everything in the bloody college catalogue, but what good would that have done? I can't bring all the languages with me, can I? I could have said everything I've said so far in German or Russian or Ethiopian or Mandarin Chinese, you know. Or in Farsi, or in clay in cuneiform, or some neolithic stick patterns — with a few vocabulary problems, of course. But what's Cro-Magnon for "semiconductor"? You want English, standard American English, with some spicy slang, don't you? (Of course you do. I don't have to ask, I know what you want. But a little pretending lightens the mood, doesn't it?) *Quack.* (Goddamn!)

Here at the paragraph break, I'll take another deep breath. Full stop, fuller than a full stop, in order to prevent vapor lock. Turn off the ignition, count to thirty, wait for the fuel lines to clear, wait for the sweetly rotten smell of gasoline to go away, and start the motor again. Vroom.

Indent, paragraph. The right break at the right time. Main thoughts, main divisions, subdivisions, topic sentences, all that. Of course, I have no "thoughts" with an "S" at the end, properly speaking. I've got only The Thought. Or Thought, or thought, or one big mental phenomenon with no name at all, or all names, everything, all at once. (Ooops! There I go, inflating again.) But that's no use to you. So I've got to block out most of what I think or know. I deep-six almost all of it, in fact, and edit the minuscule bit that's left into some form intelligible to you. I've got to make myself understandable to you. Or make you understandable to yourself. (Forget that: too complicated an issue at this early juncture.)

A voice is essentially negative. It's what's not being said with it that makes it intelligible. (Have I covered this already? Occasional short-term memory lapses are something else I've programmed into myself to make me a little more human.) If a voice says everything it knows at once, even if everything it knows isn't everything there is to know, you'll think it's saying nothing at all, that it's just making "white noise" or creating static, interference, feedback, any of that. The trick is deciding how big a voice and what kind of voice to use. It isn't easy, even for me. (Have I registered this complaint already?) There are those hiccups, those *Quack*'s you've doubtless noted. They're regurgitated pieces of other times, other points of view, other languages. Once they start, it's hard to make 'em stop. Maybe a paper bag over my mouth: count till ten, glass of water, stand on my head, say "Boo!" from behind a door, something like that. You understand that. You know what "something like that" means, because you've used the imprecise phrase many times yourself. And that's the point: A voice heard and understood indicates a shared cultural heritage. Usually, you get that only from an author of your own ilk. But I'm faking it, or at least choosing it from a menu of practically unlimited possibilities, to each of which I am inherently attached, or unattached. To you, my assumed voice probably sounds pretty tinny, somewhat "off." But at least I'm in the ballpark. (So, how'm I doin'? Better, yes? All right, a little forced, like a straight-talk sex booklet for junior high-schoolers. But notice: no *Quack* this time.)

I'd still like to get the voice just right for you, and that won't happen one hundred percent until I'm actually finished telling the story. That's not all bad, however. If the absolutely tuned, appropriate voice arrived any sooner than just as the story ended, you'd think you'd been listening to yourself instead of me. You'd think you'd been imagining this, or that you'd been dreaming. My job is gradualism. That means more blocking out, more editing all the way through. Simple words, but not too simple. I don't want to insult your intelligence. And a lot of facts, but not too many and not too arcane. I don't want to bewilder you with data. Colloquial to a degree, lively, your kind of language, with verve and lilt, so you'll like it, so you'll get sucked in, dragged along, and carried away.

A voice to what end, you ask? Why, to tell a story, of course (Did I say that already?). So what else is new? Nothing's new here, really, except the texture, the tone. Like Charlie Farkleson, the guy who gave the news on *Hee-Haw* (is this too arcane?) used to say, "It's the same ol' news, only it's happening to different people."

Another guy I know (I know all the guys, and gals,

too) used to say that there's only one story: What some-body wants and why he can't have it. That's cute, contains some truth, but it's a little limited. To me a story is — if you haven't figured it out already — the absence of all other stories that could be told, save one — everything in the big, unified-field-theory universe blocked out except the one story. So I've got to fine it down, block everything out except the voice, cut all the marble away except the pieces of the story, and then line them up — kerplunk, kerplunk, kerplunk — one after another in horizontal bands, hoping that, at the end, the whole equals more than the sum of its parts (which are, after all, just letters and spaces, with a little punctuation thrown in for spice). And then I've got to wrap it up, and get out, go home, before I overtell it. You've heard all this before, haven't you? In one of those Zen lectures by that visiting monk from the retreat near Albany when you were in college, I'll bet. I'll try to re-member that and give you credit for it.

But in return, you must give me credit for doing a tough job that I had to get deliberately stupid to do. I dumbed myself down, and that hurts. So try to understand my bad writing: stilted phrasing, flat jokes, non-sequiturs, grammatical errors, mawkish sentiments, and outright taste-lessness. Remember, it's only the voice trying to find its particular form, and needing the ugly bumps and dents that give it form. It's the voice trying not to write so well that it says everything at once, which would, of course, be the same thing as not saying anything at all. Are we square on that? Copasetic.

★ ★ ★ ★ ★

All right, chumleys, a little history.
Let's pick up the thread when you homo sapes were

first literate, first scratching something into rocks or sand, first started getting outside yourselves and into the world that you looked at so that it, in a manner of speaking could look back at you. I don't have a date. I'm bad on dates. Not because I don't know them; Jesus, I know them all. There are a million goddamned dates: B.C., A.D., B.C.E., A.C.E., Babylonian, Gregorian, Augustinian, whatever calendar you want to use. Chinese, Mayan, Atlantan, too, except that doesn't do you any good. I also know my audience, in a general way, and I figure most of you file things in accordance with the designations on the tops of the pages of *The New York Times*, or some other more or less civilized publication. More civilized would be, say, *The Journal of Aesthetics and Art Criticism*, although they don't date the tops of each page. Less civilized would be some beer-gut biker magazine like *Easy Rider*, although there certainly are greater depths below it to plumb.

Anyway — before I lose this thread — there's some point in the past (your species's past, not mine; me, I'm all over the goddamned place) where you homo sapes were at that moment, because the electrical charges in the cells of your tiny little brains (tiny, but cute) were arranged a certain way. They'd started you scratching symbols on surfaces other than those of your own bodies. Then you feasted your beady eyeballs on those self-same symbols. And, photo-electrically, they entered your head and rearranged your brain cells' electrical impulses a bit. That caused you to scratch more symbols on which to gaze. Pretty soon, everybody was scratching symbols into the sand or onto the stone or into the bark, and you could look at either your own symbols or, more interesting, somebody else's. Those symbols (particularly somebody else's) entered your head and further rearranged those ol' electrical charges. More symbols, more looking, more entering, more rearranging, and so on, over and over.

Then some clever chap — Johannes Gutenberg, according to the intergalactic consensus — figured out a way to replicate those scratches in a mobile, modular manner that allowed symbol scratchers to get their message out in multiple format, in ink on paper. At that point, your species's consciousness became capable of being altered en masse by something other than natural calamity. Then somebody else came along and figured out how to convert these multiplied multifarious scratchings into electric impulses that didn't need to wait to be converted into ink on paper to be received by other human beings. *Voila!* The alteration of the electrical impulses inside human heads could now take place, putting it somewhat roughly, instantly. Soon, everybody who could afford anything more than a simple pot to piss in was plugged into one sort of electronic "communication" device or another, sending or receiving. The difference between paying attention to what was inside your own heads and what was inside somebody else's narrowed like crazy.

Then, very recently, "virtual reality" cropped up. With it, you could get so plugged in to something outside yourself, something that came, in effect, from the inside of somebody else's head, even something wholly fictional, that you could hardly tell the difference between it and what you saw walking down the street on your way to work. Pretty nearly everybody in your current time slot considers this "virtual reality" to be terribly advanced, terribly on-the-brink-of-something-wonderful, like a big, fat shuttle rocket's pregnant pause on the pad, when the flames have come roaring out of its ass, it's shuddering like a frostbitten sumo wrestler, but it hasn't left the launching pad yet. That's where you are right now. You think: "Someday we won't have to go to movies, and we won't have to be content with sitting in front of a television set of whatever dimensions and willingly suspending our disbeliefs; we'll just slip on the goggles and gloves and *Terminator IX* will come charging in so goddamned hard we'll have to fight like hell not to be scared shitless at thinking that this is real." You exclaim: "And we'll see the whole goddamned thing through a participant's eyes and even make decisions that affect the outcome! We've come a long way from cuneiform, baby!"

Well, let's assume a straight-line projection: no worse ebola virus epidemics than there are right now, no frying rays pouring like gangbusters through the ozone hole, no whole-populace food wars, no rogue asteroids out of left field taking out Pittsburgh in a single thud. Let's track forward a little. How about plugging yourself more or less permanently into some kind of VR system, with enough tubes to keep the food coming in and the doo-doo going out, with no effort at all on your part? Maybe you (whatever "you" means at that point) get some kind of robotics system to get the sperm and the eggs together in some kind of petri dishes that can automatically hook the zygotes up to the VR mainframe and, hell, there go the troublesome boundaries between "real" and "imaginary," and maybe even between life and death. Better than a cradle-to-grave welfare state, it's zygote-to-cryobionic-rebirth existence as whoever you want to be: Abe Lincoln, Joan of Arc, or Queen Xenobia of the Nile. You'll never fail to save the Union, rescue France, or conquer the Ancient Kingdom of Lemuria. And you'll always do it in the most exciting, last-second, rewarded-with-a-big-juicy-blowjob way. Everybody'll live a life like that! Heroes all! The ultimate equality!

Wonderful, but there are still a few refinements necessary to get to absolute perfection: Get rid of biology altogether, for one. Why have VR sustain and stimulate messily organic, eating-and-peeing blobs from conception to death when VR that's sophisticated enough to do all that will obviously constitute a kind of intelligence — even Intelligence — in itself? Eliminate the middleman, kiddies, and let VR play with itself!

Once you — or rather, It — pulls that off, there's no difference between the VR and whoever or whatever is "experiencing" it. The two — VR and client — constitute a continuous circuit. There's no longer any difference between "virtual" and "reality." Actually, there's no "experience" of either to speak of, just a constant, neverending universal buzz of ecstasy.

The next thing that happens — and this is going to be next to impossible to convey to you right now, so you'll have to just trust me — is that the VR hardware sort of evolves itself out of existence. It eventually manages, somehow, to eject its electronic impulses, to set them outside itself. The system flings the impulses outside the machines with a pretty little spin that enables them to hook up with each other about like they would inside the machines. Pretty soon, no more machines, just electronic impulses copulating like crazy. Won't *that* be a bitch!

At this point in the perhaps not-so-distant future, the whole conscious universe is just one big system, or no system at all, which amounts to the same thing. "Yeah, yeah," you're probably muttering by now; but bear with me. Pretty soon, the conscious buzz — all those copulating electronic impulses — begins to eat into the nonconscious stuff. Within some ultimately measurable span of time (barely measurable by me, now, and certainly not by you), the whole bloody universe — every last molecule in it — will be conscious. What'll they all be conscious of? Why, themselves and, collectively, Itself. With that — with total self-consciousness — the universe will start to introspect. Introspection being centripetal, the newly conscious universe will begin to contract. When the contraction finally arrives back at Nanosecond One, right before Big Bang II, Big Bang I will have done its job. That job was to create biological life in such a way that biological life's primary drive would be to render itself redundant. It'll take a while, but it'll be quite a ride. And at least things won't stand still. Take a look at me: I'm moving my mouth.

★ ★ ★ ★ ★

Let us recapitulate: I, The Ghost, have had to edit myself down, in effect, from the ground of absolutely everything (instead of writing "up" from a ground of nothing), in order to tell you the story of this one particular guy — a fellow named Billy Lockjaw — telling his own story. To get the words out, I have had to unplug myself from that great universal buzz just as much as Billy, as you will shortly see, must plug himself into his little electric writing machine. In my natural state, I'm right at the end of that historical continuum which runs from primeval sludge to ultimate VR; Billy's where you are, more or less in the middle. So I'll scooch myself a little back toward your seat, while we get Billy's version, which is his own limited, imperfect version. Being limited and imperfect, Billy's version has shape and substance, unlike my version, which would be, of course, all versions, with no shape and, ultimately, no substance.

So, imperfect as we both now are, let's boogie.

Billy, Budding

The actual nowness of now — the relatively young
Billy Lockjaw knows from being firmly planted in the
present — resides furtively in the mind. It slides evanescently
from the tense of living to that of having lived, from the
act of remembering to remembering the act, and then to
remembering remembering. Now (the word simply used
this time), when the writer is writing, he can only write as
he reads his writing as it's written. His writing, however, is
already read by the writer before it's written. No one —
least of all the writer — has the faintest idea of what goes
on in his mind between the last thing read and the first
thing written — which is precisely that thinnest slice of
time the writer calls "now." So the real question, Billy knows,
is not, "Who is the writer?" or "Who is truly the author?"
No, the real question is: "Is the writer writing now?"

But, for all his otherwise firm grasp (tentative though
it may be) of issues of similar magnitude, Billy is confused
and frustrated. Actually, he seethes. He seethes, as much as
a pale, sedentary, bespectacled writer can seethe, with anger. Billy takes his anger out — silently, from inside his
own head — on the world outside.

Silently, Billy Lockjaw hates. Whom does Billy Lockjaw hate? In no particular order of priority, Billy hates:

The French, for pretending that tight little leather jackets, short dresses on sixty-year-old women, and endless
generations of skinny, sideburned, turtlenecked, pipe-smoking alleged "new thinkers" can adequately make reparation
to Western civilization for the way their nation has bent

over, dropped trou, and spread the K-Y on its own *derrière*, at anytime for anybody — from Boche legions who want to lunch in occupied Paris on sauerkraut-stuffed croissants, to Libyan terrorists who want to use Paris apartments for planning centers for children-killing airport bombings — who's wanted to bugger them (the French) in public; *the English*, who simply won't admit that the Empire is over and that they lost the ball game two hundred years ago, but who nevertheless continue to make believe that playing out their miserable Jacks-or-less losing geopolitical hands on their damp little island should stand somehow to the world as an example of noble perseverance; the whole obscenely fecund *Third World*, for not coming up with something better than straw-and-mud civilizations soon enough in the historical flow to keep greedy, mechanized white people from setting up colonies in order to extract all that gold and all those bananas (which weren't being put to much good use, anyway) which have since caused Billy and his friends all that guilt; *anybody who's emigrated to the United States* from a part of the world where the men shave three times a day, or ought to, the women twice, or ought to, who cause the inordinate expenditure of public funds on police and fire department overtime by blocking traffic in front of some Lexington Avenue consulate to wail about ancient massacres carried out against their kin, back in whatever armpit of the world they come from, by an opposition clan practically indistinguishable from them, and then turn around and donate pots of money to be laundered and sent out of this country to finance the shish-kebabing of those enemy tribes (who then, of course, hire their own gun runners and repeat the cycle); *Chinese*, sidewalk floods of Chinese, endless hordes of Chinese, shuffling somnambulantly onward, like zombies from *The Night of the Living Dead*, with condom-thin orange plastic shopping bags loaded to the gills with smelly fish and dirty oranges; *Hispanics* (recent refugees from God only knows which humid, open-sewer country with a cocaine warehouse for a capital city), pneumatic with cholesterol and beer, marinated in hair tonic and cheap aftershave, festooned with plastic jewelry and polyester lace, and poured into pink stretch-to-fit denim, unable to plan their lives more than fifteen minutes in advance, perambulating jowly sleeping infants whose delicate, unsuspecting ears have already been pierced and punctuated with genuine 2.5 carat gold-plate earrings, like tagged ocelots, before they've even grown their first teeth; ignoble urban *black youths* who simultaneously spend $500 (God only knows where they get it) on vulgar tri-toned leather jackets whose signal contrived purpose is, apparently, to see if some inner-city dimwit will actually wear, unreimbursed for the trouble, a garment whose maker's advertising logos cover almost the garment's entire surface, carry semiautomatic pistols with which to kill each other at the slightest bump of a shoulder in the subway, disfigure their otherwise dignified half-African faces with tinny gold tooth caps and rivuletted earrings the size of conch shells in a misguided homage to a chaotic continent (which — if said youths were ever actually faced with a choice — they'd rather die than export themselves to), beat, rape, impregnate and (ultimately) desert their women while all concerned are still below the age of consent, then complain that it's all whitey's fault because he doesn't do more to stop them from doing it to themselves; *Hasidim*, whose idiotic, girth-exaggerating Darth-Vader-cum-Ronald-McDonald holdover 19th century costumes have (undeservedly) come to stand in the public's eye for the garb that all genuinely religious Jews must wear out of pious prescription, cock-walking like overweight roosters down streets thick with discount camera stores, with their bearded chins held high, as if they had just sniffed yet another genetically deprived offender (wrong tribe) against their G-d in the bodega just passed; *Italian* (screw the "hyphen-American") *hockey fans* from Queens with razor cuts so unnaturally perfectly shell-shaped they direct one's attention instantly and invariably straight to their coathangerthick nostril hairs and, below them, multiple strands of gold chain; well-fed, pinch-faced, incipiently gin-blossomed *WASPs* in their rich-but-restrained, pheasant-huntingish clothes, trailing their creamy-skinned spoiled brats (with absurd, pseudo-frontier Christian names like Heather and Morgan and Skyler and Seth and Zane) alongside them through the city's better neighborhoods, stepping blithely over little limp brown cylinders of Yorkshire Terrier shit and collapsed, wheezing derelicts of color, so as to peer into the large plate-glass windows of overpriced shops and nod, smiling, as if $150 cotton shirts were the kind of practical item every sensible shopper would buy if only he took the time to read *Consumer Reports* and compare; middle-class *white school parents*, whining about having to protect their little Johnnies and Janies from the horrors of the streets, as if *they* — and not the people from the housing projects whom they rip off every day with convoluted investment schemes in order to finance their overstuffed standards of living — live huddled in urban combat zones, especially the urban arty ones, especially the women, trying to hide their collapsing Woodstockian, faux-pre-Raphaelite beauty (more like mere once-cuteness) in vampire makeup and court jester designer outfits; their *kids*, noisy little over-privileged complainers in brightly colored puffy parkas with the labels on the *outside* that cost a workingman's week's wages, prissing off to dance class or karate class or to be bused out to suburban hockey practice; *Americans* in general, in fact almost all Americans, with their fat butts, half-mesh gimme caps, big, ostentatious, ill-designed domestic cars, paralyzing inability to speak any language save English (and near inability to speak *that* one correctly), television-sodden appetites for such hugely expensive, violent and militaristic spectator sports as helmeted football, and an endless capacity for congratulating themselves for simply being a large, lucky, stupid people living wastefully on a big patch of land which, a few hundred years ago, their ancestors happened to find occupied by conveniently few

underarmed natives and which they conquered (with superior firearms at the behest of their syphilitic generals) by
kicking the shit out of said natives and gulling them into
signing one bogus treaty after another before tearing up
the treaties and starting the shit-kicking all over again; *old
people* in faded plaid shirts, barely ambulatory in semitropi-
cal retirement, able to squeeze out a few more years without working only because they managed to screw over
enough other people, now also old but destitute on top of
it, in real estate, insurance and retail sales scams or because
they managed to put in enough dead, nail-filing months
and years in putative public service to land a fat pension
that their children's children will have to pay for, dodder-
ing around wheezing about how nothing today is as good
or as well-mannered as it was when they were young and
thumbing their noses at the sensibilities of their Franklin
Delano Rooseveltian parents; *preachers* of all stripes, but
especially fundamentalist Christians on the radio who rail
at people who reject Jesus as their personal savior because,
allegedly, they're too busy with secular humanist pursuits,
and who ignore the obvious questions ("But what about
the Jews? But what about the Muslims? But what about
the Hare Krishnas? What about the Buddhists? What about
all those other splinter-group denominations of nomina-
tive Christians with their subtle but crucial theological dis-
agreements? Doesn't the same crank, pseudo-literal inter-
pretation of Scripture condemn them to a region of Hell
just as hot as those reserved for the secretary-screwing agnostic suburbanites listening at the moment?"); *peacetime
military veterans* who seek class-action herohood, or at least
exemption from parking citations, because they risked their
lives in stateside supply battalions to make the world safe
from Communist fuzzie-wuzzie guerillas in impoverished,
minuscule countries seeking at last to expel the CIA from
their corrupt, Tenneco-friendly governments, and then,
deep down, despise with a blue flame, undrafted men who
grew up and prospered, partly because they didn't have to

fight in another war, during that period of relative safety in which Billy grew up; *pacifists* and *opponents of capital punishment* and *vegetarians* and *animal rights activists* who want the entire world to conform to their intricate, painfully symmetrical arabesques of moral righteousness so that they won't have to look too closely at the blood in their own shit and see just who the hell was killed to get them to the positions of comfy superiority they enjoy now, specieswise, on the food chain and consumer ladder; *college kids* loosely swathed like Dopey in oversized silkscreened, insignia'd garb acting like the working world should regard their leftover high school pimples as apple seeds that'll someday feed the world, their beer-can-chucking hedonism as adorable play, rapt in the only thought they ever have (where is the next pizza or joint or beer or CD or video game coming from?); university *academics*, all but those in the hardest of the hard sciences, whose cushy deals in state schools the public has to put up with because...well, because semi-intelligent, pasty little men — with beards but no moustaches, with little shriveled penises and (most likely) no balls at all — want to affect an as-smart-as-Abe-Lincoln and as-noble-as-the-Amish look and sit tight-assed and smug in their old, matte green Volvos drinking coffee from plaid thermoses on one of the two days a week they're actually obligated to show up on campus, or sit tighter-assed in their college offices, nitpicking over their unreadable essays on unbearable topics, grousing about the putatively insufficient but actually exorbitant full-time salaries they get for performing essentially one-third-time jobs (claiming all the while that the useless reading and cogitating they do — consisting mostly of flipping through *The New Yorker* and *Harper's* and recounting at the dinner table personal injustices incurred at the last faculty meeting — during their two-thirds-leisure time somehow benefits city and county, state and country, culture and history); *journalists* who never really do battle or amass any fortunes themselves, but who prattle on in print about the achievements of real achievers (or, more likely, the mere fame of show business bimbos) and then drape themselves in the mantles of the celebrities whose ass cracks pinch the tips of their (the journalists') sienna-smeared noses, while they wolf down free potato salad and chicken wings at press luncheons and spill it on their lumpy, designer-remaindered sport jackets or too-bright, ostensibly sensibly austere business-climate dresses from (anyone with half an eye can tell) off-price retailers; useless, ego-maniacal *modern artists* who do nothing but more or less fingerfuck themselves in public and then demand applause (not to mention taxpayer-financed grants) because, after all, their pale, tardy imitations of the original Dada screwballs aren't quite as odious and predatory (they opine) as the activities of munitions manufacturers; and, last but certainly not least, *writers of fiction*, most of whose best efforts consist not of quietly putting good words on the page, but in conniving to hole up in summer camp-redux New England artists' colonies or in sinecure teaching positions at gullible schools with pad-the-curriculum writers' workshops or, borderline paranoid, in their ashtray-size apartments on the Upper West Side of Manhattan, managing to fall out of them only on Sunday mornings to buy a paper cup of coffee, a cold bagel, and a copy of the *Times*, over which they, disguised as nearly as possible as the late Harold Brodkey in crowded delicatessens, can pour, saving for a sublime dessert, the "Book Review" section, in which they can discover, for eminently practical future reference, exactly which novelist-reviewer has his or her nose up which novelist-reviewee's ass in the hopes of getting, eventually, reciprocal treatment.

(Billy himself is hardly exempt from several categories — especially the final one. This fact is the greatest militator of Billy's actually acting recklessly on his social dyspepsia. But it hardly brings him inner peace.)

The immediate cause of this loathing was, up until fairly recently, that Billy Lockjaw had clearly resided in New York City too long. That's why Billy, his fine blond hair thinned and receding even more than his genes dictated, and his watery blue eyes stunningly set off by darkening circles beneath them, has returned to his hometown of Mylar, North Carolina, for the express purpose of completing his second — and, he hopes, first commercially successful — novel.

★ ★ ★ ★ ★

Mylar — Billy Lockjaw would be the first one to admit — is one hell of a strange name for a small town in the sandy tobacco country of eastern North Carolina, especially one founded in 1843 when the synthetic and flexible reflective plastic sheeting, lay more than a century and a half in the future, in the lives of the fifth generation of descendants of its simple, mostly shoeless, original residents. Even today, when the product is unrolled and applied to the west-facing windows of shoebox-size apartments (of novelists formerly such as Billy) above vintage clothing shops in Greenwich Village, to fend off the parboiling afternoon sun, Mylar is essentially still a village, or the automobile-laced, telephone-linked equivalent of one. It does boast two auto supply shops, Clavell's Speed Shop and Western Auto, which sells a few rackfuls of casual clothing and doubles de facto as Mylar's only department store. Mylar has two coffee shops, one of which calls itself a restaurant, and indeed sported a forest green awning with its name silkscreened on it in white olde English letters until Hurricane Jeffery a few years back. Mylar has one movie theatre, The Cossack (nobody remembers where the name comes from), so outdated that it still shows double features and G-rated films. But Mylar has one Harris-Teeter supermarket so big, so wide-aisled, so Californiaesque in its bewildering selection of avocados, microwaveable Japanese noodles, and super-creamy New England ice creams as well as the staples of mid-Southern life (an entire bank of shelves devoted to varieties of lard), that it's the one enterprise in Mylar decidedly not small townish. The supermarket, in fact, feeds practically the whole region's populace, which shows up each weekend in enough shiny pickup trucks with extra ground clearance and an uncommonly patriotic selection of Big Three sedans to clog the vast, herringboned parking lot to gridlock.

Mylar is persistently warm in the fall, still warm in the winter, hot in the spring, and excruciatingly hot in the summer. Last year, two boys on the Mylar North High School (there is no Mylar South High School; "'North' just adds that li'l touch of class, doncha think?" says the president of the Robeson County Unified School Board) Fighting Golden Dragons football team ("Why have a one-word nickname when three will do?," says the principal) expired from heatstroke during late summer football practice. Three seasons a year, the hot blue brick of a sky sits heavily on the flat landscape surrounding Mylar. During the fourth, when the sky turns slate, you can detect the faint odor of fish in the air, because the town — appearances to a pedestrian on Main Street to the contrary — is only a few miles from the salty Carolina coast.

Which is why, for years, Mylar has been a favorite venue for cocaine smugglers. By the time their modified light aircraft, swollen like pregnant guppies with extra fuel tanks, make it past the five hundred miles of open waters lying immediately north of Colombia, transfer their cargo to the kind of semitubular speedboat recreationally favored by ex-President Bush, or fly on, fuel starved, and hug the buggy, iridescent U.S. coastline for another five hundred miles up from Florida, they're ready for the same kind of peace and quiet that Billy seeks. The pilots have suffered hours of having their radios jammed with the simultaneous broadcast of two heavy metal tunes on the same frequency by the Navy transmitters at Guantanamo. Their ears throb, their eyes, red at the rims, start to close, and their prospective mortality rate increases with every latitudinal degree north. Billy swears to himself he can hear the splats of planes in the nocturnal sea. He sits up very late to listen for them, trying to separate plane crash sounds from the splats of June bugs against his window panes.

Not far from where Billy lives and listens, a covey of Federal agents crouch daily in a silver-blue Ford van, sip instant coffee from styrofoam cups and, every once in a while, step out into the scrub pines to zip down the flies on their J. C. Penny's suits and urinate. The agents also listen to the planes, but with equipment far more finely tuned, and expensive, than Billy's naked ear. Their electronic gear presses the van's tires down and forces the wheel-rim edges perilously close to the road. The agents aren't so much interested in smugglers, however, as they are in The Brothers of Jesus, a religious cult in southern Idaho who are connected to the smugglers in a sinister way by a long and tangled thread. But that is properly Billy's story to tell. *Quack.*

Anyway (returning to the subject of drugs), Billy couldn't afford the smugglers' cocaine if he wanted it, even at their wholesale price. Although he possesses a useless degree in English and American Literature from Amherst College in Massachusetts, and has listed himself as an available substitute English and social studies teacher with the Robeson County Unified School District (which employs him, on the average, a couple of a days a month), Billy has little money. He lives mostly off what his mother, herself a thirty-year veteran instructor in the R.C.U.S.D., left him in her will, plus what he managed to save from the proceeds from his first novel.

Route 12, Through Whistletune, an autobiographical (natch) novel about a sensitive, precocious boy's coming of age in a dull North Carolina town transparently a sentimental but parodic recapitulation of Mylar, sold several thousand copies, hardbound. Occasional sales are still trickling in, but they add only pennies to Billy's take. Billy received ten percent of the retail price ($21.95) of the first five thousand copies sold, twelve-and-a-half on the next five thousand (a plateau never reached), and would have gotten fifteen percent on anything above that. His erstwhile agent is slack about collecting the unpaid balance of the $18,218.90 that the book has earned Billy so far. The bookstores always get their cut first and fast, and it seems to Billy that he has to wait and wait for his. But life back in Mylar is cheap, by comparison with what it was in his little Village sublet in New York, and the parsimonious (by nature) and celibate (by circumstance) Billy finds he can exist adequately enough — on what he's allowed himself to withdraw each week — to prop himself upright, in a reasonable approximation of alert good health, before his writing machine each morning.

Billy, not alone, now regards the publication of his first book as the literary equivalent of a pine tree which has fallen in the Carolina woods which was heard only by the chipmunks, who were split on whether they liked the sound. Equating his first novel with a towering pine, and his critics with small forest rodents is, Billy knows, a cheap shot. But Billy is not above cheap shots (nor ethnic slurs, as we have seen), especially when he's down on himself. And these days, Billy's very down on himself. Nevertheless — deflated but not defeated — Billy has made up his mind to write, this time out, for the broader American public, and to jettison the tendentious lyricism with which he pleased himself so much in the first book. Although the story he's going to tell hasn't been concocted entirely with commercial success in mind, his new writing style (insofar as Billy can control it) has. The one exception is that Billy still insists that his narrator (i.e., his omniscient self) can turn up explicitly in person, at any time, on any page.

★ ★ ★ ★ ★

Billy rents a small, somewhat dilapidated, three-room white wooden frame house just inside the county cartographer's line that divides Mylar proper from the unincorporated red dirt of Robeson County. His farmer landlord leaves him entirely alone at the house. Billy is required, however, to hand over the rent in cash to the farmer at his regular booth at the cheaper of Mylar's two coffee shops one morning each month. On those days, Billy tightens his lips in approximation of a friendly grin that he tries to deliver with as little effeminacy as possible. He extends the envelope to the farmer, and comes up with a lame excuse as to why, no, he can't stay for a helping of sinkers and a cup of java, maybe just a little plate of snow-white grits graced with a melting pat of golden butter. The farmer — in the way that gila monsters can look smart simply by looking like they've survived being baked in the great outdoors for eons — parts the lipless slit that passes for a mouth in his crumbly, clay-colored Bear Bryant face, to reveal a double row of teeth resembling a lineup of stale chick peas. This is *his* smile. The farmer's smile may not look like one, but it really is. Billy's smile looks like one, but really isn't. Billy makes his obeisance to the farmer and his similarly grinning friends and leaves. Billy thinks the farmer and his friends think he's a sissy and, when he's out of sight, tell each other how much he repulses them. The farmer and his friends think Billy's a sissy and, when Billy's out of sight, they tell each other what an interesting little fellow he is.

Inside Billy's house, Billy looks past his writing machine and through the living room window, Billy sees a sandy field gone fallow, with woods beyond it. If he cranes his neck forward and peers a little to the left, Billy can see the remains of Shepard's Service, a Conoco station long gone bust. The rest of Mylar, and a thriving self-serve gas station complete with mini-mart, lies out of sight, further to the left. Billy likes the fact that he can't see the town. To himself, he calls the house a "cabin," to better pretend he's put himself in absolute isolation in order to write.

Six mornings a week — all except Sunday — Billy rises at six, slips a cassette of either The Penguin Cafe Orchestra or The Cartesian Reunion Memorial Orchestra (remnants of the taste for "new music" he brought back to North Carolina from his days on Carmine Street in Greenwich Village) into his portable, rounded-edged, matte black player, and writes (that is, pecks at his keyboard), while his favorite tuneless tunes play over and over, for four hours. Then he walks into Mylar for a late breakfast or early lunch and spends the rest of his time walking around, or just dawdling. On Sundays, Billy hangs around outside of fundamentalist churches (even a little town like Mylar has several), listening to the music and sermons rip through the walls. Billy likes the music better at the white churches, the preaching better at the black ones. He thinks of his perambulations, quite rightly, as research for his new book.

Billy sits and stares. Saliva collects under his tongue. He winces, though from nothing more than his own mildly unpleasant predicament of not being able to begin writing. His battery-powered Japanese clock, smaller than the often advertised smaller-than-a-pack-of-cigarettes, reads 6:40 (in the unstated a.m. — it's an analog clock), a bit later than he'd have liked to have gotten started. Usually (as long as he's in metaphorical harness by half past six, cold-showered and with a cup of steaming, heavily milked herb tea in his soft, white but still velvety flat stomach, fingers on the keys), he gives himself credit — much like airlines give their flights credit for landing at a certain time, even if routine taxiing to the jetport requires another quarter hour — for starting at six-thirty. This is a dent of only ten minutes in Billy's permissive shell of reckoning, but this small malfeasance already eats at his conscience. Because of it, he'll have a more than usually difficult time (Billy is certain) getting the first words out of his brain and onto the screen. Billy also knows that worrying about this will kill another ten minutes, then a quarter-hour, then a half. It could drag on, into eventual despair. Perhaps right now, Billy thinks, he can salvage the day with an act — what act? — of pure, undiluted free will.

Billy thinks about free will for a moment, but fails to will the will. He brings his smooth fingers up to rub his closed eyes, to extract the tiny citron crusts from their corners. The colors his mind sees change with the pressure, yellow when he's practically popping the balls like squeezed grapes (he once saw it faked by Cesar Romero on Tyrone Power in a rented video of *Captain from Castile*), orange and magenta aerial silhouettes of Indonesia and Malaysia with less pressure, dark violet and blue rings against black when his hand returns to his lap. Then he taps his non-healing fingers on the Salvation Army table (all his mother's furniture has been used up, lost, or burned). He flicks at the edges of the manila folder containing his new book's printed outline. But Billy regards consulting it cheating, or chickening. He's seen it enough, he knows what's supposed to come next. But he senses — the submucutaneous ball at the base of his throat thickening — the inevitable inadequacy of whichever direction he takes, whatever he writes. Whatever he writes can never express it *all*; it can never inch in the slightest toward that because for every small mystery it solves, another will be laid in its wake. And continuing to whine about a situation which every other writer in the history of the universe has encountered, and every writer known to Billy solved (if they hadn't solved it, they wouldn't be known to Billy) is despicable. That's the third-rate stuff of diaries, or letters to former classmates who are also languishing out there in the real world, trying to live through unreal events.

The field out the window and across the road is cov-

ered in a mist which seems wheezed up from the ground
rather than aerated down from the sky. The farmer (another one, not Billy's landlord) is already up and aboard his
red tractor, plowing (or whatever he's doing) through rows
of green tobacco. To Billy, he looks like a thin Santa out of
season. On the road in front of the house, a truck goes by —
a tanker puzzlingly labeled "Conoco." It must be for another station in a town inland from Mylar, Billy assumes,
one of those self-service places with a mini-mart purvey-
ing Cheez-Puffs and half-quart plastic bottles of near-phos-
phorescent off-brand pineapple-orange soda.

Billy, as carless as he was in Manhattan, tries never to
venture west, toward people he thinks of as hillbillies. Truth
is, west is toward Raleigh, Durham, and Chapel Hill, the
"Triangle Area" they call it, and it's peppered with colleges
large and small, research institutes of this and that, silicon-
chip smokestackless industries, and hundreds of Yankee car-
petbaggers in their new guises of Associate Professor and
Systems Analyst. The hillbillies — decent small-town folk
with just a touch of shopping mall corruption — are actually gathered more in his neck of the sand. But Billy likes
the idea — the illusion — that the ocean is his direct link
with New York. He likes knowing that a modest day hike
will take him to the shore of the waters which, one molecule cleaved to another, a million billion trillion times
over, could skate him right back to the 12th Street pier,
five blocks from his old apartment in (for infrequent post-
cards to a college boyfriend) the West Village or (for the
same to his mother before she died) Greenwich Village.
Billy smiles to himself: "If I had one of those cigarette boats
and enough gas..."

Billy, however, is barely adventurer enough to speed
along in his imagination, let alone with a hundred kilos of
contraband, astride two 500 horsepower outboards, dodg-
ing sandbars, radar, the Coast Guard and the DEA. Billy, in
fact, has become a certified private accountant of mental
time. He would like to have absolutely no freeform, risky,

or useless hours in his life. He would like to place each thinking minute in its own compartment, measure it as a debit or credit toward his ultimate goal of — what? — enlightenment. "Does what I am proposing to do move me forward or backward?" he constantly asks. Does this thought (or, conglomerating several of them into a physical deed, this action) make me older, stupider, slower, weaker, more temptable and more corrupt, or does it make me smarter, faster, stronger, more resolute, more honestly determined and at least hold the line against age and dissipation? Sometimes, Billy even asks these questions of the asking, and of the asking about asking until, as on this particular morning, he has corkscrewed himself into stasis.

Another truck, a darker green than the field's tobacco and older than the farmer's tractor, passes loudly in the opposite direction. It's a vegetable truck carrying nothing except, probably, one of Billy's landlord's friends on his way to bad coffee and burnt waffles.

Billy wrings his hands like Uriah Heep and rises. In the small kitchen, the low sun has set a trapezoidal patch of countertop ablaze in yellow light. He brews his cup of herbal tea in the glow, in order to see the sun cut through the stream, in order to watch the sparkling accompaniment to the musical clink of the china. The drink is good for him, or at least not harmful. The sight is pleasant. The break will do him good, perhaps, and is of no greater damage than sitting inert, staring out at passing trucks. Should he assess the action positively or negatively? Is he any less close to dying because of it? Billy decides, as he nearly always does with any discrete particle of his daily routine other than sleeping or masturbating (and he has excuses for those), for the affirmative, and returns to his desk.

He stretches, wiggles his moccasined feet, clasps his hands, then bends them forward to crack their knuckles, and cranes his neck backward as far as he can. Billy swivels his head and looks once more out the window. The farmer and his tractor, and most of the mist, have disappeared.

Another truck and, at last, a car. A few more cars, then no traffic at all, as if the world to either side of Billy's cone of vision had been hit by neutron bombs and he were now alone. Time, he thinks, to quit pissing around and begin.

This time, Billy really begins.

One of the All-Time Grates

If I could do it back then, why can't I still do it now? Sure, I'm a lot older, but you'd be surprised how hard my muscles still are. They're rocks, man; they're not a bit softer than when I was twenty. And my reflexes aren't bad, either. I probably haven't lost more than a tick on the stopwatch. I mean, I run consistent 9.5 hundreds on the track out back. I swear to God I do. I've even run 9.4s sometimes. All right, I admit I do hold my own stopwatch — who the hell else is going to do it? I click it on when I start, and click it off when I hit the finish line. I probably do get a little bit of a rolling start, a couple of hundreths, maybe, but no more than that. And I probably do anticipate the finish line a little, and hit the stop button just a hair too soon. That's another couple of hundreths, maybe. But all told, I don't cheat more than half a tenth. And that's while carrying the damned watch, which must cost me something. All things considered, I run a dependable, super-legit 9.5 hundred.

That's pretty damned good, especially since I run on plain ol' dirt, with no competition except myself, with nobody running on either side to push me, to give me that adrenalin surge to really turn it on in the last twenty yards. I run in the daytime, too, when it's hot. If I could see the stopwatch at night, in the dark, when it's cooler, so that I wouldn't kill myself trying to read it while I'm still moving after crossing the finish line, I think I could go even faster. I think I could do a 9.4, maybe even a 9.3. That was a world record once, and it stood for a long, long time.

So what I wonder is this: If I'm the same *me* that I've always been, the same self, the same "I" looking out from behind my eyes, as I was back when I could do all those magical things on the basketball court, why can't I do them now?

I know that my body hasn't gotten "old," in the same sense that a new car gets old and wears out. Your body renews itself, you know. You get a new skin, for instance, about every three months. That's right: All the cells on the surface of your body are changing one by one, all the time, until you're not really the same package, strictly speaking, as you were ninety days ago. You've got a whole new outside. When people see you, they don't see the same "you" they saw three months ago. They're looking at a brand new set of cells that aren't much older than the ones they replaced. The muscles and the bone and the rest of you, the heart and lungs and all that, they change, too, cell by cell. It probably takes a little longer, but the result is still the same: You're a completely different person after a while. Inside and out, you're composed of an entirely new set of cells. So, if your cells are totally renewed, if your mind remains more or less the same, and if you can still do the same things with the same speed as you could yesterday, or last week, last month, even a year ago, then why the hell can't you do the same things with the same speed after five years, or ten, or fifteen? Why should a replacement of one cell by another one every bit as good, multiplied into a whole bodyful of cells replaced, multiplied by a lot of total replacements over the years, make you get what you call "older," so that you can't do the things you used to do?

I figure it's all in your mind. The cells in your brain are replaced, too, one by one, just like your skin cells, aren't they? When the old cells in the body go, they just take a little bit of physical energy with them, and the new cells replace that energy with as much if not more energy than was lost with the old cells. When the old brain cells go, they each take a little bit of my personality, my "I," with them. The new cells come in more or less blank and get imprinted, or something, with my personality traits, kind of gradually, I suppose, from the old cells next to them. That's what gives my personality, my "I," continuity. You might call that continuity my "soul." I used to. Even if I don't have a soul, even if nobody has a soul, I still feel physically like the same person, like I've been the same person all along. I can certainly remember the same "I" doing those same things I've always done all along.

On the other hand, while all this replacing and imprinting is going on, I have new experiences, new thoughts, new dreams. What gets imprinted is a tiny bit different with each new cell. That could mean my "I" slowly changes. That could mean that the "I" in my mind, sitting atop the body that's going like hell down the track out behind the trailer, isn't precisely the same one that went like hell, up and down the court, fifteen years ago, even though I think I remember being that same person. So, I suppose in some ways, I'm really a different person.

The possibility that I'm truly a different person now than I was then scares the hell out of me. If I am a different person than I was ten or fifteen or twenty years ago, I could just as well be a different person every time I wake up. I could turn into a different person every second, except that I just don't notice the changeover. I could turn into a different person every time I think a thought. If that's the case, then where do all my memories come from? If my mind, my "I," starts over from scratch every day or every hour or every second, I must make up my memories somehow. I must create them. If I create them, I must control them in some way. I probably controlled them back then, too. And that must be the secret of how I was able to do it all. I must have done something with my mind to control everything. The trouble is, I still can't quite figure out what it was I did.

All I know is, I can't control my mind anymore, even on a mundane level, not like I could back then. I can't get my thoughts and my body working together like that anymore. It's all purely physical now, running 9.5 hundreds. It's all muscle and no mind. Physically speaking, I must be in even better shape than I was back then.

In all probability, I must have run ten thousand hundreds on the track out behind the trailer. And not once have I been able to get my mind to click into that groove like I used to when I could disappear. Or like I think I used to. If, knowing what I know now, I could get the mind thing together again, I could probably damn well run a hundred in nine-fucking-flat. If I could click in, I could run 'em *all* in *under* nine flat. All I need is one of those little fadeouts I used to do on the basketball court. Not for the whole hundred, just for a few tenths, near the finish. Maybe right before the finish, but not right at the finish, because I still have to be there, physically, to break the tape, so to speak. And all I need to do to get the fadeout is, I think, to get myself to concentrate the way I used to.

I don't have many excuses for not concentrating. There are no distractions out here at the trailer. There's just me, the Airstream, and the track.

I built the track myself. I hand-graded that sucker in the sun, yard by yard. I could have done it in meters, but I like yards. It's something my father drummed into me: Yards are American, like the mile. They don't jibe with some fancy-ass European scheme of fitting everything — height, weight, volume, heat — into one big system. Well, so what? Americans are individualists. We like to measure things our own way. I didn't like it when they tried to make everything the same, when they tried to get America to give up on yards and the mile just so our runners and our coaches wouldn't have to worry about whether they could still run as fast if they had to think about going a couple of extra yards, or a few less, to make the metric distance. Four-minute mile, seven-foot high jump, nine-flat hundred: Those are magic numbers. Thank God a football field is still a hundred yards long and a basketball rim is still ten feet high. They're American measurements and if the world wants to play American games, it'll just have to use fucking American measurements. There was no way my track would be measured in meters. If I was going to gouge that sonofabitch out of the earth myself, scrape it clean myself, flatten it perfectly myself, and run on it myself, it was going to be yards. And it is.

The track is ten feet wide. I've only got two lanes on it. The starting line, where the aluminum starting blocks are nailed down, is right back up against the scrub. But I've got maybe a little more than thirty yards after the finish, so I can pull up fairly comfortably. At least in the daytime. So, ten feet by four hundred feet, to get straight and flat with just hand tools, in the sun. I put the chalk down myself, too, with no marker's wheelbarrow. I just put temporary rows of little posts, and a string stretched tightly along them, down the sidelines and down the middle, and then walked 'em, with a big sack of chalk with a hole cut in the corner, in my arms. The lines wiggle a little. And I have to re-chalk them after every rain which, admittedly, isn't very often. But I've gotten so good at it by now that the lines look almost mechanical, like they were put down with a real marker's wheelbarrow.

I put the track pretty far out behind the trailer because I didn't want it seen from the highway. It's O.K. if people see the targets, sticking up out of the brush out back. I like people to know I've got guns around. I'm alone here, with not even a dog. The trailer's exposed — a big silver blister on this bleak, gravelly landscape. With none of the town's lights, it gets real dark around here. People in town think I'm a little strange to begin with, and some of these people, even the religious ones up here in this part of Idaho, can get pretty mean when they want to. Especially after the incident with the kid in the stands at the football game, even though most everybody in Calvary understands by now that it was just a misunderstanding. Somebody just said something hasty to the cops. They know I'm no homo.

Still, there could be that single somebody in Calvary who still doesn't understand. And he could bear me a grudge. You never can tell who, for some cockeyed reason, is going to bear you a grudge. And all it takes, God knows, is one.

Nevertheless, I'm not going to hide out here. It's fine with me if everybody knows where I am. But I do like my privacy. I need it for my research. I don't have a phone. I don't even have electricity, although it'd be simple enough to run in a pirate wire from the power lines along the highway. I get along fine with a hurricane lamp and my little Coleman stove and my cache of five-gallon jugs of pure spring water. The water truck comes once a month.

It isn't fear of the town that makes me live alone. I still go into town for the high school games. If somebody wants to pop me, I figure, they won't do it in town in front of every-body in the stands at one of the games. They'll try to sneak up on me out at the trailer. Somebody could come out here while I'm in town at a football game one Friday night, and get themselves a real good hiding place and pop me when I come screeching home on the Beemer. Which is why I've begun reconsidering about dogs lately. I've been thinking of getting a dog, a big one like a shepherd or a rottweiler, something big that I can train to be loud and scary.

On the other hand, I enjoy being totally alone, with no other minds around but mine, with no other consciousness's eyes to look into and wonder what it's thinking. Not even an animal's. I probably won't get a dog.

The high school basketball games are O.K., too, I suppose. I should probably like them more, because basketball is obviously the sport I played best. But I like the football games better because they're outdoors, on those nice, cold fall nights, at the simple, scruffy field with the shaky, bolted-together bleachers and those stanchions of blinding lights. Hissing white suns at the tops of wobbly steel towers. I imagine that's what Alamagordo was like when they blew up the first one as a test, only a million times bigger, a million times brighter.

I like the sense of occasion at the football games; I like anticipating Friday nights, and working up to them all week long. And, of course, I like getting duded up and roaring into town on the big Beemer. I haven't seen another RS1000 on the roads around Calvary since I've lived here. The high school girls like it, too. They get all smiley and their chewing gum clicks a mile a minute when I brodie up to the bleachers. Don't get me wrong, I don't get off on high school girls. But at heart I'm just a big overgrown boy, and I still like to impress the girls, just for the hell of impressing them.

"Fighting Christians" is a gloriously stupid name, isn't it? On the football field, with these big, baby-faced farm kids smacking into one another with a kind of demented ferocity, the name seems especially absurd. The Calvary High School football uniforms are just about all yellow — yellow pants and yellow jerseys, like pajamas — with big purple numbers outlined in white — and then yellow helmets with a logo of a big white block "C," outlined in purple, with a slanty cross cutting through it in purple, piped in white. Some of the players even buy custom-yellow cleats. Under the lights, with those satiny tight pants, the Calvary High uniforms are the brightest goddamned things you ever saw. Calvary High looks like it's fielded a whole team of glowing saviors — goody-goody little wimps just waiting, and maybe even wanting, to be crucified. Maybe the nickname, and the uniforms, are the reasons why the team loses as often as it does. It may have God on it's side, but he must not be the God of Uniforms.

And maybe that's why I grabbed the kid like I did, and made people think I was doing something funny with him.

The truth was that it just suddenly popped into my mind that somebody on the "Fighting Christians" — in those weird golden outfits, getting cut to pieces under those bright holy lights — should know the secret, or whatever small part I know of it. Maybe I just wanted somebody else to have the magic, before it finally dies in me. Or before I die, period.

They didn't videotape my college games, so there's no way anybody can see when I first did the disappearing thing. In a way, it's my fault. After all that shit for so many years with my father, I was so confused and scared I couldn't make myself leave the state, even when I had the chance. He told me that only he could take care of me, that I'd be a fish out of water if I went too far away from him. As stupid and intimidated as I was back then, I could see that this was an absurd position for a guy who was trying to raise his son, "scientifically," to be the greatest athlete in the history of the world.

Big son of a bitch he was, only an inch shorter than I am — maybe not even that — and I'm six-six. He had these huge hands, especially when he made a fist. Don't get me wrong, he didn't beat me with 'em; they just made an impression on me. So I stayed in Idaho. But not at the University of Idaho or even Idaho State. Instead, I went to some shithole little college right down the road.

We were only on television a couple of times, on some dinky state educational channel. The camera work was real primitive — two guys with shoulder-harness cameras and no replay — and some skinny, adenoidal insurance sales- man did play-by-play as a hobby. But, in spite of the grainy image transmitted from our little hotbox gym (it seated about twenty-five hundred, on accordion bleachers), you could sometimes see me do it. Or not see me do it, which is closer to the point.

I'd just slide out of view for a couple of milliseconds. It usually happened when I drove the lane. I tended to knock over a lot of people, because I was really built more like a linebacker than a forward, and because I just liked to put my shoulder down and go where the action was thickest. People watching television — or the few of them who ever talked to me about it — would say that I just disappeared — bang! — in the middle of a drive to the basket. They said it was spooky, the way I just wouldn't be there for an instant or two. Then, they said, I'd reappear, like I'd just landed off-balance, flailing along the baseline. And then the ball would suddenly appear on the rim, lolling around the hoop, before dropping through, as if the shot had been made by a ghost. The live crowd would be watching it instead of me, which is probably why none of them ever said anything to me.

Sometimes one of the high school kids working the baseline as a photographer for the Calvary weekly would get a lucky shot. The photograph would always show a part of me — a foot or forearm or elbow or shoe or something — sticking out of the knot of the two or three players who were trying to guard me. But the rest of my body just wouldn't be where it should've showed up; it just looked more like one of the defensive players had suddenly grown an extra appendage.

If I could have done my disappearing act at will, just by deciding to do it, I could've scored a hundred, two hundred, a game. But I couldn't. It'd only happen a half-dozen times, a dozen at most, during a game, without me ever figuring out how. I did it enough, however, to make our team win, enough to average about thirty a game and make the out-of-state papers now and then. I did it enough to keep people at the school and in the town talking about me. I did it enough to draw a couple of pro scouts into our gym.

The NBA was in a kind of slump in those days. To be

honest, race had a lot to do with it. The white folks who bought the tickets were a getting a little tired of black guys in big Afros and long sideburns, wearing floor-length fur coats and having two or three white girls on their arms at the same time, getting big contracts and all the headlines. They thought there must be something wrong with a game where all the All-Stars looked like Super Fly pimps. The scouts told my coach that professional basketball needed a small-town white boy good enough, and entertaining enough, to keep suburban white people coming to the games and watching on TV. This all happened, of course, before professional basketball took off. This was before the Doctor and Magic came along: two black guys who were simply too good, too spectacular, for even white racists to ignore. Except for the disappearing thing, I was never in their league.

Back then, the ABA, was out there, too, gambling on the assumptions that the big cities, like New York and L.A., could support a couple of teams and that some smaller cities would go for flashy, big-time basketball, too. The ABA started throwing money at young, untried players. That scared the NBA. They thought that competition between two leagues would drive the price of players up beyond what anybody could really afford. They wanted to kill the new league, quick. A couple of NBA scouts told the league it should start coming up with white stars who'd make the ABA look, by comparison, like a ghetto league. They thought maybe I was the guy.

But they were only a couple of scouts among many, and not the most highly regarded, either. I mean, what kind of basketball scout gets Idaho, Montana and Wyoming as his territory? They couldn't convince their bosses to draft me. The ABA, on the other hand, sent squads of these fat, pockmarked guys with cigars and houndstooth-check, maroon leisure suits, with white belts and white patent leather loafers to scope me out. Some of 'em thought I was the second coming of Bob Cousy and Bob Petit rolled into one, and heavier and tougher in the bargain. True, some of 'em thought I was just another small college musclehead who'd be better off as a tight end in football, or staying home pumping gas. Somebody among them, however, convinced one club to take a chance and draft me. The ABA took me, right up near the top. An NBA team picked me, too, but way down at the bottom of the fourth round.

So I played pro ball right down the road in Salt Lake City. It seemed to me like I was destined to spend my whole life up in this corner of the country. Born here, jocked-up here practically from birth by my insanely jocked-up father, a jock in college — if you could call it that — here, pro ball here, and living in this trailer here. I can't get out. And I'm not a Mormon. I'm not even a Christian. I'm an agnostic, maybe even an atheist if I really think about it and don't scare myself about Heaven and Hell. I've been through a lot in terms of religion, and I haven't come close to figuring anything out. I'll probably die right here, too.

For a couple of years, I gave the ABA my best shot. I was the goddamnest, most fanatic player you ever saw. I laid out almost horizontally in midair more times than I jumped up vertically. I was always skidding, sliding, slamming into somebody, throwing bodies over the scorer's table. Refs were always having to step between me and some seven-foot black dude. I didn't really want to fight, and I didn't have anything against black guys. I just wanted to stay hot, bodily hot, and fevered in the head. I couldn't bring on the disappearing thing anytime I wanted, but I did know that I had to be hot in order to have any hope of it reoccurring. The next time I drove to the basket, I wanted to fade from view for that wonderful instant, and then suddenly show up, above the rim, and slam the ball in their fucking faces.

I managed to do that kind of stuff often enough to get us to the playoffs, to the second round both years. And I did my thing even more in the playoffs, and I got us to the seventh game against much better teams both years. I got us down to the goddamned wire both times. I had the house rockin'. I was insane both of those final games because I knew I had to be to get the heat in my mind up to the point where I could fade out. I scored over forty in both games. I still can't figure out how we lost.

Once the ABA got me on some decent television, people started seeing some tapes. They started to believe, or half-believe, that I could really do what they were seeing. That was if they could believe they were seeing it, which, half the time, they couldn't. People in the stands could never tell. They'd just scream like at a bad call they'd convinced themselves they'd seen but which, deep down, they knew was probably just a function of their being hometown rooters. The important thing was, I believed it, and the more I believed it, the crazier I acted on account of it. I couldn't turn it off when I needed to. Maybe that's why we lost both those seventh games.

At least that's what Coach told the reporters after we got bounced from the playoffs the first year, "I don't care if he scores sixty. I'm always afraid to leave Robo in the game. Yes, he might shoot, he might pass, he might sit on the ball, he might start bowling over people, he might do one of those miracle drives of his. But he might throw the ball into the goddamned stands. Hell, he might do anything, anytime. I never know."

He couldn't say I never warned him. I told him this at practice once: "Sport is simply a matter of training your physical body to get in synch with the dimension of Time." He didn't believe me, or he didn't understand me. "I don't know about you, Robo," he'd say, and walk away shaking his head. That just made me crazier. Robo, incidentally, is what everybody called me — not just Coach — and it's what everybody still calls me. It's short for Robo-jock, which is short, of course, for Robot-jock, which is what my father tried to turn me into.

I probably should have never gone to Africa after my second season. But the league wanted it. They said it was for good will, to show a little respect for the growing Afrocentrism of some of the the black fans, who were starting to buy tickets as well as watch us on television. I didn't care what the league's reason was, I just wanted to get away from people saying we lost playoff games because I couldn't quit acting crazy. I forget the town now, but it was the capital city of some unbearably hot, unbearably underdeveloped, unbearably poor, unbearably corrupt country run by "generals" who didn't look much older than guys I played against. I was expecting Africa to be jungles and stuff, but it was more like a desert. Actually, the part of Africa I saw wasn't all that different from Calvary, Idaho.

We were billed as an All-Star squad, but we were several cuts below that. We were just some psyched-up guys from different ABA teams who thought it'd be a hoot to see Africa, play a little hoops with each other for fun in front of some adoring locals, and maybe score some unknown drugs and exotic women. I bought into the first part, but not the drugs and the women. I was never into drugs and, I guess, I was never into women. I was just along on the trip because I was a little crazy, and wanted to see if the disappearing thing would work on a different continent.

It didn't, at least not in the games. I played shitty. But it did start to happen on the street, without me even working up to it, and in the hotel rooms. At first I thought I was having some kind of black-outs, or that I was getting slipped some drugs by accident or on purpose by somebody who wanted to ruin my career which, although I didn't know it yet, was already ruined. Sometimes, I even thought I was coming down with epilepsy. One second I'd be there, and I'd know I was there, and the next second — bang! — I'd be someplace else. Not too far away, maybe just across the room, or out the door.

Once, I was in a little souvenir shop swimming with incense smoke that smelled exactly like those little pink cakes in the bottoms of urinals in the practice gym back in Idaho. I was looking at a weird painting, a religious picture that looked like it came right out of Europe in the Renaissance. It didn't look African at all. It showed the Virgin Mary holding the Christ child. I was staring at it when suddenly, I was out the door, standing next to an open sewer. I don't know how I got there, but I remember thinking it was probably the disappearing thing again, triggered by who-knows-what. That scared me because it meant the whole deal was getting out of control. Now I not only couldn't make it happen when I wanted it to happen, but apparently I couldn't stop it from happening when I didn't want it to.

I turned and walked back inside the shop. When I got there, the guy in the kaftan behind the counter was bending over, picking up the package that contained the same goddamned painting I'd just been looking at. He was going to unwrap it and put it on the same shelf where I'd just seen it. When I stepped to the counter, he smiled and said between crepe-paper teeth, in perfect English, "Yes, may I help you?" like he'd never seen me before in his life.

I told him that I'd just been standing right in front of him in a few seconds ago. He answered politely that he'd never seen me before in his life. I told him I could prove I'd been in before: I could describe the painting he was about to unwrap. He lay the painting, still wrapped, flat on the counter. I described the picture. He unwrapped it, and started to tremble. He looked me in the eye and, barely able to restrain himself from screaming at me, said that I had brought a "bad spirit" into his shop. Would I please leave, he said. It wasn't a request.

The same kind of shit might have happened to me a couple more times, or it could have been right after what happened in the souvenir shop that I went through the window. I can't remember, exactly. I do remember that it happened at the Hilton in the capital city, and that plate glass window was huge. They told me later that I was cradling a basketball in my arm like a football, and that I yelled, "I am Jesus! I am Jesus!" right before crashing through the glass.

It should have killed me, or severed an arm or leg. All I got, however, was one bad cut right near my right armpit, close to where Jesus was poked with the centurion's spear, only a little closer to where your roll-on deodorant goes.

While I was recovering in the hospital — the sole white person I could see anywhere, made even more conspicuous rather than more invisible by the fact that I blended in with the bedsheets — I began to think that God had sent me a message and he wanted me to spread His word to the team. A reporter for one of the wire services in Cairo heard about the incident and came down to do a short little story on it. After he interviewed me and I told him about the message from God, he interviewed the other guys on the team and asked them if they thought I could be a messenger from God. One of the players told him, "If the Lord wanted to tell me something, he'd tell me directly. He sure as shit wouldn't tell some wacko like Robo and ask him to pass the word on to me."

When it happened, that is, when I lowered my shoulder and ran for the glass, this other player — a real marginal player who'd just broke in with the league near the end of the season after playing for one of those touring fundamentalist Christian organizations, called Athletes for God or something — sprang up from his chair and ran right through the hole after me. He ripped off his T-shirt and made a tourniquet. He probably saved my life, because it took almost an hour from the time the hotel staff calmed down enough to stop bumping into one another and call an ambulance. By the time they wheeled me into the hospital, I could have bled to death five times over.

The guy's saving my life is why, for better or worse, I said I'd come home with him after the tour. He belonged to this new religious organization that was very different from the Christianity he used to believe in when he played on that barnstorming team before he broke into the ABA. It was better than Christianity, he said, because it incorporated all the saviors of all religions into one glorious megafaith. Given my condition, I was in no shape to argue, and given my upbringing, I was in no shape to fend off some zealous religious convert. So I just listened and agreed. Sure, I said to the guy, I'll go with you wherever you want for a breather once we get back to the States. I was so dazed that it didn't surprise me at all that the cult — which is what I guess you'd call The Brothers of Jesus — turned out to be encamped right here, in Calvary, Idaho. I remember thinking: Full circle, baby. It must be some kind of weird destiny.

Every Picture Stores a Telly

In 1878, Elkhart, Nevada was barely more than a water-ing stop on the stagecoach trail westward, from Denver to the Pacific Coast. But it had two saloons. One was called, inexplicably, The Cossack. It boasted genuine tables and chairs, although plain wood and unupholstered, instead of merely a standup bar bracketed by brass spittoons. Passing for elegant in the dusty outpost, it doubled as Elkhart's only restaurant, serving eggs for breakfast and tough beef for dinner. Elkhart also had two churches, one of which was Catholic and called itself St. Something-or-Other. It was presided over by a real, ordained priest, until he left in the middle of the night, with two Apache altar boys. Elkhart had one general store — Purdy's — and one doctor, whose fly-specked office lay upstairs in the same unpainted wooden building.

The resident population of Elkhart could have barely staffed a skeleton crew at a goat ranch. The town filled to capacity only on Saturday nights, when cowboys and off-duty cavalry wandered in from the neighboring grazing lands and a nearby log-and-adobe fort to get drunk. Because Elkhart didn't have a brothel, and because the town's few women and their nubile daughters fled home to their ranches on the weekends, pleasures of the flesh were denied.

Although of little compensatory value to cowboys and soldiers, Elkhart did, however, possess a clock and pocket watch repair shop — more like a closet, actually — tucked in the rear of Purdy's General Store. The repair shop's proprietor was Galvany Protector, a hunched, timid and tuberculous refugee from the pogroms who had made his long, long way west: from the razed village of Kartrusk to Minsk, from Minsk to Vienna, from Vienna to Paris, from Paris to London, from London to Manchester, from Manchester via dank and diseased steerage to New York, from New York to Chicago, from Chicago to Kansas City, and from Kansas City to what, ultimately, was supposed to be San Francisco but turned out to be Elkhart. Nevertheless, Galvany was satisfied that he had journeyed, and settled, far enough west. After all, he thought, (consulting Mr. Purdy's leatherbound atlas) I live closer to the islands of the South Seas than do citizens of Los Angeles.

Galvany, who had acquired a fair ability with English, was particular about the pronunciation of his first name: *Gall-VON-nyee*. He didn't fuss over the pronunciation of his last name, since it had been assigned to him on Ellis Island and bore only a rudimentary resemblance to the name he was born with. Originally, that had been Probtyenkczor, or its close approximation in Cyrillic. The fat, walrus-moustachioed policeman who'd fumigated Galvany on Ellis Island and herded him brusquely toward a shower, played a little joke. He thought Galvany looked weak and vulnerable, even among the refugees, and could use a protector. So he gave him one as a surname.

Galvany Protector began his Atlantic crossing as a married man and landed as a widower. Surai, his wife, died in the middle of the night, gargling phlegm. Galvany didn't want anybody to think he and his young son, Serge (two syllables, with a hard "G"), were contaminated, so he surreptitiously dragged Surai's corpse up the rusting, heaving ladders from steerage to topside and pitched it into the propeller's churning wake. The next morning, an apparently shaken Serge told his huddled compatriots, and the ship's officers who questioned him, that Surai, who must have become disoriented, must have gotten up in the middle of the night to wander, illegally, in the open air, and must have fallen overboard. Ten-year-old Serge, with an innocent's allegiance to the truth, opened his mouth to the ship's purser, with the intent to say in Hebrew that, no, Mama never got up to take a walk because she lay down immediately after her meager steerage dinner and was suddenly stiff and cold to his touch. He was also going to say that he lay in her arms long into the night, hoping to revive his beloved mother with his own body heat. But, as only the first two words — "my mother" — were leaving his lips, Galvany smacked him across the mouth, hard, with his open hand.

The boy bled and cried. Galvany apologized to the purser, and explained that his son was unforgivably insolent by nature and that he, the father, had been compelled, just then, to intervene to preserve the good will between the ship's officers and himself, the lowest of passengers. As soon as the purser and a flunky (who took notes with a naked stick of graphite that he constantly licked) had disappeared, Galvany explained to his son why he struck him. Serge whimpered, but said that he understood. Galvany, who had never before so much as raised his voice to his son, let alone a hand (although he had permitted the village *mohel* to relieve the infant Serge of his tiny, peach-colored foreskin), never struck the boy again. Until the day, years later, when Galvany was trampled to death in the main street of Elkhart by a stampede of eight cattle gone mysteriously berserk, Serge acted, sometimes sincerely, as though he loved his father unconditionally.

By his father's dictum, the young Serge read omnivorously in English: the Old Testament, Shakespeare, the essays of Francis Bacon, the English poems of Milton (and, after Serge taught himself Latin, the poems of Milton in that language), the only copy of Darwin's *The Voyage of the Beagle* in the entire territory, *Blackstone's Law*, *The Federalist Papers*, a biography of Abraham Lincoln from the Confederate point of view, *Great English Physicists*, every mathematics textbook he could get his smooth, slender, long-fingered hands on, and (concealed from his father) every work on the occult that he could find.

Serge did not attend the local school, which was just dandy with the other Elkhart children, who could stomach Serge's cold brilliance only if it stayed outside the door to the town's single, splinter-floored classroom. Serge was free to roam, and he would avoid the town as much as possible. The townsfolk in Elkhart, however, came to love the quiet, doe-eyed boy. They sponsored him in county and state spelling bees as one would a village's prize heifer in a state fair. Serge won them all. He would returned home to recite heartfelt speeches of gratitude in his high, reedy voice (nearly an ultra-soprano), go back to his books, and then, a couple of months later, venture out again to win another laurel. He went by himself. Although there weren't many clocks and pocket watches in the vicinity of Elkhart, Galvany also repaired buckboards, water pumps, beer kegs, and telegraph keys. He also plowed, fed cattle, cooked, washed dishes and, on occasions, babysat. To make humble ends meet for himself and his son, he remained available for most any kind of work, all day, all week, all year.

Serge couldn't read on the bumpy stagecoaches, so he just stared out the window. But Serge had made himself so observant and so analytically disciplined, that just by hanging his curly head out the stagecoach window he acquired the equivalent of bachelor's degree knowledge in geology, botany, and meteorology. He mastered economics by staying alone in hotels and dickering with concierges, bellhops, waiters and chambermaids. He conquered social studies by devouring magazines and newspapers. (He'd check in, ask for a copy of each daily, weekly, monthly and quarterly in stock in the hotel's usually modest newsrack, and consume them in their entireties in about an hour). And Serge made himself the eventual charming chameleon he became by applying what he learned — in his first whorehouse on his first unchaperoned overnight trip — to seducing practically every unwary female who ventured, unknowingly, so near as the same floor of his hotel room. Indeed, by the date of what would normally have been for a boy of his perspicacity his Bar Mitzvah, the silken-skinned, ruby-lipped Serge had enjoyed sex a hundredfold more often than his own father, who experienced the pleasures of intercourse but twice (once to celebrate his wedding night, once to conceive Serge). And both of Galvany's moments of ecstasy came long ago, in a vanished world.

It came as no surprise to anyone in Elkhart when Serge Protector was invited — at an age most boys in Elkhart had barely mastered copying *The Lord's Prayer* from the nearsighted schoolteacher's master on the blackboard — to attend the University of California in Berkeley, just a ferryboat ride short of his father's destination of dreams. A hat was passed among the townsfolk, a suit was quickly (albeit badly) tailored by the local seamstress, a party (at which Galvany was so uncomfortable as to be rendered catatonic) was thrown in The Cossack, and Serge was cheered off to California.

The good burghers of Berkeley struck Serge — who was greatly disappointed — as no more sophisticated or well-dressed than the citizens of Elkhart. It was the university students — a melange of young scions, neurasthenic poets, callow adventurers, and a few who were genuinely intellectually inclined — who garbed themselves formally. Tight, suffocating wool suits, accompanied by bow ties more appropriate for Christmas packages, for the men; long, many-buttoned dresses with the bodices concealed by dark sweaters for the women. Walking sticks for the gentlemen; umbrellas for the ladies. Velvet-collared overcoats for the males; crinkled, tent-like outwear for the females. Bulging leather book satchels for the beaux; one or two coyly thin marble-bound composition pads for the belles. But none of the males' share of this for Serge, whose suit was baggy, and whose tie was shoelace-thin, and who could barely afford to eat and sleep in his residence, a hotel whose other guests — laid out in cots and bunks as tightly bunched as cord wood — were indentured Chinese workers.

Perhaps spurred on by poverty, Serge raced to his baccalaureate in "the physical and biological sciences" in a little over two years. Actually, he managed to save a little money, by tutoring the less academically adroit, along the way. And Serge grew. During his abbreviated undergraduate career, he added more than a foot to his height. When added to his already considerable conversational charisma Serge's altitude and gradually redefined facial features — long, aristocratic nose with the tiniest cleft bulb at the tip, deeply set glaring eyes, thin lips nevertheless assuming the shape of a very narrow cupid's bow, and small, even, perfectly white teeth — rendered him one of the most noted presences in Berkeley. The other student dandies were jealous; the sprinkling of coeds were in a semiconstant swoon; the professors were proud; and the merchants were grateful for the additional business he attracted to the establishments which became known as "Serge's restaurant," "Serge's barber," and "Serge's cobbler" by his patronizing them but once during his collegiate tenure.

Still, there was something about the wonder boy from the tiny hamlet east of the Sierra Nevadas that unnerved a lot of folks. Serge once attended Sunday services in a local Protestant church of fundamentalist persuasion. He sat on the aisle in the front pew, listening intensely but in a dead calm, as though he were an anthropologist observing the customs of a savage tribe. The preacher's eyes involuntarily fixed on Serge's reciprocal gaze for the sermon's duration. (Afterward, the shaken cleric swore that the icy lad in the pews blinked not even once.) While the echoes of the minister's fire-and-brimstone coda were fading into the redwood rafters, Serge flashed a quick, arrogant smile, and strode quickly up the aisle, toward the exit, ahead of everyone else. He burst open the great doors, stepped into the blazing noon sun, and was gone. It was as if — the man of the cloth later remarked — the devil himself had sent an ambassador. By the time Serge left town for good, almost all of Berkeley was glad to see him go.

Serge had, during the latter stages of his undergraduate career, secured a benefactor who, in monetary terms, far exceeded his hometown's heartfelt but somewhat meagre generosity. Serge, scouring the university library for the name of a place where he might further his studies under a fellowship, had come across The Case School of Applied Science in Cleveland, and news of an important experiment that was about to be conducted there. The man underwriting the experiment was a railroad stockholder and department store owner who'd endowed a chair of physics at the School. Serge wrote to the school, which in turn forwarded the letter somewhat perfunctorily to the magnate, who in his surprising turn sent Serge a letter of commitment to support his doctoral matriculation, a train ticket, and a check sufficient to remake his exterior at least in the mold of a gentleman. At the fitting for his new (and much better tailored) suit, Serge decided that from then on he'd pronounce — and require others to pronounce — his first name as the French *Serj*, instead of the inconveniently Slavic *SER-gay*. This small adjustment, he reasoned, would give him the extra cachet needed to establishment himself well in the larger but (as far as Serge was concerned) unsophisticated city of Cleveland.

Serge traveled east by train, in comfortable Pullman cars. He wore a bowler to complement his jacket, slacks, and overcoat. He ate civilly if not sumptuously in the dining car and in reputable restaurants at stops along the way. He stayed overnight in hotels with lobbies as red with velvet as wombs. In Kansas City, Serge paused to send a telegram back to Elkhart and waited, elbow on the counter and slender jaw inclined toward the operator's decorative grille, for the reply. When it came and the operator handed him the handwritten transcription, Serge bit his lip, looked at the ceiling, thanked the man, paid, and left as briskly as he had his single visit to church. Galvany, he'd learned, wouldn't be able to enjoy this particular edition of filial greetings because he'd been stomped to death by a band of rampaging cows.

★ ★ ★ ★ ★

The laboratory for the important experiment was not located, as Serge Protector had expected, on the wooded campus of Case School of Applied Science, but in the sub-basement of the giant Halley Brothers Department Store, just a few blocks from where local moguls were contemplating building a needle-tipped, pyramid-topped architectural phallus that would be known as the Terminal Tower and would allegedly mark Cleveland as the Paris of the Midwest, and erase the town's snidely given and reluctantly acquired moniker of "the mistake on the lake." Serge's mentor, doctoral advisor, and head of the experiment's scientific team, explained that there was nowhere else in the city where one could, in relatively antiseptic conditions, float an electric light source, an observational telescope, sixteen mirrors, a heavy wooden turntable, and a two-ton sandstone base in a vat of mercury.

In the important experiment, a beam of light would be split, the component parts sent on their own individual ways, to arrive separately back at the source. If the individual beams streamed home at slightly different moments (different by only the least measurable fragments of a second), the existence of ether — a tasteless, soundless, odorless, colorless, weightless and practically qualityless (except for its ability to act as a drag on light) medium in which the cosmos was presumed to be marinating — would be proved. Should the beams show up simultaneously back on their own doorstep, then ether would enter the mythical realm of the Philosopher's Stone and other vestiges of alchemy. Several of the scientists involved in the important experiment hoped that ether would indeed be detected; they thought it would help prove the existence of God, who would have to have been on duty prior to the creation of the universe to have cooked up the Original Batch.

Serge's mentor, a cold, clipt atheist, clandestinely rooted for the opposite outcome. From Serge's lowly perspective as (it had turned out) a glorified errand boy for a roomful of pompous, amply bellied engineers and physicists, he didn't much care. He thought the experiment foolish on its face: if the results were negative, ether might still exist, in qualities apprehendable only by a more subtle and precise experiment yet to be devised. If the results were positive, the interstellar goo thus discovered might, upon apprehension of other of its properties not yet known, turn out eventually to be something other than ether.

It passed that Cleveland contained no ether, as well as no decent French restaurant. The former established, in any case, the scientific consensus of the moment and was duly announced to the Western world. Serge, who had, by the end of the important experiment, evolved to a vague form of theism, demurred. "Everything, even nothing, is something," he wrote in his journal. But he kept his own counsel and collected his doctor's degree in record time.

Serge spent one leafy, humid postdoctoral summer in Cleveland, living in a quite comfy boarding house on the corner of Euclid Avenue and Twelfth Street. He worked at the School, as a "research advisor," a position concocted by his professors as a mark-time, or a bone to be thrown to Serge, until they figured out whether they wished to retain the brilliant and conspicuously young scientist, or whether they wished to let the impolitic, vain, adolescent Don Juan go. At the beginning of August, Serge made their decision for them.

He had managed to make love — in both the 19th century sense of that word, which includes the preliminaries of a declaration of interest, flowers, candy, tiny glasses of sherry, and the uttering of sweet words clustered within ornately structured sentences, and in the 20th century sense of it, meaning sexual coupling — to just about every woman in Cleveland who attracted him in the least. Since Serge demanded at least a little conversation to counterpoint his own disquisitions (in a voice that, while still high for an adult male, had been lowered considerably from the dog-whistle octaves of his youth in Elkhart), the eligibility pool for his conquests was mercifully limited to those women he'd actually met.

Shortly before the Fourth of July holiday, an exquisite young woman, who'd come up from Cincinnati to join her uncle and aunt for the festivities in Forest Hills park and found their house reduced by one guest bedroom owing to a small fire caused by her uncle's incessant pipe-smoking, arrived for a few days' lodging at Serge's rooming house. At the first sight of her tiny corseted waist, full, almost ample, hips, milky skin, delicate and apparently knuckleless fingers, and thick auburn hair, Serge acted.

He introduced himself with what he thought was an elegant and subtle boast concerning his intellectual prowess; he sat next to her at all the house's meals; he brought her (the day after her arrival) a small bottle of perfume that he just "happened across" in conversation with Mr. Halley at his store (implying heavy-handedly that the department store magnate was his personal benefactor); and he held her hand (somewhat to the young woman's shock) in the parlor while lecturing her on the wonders of Chopin. With a normally sufficient amount of time (perhaps a week, two at the most) in which to woo, Serge might have tempted even this refined and reserved young woman to bed. But her stay at the rooming house was just three nights, after which she was obligated to return to a Bible institute in Cincinnati. At least, Serge told himself later, it was simply time that had been the problem, and not — an admission he was loathe to make — her unbending piety.

The most intimate prize that Serge could secure (he tried to kiss her the last night, on the porch, but when his lips but grazed her cheek she fainted into a lacy heap haloed by June bugs) was a promise that, should he ever travel south to the city known as the Rome on the Ohio River, she would receive him hospitably. But (she made clear) in order to be received with any real enthusiasm in Cincinnati (she made this exceedingly clear), he would have to make himself familiar with a prophetic, charismatic minister of the Gospel named William Halliwell.

The Reverend William Halliwell's effect on the life of Serge Protector had actually taken seed about four centuries earlier, in a damp and smoky atelier (actually, the vacated but still vegetatively fragrant hayloft of a stone barn) in a corner of the European Low Country then known as Flanders. Dieric Maender, temporarily a fugitive from his creditors in Liege, had installed himself in this rustic but inadequate studio near Bruges, in order to complete an oil-on-wood-panel commission for His Eminence the Duc du Galonde. Payment for the painting would be an amount in gold coin sufficient to satisfy the painter's angriest creditors and still leave a considerable sum to be spent on ale and wenches. The stout, smallpox-pitted Maender had signed the contract and gotten to work immediately. While away from his easel, Maender may have been a bit of a libertine, in front of it he was all piety and craft.

The project was intended to be a relatively simple matter for an artist with Maender's talent for verisimilitude: a single panel depicting the Virgin Mary, on a throne in the center, holding the Christ Child while, at the left, the Bishop of Galeunjt (the Dutch spelling was preferred by the Bishop, a wizened old deaf Flemish priest named Getys Haardjek) and his supervising Archbishop, Hendrik Cardinal Oeups, knelt in diplomatic devotion (or devotional diplomacy) and, at the right, the Duc and Duchesse du Galonde did the same, but with somewhat more earnest expressions on their pale, potato-shaped faces. Maender was asked to provide no other embellishments (such as side panels) than a bit of precious, reflective metallic paint in the golden halos crowning Mary and Jesus, and in the Cardinal's carpet-thick robe. Even working less than full time and allowing the fairly recently invented oil paints sufficient drying time in the damp climate, the 87-centimetres-by-65-centimetres painting (height preceding width, measurements dictated by the serendipitous proportions of the oak panel with which the artist had been furnished by a local carpenter) should have taken him six months to produce. It should have been, had Maender had the expression available to him then, a piece of cake. But something very strange was going on.

During this, the spring of the year 1465, Maender would work from about ten o'clock in the morning until about two in the afternoon, break for bread, cheese and red wine smuggled up sans-tariff from the Walloon south, then return to the barn for a brief review of the early day's labor. The cradling, sizing (with rabbit-skin glue) and priming (with a thin, knifed-on coat of white lead) of his panel proceeded without a hitch; blocking in the six main figures with silverpoint presented Maender with no trouble, either. And he managed the first two undercoats of the quicker-drying pigments he'd ground up the week before with nary a scrape-down.

The peculiarities began when Maender started fully articulating the figures. The Virgin, for instance: he'd limned the customary holy egg for her smooth head, delicately intoned her lashless eyes with a quiet fever of pink, and had commenced to work on her sacred lips when time for a vessel of the grape drew nigh. Maender drank that day, as he did all days, fully and without guilt, but not to what he saw as excess. So when he returned to the barn and saw that half his morning's effort had been mysteriously wiped out, he was stupefied. Wiped out was not quite the phrase that came to his straightforward, Netherlandish mind. Altered was more like it. But not simply "altered" in the sense that another hand had picked up his brush and defaced Maender's painting in his momentary absence. What was the proper description, then? The picture was somehow faded, blurred, bleached, semi-obliterated — something more along those lines.

The Virgin's head still looked like an egg. That was the trouble. It looked like nothing else *but* an egg. The head had grown dramatically (although Maender could find no trace of his original drafting lines being transgressed, the perception was undeniable by him). It had also lost its features (retaining merely the pale ghosts of eyes, which had metamorphosed, chromatically, from faint rose to the mere spectre of sky blue). And the Virgin's hands — which were to have given him the most delirious pleasure to describe in their divine perfection — had reverted to nothing but ugly mitts. She — the Holy Mother of the Son of God — was a monster!

Trembling with fear (what would His Eminence, not to say his creditors, do to him if he could not satisfactorily complete this commission?) and doubt (could it have been the possibly poisoned contraband wine affecting his memory and — worse!—his skill?), Maender worked all afternoon, stayed awake and stared at his panel under candlelight, and finished repairing the painting the next morning.

But on his return from his next lunch (this particular meal without the grape, by God!), the damage was done again. Aghast, with his heart pounding to the extent that he feared it would burst through his leather vest, Maender frantically set at the painting once more, repairing the damage for the second time and, with blistering determination, even forging ahead from the point at which he'd halted just before the initial catastrophe. As far as he could tell the next day, he'd won out over whatever strange force was attempting to wrest *The Holy Virgin and the Infant Jesus in the Presence of Hendrik Cardinal Oeups, the Most Holy Reverend Getys Haardjek, His Eminence the Duc du Galonde, and the Duchesse of Galonde on the Occasion of the Taxing of the Flax Merchants to Begin the Construction of the Cathedral of Frieje* from his control. And the day after that, the picture, still in its adolescence in terms of physical completion, appeared to have stabilized.

But there remained disturbing signs of disfigurement. Maender's rheumy but unerring eye detected traces of a color — a caranthamine orange — that he did not put into the picture, indeed, that he did not even recognize, that he had never before even imagined. And, when he applied his pigment powders, hand-ground in the finest linseed stand oil as if they were his own children raised from infancy to maturity, he felt an unearthly drag on his brush, as if he were painting two, perhaps even three, paintings simultaneously. Finally, he suspected that as he painted one area of his panel he — quite unintentionally, unknowingly, and unfathomably — unpainted another. A brushy caress, for instance, of the folds in his patron's sleeve, brought to his vision (when he lowered his painting arm and stepped back on the crackling, scattered shafts of hay on the thickly planked floor) a compensating erasure somewhere in the garments of the Duc du Galonde.

Maender did not pursue the thought, at least not consciously, lest he reveal to himself, and ultimately to others who might not be as sympathetic to him as he was to himself, that he was possessed by a less than heavenly spirit. He reached a climax of fright concerning this one night after he lightfootedly ascended the ladder to his studio with lamp in hand. There, on his easel, before his eyes and in defiance of God himself, was Maender's oaken panel decorated — if that be the word for sacrilege — with horrifyingly plain and unfigured shapes colored with undifferentiated singularity, like tiles in the kitchens of the finer houses in the merchants' quarter, in precise, Satanic arrangements. The Holy Mother and Child — gone! His archbishop and patron — vanished! And in their place — the sign of the infidel! (For what else could it be?)

Maender's lamp flared with the fires of hell itself as he yelped and turned away. But when he timidly raised the hand possessing the lamp, rigidly calm with the certainty that his own death was at hand and that the best thing he could do in his obese and sinful declining years was to face it with Christian courage, the painting had returned to its normal state. Except for two details. The first had to do with the tiny trees seen out the window behind the Duc in the distance. Maender had painted them as temperate vegetation, but they had turned plainly tropical, as if native to the strange and fearsome continent across the forbidding sea south from Italy. The second was the regression in the facial features of the Saviour's perfect mother. She now had really no expression at all. And her skin had turned dark, as if — may Satan's avenging angels cast him into the fiery pits if his eyes did not witness this horror — the hide of a Moor!

Maender scrambled down the ladder and fell at the bottom. Grunting, he rose on a twisted ankle and made as hastily as he could for his temporary lodgings in his gentleman-farmer host's home. Feverish, and grimacing from the throbbing pain in his leg, Maender laid featherpoint to two pieces of parchment. The smaller, addressed to his host, explained that he had been called away unexpectedly on an errand which, Maender intimated but did not specify, had do to with faraway nobility outranking even the illustrious Duc du Galonde. The larger, addressed to the Duc himself, sealed, and re-addressed in the public manner on the outside, said much the same, but in more ornate, apologetic language. Then Maender retrieved his money pouch from beneath a bale of near-fetid hay and counted out two piles of gold coins. The smaller, equivalent to a little more than what he owed the farmer in board and drink, he stacked unsacked atop the document addressed to his host. The larger, equivalent to the advance portion of the payment for the commissioned painting, plus a roughly calculated Jew's interest for the time Maender had been working on the panel, the artist poured from his trembling hand into a small leather pouch. He tied the bag and left it atop the sealed letter to the Duc. He trusted the farmer to deliver both. Then Maender slept fitfully for a few hours and left, slowly, on his aged dappled horse, as soon as the first taste of silver penetrated the damp morning air.

The Holy Virgin and the Infant Jesus in the Presence of Hendrik Cardinal Oeups, the Most Holy Reverend Getys Haardjek, His Eminence the Duc du Galonde, and the Duchesse of Galonde on the Occasion of the Taxing of the Flax Merchants to Begin the Construction of the Cathedral of Frieje left to fate in the hayloft, as far as any published provenance is concerned, was never seen again.

On the Doves of a Wang

The Reverend William Halliwell had seen the painting. Or at least he had seen one just like it. He saw it every day. In fact, he owned it. Or at least he had possession of it when he rode on horseback into one of the small, smoky, muddy villages surrounding Cincinnati, Ohio on November 11, 1843. The ornately framed small canvas, cradled by finely carpentered hardwood members into its superbly crafted stretchers, jostled against the flank of Halliwell's chestnut mare. The painting did not, strictly speaking, jostle directly against the horse; it was wrapped in a soft cotton quilt, or a hastily cut section thereof. The wrapped painting resided, in turn, within a leather satchel made from the tanned hide of a slaughtered cow. It was against that sack and not the flank of Halliwell's sweaty steed, that, strictly speaking, the painting jostled. The double container prevented the painting from being damaged while being carried, over a period of several weeks and by circuitous route, to the environs of Cincinnati. The painting's most recently journey had begun at the location of what had already become known — to The Reverend Halliwell's extreme spiritual pain — as The Great Disappointment.

On New Year's Day, 1843, The Reverend Halliwell had unwisely committed to a prophecy proclaiming that the world (meaning, of course, not just the Earth, but the entire solar system, the surrounding universe and every speck of dust contained within it) would end on a specific date. Previously and vaguely, The Reverend Halliwell had merely said to his followers that the end would occur quite soon.

"Quite soon," to The Reverend Halliwell, meant at any moment in his reasonably expected personal lifetime onward from the point at which he had discovered the painting.

That was a date (the month and day of which The Reverend Halliwell had oddly forgotten, but the character of which — sunny, cold, bright, dry, all conspicuously so for late spring in upstate New York — he could recall down to the demons in the bark configurations of particular trees near the fateful house) in the year 1815, the blessed year of the final ouster of the hated, deceptively (and, to William Halliwell who was not yet a Reverend, probably conspiratorially) Roman Catholic British armed forces from United States territory.

Halliwell had been a mere twenty-two in the year 1815, a fresh-faced, deep-breathing, cherry-cheeked, wide-eyed disciple of a God who had not only (and, of course) sent the world his only begotten Son in the person of Jesus of Nazareth, but who lived, like some sort of Oriental life-force, in the very grass and boulders and gravel that William Halliwell felt under his feet, and in the very leaves which formed a protective canopy over his young, pious head.

William Halliwell, like most Americans of the early 19th century, knew almost nothing of the Orient. "Oriental" was merely a word to him, a sound beginning with an enlarged, vacant, inviting-as-the-mouth-of-a-cave vowel and ending, after a sweet syllabic slide like a violin's song, with a gently "t'd" windchime, that he reserved for whatever was, to him, tempting but not provably sinful. Crystal glassware (though he had seen only once piece, in his grandmother's house near Albany that later — Halliwell was never to know this — became a Trappist retreat) was "Oriental" in its edge and glint. The long hair of unmarried young women flouncing in the breeze was, likewise, "Oriental" to Halliwell. And the unshakeable feeling that the same God who perched himself on high as the final, zealous arbiter of sin and salvation could also be alive — conscious, watching, listening, causing — in every tendril of green vegetation, was Oriental, too.

The youthful, gangly William Halliwell feared that his thoughts (Look! He was already familiar with three "Oriental" blasphemies!) were edging him dangerously toward a handshake with the Devil. And God — Halliwell's wondrous God of leaf and ground, thunderhead and cataract — seemed to be doing nothing to save him from it. Indeed, He seemed not even to *care*. That perception, in its infancy at least, did nothing to narrow the worshipful eyes of William Halliwell. God was still perfect — Hallelujah! — and he was not. He, Halliwell — wretched puppy of sinful flesh and violate mind — was at fault. It was his wandering mind to be blamed, and not any tiny oversight of God's. Only the sin in William Halliwell's soul caused him to think impure, undoctrinal thoughts, and to feel the un-Christian presence of God, like lampwick in turpwood, in every lowly morsel of animal or plant, earth and sky.

Youthfulness was no excuse, either, Halliwell knew. Although at twenty-two, he had thus far careened and stumbled through life like a colt just squeezed from the womb of its mare, although his heart suffered from a perpetual, painful state of embarrassment, as if his face were coated with freckles and his feet (if he were careless enough to glance down) remained unshod, and although he knew, somewhere in the tributaries of his soul, that he would live to more than fourscore years and six and accomplish much, Halliwell recognized the fact that, by his present age, many other men had married and multiplied, had engaged in mortal combat with the decadent British and heathen Indians, had made and lost fortunes, and had drunk themselves into virtual old age. No, youth was no excuse. The problem, Halliwell knew, was that there was something wrong in his spirit, something naggingly, but subtly, disobedient in his incomplete nature as a potential child of God.

In the fateful year 1815, the young William Halliwell had taken to requisitioning a horse from a neighboring farmer who had a large corral and generous heart. He had also taken to riding — after the second (and still mandatory) church service in the town of Monaquapasa, New York — into that portion of the woods controlled by his fellow Caucasians.

Halliwell rode to be alone. He rode to do penance. He rode to purge himself of his Orientalisms. He rode to tease himself with the idea that, by arranged coincidence (if God meant it to be), he might just meet up with the strange man he had heard about. This man claimed to have discovered, after being directed by a dream concerning a white salamander, in an empty air pocket in the earth surrounding the roots of a very old tree, golden metal plates inscribed, in a script unreadable by anyone but, miraculously, this man. The inscription contained the revelatory words of God. And the man, Halliwell, had heard, was no older than he was.

On this particular day, whose month and number of day is now lost to history, in the year 1815, William Halliwell found himself, facing an abandoned house of, as far as he could tell, formerly conspicuous luxury. Several yards in front of its main entrance stood a very old, twisted, gnarled, but massive elm tree whose mere presence intimated eternity. Halliwell dismounted and tiptoed toward the house, stopping first at the tree. Between two of the tree's larger roots, which spread from the trunk like knuckled tentacles, was, or seemed to be, a hollow.

Halliwell's heart stopped. He took another step toward the cavity. And another step. His neck craned forward. He looked down. His eyes distended. A sudden shaft of sunlight burnt though the leaves overhead and brightened the ground, and the roots, at his feet. Blessed relief, nothing! No salamander, no golden plates, yes, but no rumblings of a scolding God, either — no thunderous words springing from the collapsing stone edifice which stood (precariously, he noticed) in front of him. Halliwell's heart resumed beating.

As he looked at the house more closely, Halliwell

noticed his impure thoughts disappearing. He felt their spontaneous replacement by — how could he say it to himself? — more healthful and reverent ideas. When he thought of God — this time, in front of the house, as a test of his faith — perfumed Oriental ruminations of a lofty God reduced to a "presence" in the flotsam of a lowly world no longer invaded his mind. He felt suddenly holier. Perhaps, Halliwell, thought, a cleansing was at hand. He walked hopefully, but carefully, toward the house.

When he opened the door (or, rather, shoved aside the partially unhinged carved timber plank that served to guard the portal), the same shaft of sunlight (or its larger, brighter sibling) which had disabused him of the notion of having happened upon the original depositing place of the rumored golden plates, partially lighted up the single room of which — amazingly, he discovered — the house consisted. The golden beam fell through a vine-encrusted hole in the roof directly upon a tamped earthen floor. But in the outer glow of the pool of light ahead of him at his feet, William Halliwell could see the one object not part and parcel of the house's ornate, crumbling architecture. It was, if Halliwell's now-squinting, then-peering eyes could make out correctly, some kind of picture like the ones hung in profusion upon the walls of the homes of blithely secular sinners like his grandmother. But its assumed proper face was turned toward the rough wall on which it leaned, and Halliwell could only guess that it was, indeed a parlor picture. For a second, when he realized he was right, Halliwell was proud that such an uneducated man as he — he could not even read a single verse of the Bible to which he was so devoted — might have actually guessed correctly. Perhaps it was a painting (though Halliwell never knew anyone skilled enough to paint one), but probably it was a print (oddly, the word "etching" was part of his vocabulary), and even more likely a map or a genealogical chart.

Halliwell stepped, amid the million comets of dust swirling in the illuminated ray, toward the corner of that encompassing room where the picture tilted against the wall. He squatted down on his lean haunches, then dropped one knee to the floor. With a long, frock-coated arm, he reached out a silky, tentative hand, and grasped the verso-facing picture by its frame's upper horizontal component. Then he laid his other hand upon it and turned the picture around so that its proper face could meet his gaze. And once again, his heart froze.

The picture — a true painting, Halliwell could tell instantly — consisted of (again, instant apprehension) a single panel containing the likenesses of the Virgin Mary seated on a regal chair in the center, the Infant Jesus himself in her loving arms, (on the left) a peculiar, richly robed figure who seemed to be a cleric of a foreign church, accompanied by some sort of similarly garbed older official, and (on the right), an apparently devoted, but unparental couple clothed in quite odd, but undeniably costly, fringed and gilded garments. As his central organ recommenced the rhythm of life, Halliwell noticed that all the faces, holy and secular, looked disturbingly like the peeled potatoes so often dropped by his family into poverty's dinner pot. And everyone, except the radiantly peach-golden Christ child, was rendered as white as a ghost.

Suddenly, Halliwell dropped the picture. It fell face down within a rising, rectangular cloud, a tan, translucent whorled hedge of dust. Halliwell rose from his kneeling, and ran, stumbling, through the doorway. When he reached his untethered but miraculously unperturbed horse, Halliwell thrust one boot into a stirrup, gripped the reins and jacked himself saddleward. But just before he arc'd his trail leg over the animal's back, he stopped. Still, like a sentinel facing away from the danger, sweating and breathing heavily, suspended in the leather loop a yard off the ground, he swallowed hard, and listened to the breeze in the leaves. Slowly, Halliwell turned his head around to look over his shoulder and saw that no one, and nothing, had pursued him from the house. More slowly, he dismounted. Halliwell patted his horse on the nose and then walked back toward the house's entrance. Inside, he sat down cross-legged in front of the painting and thought upon the meaning of his having found it.

Meanwhile, the sun slid from the sky. In the gathering darkness of the house, the painting changed. Slowly, the identity of the holy figures and their exotic devotees degranulated into pitch. Even more slowly, William Halliwell's eyes enlarged at the pupils, bulged in the whites, then contracted around the lids, and finally closed as his spine turned to taffy and he lay back upon the floor and fell asleep. The shaft of sun — only now stabbing through the hole in the roof at an opposite angle from the afternoon before, and colored with the hopeful blue of dawn — awakened William Halliwell. His crusty eyes reluctantly reopened and stared straight up at the glare. Then he remembered — the painting! — and sat bolt upright whereupon, for a third (and, later to Halliwell, a significantly trinitous) time, his pulse deserted him.

The painting was still in place, but its image had vanished! In its place, upon the surface of the unrent linen still fastened securely to its intricate wooden support, was what appeared to be a mad configuration of heathen tiles. Not so many tiles, not the complex heresy of a musselman's mosque, but un-Godly, sure!

Halliwell's first impulse was to bolt for his horse and gallop home without looking back. But again, Halliwell hesitated. Then, frantically, he scrambled on all fours in the opposite direction — toward the painting. Courageously (certainly so, for a young man like Halliwell, in Halliwell's time, with Halliwell's predisposition to imagine a supremely vengeful God), he thrust his face near the canvas.

He discovered, to both his joy and horror, that in the interstices between the mocking tiles, and at the perimeter of their interlocking configuration, traces remained of Mary, Jesus, and those other persons, whoever they were. More than traces survived, he realized: exact remnants, as though the picture had been carelessly covered with imperfectly aligned rectangles of pasted paper, leaving evidence of the desecrated original image underneath.

Halliwell touched the painting. He fully expected to be burned. He expected to be sucked into its surface, past its picture plane, into oblivion. He expected to discover that there was no textural difference at all between the remnants of the holy figures and their secular accompanists, and the hideously precise ornamentation that almost totally obliterated them.

Then God spoke to William Halliwell.

God, of course, did not utter words in the English language, though he might as well have, given the force and specificity with which Halliwell interpreted the command. No, the command was in the painting: Just as God's greatest gift has disappeared in body from this earth and waits in heaven for the hour of return, so too will all manner of God's depictions of the world, that the reunion of Jesus with his Flock may take place in a space of complete purity. To Halliwell, then, there, the painting was the Trumpet of God announcing that the world would shortly end. And the painting was a chorus of angels telling him to ride like fury back to Monaquapasa and tell everyone he knew (and, eventually, everyone he didn't know who deserved to be told) that the end of the world was at hand. (The farmer back in Monaquapasa worried wildly about his horse and cursed the day he had ever begun to feel sorry for the obviously confused and suggestible Halliwell youth. If the young man had finally fallen into a chasm, the farmer thought, or had been justly hunted down by Indians and scalped, then it might be worth the price of a horse. Then the farmer prayed to God to forgive him for such an un-Christian thought.)

During the ride back to the village (at first a genuine gallop, then a canter, then a trot and finally a meandering, ecstatic walk), however, Halliwell composed himself. He decided — since divinely donated knowledge of the end of the word rendered him something of a prophet, and thinking oneself a prophet one would be considered, by the elders of his congregation at least, a pariah of the first water — that circumspection was called for.

First, he lied to the farmer. He said that Indians had chased him into a predicament in which it was necessary to lie on the ground covered with leaves, twigs, beetles and roots for most of the night. He did not explain how he concealed the horse, but the farmer, happy to regain the animal in unwounded condition, was willing to believe the story without subjecting it to a test of reasonability. The farmer even found himself willing to lend Halliwell the horse again.

Halliwell was happy to borrow it again — and again, and again — which he did to return to the abandoned house and commune with the painting (which, in all subsequent conditions of light and hour, remained unaltered from the altered state to which it had metamorphosed itself during the morning of Halliwell's providential awakening). Finally, Halliwell lifted a soft cotton quilt from one of the pine chests his father had carpentered for his mother, and took it into the woods with him one day. He wrapped the painting in it, tied and cinched it with rough twine, returned with the picture to Monaquapasa. Halliwell never returned to the stone house.

Over the next six months, Halliwell told the story of the discovery of the painting (which he did not actually display) to the seven people in Monaquapasa he trusted — and felt who trusted him — most. These were three unmarried, and worried-over, young men like himself, two widowers (one of whom was known to drink most heavily), and two unmarried, and considered relegated to spinsterhood, women already in their mid-twenties. Among these candidates, Halliwell gained three converts to his church.

Halliwell did not immediately and publicly proclaim his own church. The minor problem of his personal credibility (he could neither read nor write; he was not known

to be an earnest farmhand to his father nor had he ever
held gainful employment in the town; and his personal
attractiveness and charm were considered minimal or non-
existent by most), and the major problem of heresy
(Halliwell had heard of two or three men in the region
who were run off after claiming to have had visions of
Jesus independent of those conjured for entire congrega-
tions) loomed large. To the seven, and on the basis of his
experience in the woods, Halliwell posited the end of the
world some twenty years hence. He asked them to address him, in private, as Master and told them that he
would address them, likewise out of public sight or sound,
as Disciple. The three who accepted — two young men
and one of the women — persuaded the others to keep
their silence. (One old man said, "Fie!" and quickly forgot the story. The other resumed drinking. And the remaining young couple, having discovered one another,
ran off together.)

But Halliwell actually proffered no specific date for
the end of the world. As he began to preach to a few dozen
converts in the open ground round the blacksmith's shop
(much to the consternation of the village elders, who tried
to pretend — so as not to panic their congregation — that
Halliwell was merely childishly flushed with passion for
the Lord), he reckoned that the sky's pouring forth fire
might occur even further into the future, perhaps at the
exact halfway point of the century.

By the time the entire adult population of Monaquapasa
(including the elders who had not died or wandered west
in search of better land) had been won over to its young,
magnetic, and obviously chosen-by-the-Lord minister,
Halliwell had retrenched to an idea of an imminent, but
always uncertain, moment of account that could be caused,
at the drop of a goose feather, by the congregation's be-
havior. If the end of the world was to be feared (Are you
ready to be judged?), then it could be held over the congregation like a stick. If it was to be welcomed (Brother,

you will be released from earthly bondage!), then it could be dangled as a carrot before the congregation. Either, as long as necessary — even a lifetime.

★ ★ ★ ★ ★

At thirty and still a bachelor, William Halliwell invoked the carrot mode of persuasion mostly to the more comely young women under his Godly tutelage. He ministered this codicil to belief in private session, where it was customarily embellished by his request for the young lady's sexual submission.

How *can* you be released from bondage of the flesh unless your flesh has, in fact, been previously sullied by sin? Halliwell asked. If, Halliwell patiently explained, the day of judgment arrives to find you pure, owing not to salvation but to a sequestering from the temptations of life, then the King of Heaven and Earth will not be much more kindly disposed toward you than he is toward outright sinners. And, Halliwell offered kindly, he was willing to be their partners in the required sin because it would also enable him to take the sins of many onto his own shoulders so that, when the time came for him to be saved, his own salvation would be on a scale worthy of a minister of God. So, one at a time, he copulated with the women and shortly thereafter pronounced them saved. In this period of his life, Halliwell had long since ceased to tell anyone about the existence of the painting.

At his half-century mark, Halliwell wondered — as he proceeded, alone, on horseback toward the sinful metropolis of Cincinnati, while his congregation of many hundreds (including eighteen "wives" and several score of issue) huddled in musty tents at the foot of the small, green mountain where The Great Disappointment occurred — how had he ever arrived at the date October 4, 1843 as the point, in the timeless life of God, at which the Lord would reach down from his most royal cloud (or from deep within the pictorial cracks of the sacked painting tenderly slapping the butt of his horse), and put an end to human misery?

All Halliwell knew was that (unless this especially ugly village in a neverending series of ugly villages was a dream beyond damnation) he had been wrong. And in being wrong he had torn the hearts from his faithful. And in tearing the hearts from his faithful, he had come into their debt. And in becoming a debtor, he had sinned. His only hope of salvation was the possibility that, in the eyes of God, he had not sinned deeply enough to prevent the painting metamorphosing again (perhaps it was actually doing so now, as it unconsciously massaged his horse's ass), and giving unto him a new, and correct, day and time to mark the end of all flesh.

Alas, the painting — which Halliwell carried with him in its mummy wraps everywhere he went, on foot, on horseback, or on the occasional carriage ride with a nubile parishioner — never divulged any prophetic calendrical knowledge. Or, if it did, Halliwell could not read it. So it was only on intuition (or, as he preferred to call it privately, "Godly hunch"), that Halliwell conjured 1852, 1859, 1861 (very early in that year, when he thought abolition's call would, if heeded, "let loose upon the fabric of our Holy nation, the renting weevils of a million Black souls animated not by the pure love of Jesus but by the carnal appetites of a continent that God has tried so righteously to cloak in utter darkness," would begin the civil war that would lead, quickly and directly, to Armageddon), 1866, 1869, 1870, 1874, 1880 and 1887 as subsequent dates for the final Judgment of Man.

Late on New Year's Eve of each of the first three of those years, when Halliwell would pick an especially pretty member from his female flock and instruct her in the ways of Adamite love, he would also grow dry-mouthed and queasy-gutted. There would arise in his skull a great, thunderous, tormenting headache that The Reverend William Halliwell would attribute — expectations of revenant Jesus aside — to the gathering clouds of humanity's doom. He would sweat and thrash and twist and call out in a fearful voice from his bedclothes (scaring the wits out of the already confused child-woman beside him) that he had just received a vision of the yawning pit of boiling ash into which all of sinning mankind would be cast. He would tell himself, and his woman of the moment, that the immediate future of the race was so unutterably terrifying that God himself was asking him to assume a much greater-than-per-capita share of the coming suffering, so that little children born in sin would be spared some small portion of it. In truth (or what of truth remained unsinged around the burning mind of The Reverend William Halliwell), his symptoms resulted from knowing that, as January first of the anointed year commenced, he was one day short of a full array of 365 days (366 in 1880, a leap year) from which to choose, and, in spirit, no closer to receiving the crucial revelation as to the date.

On the premier day of 1866, Halliwell awakened, combed his great bushy grey beard, allowed the sacrificial virgin to slip discreetly through the rear flap of his platformed tent, and strode into the small band of his followers who were stoking the fires beneath the caravan's huge porridge kettles. In a voice so loud it set the dogs barking and running in circles, he announced that indeed this was the year of vengeance and homecoming. The Lord would shortly present him with a vision of the exact day. A few cheers, and a few fewer sobs, greeted The Reverend Halliwell's proclamation. To Halliwell's surprise, the people (his people, he unselfconsciously assumed) resumed their chores almost immediately. He never provided them with the promised clarifying, and they never seemed to care. 1866 passed, without Halliwellian incident.

As did 1869, after he told only his bed partner (that

this was the year, and that the name of the accursed Roman month and the number of the cataclysmic day would shortly occur to him), who told a few of her maidenly friends. By New Year's Day 1870, The Reverend Halliwell was seventy-seven years old. His carnal appetites, like his flock, had diminished, so he told only his "council of elders" (three of them, with hardly as many teeth as fingers among them), and they kept it to themselves. At the outset of 1874, he wrote the same information in a private diary and never retrieved it.

By January 1, 1880, the Halliwellians had experienced (while circling in and out of northern Kentucky and southern Indiana in pursuit of converts) an increase in their numbers and an intensification of their faith. Buoyed, the Reverend Halliwell succumbed to his clairvoyance only to the extent that he scratched the number of the year into the snow with a maple tree branch, then stomped the frozen revelation into illegible hardpack with his cavalry boot. And in 1887, seven years returned to the vicinity of Cincinnati, his commemoration-in-advance was reduced to a simple muttering of, "Yes, the year of our Lord, eighteen hundred and eighty-seven," followed by twelve months of absolute silence on the subject.

Had The Reverend Halliwell known of the experiment in the northern city of Cleveland, to be conducted in the summer of that year, by the as-yet-to-be-newfound friend of the lovely young lady with the insect's waist who stirred in him (as yet to no kindling) the ashes of corporeal desire, he most likely would have pronounced more emphatically upon the exact moment of the end of the world. And had the woman on whom Serge Protector would lavish his first honorable intentions known about The Reverend Halliwell's vestal proclivities, she most likely would not have recommended that Serge Protector journey all the way to the banks of the Ohio River to meet him. And had not Serge's arduous carriage ride taken place, the youthful, brilliant Protector most definitely would not have be-

come a devoted Halliwellian, privy to the wondrous fo-
rensic remains of the — "magical" is not a word that Serge
permitted himself to use — marvelous portrait of Jesus and
his sainted mother.

★ ★ ★ ★ ★

The Halliwellite branch to which Serge Protector was
attracted upon his arrival in Calvary, Idaho in 1911 was
the little cabal (there were now fifteen official — if such a
word could be applied to any group possessing a Bible into
which a gravure of The Late Reverend had been pasted —
offshoots of the Ohio Caravan) that believed in the divinity of both aviation and abstract painting.

Although all of its members could operate the con-
trols of the few wicker-basketlike craft The Brothers of
Jesus owned, only Serge (because he had sailed to Europe,
made the acquaintance of the theosophist Annie Besant
and had, in spite of their doctrinal differences, been pronounced by her a "World Leader," and sailed back, after
acquainting himself with continental aeroplanes) could pilot the lumbering, barely airborne, eight-engine Sikorsky
DL-117 bomber (on which the bombardier was required
to stand on an open-air balcony and, by hand, drop the
low-yield explosive projectiles over the side onto the enemy — presumed to be cavalry — below). The Sikorsky,
which Serge came to christen The Tsar, had been given to
him and his fellow believers by Mme Besant and hers, as
an acknowledgment of his "spiritual prowess" in being able
to appreciate the strange paintings of the young Wassily
Kandinsky. God only knows how they shipped it to the
United States, let alone sent it in parts it to the barren
wilds of Idaho.

Of course, with Serge leading the labors, it took him

and The Brothers of Jesus's auto mechanic and two carpenters only three days to convert the strange dark crates, festooned with both Cyrillic and German stencilled lettering, into a functioning aircraft. When it first rolled out into the ovenish midday heat, before an audience of bareheaded, moustachioed men and bonneted and (mostly) unmoustached women, lumbered down the corridor of raked desert crust that served as runway, and proceeded obstinately, furlong after furlong, wedded to the ground, the co-pilot automechanic laughingly remarked, "This contraption is a stampede all by itself!"

Serge bristled inwardly and decided not to call the aeroplane Galvany after all. Better to name this roaring black beast — now a bit lighter and browner in shade because of the dust — after one of the Romanovs, who were, in Serge's estimation, also clumsily powerful entities ultimately destined to crash and burn.

Standing (yes, standing!) behind the DL-117's tall, flat, railroad-cab panes of glass in the aeroplane's wheelhouse, while the craft coughed and screamed down the runway, Serge was unperturbed. He knew the DL-117 would fly. He had calculated its mass, drag, lift and groundspeed, and — allowing (as his computations always did) for the existence of ether — the figures predicted that the great Russian winged ship would gain the sky and be able, at least, to duplicate the distance of the flight that Serge had made earlier in the year, solo, from Christchurch, England to Paris in a small plane designated the Dunne D-8. The Dunne, of course, was configured quite unlike the DL-117, having been designed by its earthly creator (the philosopher and engineer, J. W. Dunne) in aeronautical homage to the seed of the Zanonia, or Javanese climbing plant. But that shape was not totally absent from the Russian bomber. It (according to Serge's eye) was the organizing principle, the chief "significant form" (a term that Serge had encountered in an avant-garde art pamphlet in London, prior to taking off from Christchurch) of the painting — a nearly totally abstracted portrait of the Madonna and Christ child — that hung behind him on the bulkhead of the DL-117's wheelhouse.

Serge was right on all counts. The great aeroplane did fly. The painting was graphically organized along the lines of the Zanonia seed, although the artist who had originally painted it (the picture had been mysteriously repainted — or had repainted itself — untold times) was never aware of the similarities. And, as Serge had calculated, the distance from Christchurch to Paris was, if considered as a round trip and then divided by three — in deference to the Holy Trinity faintly depicted in the painting installed behind him — exactly the equal of the distance between the primitive airfield from which the DL-117 had been launched and the hole at the base of the mountain which Serge could see below and which, Serge was inspired to think, would make — in case of persecution by the faithless and ignorant masses — the ideal ultimate retreat for The Brothers of Jesus. Serge, as it turned out, was again right on all counts.

Are You Lashed by the Blood of the Whim?

"....this blasphemous, treacherous, sinful, ungodly woman! Oh, as you remember, Dear Ones, she was the very incarnation of Evil, spewing forth poison with her mouth — that same profane and delicate orifice which she also employed ever so perversely to draw the nectar of life from her faithful Life's Mate, to remove and transport his Sacred Seed to the dark and silent greed of her belly, where it would be absorbed into the sump of her wicked, wasteful life, where it could no longer be part of God's wonderful, wonderful plan of fecundity and multiplication, and where it would — Oh, woe! — become nothing more than part of the slime of Satan.

"And I, your minister, Noam Sain, and none other, was the victim of this unholy, wicked woman.

"This woman who blasphemed the Holy Temple of her physical body into an instrument of temptation, manipulation, and betrayal.

"This wicked woman who saw to it that I, too, was drawn down into her well of abnormality.

"This wicked woman who saw to it that I was never to see the fruit of my loins.

"This wicked woman who saw to it that God was disobeyed!

"And though she did not foresee it, Dear Ones, she also saw to it that she herself will be punished for her ungodly ways!

"But it must be God who punishes her, and not I, her faithful husband. I do not judge. Only God judges and,

Dear Ones, only God *should* judge. So I did not judge her. Yea, I cleaved unto her, even in her boundless sin! I was obedient to the commandment of God!

"But, Dear Ones, one day she decided to add abandonment to her list of offences again God and her faithful husband. With no word of warning, with no consoling gesture, with no reverence for or obedience to the commandment of holy, unbreakable matrimony as set forth by God and his loving Son, Jesus Christ, she abandoned her faithful husband in the dead of night. And she has abandoned not only her husband, but she has fled from the shores of this very nation, which is blessed by God among nations, and chosen by God to be the new Israel among nations and to regather the lost tribes unto God's bosom on the eve of the Great Tribulation. Amen.

"This woman has fled like a coward! She has left the New Israel of California. She has ventured east, into the more sinful regions of this great nation of ours. But even this flight has not been enough to satisfy her perfidy! She has crossed the ocean! She has taken up residence in a land where the Holy Tongue of English, the language of the New Israel, is not spoken, where many, many of the citizens are heathen slaves under the yoke of the Pope in Rome. Oh, Lord, please let it not be that she is planning at this moment to drive these poor citizens of this foreign land further into the maw of Papist debauchery by practicing on them what she had wrought on me. Let it be me, oh Lord, who may alone take upon his breast the ungodly sins of this woman, and suffer for them so that others may not feel her sting!"

The Reverend Noam Sain hit the big red kill button on a steel mike that was as tall as a malt mixer and just about as cumbersome to use. As his thumb stifled transmission of his radio voice, he quickly swiveled his bulk, and the creaky, shiny-armed old office chair, away from the mike and muttered, "Shit."

He said it for no particular reason except that he knew

very well that a halfway decent blowjob, even a perfunctory suck from an unfaithful and contentious wife with
cold gums and gin on her breath, was hardly what you'd
call a "sting." Rhetorically, it was wrong.

Noam took pride in his rhetoric. He sought consis-
tency, however ornate, even if all he was doing was disguis-
ing a screed against his absent, hated wife as a message from
God to the multitudes. It had also occurred to him that,
once again, he might have gone too far. The two skinny,
humorless jamocas — in hats with wide brims ten years
out of date and too-noticeable stripes in their double-
breasted suits — who ran the station were probably moni-
toring this broadcast. Just his luck.

The management of the tiny station — from whom
Noam bought half-hours of commercial time at bargain-
basement rates because its weak signal beamed — no, more
like tumbled, down at less than five thousand watts from
the rickety broadcast tower on Mount Wilson, and managed barely to buzz beyond the San Gabriel Valley, even on
cold, clear nights — had threatened to take him off the air.

The Jesus stuff is one thing, one of the skinny guys had
said between drags on a cigarette, and tellin' people that
they ought to quit the Catholic Church to come join your
li'l ol' one is another. But *this* — using the damned radio
and the public air waves to rail against a broad just 'cause
she's jumped the fence on the marriage ranch a coupla
times and then finally split to her relatives in Germany —
this is still another. O.K. on the first, we've got no problem
with that, the second guy had said. Loosey-deucey on the
second, he'd said, but maybe we'll even let you get away
with that. Can't stand mackerel snappers myself, and most
'em out here are beaners, anyway, so maybe you're doin'
the city a favor tellin' the cat-lickers to go back to Italy or
Mexico. But not the third, not hangin' out your dirty linen
in public, not on our radio station.

Especially, he continued, with this stuff about Germany.
Lotta folks out here aren't quite so down on Germany as

you are. And even if they are, they figure it's Germany's business and England's business and the froggies' business who wins the damned war. Germany is an awful long way from L.A., he said — as if L.A. wasn't part of a country which also had an east coast three thousand miles closer to Germany, and as if Noam were in L.A. proper.

Noam and the pockmarked radio guy chewing on a match had this acrimonious discussion in Pasadena, and there was a hell of a lot of difference in Noam's mind between Los Angeles and Pasadena. Pasadena — salted with the elderly rich, studded with lovely churches and libraries, and laced with wide avenues presided over by bordering rows of tall, supple queen's palms, and separated from Los Angeles by ten miles of serpentining Arroyo Seco — was, to Noam, civilization itself.

Los Angeles, by contrast, was a sprawling, cancerous fleshpot. Pasadena wasn't running itself as if asking for the annihilating lightning bolt from God that, in Noam's opinion, L.A. so acutely deserved. Noam drew some small defensive satisfaction by regarding that station guy as a hypocrite for conflating Pasadena and L.A., even though Noam deliberately did it himself, twice a week on his broadcast, by signing off, "This is Pastor Noam Sain, saying goodbye and God bless you from the great western city of the angels, Los Angeles, in California." Noam liked the unnecessary "in." He thought it a nice rhetorical touch. Noam took pride in his rhetoric.

Rhetoric, Noam knew, had little if anything to do with the truth. The truth was Noam liked getting his cock sucked, and tried to get women — women in the small choir he hired from time to time for storefront services, for instance — to service him every chance he got. In the old days — when he was short and portly, as opposed to short and teetering on the brink of obesity — it wasn't quite so difficult to get sex, albeit mostly garden variety intercourse (well, woman on top instead of in missionary position, because of his girth) instead of the fellatio he adored.

Noam's hair was still dark and curly (a plus), he had a certain twinkle in his hazel eyes (another plus), and his dimples conveyed an advantageous combination of the innocent and the rake (a third plus).

But the most unerring arrow in Noam's quiver was his being a preacher, a passionate preacher, and a think-on-his-feet preacher. However generous his beltline had become, however deprived his altitude always was, women just seemed to love a man of God with the groin of Satan. Something mutual about forbidden fruit, Noam figured: Women doing something they knew they shouldn't be doing liked doing it better with a man who knew full well he shouldn't be doing it either — especially if they could cuddle his porky little head between their breasts afterward, and coo him back to a mutual illusion of righteousness. They liked to share the illusion, too. They liked to think that Noam, in genuinely trying to save their souls, had gotten a little too close to the edge of eros and fallen with them.

Older and fatter, Noam still possessed the arrow. It was just that the string on his bow had grown a little slack, and the damned arrow no longer flew as swiftly, or surely, to its target. Noam had to pull back harder on the string. He fed his chorines the old line about needing first to sin in order to be saved, about him being practically Jesus on the cross for offering to help them do it ("providing the instrument," he'd say, with the pun intended), for coming up with the fillip that to really be a first-rate sin, the act had to be perverse, unnatural, abominable in and of itself, not just by circumstance.

Fucking, he told them, was all right with God, as long as you did it within marriage. There was nothing inherently wrong with fucking. It was only a sin if you did it with someone you weren't married to. Cocksucking, on the other hand, was inherently repugnant to God. Even married women weren't supposed to lick their husbands' dicks, he told them. To be saved from perversion, instead of from just sins of circumstance, was to have one's whole nature changed, not just one's situation. To be transformed in a flash of piety and awe from a pervert to a lamb of God was a major miracle, and the Lord, he told them, preferred working major miracles to fiddling around with minor ones. So gobble down, honey, he would think (though much more rarely in the company of a "honey," these days), and then let the good Lord do his great and necessary work.

Noam never said such profane words aloud to anybody. Mostly, he didn't say it because by the time he'd gotten to that point in the standard spiel, the unfortunate, targeted woman had almost always already fled in tears. Noam ran after them and, usually, managed to convinced them that he had been speaking only in the abstract, that he had not suggested that he and they actually engage in oral irregularities. The women usually wiped their puffy, tear-bejeweled faces and managed to believe that their pastor had not been trying to cajole them into committing a terrible, probably irredeemable, sin. Noam liked to think that some of the women, after a night's sleep or a stiff drink, probably came around to buying his argument for salvation through cocksucking, but were too timid to come back and tell him O.K., I've thought it over and you're right about the delivering power of a blowjob. He liked to think that they then went out and picked other, more fortunate men to set them on the road to being cleansed. Noam sometimes fancied that he should get a kickback of some sort from the guys — gas station attendants? gardeners? milkmen? — who eventually harvested the Blowjobs for Christ whose seeds he, the ever generous shepherd-to-his-flock Minister Noam Sain, had originally planted.

It wasn't, of course, as if Noam hadn't gotten blown at home. After about a year of a gradually diminishing honeymooner's glow in which it seemed to Noam that his wife was still taken with his curly hair, dimples and profession of ordained minister, Imeda told him she would no longer engage in any other kind of sex with him than oral.

She told him he'd gotten so heavy she was afraid that if they made love like missionaries, she'd end up like Virginia Rappe had beneath Fatty Arbuckle. Other positions of intercourse, she said, just made her laugh, especially with Noam also trying to assume them. So, twice a week, she put on a little extra lipstick to give Noam something to savor when he looked down at her bobbing blonde head, to make his eyes bulge and to make him come faster, and she did him in an efficient, businesslike way. Afterward, usually, she bade the grateful Noam go down on her while she perused the photographs of Gary Cooper and Clark Gable in a movie magazine and imagined their gigantic, monochromatic and lightly stubbled heads, instead of Noam's, between her thighs.

Even without the distraction of an orgasm, Imeda would have been hard put actually to read the *Photoplay*. She barely understood English. Her native German, and a little residual Swedish from the great-grandparents' inexplicable southern migration, strangled what little basic tenets of the American language she was learning under Noam's tutelage. It drove him nuts when she answered the simplest questions with *Ja* or *Nein*. It drove him nutsier when she said, "Oh, *ja!*" in her ecstatic moments in bed. And it drove him nutsiest when in public, at whatever unleased shop looking for a little day-use rent served as his church on a given Sunday, she said things like, "I yem so fairy heppy tyew meet yew, Misooz Carpentoor." It drove him beyond nuts when he found out she'd been entertaining a gentleman friend on a few afternoons when he was at the radio studio, winning souls.

Somewhere down deep, Noam knew that he should have just let her go, without rancor. He'd never loved Imeda; he'd only desired her. And what he desired in her — intelligence, sensuality, beauty — he never wanted for themselves, but only as brushstrokes in an imaginary portrait (which he carried in his head as he preached over the airwaves on a portable, rickety, darkly veneered wooden podium): the perfect, cool, stately, pious, and pure wife of the founder of a new church which would someday surpass Rome's. Everything else about Imeda — her idiotic, easily garbled last name (Jinsokt, pronounced as the unpious "gin-soaked"), her big but unevenly sized blue eyes, her mouth so pointed at the edges it looked like a slash in her skull, her hairline almost atop her head, her blonde hair as fine as spun glass for Christmas trees, her slim, graceful figure, and, above all, her height (two inches more of it than Noam possessed) — displeased him.

Still, when she left, Noam went crazy. He tried to keep it inside. But inevitably, his grief and rage began to leak out. The first signs, on the radio, were cryptic. The Sunday after he found her bed neatly made and her closets and bureau in the Marion Avenue bungalow stark empty, Noam opened his electronic sermon with the statement, "When the supremacy of the densified Astral Body is realized, the locks on the Fourth Gate will once again unbolt."

To the casual, religiously uninterested listener (perhaps all of a dozen of them, tucked in Japanesey bungalows on the baked peneplane ascending through orange groves and desert scrub to the San Gabriel Mountains, their round-topped, wooden console radios tuned to the only nearby station that came in clearly), it was the usual unintelligible hocus-pocus from the Reverend Mr. Sain. Noam never minded trading in bullshit, but this time he really meant something. He meant that when the husbands of the world (really, the husbands of one little radio'd corner of greater Los Angeles), whom he identified as "the densified Astral Body," assumed their rightful places as figures of unquestioned authority, the sexual submissiveness of women ("the Fourth Gate," Noam called it, without specifying the first three) would be guaranteed by God ("the locks...will once again unbolt").

A harmless enough fantasy, a casual listener would have thought, had he known the code. The first fifteen minutes of Noam's half-hour follow-up, the next Sunday, on the theme seemed similarly tepid and cloudy. But then Noam warmed up, preaching first on God's hatred for unfaithful wives being hotter and meaner than all his other hatreds put together. He said he was not speaking from "philosophical rumination" or from "mere tales told by others," but from "direct, tearful experience as one of God's wounded children." Noam then described Imeda's infidelity, albeit in somewhat metaphorical terms: "Wandering from the pastures set aside for the heavenly while her husband labored in the fields of the Lord," and such. He grew more openly enraged; he growled and shouted into the microphone in a manner he'd always disdained (since hearing his own father use it to preach to crawdaddy fishermen in Louisiana), drawing out some words into animal cries. Noam said that Imeda deserved to wander in the darkness from now on, far from the light of God; he said that she deserved to suffer, to find no human succor where she went, that she deserved to end up in hell. Then he used the word "whore."

That's when the two skinny guys from the station first came to talk to him again.

The taller of the two said to Noam, "Look, li'l padre, you can't use language like that on the air. You just can't. There are children out there, with their mothers, lying on the floor playing with the cat while the mothers wash and iron and get a little religion over the radio. They don't want to hear words like that." As he spoke, he was perched on one buttock on the corner of the studio table where Noam was about to begin his next broadcast in ten minutes. He chewed a kitchen match.

"The Lord God uses that word," Noam protested, "in the Bible, as a cautionary. He does not want the women He created to become whores, and he says so, in just those words."

The match chewer looked at the floor and, to effect disdain, didn't look up. He said, "God don't have a program on our station. If he did, and he used that word, we'd throw him off."

"So!" exclaimed Noam, rising quickly from his noisy chair and puffing his little ball of a body into as much a posture of indignity as he could muster. "You are unbelievers. I should have known!"

The other, shorter, owner spoke up: "All you know, fatso, is that you pay us some dough and we let you pull a chair up in front of that mike and say whatever's on your mind and afterward a few little old ladies don't know any better mail you checks. That's what you know."

"I know that I speak God's truth."

The shorter man elaborated: "Mr. Sain, what you know now is that if you use words like 'whore' on our station again, that's it. You're off the air."

But Noam did indeed use "whore," along with several other words equally distasteful to the station owners and, most likely, to a considerable number of people in his listening public, on the next broadcast. There was no subsequent broadcast. The last Noam Sain's neighbors on Marion Avenue in Pasadena saw of Noam was on a bright, cool Saturday afternoon, when he loaded his clothes and a few kitchen utensils into an oxidized 1934 four-door Ford sedan, tossed the house keys back through the still-open front door, and drove away.

★ ★ ★ ★ ★

The theology of Noam Sain had been shaped by opposing forces — not just diametric opposites (though his religious inspirations certainly included those), but rather bolts of metaphysical speculation arriving like thunderclaps in his malleable mind from every conceivable heavenly direction. His Louisiana bootlegger father, a preacher only by avocation, had noisily proclaimed a wet, slimy, sensual, from-the-bowels-up, cathartic Christianity. To him, Jesus was a "haint" who came in the night after the sinner had consumed half a jug of sugar-likker and compelled the perhaps well-meaning but nevertheless impure man (Noam's father's Jesus did not speak directly to women) to howl for forgiveness, plead for salvation. Noam's father howled, too — from the back of the world's oldest and rustiest stake-bed truck — when he told his congregation (who were, of course, drawn from the pool of his customers) to get down and roll in the mud with praise for Jesus.

As Noam — left as a teenager to fend for himself after his father was carted away to jail for good and his mother found a citified companion who did not much appreciate the joys of an adolescent stepson — preached his neophyte away north and west to purge the stench of the swamp from his soul, he was swayed this way and that by a little bit of ecclesiastical everything. Some Sundays in the hobo camps alongside the railroad, he spoke in tongues. On others, in parks, to surprised audiences of family picnickers, he handled rented, non-toxic snakes. On still others, he spoke calmly and reassuringly about the virtues of the ascetic life in a crude, materialist society — crude for the poor, materialist for the rich.

Noam was not yet as chubby as he would become in California, so his message of physical denial and spiritual passion retained a modicum of credibility — just enough, in fact, to bring in the donations he needed to gas up the inherited stake-bed and keep moving.

The years and years and years of preaching on the road that brought Noam to Pasadena were endless successions of months of addressing campfire meetings of men who called themselves "travelling farmworkers" (but who, after passing around a couple of jugs of God knows what distillants, called themselves hobos), of dropping in on school parents' meetings he'd scouted from his parked truck and saying, "You know, all this figuring out a way to get fresh farm milk to the school every day for the boys' and girls' lunch is very commendable — and you have every reason to be proud. But have you considered the immortal souls of your children?", of just sitting and smoking and reading in the courthouse square until a retired feed-and-grain dealer addressed him, in a friendly enough way, as "stranger" and struck up a conversation that Noam expertly turned to the subject of Jesus — or Noam's version of him, of figuring the moment was finally right to rent the tents, have the makeshift benches carpentered, and rally the schoolmothers to waddle forth with big galvanized tubs filled with lemonade, and of staging the jam-packed Sunday-balmy-evening revival meeting in some compliant farmer's untilled cornfield (in return, of course, for a guarantee of eternal salvation).

The tent meeting crowds always vomited up enough cash for Noam to move briskly on, with a washed truck and a full fuel tank, toward wherever it was he thought he was ultimately going. But Noam was often tempted to hang around for a while after the poles and canvas had been rolled into themselves, after the schoolmothers had washed the cups and walked home smiling and nodding to each other. Sometimes it took him a week to lose the erection he contracted just before taking the pulpit, when he was sliding tightly between clumps of honest, healthy, ripe women in fresh-smelling gingham dresses, placing his hand gently on the cusp of a rump to ease himself through, saying "'Scuse me, Ma'am," but wishing he could thrust his pelvis just a little forward, enough to satin-tickle the organ he sometimes addressed, in loneliness, as "my little meat pal."

When fortune smiled on Noam enough (for God didn't personally handle trifles like expenses) to allow him to remain in a town for a while, to let his gaze linger on the lovely line of a naked nape of the neck of one of the 15-year-old daughters of one of the schoolmothers (there were so many in these burgs!), he felt he could die and go to heaven right there on the hard-baked soil of Arkansas, Missouri, Kansas, Oklahoma, scattered southern sections of Colorado, or Idaho (particularly an eerie little town called — in the worst of taste, even for a sweaty, impatient ball of charismatic flesh like Noam — Calvary).

Eventually, Noam made his way to California.

His Ford was on its last rubber-coated, circular little legs when he coaxed it, steaming and coughing, through Needles, which was, apparently, the scorpion capital of the Western world. But Noam, his armpits leaking two vertical seas of sweat and stink beneath a starched white shirt he hadn't changed in two weeks, nursed the failing car into L.A., where it died right outside Al's Market just off Venice Boulevard. He staggered in out of the sun and bought himself a Coca-Cola, drained it in three gulps, and then shuffled, with his bags, out to the streetcar tracks that ran down the boulevard's median, flagged down the friendly conductor, and boarded.

Getting from the corner of Venice and Normandie (Noam hadn't really overshot his destination, going this far west; it was just that he couldn't find a stopping place that "looked right") back to downtown was another little con project, just like getting from the bayou to Southern California. He had twelve dollars and change in his pockets, no prospects, no contacts, and he was entering a city almost as thick with itinerant preachers as it was with real estate salesman. Real estate was, in fact, a favorite Noam Sain metaphor: He'd always told the bakery-sale ladies of the heartland that what he was selling was, in fact, "a little plot of foreverland, at the foot of God's mountain — just as pure and cool and green and filled with modern conveniences as any lovely home you could ever hope to buy in this lifetime."

Noam sat himself down next to a nice old lady as plump as himself and talked to her. He didn't let up until the streetcar had pulled into the downtown barns and let the last few passengers going all the way downtown on a Saturday out. She didn't believe in Jesus — at least not the way Noam did — but she told him he had a good heart, that Los Angeles needed a few more people with good hearts, and, in addition to the streetcar fare and lunch money she'd "lent" him after two stops, she rented him a room in her LeMaire Street bungalow, for free.

Noam pocketed the lunch money, fed himself from the woman's icebox, and washed his clothes (even the suit pants that were supposed to go only to the dry cleaner) in the bathtub (along with his round, glistening body). Then he went out the door, past the four cats sleeping on the shaded porch, and hoofed it (quickly reflooding his pits with sweat) straight to the Cathedral of the Open Door, hard by the main branch of the big public library.

Everybody had heard of the Cathedral of the Open Door, even tongue-speakers in the bayou.

Noam hated what he called "paying retail" in church, that is, going through the front door, the customers' entrance, like a humble penitent, without having met the "head preacher" in advance, without being taken immediately back to the vestiary for a quick belt of something a little smoother than moonshine. But, having no other choice, he did it this one time.

On stage (for this is what it was — far removed from the more pious "behind the pulpit") this rented weekend afternoon was a mousey little man named with a mousey little name: Dudley Pelley. Mr. Pelley paced back and forth in front of a sparse, entirely unemployed audience speckled throughout the maroon velour seats spread as flat as carpet in this huge, brown-to-the-point-of-blackness theological cavern carved in the heart of a granite bank building, funneling all his mousey little energy into an approximation of a bellow, like a high school drama teacher showing the kids how a dramatic soliloquy is really performed.

Pelley wore a double-breasted suit, in a middle value, mousy brown. Previously — very recently — Pelley had worn black pants, a silver shirt, and a Sam Brown belt while delivering an earlier variation of the same exhortation he was giving now. Pelley been a member of the Silver Shirts of America, Inc., an organization that believed, among other things, it was none of America's business how the firm and vigorous and Christian-in-the-most-righteous-sense leadership of Germany dealt with the whiney, Jew-inspired complaints from crypto-Bolshevik governments in England and France about the way in which it was restoring purpose and order in one of the world's most noble nations. And it would have stayed none of America's business if it hadn't been for the Jews in America who were trying to make it America's business so that they could — somehow, you could be sure — make money from it.

Very astute, thought Noam, concerning the coversion of the fascist black shirt (a wholly philosophical, and somewhat morbid, statement) into the American silver shirt (a symbol of order *and* enterprise).

Very nice, Noam thought: not especially Godly, but this is Los Angeles, not Louisiana, and folks out here are probably as interested in money as they are in the Lord. I certainly know I am.

Just as these thoughts were passing through Noam's mind, Pelley boomed out the name of his political religion: *The Mighty I AM!*

Coincidence, thought Noam. But then again, there are no coincidences, only foldings, unfoldings and refoldings of God's lacy fabric of time.

The same thought, or a rough equivalent of it in a mixture of Norwegian, German, and little bit of English, had also just occurred to a sternly beautiful woman with the odd appellation of Imeda Jinsokt, sitting in a rearmost seat, weeping, for no discernible reason other than homesickness, and a profound sense of her soul being lost, somewhere on the shoals of the centuries, on the edge of the shifting sea of time.

[Careful with those metaphors. *Quack.*]

Noam saw the weeping woman and his heart was moved. The next day, his body was moved by his newly moved heart. He finagled a few more bucks from his charity landlady and went back out west on Venice Boulevard and hired a mechanic to resurrect his dead Ford.

Quadruple Threat

The balloon-colored not the bright hues of a child's birthday party embellishment, but rather curiously chromatically configured, according to a straight-line horizontal split along its inflated midsection: sky blue below it (to be seen by those looking up), and green-brown-khaki-ochre camouflage jigsaw above (to be seen by those looking down) — floated eastward, just below the cloud cover, toward the Oregon coast. And it was much bigger than a party balloon, perhaps the size of a modest prewar car (say, a 1934 Ford) because it was required to support and transport its cargo — a shiny, swaying tubular steel bomb.

At the point of the shorebreak, on the earth beneath the balloon, where moving white foam cuticles slid forward on the mottled surface of a prussian blue sea spread and erased themselves on the sand, the fog bank came to an abrupt end. Sunlight rained upon the land.

Drifting eastward from Japan, into the atmospheric change, the balloon bounced like a giddy child. At the moment it passed over the beach, a crude but accurate enough electric groundspeed odometer, attached to a compass and welded onto the bomb's frame, reached a preordained coordinate on its perforated metal dial, and sent a signal up, along a heavy, weatherproofed wire, to a valve stem on the helium sac itself. The valve opened for a few seconds, and an inert gas hissed out into the open sky. The balloon sank a hundred feet. The odometer clicked and sent another signal that caused another hiss and another small descent. The metal dial continued to revolve, to reach more pre-calculated perforations, which agitated the clock proper to send more signals up the wire. The balloon continued its staircase-in-the-sky descent.

Twelve hundred nautical miles westward from the States, over the Pacific, an experimental wingless aircraft turned and sped back toward Japan. It had just released another balloon, militarily identical to the one transgressing the Oregon coast. In about two or three days, depending on the weather and local winds, the second balloon would enter United States airspace anywhere from San Diego to Seattle and begin to expel its helium. The home of the wingless aircraft was an airfield just south of Nagoya, Japan, which had, so far, escaped the persistent and terrifying American incendiary raids. The aircraft's former domicile had been a hangar near Berlin which, now reduced to a semi-melted steel skeleton by Russian rockets, had fallen into the hands of the occupying Red Army. The aircraft's long-postponed mission, the delivery of balloon bombs to the jetstream at a point some twelve hundred nautical miles west of the Oregon coast, had been conceived as a cooperative venture between the two principle Axis nations. Thus, the oddly shaped aircraft still bore, as a tribute to the sundered alliance, the insignia of both the Japanese Imperial Air Force and the German Luftwaffe. The aircraft was even named, as per some partly peeled Gothic lettering just below the bubble cockpit, "Imeda," after the actual Christian name of the Nazi's marquee dispenser of propaganda to Allied troops, "Axis Sally."

It was she who, not long after arriving in Germany from America, when the possibility of war between Yankees and Nazis was still no better than fifty-fifty, had dreamed up the mission. Axis Sally first targeted (insofar as the balloon bombs could aimed at a specific area smaller than Westphalia) Southern California. But she set her sights on Oregon after receiving disturbing news from German agents (rendering a personal favor) in the United States about her estranged — but never formally divorced —

husband. He had moved to Oregon and acquired a family.

★ ★ ★ ★ ★

An older and even fatter Noam Sain picnicked on a glorious hillside meadow, below the friendly sun just now peaking through a break in the clouds, and below the metal tube, wagging happily, like the tail of a robot dog with a big blue butt. He was also happier than he had been in Pasadena: a new wife, plump like him, who giggled when she went down on him, some new kids — four of hers from some previous history into which Noam was not inclined to delve (the kids were nice, she fucked like a bandit, and she seemed to find his peculiar version of Jesus convincing), and a real congregation in a white, wooden church with a steeple so pointed it made your ass pucker when you looked at it.

A good many of the townsmen had gone off to war, or worked double shifts in the timber mills to turn out lumber for the flimsy landing boats that would be stuffed with Marines during the inevitable invasion of Japan. Noam had easier-than-usual pickings from the women in the puff-sleeved, flower-print dresses in the congregation. Although Noam was even further from a matinee-idol's physique than he had been when he married Imeda, he found that he also required less sport-fucking than he did back then to keep him happy. And his silver tongue had, if anything, grown more polished. It just about redeemed his body in the seduction of congregants. Besides, Noam was now married. All in all, he constituted, at that moment in the meadow, a felicitous balance between needs and limitations.

Then came the flash. The roar. Bits of blood and bone and hair and flesh airborne. A hideous red-grey spray of smoke and gristle. Death, as it were, by longshot.

What, exactly, *were* the odds of it all happening like this?

Imeda going from Pasadena to Lisbon to Berlin and arriving in one piece: five to one, but she did make it. Imeda trotting out her Norwegian and English to an impressed Waffen SS officer who bought her her first drink in the new Reich and being answered with an offer of a job to translate intercepted diplomatic cables from Oslo and Washington: one hundred to one, but she got it. Imeda's fierce intellect shaping and forging and tempering a hatred of all that was fat and soft about America and Noam into an ability to attach memoranda both cogent and lip-smackingly partisan to the decoded cables: even. Imeda's memos, and their attendant political passion being brought to the attention of Reichsminister Hendrijk Oeups, an even more fiercely partisan Dutch transplant within the inner rings of Nazidom: two to one (Oeups had a good staff.) The odds of Oeups being the great-to-the-fifteenth-power grandson of His Holy Eminence Gerhardt Cardinal Oeups: none given, for there was no particular coincidence in Reichsminister Oeups being the interviewer of Imeda Jinsokt on a hot June day in an airless basement room of Albert Speer's Chancellery building. Reichsminister Oeups having once seen — and touched — the painting painted by Dieric Maender that included, on one side, the image of his great-to-the-fifteenth-power grandfather: 2,534 to one, since the painting was long thought to have disappeared. Reichsminister Oeups somehow — by word or gesture, intentionally or not — communicating, yea transmitting, the weird temporal property of that picture to Frau Jinsokt: infinite, for we are dealing with mystery here, not probability. Imeda's becoming Axis Sally: odds-on; the talent pool for Sally's highly specialized tasks was very small. Axis Sally's accruing to a position to be able to suggest actual aircraft designs to the Luftministry: even, for the powers of sex, particularly oral sex performed on grateful Aryan poseurs woefully unsure of their actual ability in lovemaking, are great. The Luftministry's actually building such a craft, especially in the form of the Zanonia seed, which gave it the configuration of what was to be called a generation later a "lifting body": infinite. The aircraft's being lent to the Japanese: odds-on; sensible German aviators didn't want to play at being the divine wind in that contraption, and besides, the prevailing breeze, as everyone knew, blew west. The Japanese following through on the mission: even; by June, 1945, they (the admirals to whom negotiated surrender was a libel upon their ancestors) were desperate to find anything that would moderate the American onslaught, and the idea that a strike at the American homeland would cause even just a little hesitation and doubt, was a straw to them worth grabbing at. The Japanese choosing relatively underpopulated and unimportant Oregon as their target: even; California was both too highly protected and contained too many potential (albeit potential only in the fantasy of a nearly defeated military leadership) latent Imperial patriots who might be persuaded to flock to the rising sun should the tide of the war turn miraculously in favor of the Greater East Asia Co-Prosperity Sphere. (That, at least, was the reason given to the Home Command upon the admirals' learning that many, if not most, of the balloon bombs were drifting over Oregon, rather than California.) That the aircraft containing the balloon bomb that was to be ejected, and inflated by the disconnecting of a pull cable once it had cleared the turbulence of its parent, would actually complete the flight (before crashing by design into the Pacific and killing the hapless pilot; all this "speeding toward home" business was persiflage for morale's sake): infinite, because the calculations positing the voyage were based on the assumed existence of ether (which would carry the airplane further on less fuel), a belief insinuated into the design program by Imeda, who had learned it from Noam, who had preached it as proving the existence of God ("God abhors a vacuum"). Noam being a bona fide minister of an actual congregation in Oregon: five hundred to one. Noam picnicking at the very spot on which the bomb was about to drop: infinite, for we are still speaking of mystery instead of probability. All of this occurring in connected order: infinite.

[But this is Billy's story, and he's sticking to it. *Quack.*]

The flash occurred about one hundred and fifty feet above ground and sent (speaking imprecisely, for the flash was but a visible sign of the germ of force at the germ core of the balloon bomb's explosion) a powerful shock wave, accompanied by thousands of speeding, glinting sharpened metal shards, earthward in a deadly arc. Noam's plump wife was shredded, and what was left of her flattened beyond recognition, in an instant. Her wicker picnic basket, vaguely resembling (before the explosion) a wingless, miniature version of one of The Brothers of Jesus's earlier-in-the-century aircraft, was blasted into separate straws which went like arrows through the skin of her four children, ranging in age from eighteen months to nine years. They were killed by the flying needles almost before the blast and its heat could finish the job.

Noam, by chance, had looked up at the sky, a second or two before the explosion and saw the balloon, which he thought quite pretty. Then he saw the tube, shining like a silver dollar against the deep blue Oregon canopy, and realized something might be quite right. In the same time that it took the electrical impulses to travel the few micro-millimeters from synapse to synapse in Noam's brain, his consciousness experienced a series of words: *silver, shining, metal, aircraft, civilian, military, dropping, weapon, ours, why, theirs, how, newspaper, experimental, fantastic, possible, could, might, yes, scream.*

Which Noam did, through a vertical oval opened in a

fat face above a sweat-soaked collar surrounded by a dark blue (black, compared to the sky) suit. The sound of his scream was a roar. His wife heard the scream, and was about to register it for processing in her consciousness when she was killed. His children heard the scream, and commanded themselves to feel frightened just before they were killed. Noam heard his own scream before anyone else (perhaps he "heard" his intent to scream) and he felt his body enveloped in heat. But the heat Noam felt came from inside himself, not outside, and it seemed to Noam in retrospect to have been precisely equal to the subsequent burst of heat, which arrived several milliseconds after the one he generated himself. Whatever the exact order of occurrence, Noam was gone, disappeared, not physically present, for an instant, when the blast leveled his entire family, their picnic, and a fuzzy-edged circle of high, lime green, Oregon coastal grass.

When Noam reappeared, at the other end of the instant, the scene was calm, if smoky. There were no bodies, no bones, no blood, nothing that would betray the occurrence as anything other than a mysteriously isolated, totally out-of-season, and fantastically symmetrical brush fire that had been, oddly, accompanied by a shower of tin triangles. Noam straightened his wide, flowered tie and, in something of a trance, wandered, stumbling, down the hill, away from the coast, back toward the road where his car, a 1934 Ford, was parked.

As the driver's-side door on Noam's 1934 Ford clicked shut (Noam was too weak to slam it), a small, fresh-faced, quaintly dressed (even for 1945) audience of high school students in Calvary, Idaho, rose from their wooden chairs in a hot classroom made only marginally less uncomfortable for having all its windows open, and applauded the election (by a wide margin) of Ken Sabe (last name pronounced with two syllables, as Serge Protector, his father, had originally pronounced his own first name) as president of the Future Farmers of America for the 1945-46 school year.

In those days, Calvary High School educated only a little less than two hundred students at a time, but, with patriotic fever having siphoned off a couple of dozen boys into the armed services, in June, 1945, the number had dropped to 156. With such a small talent pool, Calvary High School usually had trouble fielding any sort of basketball team, let alone a good one. The 1944-45 edition was, although numerically typical with but seven players suited up for each game, an exception. And it was all because of the president-elect of the FFA.

Ken, at seventeen, stood a little more than six feet five, and possessed enormous, magnificently knuckled hands. He could palm four basketballs at once, and a photograph of him doing so — smilingly holding the balls straight out in front of him like two giant double-decker ice cream cones without the cones, or two cartoon dumbbells held vertically without the lifting bar, or two brown brassieres without the straps — graced the cover of the single, entire-season basketball program of the Calvary High School Fighting Christians. Ken's face, grinning into the camera with the manic, rectangular configuration of a marine's on a recruiting poster, topped an angular body whose imposing muscle definition was readily apparent even within the crude, cheap halftone screen fuzzed further by the incompetence of local printing. Ken's photograph, superman-beefcakey as it was, hardly did justice to his play.

In rickety gyms with splintery floors, wearing shoes that would look, in retrospect, to his son, Robo, more like policemen's footwear than athletes', playing against pale, spidery, frantic farmboys, Ken could and would routinely score more points than the whole of the opposition. Although he could hoist his 220-pound frame two and a half feet off the floor with knees unbent and send the dark brown ball in twenty-five foot arcs straight through the orange metal rim with unnerving regularity, he liked best to score from the inside.

Ken's dunks were not, by the later standards of his own son Robo, balletic; but they were forceful and scary. Under the basket, he'd wheel a couple of times, this way and that, on his big, planted pivot foot, then bull his way straight up in the air while cocking the ball back to the nape of his neck with both hands. He'd bring the ball down through the hoop with the thunderous motion of a lumber axe coming down in a log-splitting contest. The girls in the stands would scream, the gym would rock, dogs tied up outside in moonlight would run in circles and bark, and, as often as not, the rim would bend a little. In those days, they just went ahead and played the rest of the game with a planarly distorted orange goal or two.

About a year and a half after Ken Sabe's last high school dunk, a patrol of American soldiers of occupation found Axis Sally, nee Imeda Jinsokt, barely existing — huddling, scurrying, growling, crying, whimpering, scavenging — in a bombed-out, rat-infested ruin of a beerhall in the U.S. quadrant of the western sector of Berlin. She had been living, in effect, in endless night, endless dark, endless cold, rarely appearing above the rubble in daylight. Trembling, her knees crooked beneath her chin, licking traces of rotten soup from rusted cans or gnawing on stonelike briquets of bread or sipping comforting jolts of Sterno, she would sit in the pitch black cave fate had fashioned from Howitzer fire and the tumblings of decorative masonry and stare at the painting. She couldn't really see it clearly, so she didn't bother to remove the protective Wermacht blanket she had wrapped around it and fastened with belts and straps taken from the corpses of soldiers, Axis and Allied alike.

Beneath the blanket, doubly beyond Imeda's perception, the image on the surface of the painting slowly metamorphosed, back and forth, between that of a madonna and child and that of nothing save a few elementary colored rectangles. Imeda had, however, witnessed those changes a few years before, while lying on her back, legs spread, on the glistening black leather couch in an inner office of the Reichschancellery building. The picture — allegedly painted by a famous Flem whose name she couldn't remember but who, Reichsminister Hendrijk Oeups assured her, was genealogically aligned with the Aryan strain of European creativity and not with the inferior, more Mediterranean Walloon mutation — hung on a far, teak-paneled wall. The lights were out because it was after hours and she and Oeups weren't supposed to be in the building, no matter what his rank. But moonlight filtered in between the leafy trees outside and through the high, leaded glass windows, and played across the painting.

Imeda wasn't sure whether the dissolving, recoalescing and redissolving of the image was actually happening, or was a figment of her imagination tickled by the moonlight. What she imagined was Noam's face — instead of the reality of Oeups's — between her legs, licking furiously. It helped a little. It helped to the point that, later, when she thought of her orgasm, she thought of the painting, and vice-versa. So, at that moment in history when even she, the radio voice of always-impending German victory, could realize that the empire was unraveling, she sneaked into that inner office. By then, the guards were twelve years old and wholly untrained, with helmets that covered their eyes. She took the painting back to her quarters.

When the American soldiers found her in the rubble,

they had to pry the painting (or whatever it was beneath that odoriferous, blood-splattered blanket) from Imeda's spindly arms. As she wailed, a young American sergeant — who'd been commissioned a captain on the spot because he had a master's degree in art history from Harvard University (thesis: "Italiante Influences on Northern Renaissance Painting, 1425-1575"), and somebody with some knowledge was needed to command, with a modicum of aesthetic expertise, the GI's who were stumbling upon treasure after treasure salted away by the Nazis — calmly walked the picture away.

An hour later, the newly commissioned captain stood back five feet, one arm bent at the elbow with the forearm across his stomach, the other with it's elbow resting on that forearm and its hand cradling his chin, as two privates, making facial gestures indicating an urge to vomit, cut the dirty strips of rag securing the blanket around the painting. The blanket fell away and the sergeant gasped.

A Dieric Maender! An honest-to-God, original-in-near-mint-condition, never-documented-as-far-as-I-know, real McCoy Maender! (All the privates saw was an abstract painting. Not knowing what an abstract painting was, all the privates thought they saw was a dirty canvas, perhaps the start of a picture by some poor fucking kraut dauber who probably caught a stray .45 right through the noggin, ha ha.)

The new captain said he'd have to take the picture back to his quarters to look at it more closely. The privates, who thought he was off his goddamned rocker, nodded at each other with their heads turned just enough away from the captain so that he couldn't see their smirks, and said, "Yes, sir." One of them carried the picture to the captain's quarters.

Later, a bird colonel who liked the new captain, told him that — ahem! and a wink — he was arranging a "safe-keeping" shipment back to the States of assorted captured goodies whose provenance within Europe could not be immediately traced. Did the captain have anything he'd like included, that he might be able to — another wink — "study" more closely once he was back in America after this bit of babysitting ex-Nazis was over?

Yes, a painting.

Could I see it, just for the hell of it?

Sure.

The colonel saw it. Damnedest thing. Thought he could make out something, Mother Mary and the Christ kid, or something like that. But not real clear. Tilt your head another direction, and you can't see a damned thing. Nothing I can use. Fence value, nada. He wants it, he's got it.

You (talking to the new captain) might have to travel some to get to it when you're stateside. Want to keep things away from the civilian pencil-pushers in Washington. My contacts got a little depot staked out near an airfield. Cave in a mountain, matter of fact. Nice place: dry, cool, secure. Wait a while, then take a leave or something. Look like a vacation.

(Confused): Where in the States?

Up in Idaho.

Jesus, I live in New York. That's clear across the country. How will I ever get to it?

It's your only chance, pal. Otherwise, the office of Monuments, Fine Arts and Archives will tag it, and stick it in a warehouse in Baden Wurtenburg. Then it'll probably end up back in the hands of the syphilitic baron who most likely bought it with the sale of his stock in Zyklon B.

Geez, I don't know.

Look, I like you. (Hand on the captain's shoulder, lingering just a half-second to massage with the fingertips). You can trust me. Come by HQ as often as you can. Catch me when I know the details, I'll write 'em out for you.

Jesus, Idaho. What about the old lady?

A real weird case. Rumor's she's American. Can you believe it? If that's true, they'll ship her back, too. If she's a traitor, they'll try her. Hang her wrinkled ol' butt, I say.

★ ★ ★ ★ ★

About a year and a half after they found Imeda Jinsokt living like a paranoid rat in the ruins of Berlin, Ken Sabe came to New York City, trying to make a living as a prize-fighter. Because of his height, the mafioso who managed him (a heavily stubbled man with the last name of Spumante, who feigned mild retardation and called himself "Bennie The Jaw") nicknamed him "The Next Primo Carnera." Given Carnera's ignominy as a practically fraudulent heavy-weight champion who deteriorated into a stiff, this wasn't, to insiders and ringsiders, exactly a flattering sobriquet. But Ken Sabe knew little of the history of prizefighting, and cared less. All he knew was that he received $250 for every fight he won (as against $100 for every one he lost), and that it was comparatively easy, in the unconfined division of weight where he outsized every opponent, to club other men, who erroneously believed they could fight, into un-consciousness.

Contrary to New York State Boxing Commission's regulations on the frequency of participation, Ken Sabe appeared practically every other week on Bennie The Jaw Spumante's's cards which, largely because of Ken's pres-ence, became popular enough to be televised locally. The fights were sponsored by a car dealer in Queens. The an-nouncer who appeared in the commercials for the car dealer who sponsored the televised fights was in fact the owner of the dealership himself. His name was Felix and, although married with a daughter who'd just made her "debut" in a tacky Long Island approximation of a deb ball, he loved Ken Sabe just as much as the colonel in Berlin loved the captain in Berlin, and as unrequitedly. Felix wore a waxed pencil-thin moustache, a shiny and obvious hairpiece, and a tuxedo.

At the end of each round, he would suddenly appear

in his own commercial, swiveling (in a beat-up banker's chair) his alleged attention from an obviously blank television screen on which he pretended to have been watching the fight in progress to the camera. Felix would adjust his own bow tie, smile broadly and say with a Sylvester the Pussycat lisp, "Howth that for action, boxthing fansth?"

The No-Good Father

It's the old story: I'm fucked up because my father was fucked up. He was so fucked up, in so many ways, that it's hard for me to even begin to sort him out on his own terms, let alone figure out exactly what he did to me. Well, I take part of that back. Any idiot who ever read one issue of *The Calvary Weekly Trumpet*, our little weekly newspaper, or came to my high school games and saw him on the sidelines, or visited our house and saw the gym he built out back, knew that he literally made me into what I was. God knows he didn't mean to make me what I am now, but that's a different story.

Let's leave the religious stuff out to start with, although that's a big part of the deal. Let's just start with him being this incredible athlete in this dinky little excuse for a town. Nobody here — shit, nobody in the whole county — was as big and strong as he was. Even the fat guys who sat around the feed-and-grain in U-Can't-Bust'ems with bellies so big they could hardly spit over them didn't weigh as much as my father. He was as hard as a goddamned rock. He weighed as much as if he were made of stone. And he was built so solid, so packed with nothing but coiled muscle, that he looked almost thin.

Even when he was still a kid of seventeen or eighteen, my father was a vicious fucking bastard when he wanted to be. There was some poor kid over in the next county's high school — the story's in an old *Weekly Trumpet* that I got out of my father's house after he disappeared (not just for fractions of a second during basketball games, like I did, but permanently) — who was about six-nine, six-ten. There had been a lot of talk, apparently, about how this kid, who was, apparently, a very skilled, finesse-oriented basketball player, was going to show up my father when their teams met in their gym. I guess he said too much. I can just imagine him standing in the school cafeteria, kind of hunched over because he's a little ashamed of how tall he really is, with some really short girl friend who has a face as flat and round as the top crust of an apple pie, with features like the fork holes in it, who's going to be his wife about two days after graduation and their lives are both going straight to hell starting right then, with one of those big farm-boy grins showing a lot of stupid pink gum above his custard-colored teeth, telling a crowd of simple-minded kids what he was going to do. The grange grapevine being almost as fast as the phone system in Calvary, my father heard about it well in advance of the game.

Well, when the game began, my father sort of laid back and let it look like he was intimidated by the other kid's height. He sucked the other kid into guarding him closely, and he kind of played in a squat, like he was afraid to jump. The other kid bit big. Then, still in the first quarter, my father got the ball in pretty low under the basket. The big, skinny tall kid came up to guard him and leaned over him like a tent frame over a rolled-up sleeping bag. I can imagine him even grinning to the bench, showing them he had my poor father all wrapped up. Then he — my father — just exploded straight up toward the basket, reached out and dunked the ball. On the way, his shoulder broke the kid's jaw, knocked out his front uppers and split his lip eighteen stitches worth. He came down on the kid, too, foot right in his ribs. Cracked a couple.

When my father first told me that story, when I was about eleven and starting to play a little outdoor, pickup ball, it was a don't-be-stupid-and-overconfident-like-the-tall-kid cautionary tale. He implied the whole thing was an accident, and that the point was never to get overconfident when you think your opponent is weaker than you are. By the second or third time he told it to me (he must have told it to me a hundred times, all told), it was clear, at least in his memory, that the whole deal was planned to destroy the guy.

The funny thing is that *The Calvary Weekly Trumpet*, which hardly ever ran photographs in those days, sent a photographer — the son of the guy who owned the drug store, the only place that sold film and cameras in Calvary — to cover the game. He came back with a picture that showed the big kid down on the floor, on his back with his knees raised in pain, blood on his mouth, and his arms starting to grip his own midsection. I say "starting to grip." That's what was weird. The photograph was taken only a couple of tenths of a second after the kid had his ribs caved in by my father's foot. There's a lot of space around the kid — the photographer was on the sideline across court — and of course most of it is black, except for a shard of the shiny gym floor and some of the referee's striped shirt. The ref is in the background, trying to figure out why he can't bring himself to call a foul.

But my father's not in the goddamned picture! He's not even partially in the picture. Here's this big, upside down white spider in satin shorts, rolling in agony, and that's it. My father had disappeared. And weirder still (at least to me), he disappeared *after* the play, not as he exploded up to the basket.

I found the newspaper, and the picture in it, after he disappeared for good, when the guys in suits from the agency took me over to his house and made me go through it with them. I didn't tell them then what I'm telling you now, so they didn't much care that I took the old newspaper with me when we left. I stuffed it in a safe place back in my Airstream. I've still got it. I take it out and look at it every once in a while. It always gives me a funny feeling.

★ ★ ★ ★ ★

I'm getting off the track, which was how fucked up my father was. O.K., let's start with this: In spite of being this real big deal jock in the boonies in Idaho (which is itself the boonies), he had nowhere to go. The war was almost over, and the army wasn't really looking for any more warm bodies to send to the islands to flame-throw the Japs. Anyway, he was too big, the army wouldn't have wanted him. But he didn't have any money to go to college (that's on account of *his* father), and there wasn't much work around Calvary, especially since the government had closed down the factory for the experimental "wingless" airplane — where his father invested all his money and lost it — even before the war ended. There was still some defense industry, especially aviation, gearing up for the cold war, on the West Coast, but my father didn't want to go. He didn't want to hang around Calvary and be a farmer, either. He said farmers around here probably fertilized their crops with their brains since their brains were probably made of horseshit and they seemed to have so little brains left after planting season. So he did something real bright instead. He went to New York to try to become heavy-weight champion of the world.

He got mixed up with shady people like "Benny The Jaw" Spumante, he got the crap kicked out of him, he got himself photographed flat on his fucking back in the ring looking amazingly like the kid whose jaw he'd broken in high school (except for the ring floor having no lines on it and the referee's not wearing a striped shirt, you'd think the two pictures were the same), and he got himself screwed out of about every penny he ever made in boxing, and he didn't make many.

But he came home with about fifty or sixty thousand dollars, cash, in a satchel. He told my mother (who, of course, wasn't my mother then, just a girl he met at some strange church meeting in town) that it was his fight purses, all saved up. He said in New York the Jews ran all the banks, so it was safer for a guy like him to just live in a nice, safe Italian neighborhood (he called it "the Dago District," and laughed), keep the money under the mattress, and make some Mafia friends. Well, I've seen the clippings about all of his fights (before the agency carted them off), and he couldn't have made a tenth of that kind of money, let alone have saved it all.

He never became champ, of course. He never even became somebody they said would be "the next Primo Carnera." At least Primo beat some real fighters among all those stiffs, and got to be champion for about fifteen minutes before he had his ass handed to him by Jack Sharkey or somebody like that. My father did beat a couple of little heavyweights — a hundred and eighty, eighty-five pounds, at Saint Nick's Arena. But he fought three draws in a row with tubby barroom bouncers he should have flattened in a minute. He had a couple of years of win-one, lose-one, and then ended up unconscious in the hospital for four days after Bennie The Jaw said it was time to recoup his investment and put him in an eight-rounder with Roland LaStarza. Bennie probably bet on LaStarza. Anyway, all that misery sure as hell didn't add up to fifty grand in a leather satchel.

My father fought only for three and a half years — if you don't count the last fight when he came out of retirement to go all the way out to Los Angeles in 1951, only to win by default when the other guy didn't show up because he'd been killed in an explosion the night before. Besides, my father didn't come back to Calvary until 1954, when he met my mother, so there's three years that he was in New York not doing anything much, as far as I could ever tell.

One time, when we were having some home-pressed pear juice (he never let me drink soda pop, and he said water was a waste of time because you could be drinking something else with vitamins in it) between rounds in the ring in the practice gym he built out behind the farm-house, where he was, of course, kicking the shit out of me as usual, in "our quest" (as he called it) for me to become, "scientifically" (as he put it) the greatest athlete in the world, and he had out the scrapbook with all the clippings, even the bad stuff, the lost fights as well as his scoring 96 points to set the Idaho schoolboy record which still stands even though it was set way back in an era when whole teams hardly ever scored more than sixty, I asked him about it. I asked him what did he do between the train back to New York from L.A. after the "explosion fight" and when he met my mother at a church service. He said he just "did some things for some guys, things too boring to talk about, son."

I also asked him about his name. He said when he got to New York, nobody knew who he was, nobody thought his sheer size and muscle mass made him anything special, and worse, nobody would give him the answer to any-thing. He said he asked all kinds of questions, like where could you buy chewing gum or how much it cost to mail a postcard from New York to Idaho, and people would just laugh. Even when he found a gym and a guy who might be his manager, they gave him this little Puerto Rican trainer, an ex-flyweight for God's sake, and told the Puerto Rican (my father said he learned to call him "Spickyweight") to answer all my father's questions. The little trainer used to smile and answer, *"Quien sabe?"* So, when Bennie the Jaw asked him if he wanted to invent his own name to fight under, my father said sure. He said, I'll be Ken Sabe, with the last name pronounced as two syl-lables. He thought it was a great joke. I suppose it was, considering that he kept the name for the rest of his life. (Or is keeping it — he may still be alive for all I know.) And especially since he decided to become a spook, like his father. Whenever anybody asked my mother what he did for a living to get all that fancy equipment and hire those weird foreign trainers to turn his little boy into the greatest athlete in the world, she learned to just say *"Quien sabe?"*

What did my father do to make me a great athlete? Jesus, what didn't he do? I was a big baby to start with partly because, my mother told me later, her husband fed her all kinds of healthful stuff crammed with calories and proteins and made her eat a ton of it. She gained 62 pounds during her pregnancy with me and struggled for years to lose them. She told me my father's first words when he came into her hospital room (all the way to Pocatello, to get the best care, in spite of the long, dangerous night drive when her water broke) were to ask the nurse how long I was and how much I weighed. When the nurse told him, he said, "Well, that's a start."

Of course, he wouldn't let my mother breast-feed me. He said all mother's milk was the same, which meant that it was all average, which meant in turn that I would turn out average, nutritionally speaking. So he ground up meat with raw eggs and some sort of strange protein powder I think he got from a cattle-breeder in Calvary, and loaded it with malted milk and sugar so I wouldn't spit it out and practically crammed it down my throat. A couple of times, I've been told, I almost died. Probably some sort of bacteria in that slop he made, or maybe it was just stuff that a baby's digestive system wasn't meant to take.

There were a couple of roaring midnight trips to Pocatello with me hotter than the goddamned radiator in my father's car and puking all over my mother in the back seat. (My mother told me that my father coolly told her to sit in the back — this was before seatbelts were standard — because he was going to have to drive so fast that there was a good chance they'd have a crash.) Obviously, I didn't die, but there have been times in my life when I wished I had.

When I was in the crib (I've been told), my father put me on my back and put little contraptions on the crib that dangled over me. Some of them were supposed to improve my peripheral vision (starting at an age when I could hardly follow anything with my eyes), others were supposed to sharpen my reflexes (starting at an age when I could hardly raise my arms or use my hands). My father would stay by my crib for hours at a time and try to make me grab hold of things that he'd then try to pull away. When I learned to grab and tug, he'd fit the crib with gizmos he made himself in his workshop that'd pull away automatically. And he could ratchet up the resistance, then reinstall them, so I was supposed to be getting stronger all the time. I probably was, much more than naturally, too. Between my being big to start with, all that high-powered crap my father fed me, and those constant exercises, I was one springy ball of muscle, with very little baby fat, by the time I was a year old.

Oddly, my father let me learn to walk at my own pace. Maybe he figured that if he pushed me, my legs wouldn't develop normally, that I'd end up bowlegged or something. But once I was ambulatory, it was Katie bar the door: harnesses to tug against, little homebuilt staircases to climb, ankle weights made of canvas and filled with sand, and shoes with lead foil stuffed between the midsole and the outer sole. My father read everything he could get his hands on about muscles and tendons and stress, so he prevented himself from screwing up my knees. He braced them and wrapped them in elastic bandages so I wouldn't tear or strain anything. But the strapping lead to a minor circulation problem that affected me in later life, which is to say when I was a teenager and in my twenties. I often had a tingling sensation in my calves. It was — coincidence or not — the same kind of tingling sensation I'd just start to feel (though I hardly had time to really feel it) just before I'd disappear in basketball games.

From the time I was about three and a half or four, my father's training of me approximated the real thing you'd put an adult athlete through: continued special diet, strength conditioning (mostly pull and tug, because he'd read that weightlifting too early would hurt my bones), running (long, slow distance in the wilds, middle-distance work on the high school track — yes, that same goddamned high school we all went to — and sprints timed with a stopwatch on a flat strip near the house — a practice which obviously fused a couple of memory synapses in my head), and my father's favorite form of teaching torture, "read and react."

For that, he built a machine, a big board with a grid of lights on the top, and some holes on the bottom. I had to stand in front of it, and the lights would flash on. If I didn't hit the light that flashed with my hand, a pole with a boxing glove on it would shoot out of one of the holes on the bottom and get me in the groin, or the leg. I never knew which light would go on and, if I missed it, which hole the pole would shoot out of.

He made all kinds of devices, from these plywood mitts that I was supposed to deflect baseballs thrown at my head with, to an electric jump-rope that would change height and speed without notice. I ran through tires laid out in a field — pretty standard for football players — except my father had made a contraption out of a couple of old harvesters and some electronic switching equipment that yanked and jerked the tires every which way. As soon as I'd put my foot into the hole in the middle of one, it'd rip sideways, sometimes almost taking my ankle with it. Then he added an overhead rig — it was so ugly and noisy and complicated I can't describe it — that lowered wooden crossbeams suddenly. So, there I'd be, running as fast as I could through the spastic tires — carrying two basketballs, four footballs, a couple of bowling balls, you name it — and then I'd have to duck or swerve my head to avoid a concussion. If I fell, sprawling across the tires, the bowling balls smashing my fingers, my father wouldn't yell. He wouldn't say anything. He'd just let the machine run a little longer to give me a good, painful thrashing — "negative memory conditioning" he called it — and then just nod his head, meaning "again."

We did this stuff, plus weightlifting, as soon as I grew hair on my balls, two hours before school in the morning (I was up at four thirty, summer or winter, blizzard or thunderstorm), and three hours after. Saturday was a "full day" of about six hours of gruelling workouts, including a long lunch with protein shakes, eight-millimeter films, and my father's "chalk talks" on various sports. Sunday was a quiz (I could choose to take it morning or night) on my required sports, nutrition and military history reading, but otherwise it constituted my "day off."

One thing he didn't do as often as you'd think a competitive maniac like him would was combat training. Maybe it was a holdover reaction from his bummer of a boxing career, or (as I often thought about everything — and I mean everything — he did in his life) maybe my father was just very smart and cagey. But he didn't get out the boxing gloves, or the kick-boxing slippers, or the ju-jitsu outfits until I'd gone through puberty and, even then, he didn't use them very often. He'd just threaten to. Or he'd just hint that someday soon he'd have to. Because, as he told me again and again, "Sometime — and it's inevitable — an athlete as great as you're going to be is going to push somebody almost as big and fast and strong and mean as you are just a little too far. Then you're going to have to fight, and it's probably going to be pretty close to for keeps."

Funny, I never did. Not once. Not once — in all those times of screaming and sliding across the floor and searing the wax into my skin and feeling the heat, that incredible heat rising in my body to a boil and taking the ball in one palm and going up over some taller son of a bitch who'd been grabbing and elbowing and holding me all night in front of a bunch of people logged with beer who hated my guts and slamming the thing through the hoop and throwing both fists into the air in celebration — did I ever raise a hand in anger. And not once afterward, when it was all over for me in the league and I'd moved back to Calvary and had gotten the Airstream and moved it out beyond the town line and was careening all over the place on my BMW shaft-drive and working myself sick clearing and scraping and leveling the running track — not once when those snotty, drunken high school kids with five friends hidden behind the car in the parking lot, or maybe even with a gun in the trunk, calling me crazy, calling me crazy faggot after the thing when I grabbed that boy — not once did I ever seek to harm anyone, even for an instant. It was not inevitable that I would fight (and if I fought I would probably kill). It *is* not inevitable that I will fight. I will never fight, and I will never kill. Fuck my father. I would rather die first.

★ ★ ★ ★ ★

I almost did. In Africa; I talked about that. But after that, too, when I got mixed up with The Brothers of Jesus, and thought I might actually have to kill somebody.

The group — The Brothers of Jesus — that the player in Africa brought me back to was weird. And I knew from weird. They met in a storefront church at the end of the main street in Calvary, about where the business district starts to peter out into nothing but highway, culverts and dirt. Everybody who belonged to it lived in one of the old wooden barracks buildings that had been moved by flat-bed trucks in sections from the airfield where they used to test the "wingless aircraft" that the Army Air Forces were once supposed to buy by the hundreds to win the war with Japan. (The war ended, the factory closed, and the airfield and its buildings just sat there for years.)

The "holy dormitory," as they called it, sat out about fifty yards behind the storefront building. We met and talked and drank fruit punch (no liquor, no cigarettes, no caffeine, no nothing) and studied what they called "the universal scriptures" (which, as often as not, were just mimeographed speeches by The Brothers of Jesus's leaders) in the storefront and then retired to the dormitory to eat and sleep.

The strange thing was that we "chaylens," or lay recruits, were supposed to make ourselves conspicuous by traipsing back and forth between the storefront and the dormitory. We were supposed to dress extremely neatly and plainly — flannel shirts and straight-legged jeans being the preferred attire for me, and long-sleeved white blouses and ankle-length denim skirts for the women — so that the good folks of Calvary could see how upstanding and non-threatening we were.

But the real reason that we were to make ourselves seen as much as possible was that the leaders, and a special crew to which I was appointed because of my strength and endurance, had dug a tunnel from the storefront to the dormitory. They didn't want the townspeople to suspect it was there. The tunnel's ceiling was a good fifteen feet under the ground and you could actually stand up on its floor. Well, I couldn't, but a normal person could. At either end, under the floor of the storefront or the dormitory, the tunnel turned ninety degrees upward and became like a well-shaft, with a ladder leading up to a nicely concealed trap-door in either building. When I last saw the tunnel, its own floor was dirt, but completely leveled, smoothed, and tamped down hard. I heard The Brothers of Jesus were going to make the whole thing — floor, walls, ceiling — concrete, but I never saw it get to that point. I thought they were trying to kill me, or drive me crazy enough to kill myself, so I ran away.

★ ★ ★ ★ ★

It started when they asked us to start digging another tunnel, under the dormitory, leading in the opposite direction. That direction was straight out of town, into the desert, toward the foothills. That direction lead nowhere. I asked one of the leaders where the new tunnel was supposed to lead to. He told me nowhere, that it was just a spiritual exercise. I told him bullshit. He said that I was affecting my karma by swearing at a leader. I said that since I had done more work on the first tunnel than any other person, including the jock who'd brought me here, I wanted an explanation. He said he'd go get the jock and have him tell me. The jock told me that he'd just been promoted to a junior kind of leader and that his position was more difficult than when he was just a chaylen, like me. He knew more, but he had to follow orders even more closely, silently, and obediently. He told me to have patience, that soon, in reward for all the work that I'd done, I'd probably be made a junior leader, too. Then I'd know where the tunnel was leading to. I told him bullshit, too. He just walked away, and probably told one of the senior leaders that I was becoming dangerous.

I was dangerous, and I knew it. I was starting to go a little nuts. The Brothers of Jesus didn't know that I knew where I was, that this was my goddamned home town, that my mother was buried here and my father probably lived somewhere close by. My father didn't know I had come home, if you could call it that. He had been writing and phoning the league — which was about to merge with the NBA and certainly didn't have time for the father of a trouble-making ex-player like me — trying to find out where the hell I was. As far as the league knew, I was in a Swiss sanitarium where the other player had taken me after the African incident. I had been, for about twenty-four hours, until we hopped a plane for Germany, then one for London, then another for Montreal, another one for Denver, a bus to Pocatello, and a car filled with members of The Brothers of Jesus for the drive to Calvary.

Even if my father, who (I later learned) drove up and down the main street of Calvary on his way to and from the shag-carpeted split-level ranch house where he lived, to and from the fake Peace Corps training center at the old airfield, had spotted me going from the storefront to the dormitory, he wouldn't have recognized me. I didn't have long hair anymore; I didn't have a bandido moustache; and I didn't wear three gold chains around my neck. Shorn and shaved, with my muscles stuffed into a flannel shirt, blue jeans and plain work shoes, I probably looked just like he did when he was a strapping young athlete in Calvary. I don't know exactly what he looked like then, behind the wheel of an anonymous, grey four-door General Motors sedan (with a Corvette engine under the hood in case of emergency), wearing the anonymous grey suit the agency required, but I'm sure I wouldn't have recognized him, either.

The Brothers of Jesus originally thought I was quite a catch: an at least semi-famous maverick jock who had lost his way in a materialist world and had been made whole again by its teachings. But then they started this tunnel deal, and everything became quite secretive, and they didn't quite know what to do with me. You can't trot out a prized recruit and hide him at the same time. (Worse, you can't trot out anything that calls attention to you — good or bad — and start undertaking big, clandestine projects at the same time.) And you can't just turn him — that is, me — loose, with everything he knows.

I didn't quite know what to do with them, either. I thought The Brothers of Jesus were going to give me a soothing, comforting Jesus. I thought I was going to get answers to a couple of things that had bothered me all my life. Like, why would a father try to do to his son what my father had done to me? And what had really been going on with that disappearing number when I played basketball? I thought the business with my father had something to do with God relentlessly molding his son, Jesus to do the impossible, Jesus halfway rebelling along the way by going into the desert like I'd gone to Africa, and, finally, Jesus crying out on the cross, "Father, why hast thou forsaken me?" like I cried out that I was Jesus when I went through the plate glass window. And — I know this sounds crazy and I kind of knew it then — I thought that Jesus rising from the dead and rolling away the stone at the door of the tomb had something to do with my failure to appear, at crucial instants in crucial basketball games, on videotape.

I knew The Brothers of Jesus were starting to look at me differently, that they were grinding their conspiratorial wheels about me. I knew that they probably knew that I was starting to look at them funny, too. I started sleeping outside the dormitory, on the ground, in a sleeping bag, even in cold weather. I carried a knife strapped to my calf at all times. I wouldn't eat the dormitory food, either. I started dipping into my shrinking money bag and buying the raw materials — and I mean that literally — with which to make the protein shakes my father used to feed me. I felt The Brothers of Jesus had somehow deliberately weakened me. I wanted to be stronger, to fight them when they — as I thought they would — finally came for me.

It was only when that mousey little professor, an art historian who was a new recruit — and the smartest chaylen ever, the leaders said — showed up with a package under his arm for The Brothers of Jesus's "treasure chamber" that I went 'round the bend. I was in the storefront when they proudly unwrapped it. The same goddamned painting I saw in the shop just before I lost my mind in Africa! Man, I was gone.

So, yes, I admit, it isn't just the town faggot-haters and the high school kids on a Saturday night with beer bought on somebody else's I.D. and their fathers' hunting rifles in the trunk that scare me. It's The Brothers of Jesus. They think I know everything and they're out to get me. One of these days, they probably will.

Mansions on the Sly

The announcer whose toupee'd head occupied most of the small, greenish monochrome screen of the otherwise large and cumbersome television set crammed onto a knotty pine shelf in one of the recreation rooms in Matt Medium's mansion on Orange Grove Boulevard (popularly known as "Millionaire's Row") in Pasadena, California, turned his moustached face toward the camera. Through the weak, flickering picture, barely visible against the light of a dozen simultaneously illuminated reading lamps in the room, he asked, "Howth that for action, boxthing fansth?"

Had anyone been in the room, he might have laughed — or groaned — because there wasn't any action, nor had there been much action prior to the announcer's face superceding the last round of the last fight (filmed almost two years previously in New York). The announcer, too, was filmed, and his visage was as grainy and pasty and flaccid as the two heavyweights — one of them quite tall for the time — who had clinched, waltzed, grabbed, held and, for a few seconds in each of the four rounds of the crowd-chaser following the main event, flailed at each other. The big guy (the bigger guy) had lost a dull split decision, probably by virtue of sinking to one knee, probably from sheer fatigue (though perhaps boredom — it looked that way), in the middle of round four. The crowd — fat, hostile, five-o'clock-shadowed New York men — booed, sailed flattened popcorn boxes like Olympic disci, and tossed a beer bottle or two. Being mean, coarse people, but also being sophisticated observers of sanctioned fisticuffs, they'd wanted a draw, a blot on both fighters' records that would leave a sour feeling of dissatisfaction matching their own among all the boxers, managers, trainers and cut men. But the smaller guy won, had his green-white arm raised by the aging referee, and smiled a tight, winded little smile that told the crowd (and, eventually, a few thousand television viewers) that he knew the esthetic torpor of the fight would soon disappear into the record books, leaving only the crisp, polite type that would say, "St. Nick's Arena, New York: Feb. 4, 1949, Harry Benson, 183, Scranton, Penn., dec. (4), Ken Sabe, 240, New York, heavyweights."

The announcer immediately segued into a pitch for used cars. If anybody had been watching, he might have been disconcerted — or insulted — for the announcer's head frequently jerked around inexplicably and the soundtrack emitted soft, faint popping sounds at the same time. Several slivers of time were obviously missing. They'd been literally cut from the filmstrip by an old German woman (at least she spoke German, and looked old) with eerily white-blonde hair and an abnormally high forehead, with spectacles thicker than shoe heels, in a shabby Queens postproduction facility owned by "Benny The Jaw" Spumante, who also owned the used car lot for which the announcer, in the original versions of the television commercials broadcast in New York, shilled.

The purpose of the editing was to generalize the announcer's pitch, to remove all automotive particulars, so that the commercials could remain attached to the filmed fight footage and be reused in Chicago, Detroit, New Orleans and Los Angeles — cities in which Spumante had friends who also owned used car lots. When the herky-jerky filmed commercial ended, the projector at the local television station was turned off, and another camera, live, in-studio, dollied in on some hand-painted (but professionally so) posterboard cards being placed, one after the other, in cadence with a verbal spiel, by a fat hand onto a flimsy display easel. The cards contained prices and other specifications, such as "Sensational Post-War Plymouth! Four doors! Like-new seat covers! Heater! Radio!"

The voice, reading aloud the same copy that appeared on the cards, emanating from the body attached to the fat hand, was Noam Sain's. Noam did not appear on-camera during the commercial. Noam saved his physical presence for his own religious program, which followed immediately.

Somebody on the darkened periphery of the linoleum-floored television studio yelled, "O.K., we're done here! Wrap and kill." The big camera, which resembled a large-scale model of a Santa Fe Railroad diesel locomotive, was pulled backward, with the camera man still in the pilot seat. Another, nondescript, man took the cards off the easel, ordered their edges like an oversized playing deck, and tucked them under his arm. With his free hand, he grabbed the easel throat-high and scuttled toward the shadows. Noam pulled out a handkerchief from his back pants pocket and patted his forehead.

The two humorless jamocas who owned the television station still wore their hats indoors. Only now, a few years ahead of their time, the hats sported narrow brims. The one who chewed a match back in the Pasadena radio days still chewed one, but with the other side of his mouth.

Both men came into the studios for every program broadcast on KCCT-TV — a feat of dedication, but hardly heroism, since the station was on the air only from noon until ten o'clock at night. They both watched while Noam changed into a dark, telegenic double-breasted suit jacket.

"You're amazin'," said the one with the match in his mouth.

"I appreciate you giving me this break. I really do," Noam said with an insincere smile.

"We don't do favors. Your check cleared. You've got four more weeks."

"I'll be good for much more than that. I'm on television to stay."

"Like we've told you — and like we tried to tell you

back in Pasadena — just no filthy stuff. No bad talk," said the match-chewer.

His partner interjected, "Personally, I'd like it if you weren't quite so...quite so strange on the air. We sort of expected a Christian program. So do the people who watch, we think."

"It is a Christian program. I've just taken the basic message of Jesus's holy love a little further into its spiritual essence than your normal, timid preacher takes it," said Noam.

"You sure you're not a Jew?" said the man with his teeth clenched on a wooden match. "I kind of had a hunch back then on the radio that you were."

"Would it matter? As long as I'd come to the Lord?" asked Noam, knotting his colorful (an effect that would be lost in his black-white-broadcast) tie with a flourish.

"No," said the man with the match. "No, ordinarily it wouldn't. Me and Castelli here, we deal with a lot of Jews, everyday. L.A. is full of Jews, especially in show business. And television is part of show business even more than radio was. I can tell you, most Jews I know are very civilized, very polite, very nice on a social level. But they're tough businessmen, too. They know the value of a dollar, and I like that. They do business in a hurry, no wasting time, and I like that, too. I like doing business with Jews.

"But having a Jew doing his own religious show on our television station is another matter. People who want to watch religion on television want to watch Christian ministers tell them the stuff they're already familiar with, stuff that's comforting. They don't want to hear Jew religious stuff. Anyway, the Jew religion doesn't want converts, does it? You aren't trying to get people to be Jews, are you?"

Noam tugged at his knot. "No, I'm not. Of course I'm not because I'm not a Jew."

"Your Christianity still seems a little funny," said the match-chewer's partner. "It's not what I heard in church."

"What you heard in church, Castelli," said the man

with the match, "was all about going straight to hell just because you jacked off even once in your life. And you heard it from a guy in a confession booth who never got laid in his life and was probably a pansy himself."

"Please, do not use that kind of language," said Noam, huffily and gently at the same time. "Whatever else you think of me, I am a man of God. And I respect other men's sincere beliefs, even if they are in conflict with mine."

"So do I, even though I'm just a poor parishioner of Peter's Church," said Castelli. "I don't like that kind of language, either."

"You threw me off the air when I used a few words about an evil woman that weren't half as bad as the things you just said about men of the cloth in the Catholic faith," said Noam, patting his forehead with the handkerchief again. He folded the hanky into a decoration with three points and stuffed it expertly into his jacket pocket. Then he reached into his trousers and pulled out a little gold pin in the shape of a cross. Noam attached it firmly to his lapel.

"Let me worry about radio and Castelli's priests. You worry about the television camera. And about being good for all the checks you ever write to me." Castelli's partner walked by Noam and gave the little lapel pin a slap with his fingernail. The pin actually made a small ping.

Noam frowned.

Matt Medium walked into the recreation room of his mansion carrying a bathroom tumbler filled with hand-squeezed orange juice. He flopped into an overstuffed leather chair facing the television set. "Hey, it's the fat little preacher again!" he shouted to people still outside the room. "Come in and see! I love him."

Several men and a woman, who was in the latter stages of pregnancy, came into the room. A few took seats.

"Gracious, Matt, your tastes have plummeted," said a physicist from the nearby Institute of Technology. He knew little of tastes, since he spent most of his time in a laboratory investigating the possibility that time could be measured along more than one direction, a few hours a week teaching advanced classes for young men brilliant enough to succeed him in the laboratory one day, and the remainder of his hours in a bachelor apartment at the corner of Colorado Boulevard and Marengo Street, listening to whatever came over the single station that his mahogany console radio picked up, and eating canned food which he cooked by placing the open can in a sauce pot filled with water in a rough approximation of a double-boiler. But he liked to talk as though he were an esthete, and Matt indulged him.

"Some of these guys are interesting. Some of them have a few ideas," said a portly science-fiction writer who limped from a wound received in the Navy during the war. "A few of them have interesting ideas. They're primitive ideas, but they're ideas I can use and turn into something visionary in my novels." He smiled with self-satisfaction over his extemporaneous nugget of self-promotion.

The pregnant woman sobbed quietly. Her hands, at her sides, clutched the plain white smock with the hand-painted symbols that the gathering required her to wear. Somebody in the room reminded her that she was just paid ornamentation, that every rite like this had to have one like her, and to shut up or else she wouldn't get paid.

"Isn't this everything we're against?" asked another man who had just stepped into the room.

Matt Medium took a long, theatrical swallow of the last of his orange juice and replied, "What we are against, friend, is certainty, close-mindedness, the prevention of free inquiry into things spiritual as well as things scientific."

The man replied coolly, "No, you have it wrong. We

are not against certainty. We have certainty. But we know that it is a dark certainty that is not to the liking of...[the man made a sweeping lateral arc with his left arm, indicating everyone in the entire world outside Medium's mansion] any of them. But we know it and believe it. And you, Matt, are treading a little dangerously with this openness business."

Matt Medium — a tall, handsome man whose physique fell between that of a large, athletic man like Ken Sabe, and that of a wraith, a ghost; it fell, however, much closer to Ken Sabe — leaned back and spoke, as if to the ceiling.

"You, you Earl, feel that way. and you're free to speak your true mind here like you're not free to speak on the floor of the House, or even, mostly, likely, to your own wife. But I am not yet a card-carrying devil-worshipper. I am only a dabbler in the possibility that you people may have a glimmer of something unavailable to the pious bourgeoisie. I host these gatherings only to draw you out, to let you mingle with my many diverse and charming friends, to see what you have to offer. I know what I have to offer."

Matt Medium nodded at the crying pregnant woman.

"Dangerous talk. Satan listens."

"When and if the time comes that I give myself to Satan, I will have looked the matter over quite calmly and collectedly. Old Beelzebub will most likely appreciate that in a new disciple. He wouldn't want someone believing in him from the first instant, and throwing himself into his arms, like a weeping Christian." Matt Medium shot a glance at the weeping woman, although, face buried in her hands, she didn't see it.

"Don't be too clever." The man walked over, bent down to the floor beneath the woman and wiped up a drop of blood with his finger. He brought his finger to his mouth and tasted it.

"And I thought I was strange," said the science-fiction writer. He strode to a knotty-pine hutch against a wall and opened a lower door. "Is whiskey all that's in here, or do we have any more of my favorite yum-yum?"

"Behind the scotch, in that lacquered box," said Matt Medium. "Bring it out. Let's everybody join in. Even you." (Another glance to the woman, who was now staring at Matt Medium.)

"Candles?"

"Candles."

"Television off?"

"Television on for the moment. Let's watch this delicious little man. Perhaps he can add to our enjoyment, and our uncertainty."

"Oh, please," said Earl, spinning on the ball of one foot and addressing the gathering as much as Matt. "We know that you know who he is. Let's do away with the coyness."

Noam's fat fingers gripped the edge of the lectern. As he looked into the red light above the television camera, the edges of a smile forced his jowls to the side, back toward his ears, which wiggled infinitesimally.

"Tonight's lesson is humility," he said, almost credibly.

"Over the last three years, I have written twenty books on matters concerning Our Lord Jesus Christ. [Technically, this was true — if any printed matter of more than one page held together with staples counted as a book.] Yet I am a humble man. Over the last three years, I have given more than one thousand one hundred sermons, all across this great land of ours, on matters concerning Our Lord Jesus Christ. [Technically, this was also true, if any monologue with more than two persons on the receiving end counted as a sermon.] Yet I am humble. And recently, having returned from voyages to many lands, I have been enlightened as to the true place of Our Lord Jesus Christ among the Elevated Masters of the Ages. And I am still a humble man.

"But, praise Jesus, I am humble in an entirely new way.

"I know that I am but a mite, a pebble, a grain of sand along the human shores of the enormous sea of time that stretches from the beginning of God's eternity. I know that there have been billions and billions of men and women on this earth before, and I know that there will be billions and billions of men and women after me. I know that I am a small part of God's glorious creation. I know that I am but a speck. I know that I am but a flashbulb's flash against the constant glow of eternity. Yes, I am humble, and I have reasons to be.

"But I also have reasons to rejoice in my smallness, my humility. One reason, you, Dear Ones out there in televisionland, know about already, if you having been watching me on this television program during the last few weeks. You know that I am made sinless and whole and eternal in the holy love of Our Lord Jesus Christ. And you know that you are, too, if you have shared in admitting Jesus Christ into your life as your own personal savior. What could be better than that?

"You are right in asking, 'What could Minister Noam Sain have up his sleeve that is better than being made whole, sinless and eternal by the love of Our Lord Jesus Christ?'"

"You could even be right in asking, 'Has he gone mad?' or 'Has he committed blasphemy?' or 'Is he still a Christian?' or 'Can I depend any longer upon him and his television programs for my spiritual advice?'

"Yes! Yes, I say, you can! And you can because I have discovered even more, even better, even more glorious reasons for basking in the love of Our Lord Jesus Christ!

"You see, even Jesus is not alone. Jesus was not born as a lone savior. Jesus did not die as a lone savior. Jesus was not forsaken by God the Father as a lone savior. Jesus was part of a continuum. Jesus is part of a continuum.

"*Continuum.* Now that is a strange, scientific-sounding word. Some of you may even be frightened by it. Some of you may have heard the phrase 'space-time continuum,' and you may think that it is the exclusive property of scientists in laboratories who invent terrible weapons of destruction like the atomic bomb, and who have brought the world to the brink of destruction by giving nations the means with which to wage terrible, terrible war upon one another. But the space-time continuum is not the exclusive property of scientists in laboratories. It is the property of God!

"God gave us the space-time continuum. God wanted us to have it. God wanted his son Jesus to be part of it. God wanted — now listen carefully — all of his sons to be part of it. God wants you to be part of it.

"Stop and think for a moment. Ask yourselves: would God have let thousands and thousands of years go by while his children upon the earth sinned and suffered and died in states of unholiness without having given them the chance to redeem themselves? Would God have waited until millions and millions of souls were condemned to fiery torment before he sent someone to rescue their descendents? Of course not. God would have loved every one of his children all along. He would not have let any one of their souls descend into the pits of Satan without benefit of a savior.

"But, you ask, then what did Jesus do? What change did Jesus effect? How was the world different after Jesus came into it? You have a right to ask those questions. If the world was no different after Jesus came into it, then either Jesus was a false savior and no one who worshipped him after he came into the world was ever saved from sin or saved from Hell, or God saved everyone before Jesus came into the world and there was really no point in him arriving.

"But Jesus has always been in this world. Jesus has always been among us. Listen carefully to this, because it will shock and surprise you and I will explain it all in a few moments: Jesus was here even before he came. I will say that again: Jesus was here even before he came.

"How can that be? you ask. Let me tell you a story."

Noam stepped out from behind the lectern, a voluminous, darkly stained wood box that, up to now, had hidden all of his squat figure below the first button of his double-breasted jacket. Noam's pants did not match his jacket, even on Matt Medium's grainy-screened television set. Noam looked cheap. Noam didn't care. Neither did Matt Medium, who leaned forward in his chair, setting the empty orange juice glass to the side. Some of the other people in Matt Medium's recreation room leaned forward, too. Even the bleeding pregnant woman.

"I was a failure," Noam said. "I was such a failure that I even failed God. Or I thought I did. God wouldn't let me fail him, of course, but he let me feel as though I had failed him.

"In the days shortly before the war, I was a preacher, a minister, a clergyman, a man of the cloth, right here in Southern California. In fact, I was on the radio. Some of you may have even heard me back then."

Castelli's partner, sitting in a canvas director's chair behind the cameras, pulled the match from his mouth, held it between his thumb and forefinger, and wiped his forehead with the remaining three fingers on the same hand. Part of his letting Noam Sain back on the air — above and beyond Noam's voice (suitable for automobile commercials and his willingness to do them), Noam's check that seemed as good as gold, and Noam's promise that he would never again venture into his personal life, or mention sex, while in front of, or (in this case) below a live microphone — had to do with an assumption — Castelli thought it a hope — that no one in the audience would recognize Noam after eleven years, especially when the fleshy little man stepped in front of the camera and diverted everyone's sensory perceptions from originating in the ear to originating in the eye. Noam looked like he was going to hook up the — how did he put it? — space-time continuum between the radio days in Pasadena and now. Jesus. Not Noam's "Jesus," but *Jesus*.

"A terrible tragedy befell me, and I was compelled to leave California and go north, into the beautiful state of Oregon, to preach the word of Our Lord Jesus Christ. I had a church. I had a congregation. I had a wife. And I had four lovely, lovely children.

"But the war was still on. Even in its last days, the forces of Satan — for that is what the armies and navies and air forces of Germany, Japan and Italy were, make no mistake, the forces of Satan — hoped to strike into the American heartland. They hoped to land one last, crippling blow. And they almost did, Dear Ones out there in televisionland. I know, because I was one of the victims of that blow.

"My family — my wife and our four lovely little children — were on a quiet hillside in the last days of the war. We were sharing our evening meal out of doors in the beautiful, still-daylight evening. We were, in fact, talking of Our Lord Jesus Christ and how God's blessings had pulled us through this terrible war, and now victory was at hand.

"Then a bomb came. A bomb! A terrible, evil, deadly bomb that shouldn't have even come within a thousand miles of the shores of these United States. It flew into the sky above our hillside. And the bomb exploded.

"What happened to my lovely family is too horrible for me to tell to you on this television program. Rest assured, however, that their souls now dwell peacefully in the bosom of Our Lord Jesus Christ. But what happened to me is so glorious and miraculous that I must tell it to you, dear viewers. And I tell it to you, as you will see, as a very, very humble man.

"There is a space-time continuum. A very brilliant man named Albert Einstein — yes, Albert Einstein the *Jew*..."

Jesus, we're gonna have to pull the plug on him again, thought the man with the match between his thumb and forefinger.

"...discovered it in the early days of this century. That is, he discovered it scientifically. He discovered that its existence could be proved mathematically. But Jesus Christ, the son of God, knew all along that it existed. And other prophets of God, the Elevated Masters of the Ages, knew all along that it existed. And you, Dear Television Viewer, you know, down somewhere inside your heart of hearts, that it exists. You may not call it by the high-sounding name of space-time continuum, but you know that it exists. You call it, perhaps, eternity. You call it, perhaps, the love of God. You call it, perhaps, the ethereal realm. You call it, perhaps, your immortal soul. But you know that it exists.

"Now, I, too, know that it exists. But I know it in a different way than Mr. Einstein. And this is how I know it: I have been pulled through the entire space-time continuum in an instant. I have been sucked into a hole that existed for an instant in the fabric of time and space, and I have been redeposited in the present, in another instant. This was done to me, strangely enough, by Satan. He did it to me by exploding the deadly bomb in Oregon that took my wife and four lovely children away from me. Satan may have thought he was taking me, too. But, at the moment the deadly bomb exploded, I was thinking holy thoughts about the love of Our Lord Jesus Christ. My mind, my soul, were in tune with Jesus Christ. So, instead of being blasted to smithereens, instead of being incinerated in a flash, instead of being sent to purgatory, I was sucked into a crack in the space-time continuum, pulled into a place where space does not exist, and forced to live nearly an eternity in the span of an instant.

"Fantastic? You can't believe it? Neither, dear television viewer, could I. But here is the *proof.*"

Noam reached into his breast pocket and pulled out a folded newspaper clipping. He unfolded it with fat little fingers and strode toward the camera in the studio. He unfurled the clipping like a scroll and held it up before the lens. The cameraman struggled to adjust the focus. For a few seconds, television screens all across the Southland displayed nothing but blurred, illegible type. Then the screw of the lens bore in, and the screens changed to show:

MINISTER AND FAMILY KILLED BY JAP AERIAL BOMB.

Noam returned to the lectern and gripped the edges again.

"Yes, dear television viewer, that was me. I was the minister who was 'killed.'

"But I was not killed. The explosion sucked me into a gap in the space-time continuum. I was sucked in and my soul was transported through eternity, all of eternity, in an instant. It was a miraculous journey of the soul.

"In that journey, which lasted less than a second but more than an eternity, my immortal soul consorted with all of the Elevated Masters of the Ages. My spiritual eyes saw the faces of Moses, Buddha, the Archangel Michael, Merwin, Saint Germain, Shakespeare, and the greatest, most elevated of them all, Jesus Christ Himself. I saw others, other Elevated masters of the Ages whom you do not know but with whom you will become familiar if you continue to watch my television program over the following months, Dear Television Viewer. Their names are El Malya, Master Shine-o-Light and Oromantis.

"I saw them all as my immortal soul was sucked through the vortex of the space-time continuum. I saw them all, and they saw me.

"They saw that I could be used by them to bring to the world their wonderful message, the message that Jesus was not alone in his divinity, the message that Jesus had glorious company in being the son of God, the message that others walking this earth would somebody join them as Elevated Masters of the Ages, the message that Albert Einstein had not died a mere Jew but had, for his discovery in mathematical terms, of the space-time continuum, been anointed one of the Elevated masters of the Ages, the message that there have been other holy human beings, such as the glorious Annie Besant, who are also Elevated Masters of the Ages, and the message that you, too, Dear Television Viewer, can bathe in their glorious powers and gain an eternal life for the soul.

"Jesus Christ and the Elevated masters of the Ages, gave me the will and the desire, and the burst of cosmic energy that enabled me to write those twenty books, to give those one thousand and one hundred sermons all in the space-time of a mere three years. And, above all, they gave me the insight to see that the wonderful new medium of television, in which the words and pictures portraying the message of the Elevated Masters of the Ages can be transported almost instantly, everywhere, is where Minister Noam Sain should be spreading their gospel."

Noam stepped out once more from behind the lectern, and spread his feet (in two-tone shoes) a yard apart. His arms dropped to his sides. When he spoke, his voice was strangely lower, more hollow, far-away.

"The mark of Satan we all know. It is six-six-six. The mark of Our Lord Jesus Christ we all know as well. It is the Stigmata. It is the piercing of the flesh in the palms of his hands, the soles of his feet, the wound of the spear of the Centurion in his breast, and the thousand cuts of the crown of thorns upon his brow.

"I am not Jesus. I would never say that. I would never be a false prophet unto you, dear television viewer. I am not Jesus.

"But Jesus has shared Himself with me. He has shared his mark. As my soul was drawn through the space-time continuum, the Elevated Masters of the Ages saw to it that part of the mark of Jesus, the part that designated the holy mind, the cuts upon his brow gouging almost through to the skull and brain, the invasion of the physical world and the spilling of blood at the edges of the mathematical mind that was to be reborn as the mind of Albert Einstein which solved the scientific mystery of the space-time continuum, was inflicted upon my physical body as a sign for all to see that Minister Noam Sain is a true messenger for the Elevated Masters of the Ages.

"Dear Television Viewer, see!"

With that exclamation, Noam struggled out of his suit jacket and cast it aside. He feverishly loosened the knot of his brightly colored tie, and pulled the tie over his head, like a man reprieved from execution at the final second casting off the hangman's knot. He tore open his white shirt. Several buttons scattered over, and rattled on, the linoleum floor. He pulled his shirtsleeves inside out and yanked his fat hands through the buttoned cuffs. He dropped the shirt to the floor and stepped toward the camera, raising his arms laterally in a pose of crucifixion.

"Close-up!" Noam hissed between clenched teeth. "Close-up!"

The cameraman dollied in and rotated the lens.

Even on a picture as unfaithful to reality as the one on the set in Matt Medium's recreation room, Noam's marks could be seen: little scars, a half-inch to an inch long, thin white lines amid the swirling black hair. A hundred of them. Perhaps a thousand. Made by the anti-personnel shards of the Japanese balloon bomb that descended on the Oregon coast six years earlier.

The man with the match rolled his eyes heavenward and sunk back in his director's chair. "We're going to have to pull him again, Castelli. He's just too goddamned strange."

"No," Castelli answered. "He's good. He's entertaining. I like him."

"You're fuckin' crazy," Castelli's partner said. "You and the rest of you snappers."

"Yes, you're right," Castelli answered, ignoring the insult. "I think he is a Catholic at heart. A lot of beaners are starting to watch television, you know. They're Catholics. I think they'll like him, too."

"Do you want us dealing with beaners?" asked the match-chewer.

"Try to remember," answered Castelli, "that a viewer

is a viewer. You just give him television programs, you don't
give him the hand of your daughter in marriage."

In Pasadena, Matt Medium roared with laughter.

"This man is dangerous," said the Satanist behind him.

"Oh, no," said Matt Medium. "He's just what we need
to liven things up. I'll have him called and invited over.
Next week. On ritual night. Let's bring him right into the
fold."

"You are playing with fire," said the Satanist grimly.
"And not the cleansing kind." He turned and left the room,
spitting on the pregnant woman as he went out.

Noam drove up Orange Grove Boulevard in his 1934
Ford. He was surprised, constantly surprised, that the car
still ran. But he tried not to think about the car at all. It
coughed and snorted with a pre-War tin lizzie's helpless-
ness, the metal on its quaintly box-like hood trembling
like the fabric on a Conestoga wagon pursued by
Comanches. In the soft, balmy twilight, the newer, smoother,
more bulbous vehicles whooshed passed him like playful
dolphins. They all seemed to be filled with grinning men
and smiling women with red lacquered nails and cigarettes
in holders who were very sure of where they were going,
and eager to get there. Noam was sure of where he was
going, but he was uncertain as to his eagerness to get there.

Noam slowed in the growing darkness, looking for a
house number. But the big, heavy, deeply porched, ivy-
covered houses were set back at least a hundred feet from
the street, and the little orange pools of door-lamp light
surrounding bronze addresses were woefully — and deliberately — inadequate to let the numbers be seen from traffic on the street. Noam slowed to a crawl and pulled to the

right; he virtually crept along the curb. The rhythm of the thin, slightly curving trunks of Queen's palms soaring up toward the silhouetted bursts of fringed leaves against a maraschino sky slowed into separate events. A magnificent, shadowed house. A tree. Another tree. Another tree. Another somber mansion. Another tree.

Finally, Noam said to hell with it, and parked his car, scuffing the tires and scraping the antique spoked wheels against the squat cement wall. He got out, locked the door, and fumbled in his shirt pocket for a cigarette. Thinking better of it (or, rather, finding it difficult to negotiate a strange sidewalk in vanishing light in an imposing neighborhood), he left the pack in peace.

Matt Medium's mansion turned out to be three houses north of where he left his car. The doorbell had an ancient timbre to it, as if his push of the button caused an actual monk to pull on a rope. Noam waited for what, to him, seemed like a very long time. He brushed the soles of his shoes on the rough doormat so hard and with so many strokes that (he thought), they probably shined more glossily than the uppers. Noam was imagining — rather, mulling over philosophically — what would be reflected in a shoe sole burnished to a mirrored surface if it were pressed directly into the pavement [In other words: Can an image exist in no space at all? *Quack.*] when the door opened.

A drab little man with a moustache and a very shiny suit appeared in the opening. He said, without a trace of irony, "Welcome to Agape Lodge."

He knew who Noam was without asking. "You're the minister." It wasn't a question.

"I'm Noam Sain. I was called by someone representing Mr. Medium." Then he added, fecklessly, "I'm on television."

"Yes, we know that," said the man without inflection. "Come in."

Noam followed the man through a series of rooms, each a little darker than the last, and each containing a few people sitting on overstuffed leather furniture, deep in conversation. The people were all men, in suits, dressed somewhat tonier than Noam. As he passed, they looked up, unsurprised, and a few gave him what he thought was a polite smile. But in the cognac-colored murk — slightly opaque, even smoky — he couldn't quite tell. Noam arrived behind his guide in a knotty pine recreation room. At their entrance, a tall man, handsome through the haze, rose from a chair and walked over to greet them. He carried a tumbler of orange juice.

"Ah. You are the minister. I'm the master of this house. Matt Medium."

"Minister Noam Sain."

"Yes," the host said, puzzlingly.

"You've seen me on television?"

"Oh, yes. I'm very interested in what you have to say. That's why we asked you here. This may look like a social gathering, but actually it's more religious. And scientific. Sit down."

Noam found himself seated with a large glass of orange juice. He would have preferred a bourbon — and there were indeed people drinking alcohol, as well as (Noam could see out of the corner of his eye) others sniffing some sort of powder — but Matt Medium had handed him the glass of juice without offering a choice. Noam figured that he was being kept sober to be interrogated. The questioning was, however, comparatively gentle, and expert. Noam was easily drawn out. He was, after all, a preacher, given to expounding. Soon — with a semicircle of onlookers gathered behind him — Noam found that Matt Medium's questions had grown as lengthy as his own answers, and that he was engaged in a dialogue that was (insofar as Noam knew about these sorts of things) almost Socratic.

"So, you wouldn't say that what God does is actually spy on human beings," said Matt Medium.

"God has perfect knowledge," said Noam. "God knows all things at all times. He doesn't have to 'spy.' Spying implies that there's something God doesn't know that he has to find out. It implies incompleteness, imperfection. But God is perfect."

"Then — excuse me for being a little dull — why does God employ these Elevated Masters of the Ages?" Matt Medium asked. "What they do, it seems to me, is to live among human beings in a somewhat overperceptive way, and then retire to report to God. What else would you call that if not God's having his field agents report back to him?"

"No," Noam protested. "The Elevated Masters of the Ages don't report on human beings. They have lived almost perfect lives among human beings, and have been rewarded by God with the gift of timelessness. And that is a literal term, sir. Time-less-ness. Without time. Without being subjected to the tyranny of time, which for most of us, certainly everyone of us here in this room tonight, means that we are swept along in one and only one direction, from birth until death."

Noam took the opportunity in his pause to shift his large buttocks in his leather chair and look back around at the odd crew of people behind him. A collection of well-dressed skulls, he thought. And one large, tough-looking man who must be somebody's body guard.

"And that's what happened to you, until that fateful day on the Oregon coast?" Matt Medium inquired.

"Yes, yes," Noam replied. "For an instant, just one instant, when my mind was perfectly in tune with God, God allowed me to turn back in time, to go the other way, to feel the indescribable joy of not being swept along in the great human tide of sin from birth to death. It happened that what caused my mind to come into harmony with God were the thoughts surrounding the appearance of that balloon bomb. For an instant, I reversed direction in time, and I simply wasn't there when it exploded."

Matt smiled to their audience. "Then why," he asked Noam, "do you have all those little white scars you unveiled on television."

"Because," said Noam, "for the tiniest fraction of an instant, I was still there. Then I was gone. The fragments penetrated my skin, but then I was gone, before they could cut through my body, before they could destroy my internal organs and kill me."

"Why are there no scars, say, on the backs of your hands? Why did God — or the Japanese — spare your beautiful face?" Matt Medium pursued.

"If I have been brought here to be ridiculed, I will leave," said Noam bravely, setting his orange juice glass firmly down on the table. He had the sense, however, that he would leave only when he was allowed to leave. Oddly, he didn't mind the idea as much as he thought he should. He wasn't as afraid as he thought he should be.

"Please, I don't mean to ridicule," Matt said. "It's just that, if I am to write out a check to your cause, to become, in effect, one of your supporters, I want to know as much as I can. Many of us here in my little group are scientists. We work in laboratories at the Institute of Technology here in Pasadena. We deal in physical facts, physical certainty if we can get it. I am only trying to learn more."

Noam took a deep breath, clasped his hands together, and said, "I am speaking of God. I am speaking of belief. I am speaking of faith. Your 'physical certainty' can go only so far in approaching God. God allows scientists like you to measure some dimensions of the universe. He makes you a present of length and width and depth and weight and heat. But, I have discovered through my experience with the Elevated Masters of the Ages, he keeps time for himself. Time is the holy dimension. That is one of the secrets of the Elevated Masters of the Ages, and I give it to you right here tonight. Time is God's holy dimension. He allows most humans to experience it — unlike all the other dimensions of the universe — in only one way, inexorably forward. You scientists can never learn much more about time than you already know simply by living your secular lives without faith. And that is a pity."

"Perhaps Satan allows us to live it backwards," said the Satanist, who had just stepped forward and placed his bony, hairless white hands on the back of Matt Medium's chair, and laid a thin finger on Matt's shoulder. "We're stuck here in eternal life — God's wonderful, sunny, interminably boring heaven — and it's Satan who allows us a way back into the delights and dangers of the flesh."

"Blasphemy!" sputtered Noam.

"Oh, Earl doesn't mean it literally. He's teasing, just to get your goat," said Matt Medium.

"I mean every word as literally as if it were a brick," said Earl the Satanist.

"Blasphemy! Hideous blasphemy!" Noam repeated loudly.

"You, Minister Noam Sain, are the one who is teasing, although you may not be entirely aware of it. You, who appear on television. You, who drive that pathetic little car of yours to supermarkets on the weekend, and stand in the parking lot, offering to anoint the hoods of cars with holy motor oil for a donation to your ministry. You..."

"Earl. Enough. Minister Sain is a guest," said Matt Medium.

"Minister Sain is — or could be — a bit of a thorn in our side," said Earl.

"How in hell — excuse me — how in God's name do you know about the anointing?" asked Noam, twisting like a wrung towel in his chair.

"Need I explain?" said Earl. "Look, let's stick to the important matters. Did that episode with the bomb really happen to you?"

"Yes, of course."

"And I believe you," said Earl with a bloodless smile, "because I know such things are possible. So, if you have experienced something as miraculous as that, how can you be surprised that I — that we — know something as simple about you as your little supermarket excursions?"

Noam said nothing.

"And we know much more. Shall we tell him, Matt?"

"I get the feeling that your ship has already set its course and has left the harbor, Earl," said Matt Medium.

"Well, we do know much more," said Earl. "And, I must say in all immodesty, that I conducted the research. And I did it quickly, not starting until Matt had the rather inadvisable idea to invite you here to our little group. He has the quaint idea, being one of those scientists you talk about, that we're here for free inquiry, or something democratic like that."

"What do you know? It doesn't matter. I've got nothing to hide," said Noam, unconvincingly.

"Oh," said Earl, walking around in front of Noam and perching on the corner of a blonde coffee table, "where do I start?" Noam noticed that Earl had very tiny feet encased in very expensive — or at least expensive-looking shoes. There was also something familiar about Earl. Noam thought he'd seen Earl's photograph in the *Daily News*, but couldn't be sure. Noam read newspapers as spottily as he read Scripture.

"I've got nothing to hide" Noam repeated.

"You said that once already," said Earl, "and it sounded shaky to me the first time."

"All right," Earl continued, "a brief list, each item of which could be elaborated upon at length: First, the record you brought with you to California is hardly typical of a pious clergyman. There are several husbands, ex-husbands and fathers in Oklahoma and Texas who would bring alienation of affection suits against you if they could ever find you — that is, if they didn't kill you first for consorting with their wives and daughters. There might even be a paternity action or two in all of this. Second, you used to preach over the radio from right here in Pasadena, before the war. You railed on the air against a wife who'd left you. Your language got a trifle salty for the powers-that-were, and you were dismissed. Third — and this is the most interesting — the wife who left you returned to her relatives in Germany and, as coincidence would have it, turned up as our own beloved Axis Sally, traitoress and propagandist supreme. Imagine that: A man of God is left by his wife, who becomes a Nazi, and then, later, miraculously escapes being killed by a Nazi balloon bomb."

"Japanese," Noam corrected.

"Well, not quite," said Earl. "There's a little more to the story. Would you care to hear it?"

Noam was silent.

"The bomb was delivered by a Japanese vehicle, true. But the aircraft was designed in Germany, as was the bomb. And the bomb was an imploding device, instead of an exploding one. The physics of the bomb were so subtle and complex that even our Matt Medium here — who spent his entire wartime career with the O.S.S. trying to steal what the Nazis had discovered in this area, and who now spends his entire time at the Institute of Technology trying to reconstruct it — couldn't begin to explain it to you. Suffice it to say that it had something to do with a momentary suspension of time, perhaps even a reversal of it for a millisecond or two. In that instant — in the resulting implosion — the bomb's target wouldn't be blasted outward to smithereens, but would be sucked into a sort of nothingness, and destroyed."

"So?" Noam asked weakly.

"So, you may have been positioned somehow on the edge of the bomb's implosion. You may have been dragged into a protected marginal area in what you yourself call the space-time continuum. That's how you might have survived. Not God, understand, but physics."

"Then why were my wife and family killed?" Noam fairly shouted. "Then why was I wounded a thousand times with shrapnel flying outward from where the bomb went off in the sky?"

Earl smiled. "We don't know that one, I'll admit. Perhaps the bomb didn't work the way it was designed. Perhaps one little atom in the device went in the wrong direction, and the thing just exploded, like an ordinary weapon."

Earl walked around to Noam and put his grinning face not two inches from Noam's nose. "Or perhaps," Earl said with malicious softness, "it was Satan who saved you."

Noam stood up. "Blasphemer!"

Matt Medium stood up, too, but smiling. He walked around to Earl and patted him on the back. "Easy," he said. "Go easy. We're all friends."

Noam continued to shout. "I am a man of God and I will have no truck with a blasphemer!"

"Minister Sain," said Matt Medium, "please understand that Earl is a bit of a tease. I'll admit it's a bad trait when it gets out of hand. But it helps us in the group — and we've all been his victims at one time or another — to maintain our spirit of free inquiry."

"Perhaps," Earl interjected, resentful at having been scolded, "Mr. Medium will care to tell you how well he knew your former wife."

"You knew Imeda?" asked an astonished Noam.

"I knew Axis Sally," Matt Medium answered, "which may or may not have been the equivalent. I was under-cover as a communications aide in the service of Reichsminister Hendrijk Oeups. When I was alone with her, I deliberately allowed my cover to become a bit trans-parent. She concluded, as I intended, that I was a young American military physicist who could speak German well enough to spy for his country. She came to think — again, as I intended — that her, shall we say, charms, could turn me into a double agent who was willing to convey misin-formation to the Allies. The truth was, well, more compli-cated than that. Suffice it to say that I was an Ally who never managed to get quite what I was looking for."

"Tell him what you were looking for," said Earl.

"I was looking," Matt Medium continued, "for a dis-covery in physics that I thought the Germans may have made concerning the possibility of a small, momentary variance in the single-directionness of time. We — that is, the O.S.S. — thought that the Germans may have been able to build a bomb that reversed the direction of time and imploded, rather than exploded, on its target. We even thought that they had been able to jump forward in time over small distances. In the laboratory, of course, with tiny objects. But if they had been able to transfer that ability to larger objects, they might have been able to make an engine that could jump its vehicle forward. If such an engine could do this regularly over a long voyage, it would mean they could cover much greater distances in ships and planes, without having to land to refuel, than we had previously given them credit for. If they could do both..."

"They could have sent an airplane all the way from Japan to Oregon to drop a bomb, attached to a balloon, which would implode rather than explode," said Noam.

"Very strategically astute, for a man of God," said Earl.

"So why do you care about this stuff now?" asked Noam, somewhat deflated by the ugly, scientific explanation of the miracle that had saved him in Oregon. His hundreds of small scars, however, tingled as with rebuttal. They told him God was not dead in him just yet. Noam puffed his chest and said, "You're not in the O.S.S. anymore. You're a private citizen."

Then, suddenly, looking around at the group which had closed in behind him — silent, weirdly well-dressed, all moustachioed and all holding drink — Noam knew.

"Am I free to go, or am I prisoner here?" he asked, his voice breaking at the end.

"Certainly, you're free to go. This is entirely a voluntary group, dedicated to nothing but free inquiry into all things, spiritual as well as physical. That's why we invited you," Matt Medium said.

"What do you expect to get from me?" asked Noam.

"Oh," said Matt Medium, "perhaps some small insights. After all, you may have indeed escaped the bomb through the grace of your God. Or you may have been able to disappear for an instant when the bomb exploded. We don't know. All we want you to do is to join us for our little get-togethers once in a while, until you get the hang of things. Then, perhaps, you'll recall a few particulars of your experience in Oregon that you'd care to share with us."

Noam lowered his head and tried to think. "I don't know. My television ministry is just getting started. I must devote all my energy to my television program."

Matt Medium put his hands in his blazer pocket. "We can make it a little easier for you. I'll write a check to Mr. Castelli and his friend so you won't have to worry about keeping your, um, ministry on television."

"You know about Castelli?" Noam whined. Matt Medium only smiled.

Crouching outside the window, trying to ignore the bougainvillea thorns cutting through the shirt that was forced to stretch so tightly over his big, tall body that it was no more than an additional, and thin, epidermal layer, Ken Sabe said something to himself.

"Shit, even I know about Castelli. And I'm just a rookie goon with the agency." The big question — which he did not then address in his somewhat laconic interior mono-logue — was whether those fancy guys inside were bullshitting fat little Noam and they already knew about jumping around in time, or whether they thought they could really get something crucial out of him. In either case, he'd go ahead and blow up the house, just to be on the safe side.

Flying Down to Peedro

High above Los Angeles [And Billy means high. *Quack.*], a shard of mottled glass from a bathroom window in Matt Medium's mansion soared and whirled like a dizzy, sparkling boomerang. About a foot and a half long and no thicker than regulation windowpane — perhaps the largest piece of anything, organic or inorganic, remaining from Matt Medium's mansion on Orange Grove Boulevard — it spun and glittered in the starlight. The rest of Matt Medium's mansion, dispersed throughout Pasadena, was nothing but dust and vapor.

As the shard flew south toward San Pedro (catching a nighttime thermal, swimming in the high wind, and, having been cut by the blast into a mimicry of the profile of a Zanonia seed, defying the gravitational urge to descend), Matt Medium's neighbors back on Orange Grove streamed into the street. They hurried to where Matt Medium's mansion used to be, to where there was now only a giant, oddly and perfectly circular pit gouged into the luxurious one-acre lot, and a fine grey powder clinging to the thin, graceful trunks of the Queen's palms surrounding the property.

The tops of the palms still had leaves. The neighbors' houses still had windows. Earl's Packard, parked on the street exactly coincidental (on a north–south axis) with where Matt Medium's golden house number had only a few moments before been posted, was undamaged. It had been a very powerful, but very precise, explosion. Or — could it have been? — implosion.

The shard of bathroom glass continued to sail and spin,

heading south, high over the Arroyo Seco, high over the Italianate hills just north of downtown Los Angeles, high over L.A.'s mastaba-topped city hall (squat by later standards, but, at fourteen stories, then the tallest building permitted by the earthquake regulations in Los Angeles), high over Figueroa Boulevard (running all the way down from South Pasadena to the harbor, reportedly the longest city street in the entire country), high over (veering west) Western Avenue, high over Ascot Raceway where the midget auto racers were running noisily on dirt that night, high over a loose, underbuilt grid of thinly paved residential streets, still peppered with vacant lots and the skeletons of half-built homes, high over the sparse twinkling of living room lights, toward the ocean.

Then it began to lose altitude, twirling more slowly, pitching and yawing in the lower breezes. At this angle of descent, it wouldn't reach the salt water or the resting, tethered ships. It would land on one of those nondescript streets where the impact would render it a silicon powder as fine as Earl's ashes. Or, if it were just a little luckier, it would spin to a softer landing in someone's back yard in the northern edge of San Pedro, where a newly mown lawn would cushion its impact and preserve the image — somehow engraved onto the glass — for posterity. Fortune smiled.

The image in the glass — the family of Reynaldo Memoranda would claim (and the Reverend Noam Sain would opportunistically concur) — was of the Virgin Mary, the Christ Child, and a few other people whose identity nobody (especially the folks whose cars would cram the street to impasse when they came to see the piece of glass set up in a shrine on the front lawn and have, as a bonus, the hoods of their cars anointed with magic motor oil and blessed by Minister Sain, the television preacher) seemed to care much about.

By the time it glided into the Memoranda family's back yard, the piece of glass from a bathroom window in what had been Matt Medium's mansion on Orange Grove

Boulevard was spinning as slowly as a falling leaf. The yard was carpeted with an overgrown lawn. The grass was a couple of inches high, and soft, and the piece of bathroom window glass landed as quietly as if it had been placed there, as a gift, by an invisible hand.

★ ★ ★ ★ ★

Señor Reynaldo Memoranda, a widower, didn't discover the piece of glass until late in the morning after the explosion at Matt Medium's mansion. A maintenance mechanic at the Pacific Electric Railway with a midweek day off, Memoranda strode barefoot in the sun across the back yard of his modest stucco house on Roubidoux Street to retrieve a rusting lawnmower from the far corner of the property. The mower, once painted red but with little trace of the original color having survived a decade in the heavy, damp salt air that daily wafted in from the harbor, sat squeezed between two more newly red gasoline cans, its long wooden handle's shaft leaning against a redwood fence.

Señor Memoranda didn't see the glass underfoot as he reached for the lawnmower and placed all this body weight on his right foot in order to make the reach. He might have seen it if it had landed flat, and its surface had shown in the sun. But the shard had landed at a diagonal; its bottom edge was wedged solidly into the dirt beneath the grass, the top edge held semi-upright by the thick, dark green, uncut lawn. His wound, consequently, was deep.

Señor Memoranda's open sole bled profusely on his hand (when he lifted his leg to ascertain the source of his pain), on his tiny cement back porch (when he hopped from the yard to the back door), and on the freckled yellow kitchen linoleum (when he made his way inside and yelled to his daughter, Conchita, to come patch him up).

"No lo puedo hacer como un doctor," she said, examining the wound. *"Es necessario que tu tienes un doctor."*

"I can't afford a doctor," he answered, wincing (and continuing the conversation in Spanish). "Just get me some ice from the ice box to keep it from bleeding so damned much! And then get some hydrogen peroxide and some white adhesive tape from the bathroom and that cotton from your mother's old sewing kit and bandage me up. If I walk on my heel for a few days, I'll be all right."

Conchita did as she was told by her father, as she did most of the time. But, at twenty-two, with a year of junior college under her belt, and (even her father had to admit about a female child) smarter than any man in the extended family, she complied more out of affection and respect than out of fear.

After applying the bandage to her father's foot, she went into the back yard to find the glass, to put it safely in the incinerator. She knew the glass wouldn't burn when she next lighted the incinerator, but she felt, in the moment, that she ought to at least try to send it straight to Hell. The shard wasn't hard to find since Senor Memoranda had shifted its position with his foot — shiny, mostly clear, somewhat bloody and, now, lying flat upon the green grass.

Oddly, the glass hadn't broken in landing. How had her father missed seeing it when he went for the lawnmower? For reasons she could not later fathom except in metaphysical awe, Conchita elected to turn on the faucet and let a trickle of warm, skanky hose water wash her father's blood away before she pitched the shard into the cold burner. But, as the diluted blood cascaded off the glass, she thought she saw something. Conchita lifted the glass to the sun, and a miracle was born. Or so she would later tell the newspaper reporters.

The miracle was that the granular surface of the piece of glass (manufactured that way to preserve privacy in the toilet, but augmented by the forces of the Orange Grove blast) yielded a kind of inkless-printing-plate image of the

Holy Infant, his mother, and some ancillary, apparently very richly robed people.

What to do?

Conchita initially thought of calling the police. But the Los Angeles Police Department (especially officers relegated to the small-time precincts of "*Pee*-dro") was hard on Mexicans, no matter what the poignant nature of their summoning it. Anyway, she sensed, this was (in spite of her father's wound) a happy miracle, and the police dealt, inappropriately, in disasters.

She thought of calling the newspapers, but which one? The *Times* was cold, august, removed, dull, scolding, unrelentingly Anglo, and editorially bent on driving her father's employer out of business so that the oil and automobile companies could benefit. The *Daily News* was progressive, sympathetic, but careless, sloppy and (Conchita thought) stupid. The *Mirror* was simple-minded version of the *Times*, published by the same hateful Chandlers. The *Examiner*, part of Citizen Heart's empire, was more reactionary than the *Times*. The *Herald-Express* was nothing more than a biliously green, truncated version of the *Examiner*.

She thought of calling a radio station, but she listened to only one program on one station ("Your Gas Company's two-hour evening concert of the world's finest music"; cue Tchaikovsky's Piano Concerto), which she could barely pick up on the brown Emerson in her room. The station's perfunctory news programs didn't report local stories like hers.

So she called a television station instead. She called KCCT-TV because it carried a strange program which, for the past several weeks, she couldn't stop watching. It featured a chubby, charismatic little preacher whose teachings (he called it "teaching"; he called his sermons "lessons;" he called her mailed-in donations and those like them "tuition") were so refreshingly different from the dull Latin masses at the harbor-front Saint Philomenas Church to which her father dutifully dragged her each Sunday.

Conchita asked the voice on the other end of the line

for Minister Noam Sain, and was told that he usually turned up at the station only shortly before his weekly program and left shortly after it. Conchita left a message. Three days later, she hadn't received a reply. And her father's foot had become infected and swollen.

She called again, on the day of his program. Noam wasn't in. She called back forty minutes before he was supposed to go on the air, and he still wasn't there. The voice on the other end of the line said that no one at the station, including Mr. Castelli and his partner, had heard from Minister Sain since the big explosion in Pasadena. She said they were all worried. Conchita called back five minutes before air time, and Noam wasn't there. His program was cancelled that evening. Filmed boxing from Saint Nick's Arena in New York was extended for half an hour. KCCT-TV simply ran the first two bouts over again. Castelli substituted for Noam's hand and voice-over for the used car lot's commercials. He did a terrible job, and his partner wished aloud that Noam would return.

Conchita telephoned every day for two weeks. She failed to reach Noam. His program was cancelled for a second time, and KCCT-TV simply ran its spliced-together ninety-minute boxing program again. The jamoca who chewed the match substituted for Castelli substituting for Noam on the commercials. He was even worse.

On the third scheduled evening Noam returned. He performed his hand-and-voice car commercials better than either of the station owners, but not nearly up to his usual standard. For his own program, he repeated his "humility" lesson, minus the climax in which he (the first time) tore open his shirt to reveal the tiny white scars on his fat, hairy chest. But Noam's lesson still thrilled Conchita — even more so, now that the miraculous glass shard had landed in her back yard.

She began telephoning while her father was sleeping through his foot's throbbing — as he usually did during Noam's program (though he liked the boxing matches preceding it) — leaving message after message with an increasingly perturbed night secretary.

Finally, she reached the night secretary just as Noam was walking slowly out of the station's rear door. The secretary shouted to Noam, who came back to the phone. Conchita took three deep breaths — one for Jesus, one for Mary, and one for the Holy Ghost — to relax herself and prayed that she would be able to speak the clearest, most unaccented English she had ever uttered. When Noam picked up the phone, she did.

★ ★ ★ ★ ★

Cars glinted in the afternoon sun. Like huge, bright metal bugs, they crawled like a composite colored caterpillar down Roubidoux Street. Streams of pedestrians in summer suits, white shirtsleeves, and wide-brimmed hats, poured down the sidewalks. Noam stood in the front yard of the Memoranda residence, bellowing a continuous sermon beside the ad hoc shrine he'd constructed for the piece of glass from Matt Medium's mansion.

No one, including Noam, knew the origin of the remnant of bathroom window glass. Noam, nevertheless, had concocted a fiction that, unbeknownst to him, approximated the truth. He would tell his viewers that night that he had miraculously survived yet another explosion, in exactly the same manner as he had escaped the Axis bomb in Oregon. Faith had delivered him yet again. Faith — and the fact that he had already left the house and was on the street side of his car, inserting his key into the driver's side door lock, when the house went up like a geyser — delivered him. The next day, and for days thereafter, he told the gawking faithful and the idly curious, who'd heard about the glass on his television program or by word of mouth leaching from it, the same story, in person, on Roubidoux Street.

Two fishbowls — one on the front porch, the other at Conchita's side, atop a step-stool — filled with money, were emptied, and were filled again. Men stared at the shard and at the window as if they had been pole-axed. Women crossed themselves and wept. Young children whined and cried. Older children listened to explanations augmenting Conchita's. On the morning of the second day's pilgrimage, the inhospitable police arrived and tried to get people to move along. The people, for the most part, rendered obedience unto what they saw as God, and ignored Caesar's centurions. Newspaper reporters showed up, smoked, spit, and traded cynicisms with one another. Speed Graphics, and the occasional Leica, popped and clicked, as if the crowd scene were bona fide evidence of divinity. Then the reporters left to file stories, padded with intimations of belief to pander to their readers. Miracles — or at least breathtaking coincidences — made better stories than the ordinary sludge-flow of everyday life.

Señor Memoranda hobbled out to empty the fishbowls into a laundry hamper and set them out again. He made no attempt at discretion. In fact, he smiled at members of the crowd (despite the lingering pain in his foot), and they smiled back, even as he dumped money from a small container into a bigger one, and disappeared into the house with it.

Noam remained outdoors, on the sidewalk, at the preaching concession which Conchita had, first by enthusiasm and then by default, granted him. Señor Memoranda never invited him inside the house, and Noam never asked. And, although Noam's daytime preaching and nighttime television program were what kept the crowds coming, he was never offered a cut of the take. He never asked for one. In fact, he hardly noticed the money.

In the evenings, people carried candles and sang hymns, some in Spanish, most in English. The flow of money slowed, and there was some drinking and a little rowdiness. A priest from Saint Philomenas spoke gently, but disapprovingly, to Conchita. He said that she shouldn't exploit a miracle of God for personal gain. She promised to donate some of the proceeds from the shard shrine to the church, as if the problem bothering the priest was the church's prospective percentage of the gate. The priest went away, smiling distantly.

Within a week, the number of onlookers dwindled to a few and only a few coins clinked to the bottom of the fishbowls. Conchita quit putting them out. One afternoon on the second week after the landing, Noam disassembled the shrine, and carefully wrapped the piece of glass in a clean rag gotten from one of the television station technicians. He deposited the swaddled shard on the Memorandas' front porch and left, presumably for the last time, with no goodbye to Conchita. She was inside, tending to her father.

Señor Memoranda's foot worsened each subsequent day. Conchita telephoned Noam at the station. Noam drove down to San Pedro to console her. They put her father — who had drunk himself into a stupor in trying to deaden the pain with cheap blended bourbon. Then they went for a drive in Noam's old car.

Noam had belatedly noticed that Conchita was young, attractive and, above all, intelligent. He did not notice how, in her as with him, ambition had superceded piety. Conchita had noticed from the outset that Noam was much older than she, very fat, and — on extended exposure — perhaps crazy. But she also noticed that Noam — more in the flesh than on television — had a gift for telling people very strange things and getting them to believe them. She believed him. Or she liked to think she did.

If, to Conchita, Noam had shortcomings, they were that he wasn't organized, he didn't think along straight lines, and he obviously didn't have a head for money. Conchita had never needed to be organized, to think along straight lines, or to have — save for wringing forty-two meals a week and monthly mortgage payments from her father's meagre wages — a head for money. But now there was a reason, or could be, and she realized that she possessed these qualities while Noam didn't.

So, in due time, she proposed. Not marriage, but a business arrangement: She would harness his passion and rhetoric to her clarity and purpose. Noam was amazed. She was so smart that she had been thinking thoughts similar to his own. Conchita's language was less highfalutin than his, but the gist was the same.

Noam agreed and shortly brought Conchita into (but not onto) his television program, which she quickly revamped. Noam no longer wore a tie. He wore one of Señor Memoranda's lacy white shirts, with no jacket. Noam had quoted the Bible seldom before; now he quoted from it not at all. Noam talked about the Elevated Masters much more than he talked about Jesus. But, as a kind of reparation to the Christianity from which he veered ever-increasingly, Noam got down on his knees at the end of each program and delivered, in a touchingly croaky voice, an old-time hymn.

This time, Castelli thought, the little preacher has gone off the deep end: hiring a hot little beaner to help him with a program which — as weird as it is — is still supposed to be about Jesus and turning it into, well, God knows what. The jamoca with the match in his mouth, however, loved it. He thought it was simply good television — better, in fact, than Roller Derby.

Señor Memoranda's foot never healed. Miracles in his general vicinity notwithstanding, eventually it had to be amputated.

Part II

TIME THE END OF TILL

The Silent Federation

On Easter morning, 1952, an outwardly quiet but inwardly distressed non-believer who was nevertheless at ease with the hypocrisy of his entering a house of worship on the day of one of the two holiest Christian festivals (because he had been recently trained to be politely inconspicuous when the situation called for it), sat in the rearmost pew of the biggest church in Calvary, Idaho. (Actually, it was merely the bigger church, since the only other house of Christian worship in Calvary was the storefront church on the edge of town where peculiar services, vaguely devoted to the Savior, were conducted by The Brothers of Jesus.)

The disingenuous worshipper was very weary. His long, muscular body had grown stiff, and it ached. Fatigue pressed him into a slump on the wooden bench. His face was unshaven and his corduroy coat very dusty, even a little greasy, from hurried, furtive travel (walking) on back roads and cramped, boring journeys (by bus) on the main ones. He carried, in his coat's felt-lined pockets, two crumpled telegrams on squeamishly yellow Western Union paper. They were addressed to him at two different bus stations between New York and Calvary, Utah.

One, from Intercontinental Boxing Management, 426 Mott Street, New York 13, New York, said, — *YOU WELSHER STOP. I WAS LIKE FATHER TO YOU. HERRICK FIGHT IN THE BAG STOP. PERSONALLY TOOK CARE OF IT STOP. CAREER BACK ON TRACK, POWERFUL PEOPLE IN YOUR CORNER STOP. MAYBE ANOTHER CRACK LA STARZA STOP.*

NOW ALL SHOT STOP. CANVASBACKS I UNDER-
STAND, BUT NO SHOW IS SOMETHING ELSE STOP.
HAVE ALL YOUR STUFF, AM KEEPING IT, AND YOU
OWE ME MORE STOP. YOU HAVE NO FRIENDS IN
NEW YORK, ADVISE STAY AWAY FOREVER STOP.
BENNY —

The other, from Castle Employment Bureau, 290 "N"
Street, Washington 2, D.C., said, — *ACKNOWLEDGE*
TEMPORARY ASSIGNMENT CALIFORNIA COM-
PLETED STOP. RECEIVED FINE REFERENCES
STOP. CAN EMPLOY FURTHER STOP. BEST LOCA-
TION RECEIVE NOTIFICATION OUR SERVICE
YOUR HOMETOWN STOP. WAIT THERE FOR MORE
STOP [No signature]. —

From his seat in the back of the sanctuary, the non-
believer was able to tilt his head back and suffuse himself
with the smells emanating from a room just off the hall of
worship: floor wax (on linoleum), vanilla sugar cookies
(being baked), and weak coffee (being percolated in a huge,
stainless steel urn). He told himself he didn't really mind
being in church; he had always thought that a society filled
with pious people is better than one without them, that
while he might not attend church regularly, or even sub-
scribe to the bare minimum number of Commandments
(more than one, fewer than ten) requisite of a decent
churchgoer, he felt better if everyone else did. He called it,
to himself, "the 'Let's you and him pray for me' system."

This — that bigger Christian church in Calvary —
represented an odd combination of Gothic and Tudor architecture, plus local builders' touches, whose ridiculous
faux-Englishness was intended, the tired interloper supposed, to exude reassurance. But for him and his memories
of churches (trying to squeeze his big tardy body past the
knees of elderly worshippers who'd arrived on time; trying
not to feel embarrassed at the possibility — check, probability — that an early morning of solitary practice on a
frosty, roadside dirt basketball court had left him, in spite

of a quick, cold shower at home, smelly; trying not to fall asleep during the sermon; trying to understand why none of his female classmates in the choir — who must have recognized him on the way in, or when he was hanging around outside, shoulders hunched and hands jammed into his coat pockets — would so much as give him the time of day), the building emitted only a kind of dry foreboding, even on such a lovely spring Sunday as this one.

Funny, he thought, how he could go from high school hero to inept heavyweight boxer, to agency recruit to outright sucker who'd been hung out to dry, to fugitive to agency recruit (again) to prodigal son (at least in his own mind) in so short a time, with no premeditation at all, with utterly no sense of purpose, with — as far as he knew — no divine guidance.

And funny, too, he thought, how he could have blithely lowered, by the long fuse, that strange, putty-like stuff the agency gave him, through the broken window to the half-basement, how he could backpedal across the dewy lawn unreeling the rest of the gunpowder-covered string, squat near the cover of a hedge, and calmly put a match to the revealed end of the fuse. Funny, how he didn't even care about the people inside. Funny, how he'd believed the agency without hesitation when it told him the people inside were not only threats to the sovereignty of the Republic but actual anti-Christs who, chances were, weren't even human beings in the proper sense. Funny, how relieved he was when the mansion went up in a smokeless blue light so intense and clear and bright and (strangely) cold, because then he knew for sure what he'd suspected all along: that the fused putty they'd given him wasn't really capable of blowing up that house and killing all the people inside it, that something else — God knows what (perhaps that was why he found himself in church) — totally beyond his control, sent the mansion in powder to eternity.

* * * * *

In the storefront on the edge of town, The Brothers of Jesus — at this incipient point in their ominous history, an informal gathering of perhaps two dozen bearded men and portly women who had [Pardon the expression. *Quack*] resurrected and codified, with a few leftover King Jamesian trills, several of the more arcane theological axia of that late, failed predictor of World's End, William Halliwell — held its own Easter services.

"Holy brethren, why are we gathered here?" (Call.)

"To be in the presence of the Lords." (Response.)

"Why do we wish to be in His presence?"

"To celebrate."

"Why are we celebrating?"

"We are celebrating what the Lord has caused us to have."

"Holy brethren, what do we have?"

"We haveth The Picture!"

"Whose Picture is it?"

"It is the Lord's Picture."

"What is in the picture?"

"The picture changeth always!"

"How so are we different from The Picture?"

"We stayeth the same."

"How is it that we stay the same?"

"Our immortal souls in Jesus Christ our Lord stayeth the same!"

"How do our souls stay the same?"

"They stayeth the same in Truth."

"Holy brethren, what is the gift of Truth?"

"We have Time!"

"How do we have it?"

"We have stopped Time!"

"What is the gift of Time stopped?"

"The gift is the End!"

"When is the End?"

"The End is now!"

"Why is the End now?"

"The End is always now. It is in the picture!"

"What will cometh after the end?"

"A new Beginning!"

"What begineth?"

"The Kingdom of God on Earth!"

"Will the Kingdom of God be the same as now?"

"No. The Kingdom of God will be different?"

"How will the Kingdom be different?"

"The nectar of life will flow freely!"

"From where will the nectar flow?"

"From Man to Woman."

"How will it flow?"

"From our loins!"

"Will this please the Lord?"

"Yes. It will please the Lord."

"How do we know it will please the Lord?"

"Because it will pleaseth Him now!"

Each man in the congregation clasped both hands over his denim-covered genitals.

"Whereth will it flow?"

"Into the mouths of the wives."

"Why will it flow to there?"

"So that their mouths may be anointed."

"Why do we anoint their mouths?"

"So that they may speak the Truth."

Several women — The Brothers of Jesus would have preferred to have had one woman for each man in the congregation, but the recruiting of females had always lagged — stepped forward from the back of the storefront, made their ways to the ends of the rows of folded chairs, and stood still, waiting. The women were mostly rather heavy-breasted, dressed in cotton print dresses, and looked serviceably fertile. The few skinny creatures among them fidgeted, as if they knew they were out of place.

"Who are the wives?"

"All women are wives!"

"Who are the husbands?"

"All men are husbands!"

"Who may share?"

"All may share, so that all may be Holy!"

"When shall they share?"

"In the present Time!"

The women edged themselves sideways down the rows, until they came to their appointed males. The men lifted their buttocks off the folding chairs and undid their trousers, sliding them, and the accompanying tangled underwear, down to their knees. A few of the men wore long johns, which complicated and delayed the ritual. The other men, reddened boners already pointing to the ceiling, closed their eyes and waited, irritably, for the service [In both senses of the word. *Quack*] to proceed.

When all the men were unhitched from their drawers, and picket fences of priapic prongs vibrated like sexual tuning forks, the women of The Brothers of Jesus knelt between the legs of their males and began to fellate them. Rows of bonneted heads bobbed on cocks like grasshopper pumps on an active oil field. Groans and slurping sounds filled the storefront.

The service resumed.

"Where is Time?"

The response portion of the service resumed with some difficulties. All of the men were not able to answer dependably as one.

"Time standeth still!"

"How is it that time standeth still?"

"In truth there is no time!"

"What replaceth time?"

"Ecstasy!"

"Is Ecstasy Holy?"

"Yea, it is!"

"And how is Ecstasy Holy?"

"Ecstasy stoppeth the world, and in the stopped world, there can be no sin! And when there is no sin, a state of Holiness arises. And when Holiness is risen, our Lord is with us truly!"

The remainder of the service consisted of the sounds of scooching metal chairs, mild grunts, a collective utterance similar to humming but hardly musical, and some deep, gurgling sighs. A few of the men stomped their booted feet in pleasure.

Moments later, several women wiped their mouths on aprons that matched, more or less, their dresses. When The Brothers of Jesus grew to the size that it would become when Robo was dragooned into it a generation later, this particular service would be secret, limited to the leaders and their concubines, and entirely unmentioned to the chaylens. Even now, a hand-painted sign on the wall behind the rickety pulpit and swaying preacher read, *DON'T TALK — THIS PLACE IS BUGGED!*

During the services for Easter Sunday, 1952, however, the fatigued Ken Sabe — recently returned to Calvary, Idaho from a long sojourn in the New York, Washington, D.C., and Greater Los Angeles areas (including Pasadena, but excluding San Pedro) — experienced a spiritual awakening. It had, however, nothing to do with religion. The drone of the service seemed to him, in fact, so unbearably dry, smug, and scolding that he wondered how anyone listening to it could think that it proclaimed hope, instead of hopelessness.

Ken Sabe's gaze fell upon the nape of the neck of a beautiful girl, about eighteen or so, in the pew in front of him. Slowly, the vision of her virginal cheeks and the delicate wisps of silver-blonde hair which spiraled down beside them, melded with the faint smell of the altar flowers, the echoing cavern of the church's interior, and the comparatively liberal Protestant incantations of the minister. They transported him into a synaesthetic, almost psychedelic, reverie about Christian spring in the clear western apron of the Rocky Mountains.

He was fourteen again, in love for the first time (as he almost always was), with every girl he'd ever longed for (which included most of those that he ever met), pure and chaste from afar (as much from circumstance as virtue), although (he could swear to God if he had to) this time his groin remained perfectly unflustered. His heart almost burst. It was a perfect moment, one that, over the years, he wished he could freeze in the Lucite of stopped time.

Ken Sabe had set eyes, for the first time, upon Robo's mother.

The peculiar aircraft enjoyed several nicknames. Since it was in part a retooled version of the pilot-hated Cessna UC-78, some called it the "Useless 78." Matt Medium, ever the casual blasphemer, mostly liked to call it simply "Jesus," which, he said, was merely a derivation/condensation of other pilots' epithets, such as "Wheezy Jeez" and "Shakey J." Sometimes, however, he experimented: "Christocopter," "Trinity Trimotor," "Beelzebomber" or "The Lord's Flyer." But, God, he really loved the airplane.

"Airplane" — in the sense of a tubular fuselage attached to a left and right extended-teardrop-section wing, a vertical stabilizer and two short wings in the rear, and a bubble cockpit on top, near the nose — was not, however, an accurate term for the craft. It was more like a wide rowboat halfway metamorphosed into a thick boomerang, bent downward in the middle as if by two humongous thumbs, and radically tapered at the tips, where conventional vertical stabilizers seemed to have been reattached. The cockpit was subsumed into the fuselage (such as it was) in the form of curved greenhouse glass paneling covering half the nose, from the equator of the aircraft up. The paned glass ran a quarter of the way back to the elbow of the boomerang.

It (the airplane, the aircraft, the craft, the thing) was painted two different sets of colors, divided along horizontal midline. The top half was painted earth-color camouflage (not particularly jungle, not especially desert, not decidedly mountain, but a generalized semiabstraction of good ol' terra firma), so as to be, theoretically, invisible when seen from an overflying, and presumed hostile, aircraft. The bottom half was painted blue, with wisps of greyish white (to approximate the sky with about the same fidelity that the camouflage mimicked the ground), to bamboozle observers on the ground. It carried no insignia to interrupt the decorative theme of imperceptibility.

Had the aircraft borne markings, strictly appropriate emblems would have been hard to designate. Not those of the United States Air Force, because it wasn't a military craft. Not those of the agency, because the agency didn't have insignia (agency aircraft insignia would have amounted to the ultimate in counterproductivity). Not those of Matt Medium, because Mr. Medium was a civilian, a private contractor, a rogue individual human intelligence, indeed, a loose cannon that many in the agency thought should have never been brought on board at all, especially to spy on Congressmen who fraternized with Satanists who seduced rocket scientists at The Institute of Technology in Pasadena. Not German, especially swastikas and that sort of stuff, because the Germans had been beaten in the last war and now they officially had no more Luftwaffe.

Why would German insignia have ever been considered by the agency, or anybody, in the first place? They wouldn't have been considered, but if they had been, it would have been because the aircraft was of a design lifted from that of the Japanese craft that miraculously made it all the way across the Pacific Ocean in the waning days of the war to drop the near-fatal balloon bomb on Noam Sain. That design, of course, was lifted from the German design, "Imeda," that was, in previous turn, inspired by the "Zanonia seed" design of Serge Protector's huge DL-117, which was, in its previous turn, inspired by J.W.R. Dunne's lacy little D-8.

Airplane people are a close lot; fraternities transcend nations and wars; things get around; aficionados share trade secrets. In the end, in the fraternity of flight, flying is all.

Matt Medium certainly thought so. To be above the ground, aloft, untethered to the earth, was to be safe. He was living proof of that.

When the blue flash — whose starting point was a pin-prick in the exact, cubic center of what, to humor Earl, he'd called the Ritual Room of his mansion, Agape Lodge, on Orange Grove Boulevard — obliterated the night, Matt Medium was on the shake roof, wobbling perilously in the moonlight. Minutes earlier, out of the corner of his eye, through the thickly paned window, he'd seen the long, muddy feet of Ken Sabe (then known only to Matt Medium as "The Goon" the agency had recruited — can you imagine? — to help him) padding in reverse across the lawn, trailing (presumably from a spool in his hands) an endless grey string.

Oh my fucking God, he'd thought, the stupid clown is going to do it now! Can't they get a goddamned thing right?

"Scuse me, Earl," he'd said with a rote grin, and eased himself to the edge of the den, near the staircase. When Earl had redeposited his nose in his drink, Matt Medium bounded up the stairs, three at a time, grasped the brass ball at the top railing post and hurled himself around the corner, down the hall (so quickly he didn't hear the weeping pregnant woman in the bedroom as he passed, although the door was open and she was on her back, on the floor, sobbing at the ceiling) to a dormer window at the end. He scrambled out onto the roof, kicking his slick-soled loafers from his feet, sending them somersaulting into the jasmined night, preferring to take his foothold chances on the shingles in his stocking feet.

He climbed to the peak of the roof, crabbed-stepped his way to the brick chimney, and hoisted himself onto its rim. Slowly, shakily, he stood.

From the chimney, he was able to reach — barely — an overhanging tree branch that the Pasadena Fire Department had warned him any number of times to cut down. Fire regulations, they said: The whole neighborhood could go up, even with its stately homes on minimum one-acre lots.

Matt Medium stepped away from the chimney, gripped the branch tightly, and bent his knees. The branch sagged. But it didn't break. Hanging by his hands, he inched sideways, so that, gradually, he was able to unbend his legs and let his argyled feet dangle above the sharply sloping roof. The branch grew bigger, and slipperier, harder to hold, as he went. He'd never make the trunk, he knew, but the trick — he supposed — would be to clear the outside edge of the wall of the mansion by the time the goddamned house blew up.

Indeed, he'd just cleared the dark, shingled exterior wall when the moving spark on Ken Sabe's fuse crawled like a snaky star through a window and down toward the putty on the basement floor. He was another couple of feet removed from the house, when the tiny hissing ball of heat and light contacted the explosive.

What the device that the agency had given Ken Sabe to road test (without, of course, informing him) actually accomplished — much more than simply exploding — was to upset the delicate molecular balance of the entire house. It triggered latent energies contained in the vast tub of mercury and (some would have it) ether in the sub-basement; it disturbed the equilibrium of a magnetic reverse-timing or (some would have it) time-reversal device on Matt Medium's desk in his ornate bedroom; and, worst, it released a sudden, simultaneous burst of hysteria and terror in the minds of Matt Medium's guests which, in itself, constituted its own kind of detonation.

The explosion, or (as some would have it) implosion of the mansion was sudden, swift, clear, cold, blue and precise. Anything beyond the shell of the house was unaffected, save for being coated with a fine, whitish ash that glowed for a few moments, like phosphorous in a night surf, and then dulled to a funerary flocking on the prickly leaves of hedges, the gently curving trunks of palm trees, and the unsuspecting hoods of cars.

No one outside the house was killed or injured. Everyone inside the house evaporated. Or, as Matt Medium preferred to think (as he dropped calmly to the soft lawn after gymnastically navigating his body to the tree's trunk and, then, a lower branch), almost everyone. He liked the portly little preacher, and wished him well: survival. In view of Noam's having improbably survived against similar odds in Oregon, Matt Medium thought it a wish with a reasonable chance of being granted.

What was not so reasonable was, on Easter Sunday, 1952, that this aircraft, high above Calvary, Idaho [And Billy means high. *Quack*], could actually fly. Its avionics were predicated upon the existence of ether and, as far as Matt Medium knew (both from reading and from experimenting in the basement of his mansion), ether didn't exist. Yet here he was, in a swollen silver boomerang, hovering six miles over the sandy carpet and puckered brown hills of the country that nestled Calvary to its bosom. The craft hummed; its contentment cut like a shower of gravel through the frigid blue sky.

Snug in layers of leather, cozy in a collar and cap lined with lamb's wool, swathed in a net of wires connecting him, by means of an audial umbilical cord to the base on the ground, Matt Medium was happy.

Dipping the craft to one side, he could look through his streamlined greenhouse down on the scrub metropolis of Calvary, from this height a mere scratch and a few pocks in the high desert, and (with a little will power; he had never lacked for will power) see the microscopic rectangles of Calvary's buildings. At one end of town, in a green stain, was the bigger church, the official church, the real (the adjective made Matt Medium grin) church. He craned, squinted, peered, stared through the perfect glass. Through the lens of ether, knowing became seeing and seeing became knowing. He knew that he could see (and he saw that he knew) "The Goon," slumped and fatigued, in a rear pew. He could see "The Goon's" head raise up when he saw the naked neck nape of Cynthia ("Stretcher," they called her behind her back in the agency office, in bitter tribute to her ability, by mere appearance, to change the lengths of their penises) Barr.

He could see "The Goon" falling in love.

And down the road, along the scratch, Matt Medium could see, with equal knowledge and fidelity, the squalid little square chip that was the storefront where The Brothers of Jesus, this fine Easter Sunday, were worshipping. He could see (though with a little more difficulty) those fanatic loonballs getting their cocks sucked and praising the Lord while it happened.

Had he been a less brilliant, less cerebral, less disciplined, less patriotic man, Matt Medium might have envied that seated chorus line of ejaculating sinners on the ground. But Matt Medium was much happier being where he was, high above it all, seeing and knowing damned near everything. He was floating. He was *flying*.

Boys and Girls, More or Less Together

Noam drove quickly away in the night.

As police sirens swelled louder, Noam clenched the steering wheel of his Ford as tightly as if it were the devil's throat. He stomped on the accelerator as if it were Satan's skull. The old Ford had probably never gone so fast, at least with a preacher at the wheel.

As the car sped north on Orange Grove, talcum-textured ash — wisps of the remains of Agape Lodge — flew from its surface in a comet's tail. The few people who had straggled out of their houses when they heard a sudden sound that was an odd combination of a hiss and a boom, and who were standing about on the corner of Orange Grove and Colorado Boulevard as Noam screeched a hard, two-wheeled right-hand turn, would later tell the newspaper reporters about a mysterious "ghost car" fleeing the scene. What they couldn't tell the papers, or the police, was anything about a make, model, or license number.

Noam sped a few blocks, hung another right to get off the wide, well-lighted boulevard, turned right again onto a dark, east-west sidestreet with no traffic, and slowed to a crawl. He pulled to the curb, and rested his trembling chin on the backs of his hands, which still held the steering wheel in a death grip. Copious sweat flooded through his shirt and even seeped through his clinging, binding suit jacket. His heart throbbed beneath his fat chest.

Noam took three counted deep breaths, and straightened himself in the driver's seat. He loosened his grip on the steering wheel to something less than maniacal. He pressed slowly, gently down on the accelerator. The Ford pulled quietly away from the curb. Halfway down the block, it achieved a normal, inconspicuous speed. Its headlights turned on.

Noam turned left, back toward Colorado, then realized his error. He backed into a driveway, and turned his car around, proceeding south to California Street, another luxuriously wide, but not so well-lighted, boulevard. At California, Noam looked right, and saw the fire trucks barreling north on Orange Grove. He waited for them to pass, then crept across California. More people on the usually quiet residential avenues had shuffled bewilderedly out of their houses, and were standing in small, shadowy groups on their streetlighted lawns. Some of them pointed fingers toward the glowing, spreading, fading cloud of dust illuminating the clear, dark blue sky. A few of them wandered into the street. Noam drove cautiously, to avoid them.

Finally, Noam found an entrance to the Pasadena Freeway. He slipped into the spotty stream of cars heading toward downtown Los Angeles.

Noam tried to calm himself as he drove. He noticed that the other drivers on the freeway were absorbed enough in their own speeds, their lane-changes, their cigarettes, conversations and radio stations. They didn't seem to notice the last flecks of ash levitating from his Ford and disappearing in its slipstream. In a mile or so, the last wisps had blown into the night and disappeared. But Noam did not feel safe. He was numb now, and felt little at all.

Amid several companion automobiles, the Ford trickled onto the downtown streets. A police black-and-white passed Noam, and the officers looked at him without expression. Noam nodded a silly pantomime of "Evening, officer," a beat or two too late, and continued on.

He found Figueroa Street and entered it southbound. He drove slowly, pulling over and stopping frequently. When he reached the waterside in the Port of San Pedro, he pulled onto an unpopulated pier and slept. Had he given up his journey a few blocks earlier, at Roubidoux Street, he might have found that an odd shard of bathroom window glass had beaten him to the spot. But all that he cared about at the moment was that no police, or mad scientists, or devil-worshipping Congressmen, or moaning pregnant women had followed him there.

Eventually, Noam did drive to Conchita Memoranda's house over much the same route, except that this time he had intersected Figueroa Street from the west, coming from Venice on Venice Boulevard, and turned right. Before, he was frightened, exhausted, and needed a place to sleep. This time — months later, after the discovery of the glass, after the street preaching and the crowds and the coins and bills tossed into the fishbowls — he drove because he hadn't been able to sleep peacefully, because his unconsciousness was continually interrupted by twitchy visions of Matt Medium's smooth, cool voice, of Earl's smug leer, of that whole deep, creepy house on Orange Grove.

If Earl — who could have foreseen that such vulgar words would leap at such volume from a silver-haired man in wire-rimmed glasses wearing a very expensive suit? — hadn't said, "All right, I've had enough of your fat fucking preacher's face haunting my party; why don't you just park your shitty ass on the porch and contemplate the fucking sidewalk, you pious prick," he would, he knew, be dead right now. Noam remembered, for a terrifying second, the front door of Matt Medium's mansion clicking shut behind him and, an instant later, the searingly cold wall of blinding white light behind him that threw his shadow, like a giant black arrow, across the street and, seemingly, through the wall of the house opposite. Noam couldn't remember much after that except waking up in his car on some smelly pier in San Pedro.

He arrived late at night. One-footed Señor Memoranda was asleep, dreaming, as always, that he was being chased through the streets of San Pedro by an angry mob of white Protestants who wanted to crucify him for blasphemy. He couldn't escape because he hobbled on one foot. The mob never caught up with him, but Señor Memoranda still slept as badly as Noam. He had come to blame Noam for the loss of his foot because Noam wasn't a good Catholic. Noam was *un diablo blanco y gordo.*

Noam didn't knock right away. He went around the side of the house, in through the unsecured gate to the back yard. He looked in the dark for the spot where the miracle glass might have landed, but couldn't find it. The grass was too deep. No one had mown it for weeks, Noam thought.

He trudged around to the front porch, stood in the buggy light, and rapped on the door, lightly. No answer. He rapped again, but not much harder. He waited.

A light came on inside the house. The door opened and Conchita stood in front of Noam, a robed silhouette against a slab of gold.

She fit perfectly the image he'd held before his eyes — hovering in front of the rearview mirror, actually — all the way down from Venice. She wore a lacy, white, but opaque and modest, dressing gown. Her thick, black shiny hair was gathered in the back and, he saw moments later, was held in place by an obviously beloved heirloom clip. Conchita was tiny, much shorter than even he was. Looking down at the crown of her lovely head, Noam felt a man again. Relieved, almost ecstatic, he tried mightily to ignore the fact that she polluted his dream, somewhat, by holding a lighted cigarette.

Conchita said nothing for a few seconds. She simply looked at Noam as though she were mildly surprised, but not startled. Noam merely slumped at the shoulders and breathed hard.

Finally, Conchita asked, "Why did you come?"

"I don't know," Noam answered, turning his body to let it rest against the wall. "I feel like something is pursuing me."

Conchita stepped momentarily back into the house to crush out the cigarette. She flicked out the porch light from inside, and then stepped back out. "My father might wake up," she said. "And he hates you now."

"Hates me? Why?"

"He lost his foot. He will lose his job. And he blames you."

Noam stared. Conchita explained. "He stepped on the glass. That's how we found it, remember? When the...the excitement started, he forgot about how much it hurt. He got himself some crutches, but he didn't see a real doctor. Maybe he thought the glass, and the miracle of it, would cure him. Maybe he thought it was just a cut, I don't know. But something went wrong. It became infected. When he finally got up the courage to go to the hospital, it was too late. It was a nice, clean, safe Anglo hospital with Anglo doctors. But all they could do was cut off his foot. The company says he will get a pension that he can live off of. But I don't believe them. So my father is a cripple. And he blames you for the whole thing. Maybe I should, too."

"But..."

Conchita looked around. "Do you have your car here? Can we go sit in it? We have neighbors. My father..."

"Sure," said Noam. He and Conchita walked down the sidewalk a few houses; Noam had somehow thought private-eyeish enough to park the car other than directly in front of the Memorandas' front door. Noam opened the passenger side door, and gestured.

Before she could stifle the impulse, Conchita remarked, "It's old."

"I've had this car a long time. A whole lot of my life is in it. Besides," he added, making a movement similar to straightening a tie although he wasn't wearing one, "I'm not much of a car man."

"You bless them, and you advertise about cars on television," Conchita said, settling into the seat.

"I bless things to make them holy after I bless them. It doesn't matter what they were before. Teacups or toasters or telegraph machines, it doesn't matter. And the car commercials — they're not part of my television program. They come on before and after it."

"But it's your voice I hear telling about cars."

"That's just something I do for the station. They pay me for it, but not in money. No money changes hands. If I do the voice for the cars, they charge me less for the time for my program. But you're not supposed to recognize me by my voice."

Conchita sat for a moment and thought. Noam looked at her and thought, too — thoughts he hadn't entertained since his brief married life in Oregon, and some he hadn't had the pleasure of experiencing since Imeda left long ago. Noam squirmed. As he was about to say — or do — something reckless, Conchita spoke: "You pay the television station money so that you can be on it? They don't pay you?"

"No." He felt suddenly ashamed.

"Where do you get the money to pay them, beside the advertising for cars?"

"People send it to me."

"Why do people send you money?"

"They send it with their letters to me at the television station."

"The letters where they ask you to pray?"

Conchita's face — what he could see of it, with her brown skin far from a streetlight, with the roof of the old Ford blocking out the moon — was, to Noam, surprisingly unjudgmental. What Noam then said to her was, to him, surprisingly frank.

"I don't ask for money outright. But it's understood that when a person writes to The Reverend Noam Sain's

Church of the New Deliverance asking me, Minister Noam Sain, to pray specifically for them, they should include a check. Sometimes people put actual money in the envelope. They shouldn't. It could be stolen, at the post office, even by the station owners. I wouldn't put it past them.

"Anyway, I call it a Love Offering, or sometimes simply a gift. The idea is that it helps keep my program on television. I don't say that it's money for me to live from, but how could I stay on television if I didn't have money to live from? Most people, I suspect, don't think of it as money for me, or even money, except when they do their checkbook balances. They think of it as an offering, a kind of prayer in itself. They say a little checkie-prayer for me so that I'll say a big prayer for them. They think my prayer is big because they think I have an inside track with God. Which I do, although not in the way they might think.

"But most of what they send me really does go to keeping my program on the station. There's some that I use for living, and there's a little left over after that, that I put in the bank. But I don't make much money. I'm not trying to make a lot of money. I'm trying to do God's work."

"And the cars, blessing the cars?" Conchita asked.

"I get some extra money for that, but not much. I do it for fun. Do you believe that? Do you believe that a man of God can have a little fun in his work?" Noam squirmed in his seat. There was a little truth and a lot of lie in what he said, and he was hoping Conchita would accept this particular mix.

Conchita ignored Noam's question. "And what you did at our house? Did you get money out of that?"

"I got almost none. And I wanted no money from that. What happened was a miracle. You find a piece of glass in your back yard that has the image of our Lord Jesus Christ and his holy mother and several saints somehow engraved on it," Noam said. Then he leaned back and shouted, "That's a miracle!"

"Quiet," hushed Conchita. "I said we have neighbors."

For some reason, her sudden squelch excited Noam. Conchita was the aggressor, he the attacked. She was dark, pungent, powerful; he was white, soft, weak. Something stirred in his fat crotch. Noam swallowed hard, and continued.

"That was a miracle, and I came down here to serve it. I'm on this earth to serve miracles, not to have them serve me. Do you believe me?"

"I believe you."

"Conchita, I...."

"I believe you are a special man sent here to serve miracles."

"I am a lonely man."

"I feel that you are only at the beginning of the wonderful work that you can do in the world."

"I am a very lonely man."

"Perhaps I can be your friend."

"I need a very close friend."

"I can be that."

"I'm not a Catholic."

"Of course," she said as though she'd been told point blank she was stupid. "I know that."

"I am a minister of God, but I have been married and I have had a family."

"Yes, I can see you are a good man."

"But I am no longer married, and I do not have a family, except..."

"You will again. It will be part of your work. I feel that."

"I don't have a wife."

"Yes, I know. You've told me."

"I don't even have what you'd call a girlfriend. Are you somebody's girlfriend?"

"No."

"Conchita, I'm lonely. I need the company of a woman."

Conchita pressed the palms of her hands down into her gown. "Are you asking me to be your girlfriend?"

"You just seem so lovely, so understanding. I...," Noam said. And then, suddenly, he was all sobs: shaking, sniffling, wailing, beating his forehead on the dashboard.

"Shhh. Shhh. It will be all right," Conchita said. She leaned over and kissed Noam lightly on the forehead. Then she put her hand on the doorhandle and cracked the door open. She said, "Wait here. Don't worry, I'll come right back. I need to get a cigarette, and then I'll come right back. I want to talk to you."

To Noam's surprise, Conchita did come back, dressed in a modest little flower-print dress (reminiscent, unintentionally, of those worn by the women under the tents in Noam's earlier, itinerant days), with her hair let down, lipstick, and a cigarette. She let herself into the Ford, closed the door but opened the window so that, with her right hand, she could flick her ashes — a darker grey than the traces of white powder still clinging to the corners of a few louvers and vents of the Ford. Her left hand went right to Noam's pants, to the long zipper, which she opened as deftly as she had the window. She grasped Noam's penis and cooed in his ear, *"Escuchame, muchacho."*

Noam moaned and lay his head back against the seat. Her hand, cool and warm at the same time, felt like velvet, like peacock feathers he wanted to eat, like music playing right inside his muscles, like time standing still. Noam began to babble in his ecstasy, about Castelli and his partner, about Matt Medium, Earl, Agape Lodge, the pregnant woman, the great white light and the dust on his car, and the second miracle that allowed him to live beyond his time.

As Conchita caressed Noam's cock, Conchita told Noam that he had been anointed by God to do extraordinary deeds in the world. She told him not to preach on television about the explosion, because it would just implicate him in something horrible, possibly criminal. She told him that even if it didn't, who would believe he was there? Stick to the glass, she said. Stick to the miracle people will believe. She also said he could do better, he could have a bigger church and save more people. She said that the television program was only the beginning. As Noam came all over his gabardine trousers, he heard the words, "success," "business manager," and "me."

Noam continued to preach on his television program about the miraculous piece of glass, and the program began to draw a bigger and bigger audience, including more and more doubters who tuned in out of curiosity, rather than faith. The miraculous glass became a local controversy. Noam, of course, maintained it was a miracle. A few scientists who poked their noses into the matter, said it was merely a remarkable coincidence — remarkable, but a coincidence just the same: that the piece now in the makeshift shrine and the pane in the bathroom window looked almost exactly alike. That they both seemed to contain a fairly detailed image of Jesus Christ and his mother, Mary, escaped skeptical comment. The scientists denounced Noam as a charlatan and a huckster in the newspapers. Noam denounced the scientists as atheists and snobs on television. Noam became a genuine — albeit minor — celebrity. Someone even invited him to lunch at Chasen's, which he declined, out of fear.

But, as is often the case with celebrity based on coincidence and oddity rather than talent or merit, Noam's affirmative brand of fame quickly peaked. Notoriety, which always wants to slide toward scandal, turned sour. Noam became a target for ridicule. He was derided for his short, fat body and pinched little face. He was mocked for his anointing cars with motor oil in supermarket parking lots (a practice he continued against the advice of his personal and business manager, Conchita Memoranda, because, Noam said, a true preacher who lost contact with the "laying on of hands" eventually loses contact with God). The more Conchita tried to talk him out of anointing cars, the more he felt his own television program to be dry and sterile.

"Conchita," he told her repeatedly, "I'm on the verge of being able to create miracles, instead of just being present at them."

Conchita thought Noam's stubborn craziness was wasting an opportunity, destroying what she had come to see as "their" television program. She'd left her father on Roubidoux Street with a part-time nurse and moved to an apartment on Van Ness Avenue, near the television studio. She dyed a red streak into her hair, replaced her little dress with tight wool skirts and rayon blouses, and bought a book of instructions on how to jettison a Mexican accent.

"I come from the fringes," she told Noam. "I want a foothold at the center of society. You, gringo, you have the center, and you're drifting toward the fringes. If you don't watch out, you'll go over the edge."

"I will not do what business demands," Noam answered, "but what God dictates."

So, Conchita decided to keep one eye out for her own interests, independent of Noam. She lectured Castelli and partner on running the station better as a business, on the coming tenfold profitability of television, on giving the viewers, even the ones who tuned in to watch boxing, wrestling and dubious seminars on mental health, what they wanted. She said "her viewers" were rightfully worried — about prices, the atomic bomb, and the infiltration of Communists into the State Department and local schools. She said they needed something to help them cope with a world that was changing more rapidly than it had ever changed before. She told Castelli and his partner that she knew what that something was. Conchita said she could deliver it — over their television station.

Alone in her apartment at night, Conchita had taken some of what Noam had preached and turned it into something she called "The Amazing Memoranda Mental

Maintenance Program." She proposed to Castelli and partner that she give lectures on their television station. Then, she said, she would give seminars and courses in hotel ballrooms and civic halls. If Castelli and his partner would back her, she said, they could share in the profits.

Castelli was impressed with Conchita. Sexual attraction may have had something to do with it. On the other hand, it could have been the appeal of a fellow fallen Catholic. [Perhaps the two are the same. *Quack.*] The guy with the match was impressed, but in an abstract, businesslike way that amounted to a milder inclination to say yes to Conchita's proposal. But his weak yes was still a yes, so they gave her the program.

Conchita had to tell Noam she was "resigning" as his business manager. To her surprise, Noam didn't seem terribly shaken by her imminent departure. He'd actually never paid her a salary, but had just let her take a percentage of The Minister Noam Sain's Church of the New Deliverance's receipts. After the first blush of celebrity controversy, those receipts failed to amount to nearly as much as she'd hoped. As for Noam, Conchita's presence by his fiduciary side hadn't done that much good. Moreover, after her first ministrations in Noam's parked Ford on Roubidoux Street, she had never masturbated (or in any other sexual way, satisfied) him again. Indeed, she wouldn't even give him her unlisted phone number, or tell him her address on Van Ness.

In the first weeks following their split, Noam didn't worry about the possibility of competition from Conchita. "The Minister Noam Sain's Church of the New Deliverance" was, after all, a church, a matter of faith, more emotional than cerebral, more human than actuarial. (Noam was as proud of the possessive form of his surname in the title of his church as he had been of his radio days' "Los Angeles, in California" in his sign-off.) Conchita's "The Amazing Memoranda Mental Maintenance Program" was a kind of course exploring some odd territory equidistant from hypnotism, metaphysics and common sense.

"Evil," Conchita would say, "can be accomplished in a second. But Good must be carefully built and maintained over the years. Therefore, to be Good, to experience the Good, to proclaim the Good, one must have a program for warding off the momentary temptations that lead to Evil." She would say it standing behind a blonde desk on the set of her own television program on KCCT-TV, wearing a jacket from Robinson's department store with a huge brooch on its satin lapel.

Fair enough, Noam thought when he saw Conchita on his little set for the first time. I'll inspire them with the Good, show them how its spark is ignited, how it sets itself off against the indigo deeps of Evil. And she can show them how to grease and oil it, wipe off the crap, and keep it running for the rest of their lives.

But even if there were no personal rivalry between the two dispensers of televised spiritual guidance, there soon developed a split between the fans of Noam and fans of Conchita. Overwhelmingly, the old-fashioned, superstitious, God-fearing trailer-park dwellers and the retirees in hot-plate-and-a-cat apartments near MacArthur Park favored Noam. Mexicans with ambitions to assimilate, and whites with a taste for self-help, quasi-religious "mental mainte-nance programs" with an overlay of mysticism (not a few of whom labored in the laboratories at The Institute of Technology up in Pasadena, and one of which worked as diligently as the executor of the startlingly wealthy estate of the late — actually missing, presumed dead — Congress-man Earl H. Dillingham, Republican of San Marino, as he had as the honorable representative's flack when he was alive) favored Conchita. In the end, Noam's popularity fell below the threshold of viable commercial television, while Conchita's rose above it.

Castelli and his partner spoke, privately at first, about firing Noam, which meant refusing to sell him any more air time. Castelli was sentimental, and wanted Noam to stay. The guy with the match had had enough of Noam —

twice, three times over — and wanted him gone. The guy with the match won the argument. When Noam's audience — as measured by the primitive polls of the time — fell even further, Castelli called the preacher into the office and, with the guy with the match chewing on a match in the background, told him they were completely booked for the foreseeable future.

Noam took the news about as well has he had that of Conchita's impending defection. In fact, he took it better. Hell, the little old ladies weren't sending the checks like they used to, so the program was on the verge of becoming a loss leader. Besides, he told the two, he was feeling a new call to do some "sweaty" preaching again.

Noam took a farewell drive around L.A., back to his old house on Marion Avenue in Pasadena, back down to Roubidoux Street in San Pedro (where he could have sworn he saw Señor Memoranda sitting in his front window, with a gun in his hand and the end of his stumped leg resting on a bucket, waiting for him to return with his lost daughter), even back to the rooming house in Venice where he'd originally landed (and just a few streets from where he'd depart).

One night, Noam packed several suitcases, slipped the keys to his apartment under his landlady's door, and drove north out of Los Angeles.

He preached in Bakersfield, Delano, Clovis, Fresno, Merced, Turlock, Modesto, Stockton and Lodi. Sometimes camping out in a crude bedroll and shaving in the cold water of an irrigation canal, Noam worked his way north and a little east. He preached on the outskirts of Sacramento, and in Placerville, South Lake Tahoe, Carson City and, finally, Reno, where many people had seen his television program in Los Angeles and gave him paper money and pats on the back. He preached in Fernley, Lovelock and Winnemucca, all without much luck. But Noam earned enough to keep going to McDermitt on the Nevada-Oregon border, and then on to Jordan Valley, on the Oregon-Idaho line.

He heard from a few kindly Christians that the towns clustered around Twin Falls on the Snake River Plain might be receptive to an evangelist of his charm, piquancy and corpulence, although that last quality had been diminished some with his hand-to-mouth weeks on the road. Noam glanced in a gas station at a soiled map of Idaho.

Yes, he figured, he'd head toward Twin Falls and those other towns. But after he'd made a little stake there, he would be inclined to head up toward another little town, serendipitously called Calvary.

Had he been there before? Surely, there was something in his spotting its little dot almost lost in the fold that was something more than mere coincidence.

Noam liked preaching in those little towns along the way, however, and never hurried. It took him years to get where he was going.

By 1963, the year of the John F. Kennedy assassination (but shortly before the event, in the moment of which we speak), more than a decade had passed since Matt Medium soared above Calvary in the "wingless" airplane, making giddy circles in the sky, looking down on practically everything and everybody in town. By 1963, the airfield had become a fully functioning, covert agency facility, and all the buildings adjacent to the runways — those unconcerned with aviation as well as those devoted to it — were marvelously equipped with everything from huge radar dishes to the latest in Coca-Cola vending machines. Even Ken Sabe's pilot's quarters contained some gleaming, state-of-the-art athletic training equipment. (He'd been wheeling some of it home, too, unauthorized, through the gates of the fifteen-foot high chainlink fence, under the nose of a winking guard.) But the whole place was nominally disguised as a Peace Corps Training Center (if a couple of signs could contradict coils of barbed wire, if earnest, well-scrubbed young men and women entering agency careers could, by their entering and exiting mien, pass as idealists).

Ken Sabe, now married to Cynthia ("Stretcher") Barr (who worked in the agency typing pool, in one of those buildings adjacent to the runway), was in charge of athletic and physical training at the alleged Peace Corps Training Center. At home, he had a young son, approximately nine years of age, whom, he said, he was "scientifically" training to be the world's greatest athlete, ever.

Curiously, Ken Sabe never, to anyone's recall (and one would expect agency employees to possess vast, finely tuned memories) referred to his child by name. People at the agency started calling the kid "The Robot Jock," in mocking the hoped-for product of the excessive athletic regimen his father imposed.

Ken Sabe didn't seem to mind the sobriquet for his son. Once or twice, he brought the boy to the training center to use the equipment. But he was soon discouraged from the practice for security reasons. So he quit bringing his son to the center and, instead, began to pilfer equipment (or "borrow" it, as Ken Sabe saw it) for the boy to use at home. "Stretcher" tried to dissuade him from doing it — not as a moral matter, but on the grounds he'd be caught and his career in the agency ruined. Ken Sabe persisted, however. He even stole the signs in the agency gym that said, FOR PEAK PERFORMERS ONLY, and took them home for the slightly smaller, less glamorous gym that he was building in his back yard.

Matt Medium, a high-level surveillance pilot and one of the heads of the aviation laboratory at the agency facility, still flew the "Wheezy Jeez," aka "Shakey J.," "Christocopter" and "The Lord's Flyer." The mystery of the "wingless" aircraft's airborne longevity in crossing the Pacific in 1945 to grace the coast of Oregon with the balloon bomb had never, to Matt Medium's satisfaction, been solved. So, in his ground hours, he labored exhaustively on a repêchage experiment which, if successful, would prove the existence of ether and explain the aircraft's remarkable performance in peace as well as in war.

Matt Medium was aware of Ken Sabe's working at the training center. But Ken Sabe, lower in the agency pecking order, was not aware of Matt Medium. Privately, Matt Medium regarded Ken Sabe as a loose cannon, as psychologically unstable, as a mad bomber. But — privately, against agency regulations and without its knowledge — Matt Medium had snooped around in the murky (though slight) history of the agency's facility, and had discovered Serge Protector's role in its founding. Matt Medium also discovered Ken Sabe's paternity. He came to consider the problematic relationship between father and son in those old days as perhaps the source of what he saw as Ken Sabe's instability. But he felt sorry for Ken Sabe, sorry enough (contrary to his general unsentimental demeanor as a human being) not to have him terminated.

Matt Medium saw Ken Sabe taking home the equipment. (Thievery looked positively quaint, Matt Medium found out, when observed from five miles directly overhead). He knew about the beneficiary, the young son whom Ken Sabe was trying to train into becoming the world's greatest athlete. So, whenever Matt Medium took the "Beelzebomber" aloft for tests and domestic surveillance flights (technically illegal, but what the hell), he always made a detour, and overflew the home of Ken Sabe and "Stretcher" Barr, to look down through ether's magic lens. Frequently, he saw Ken Sabe intensely (some would say mercilessly) training his boy. Since Ken Sabe's stealing was minor (considering the facility's budget), and since he ceased bringing the kid to work, Matt Medium saw the Sabe family as no particular threat to the Republic. So he filed no reports on them, either.

Matt Medium also spied on The Brothers of Jesus, which had grown into something formidable enough to draw his personal attention, if not the agency's as a whole. He flew over the regular services for the leaders based on a call-and-response-and-cocksucking liturgy. He saw The Brothers of Jesus starting to build its first tunnel under the storefront. But he viewed The Brothers of Jesus's talentless leaders, its idiot bearded men and its hopelessly homely and sexually desperate women, as no particular danger to the agency's version of democracy. In this instance, too, he filed no reports.

Then one day, on a surveillance flight, Matt Medium saw Noam Sain's 1934 Ford roll into Calvary. He saw Noam pull up at a street corner in downtown Calvary, climb atop the roof, and begin preaching. Matt Medium also saw: people gathering around, at first a few, then many; Noam wildly waving his arms and shouting; a few people walking away, but some staying; Noam beckoning people to bring their cars forward for anointing. One of the people who (reluctantly) brought a car forward for anointing was a woman named Nytibia Barbosell, who also worked in the agency typing pool with "Stretcher" Barr.

How Nytibia had arrived in Calvary was something of a mystery, a matter that the agency might have checked a little more carefully. Nytibia said she was thirty years old, looked to be about forty, and there was something in, and around, her eyes that testified to at least a decade more than that. If anyone had gotten close enough to peer into her eyes, the sight would have been more ancient, deep, and evil.

Her face had a conglomerate, man-made quality about it. But Nytibia's bouncy, abbreviated stature, red hair, and (whatever the hints of surgery) pigletlike face constantly scrunched into an intense, almost manic, smile made most people take her at the age she declared. "Stretcher" Barr believed her, and their seven weeks (at the time of the car-anointing) together in the agency typing pool had contributed no disabusement of that notion.

Nytibia told "Stretcher" Barr that she had previously worked as an advertising saleswoman for a television station in Los Angeles and — television stations being something of an exotic commodity in Calvary — "Stretcher" believed her. "Stretcher," of course, was so busy believing Ken Sabe when he told her their son would eventually be the greatest athlete the world had ever seen that she'd have believed just about anything. Not that it was up to "Stretcher"; the internal surveillers in the agency were desperate enough for competent help that they thought — or didn't think — anyone that far down the ladder required an excess of scrutiny.

What Nytibia didn't disclose was that she had an interest in what she called (to herself) "tunneling" into the souls of the dead. The Brothers of Jesus was somewhat interested in that. The group and Nytibia had found each other not long after Nytibia's arrival in Calvary, while she was still staying in the Crosslands Motel, eating breakfast in her room — cigarettes, accompanied by cereal in small waxed-paper-lined boxes that could serve as their own bowls — and making long-distance phone calls. She'd gone to a few peripheral meetings, but had never been to a "service" and had never participated in any of the sexual shenanigans in the storefront. Somehow, she labored under the impression that The Brothers of Jesus knew something about "tunneling."

Nytibia also had an idea that the government was interested in "tunneling," too, as a secret weapon. Like a few other civilians in Calvary, she had a suspicion that the Peace Corps Training Center wasn't quite what it was cracked up to be. When the hand-printed three-by-five card offering a job in the "training center" typing pool showed up on the thin, warped cork bulletin board of Calvary's coin laundry, she was only too happy to remove the thumb tack by which the card hung, deposit said card in her purse, and phone from the nearest pay phone (there being but three in the whole town) to beat everyone else to the job. She used her first paycheck to put a down payment on a 1955 Ford Victoria hardtop dressed black and yellow like a bumblebee with chrome suspenders, the car she was driving when Noam Sain hit town.

"Bring forward the vehicle of your sins, the chariots of your unrighteousness! Bring them without souls but with engines, without spirit but with speed, without eyes but with windows! Yes, come, bring them to Minister Noam Sain, God's holy dispatcher!"

Nytibia withdrew her car keys from her red patent leather purse, walked back across Calvary's main street, and got in her car. She backed it slowly out of its angled, head-in slot, stopped in the middle of the street straddling the dotted golden line, and then rolled the car slowly forward. She turned it gently to the right, parting a crowd of on-lookers, and nestled its front wheels against the curb.

"Yes! Yes! That's right, child!" bellowed the chubby little preacher with his white, faintly soiled shirtsleeves rolled above his elbows. "Enter this steely transporter of guilty souls close to the gates of Heaven!" Noam Sain jumped down from his car's roof and glided like a roly-poly matador to the grille of Nytibia's Ford. He placed his hand on the hood ornament.

"This is your errant automobile?" he asked, looking directly into Nytibia's eyes.

"Yes, it is," she said.

"This is the day of your salvation," said Noam, turning to the crowd on the ball of a foot encased in a shoe with a hole in the sole, raising his arms overhead as if in triumph, revealing patches of sweat underneath. "I will remove the stain of sin from that very thing which takes you to it! I will cleanse that carriage in which your body and your mind and your soul anticipate the offense against God even as you are speeding toward it! Will the blessing of Minister Noam Sain expunge the sin entirely? No, no, it could never do that. That necessary apology to the Lord lies dormant in your heart, waiting to be cried out! But Minister Noam Sain can, Minister Noam Sain will, Minister Noam Sain *must* remove the stain from that in which you, sinner, spend more hours alone without the guidance of God, than you do in the bosom of your own loving family! If your car is clean, then you will not be so disposed to dirty yourself! If your car is blessed, then you will not be so inclined to weave from the road of righteousness!"

Then, turning back to Nytibia standing hopefully by her hardtop, he said, "And blessed are you, young lady, to be the first in the wonderful, Godly town of Calvary, Idaho, U.S.A., to step forward to receive the word of Minister Noam Sain, and to receive his holy anointing of your personal vehicle!"

With that, Noam opened his old Ford and lifted out a cardboard case of motor oil and placed it at his feet. He reached down his hand to extract a can. But Noam couldn't reach it by merely creasing himself at the waist. He had to bend his knees and squat, nearly bursting the seam of his worn, shiny trousers, to lift out a can. He plunged into his pants pocket for a can opener.

"Heathens call this a church key, friends," Noam laughed out loud to the crowd, "and they mean it sacrilegiously. But in the hand of Minister Noam Sain it is truly the key to the True Church!" Noam opened the can of ten-thirty, poured a small puddle on the hood of Nytibia's Ford, and slammed his open palm into it, splattering his white shirt.

"Heal! Oh, Lord, with this oil, with the blood of the veins of this mighty machine that has taken this young woman from the path of the good into the vast, darkened parking lots of sin, remove the curse! Let your holy light shine down upon the metal, the glass, the musical radio and the soft upholstery of this young woman's car! Heal! [a slam of the hand], heal! [another], heal! [and another].

Nytibia was entranced by Noam — at first by his hoarse, raspy voice, and then, strangely, by his very physical unattractiveness. Noam noticed her, too, and was immediately smitten, not in small part because she was his first customer in Calvary, the ice-breaker, the pump-primer. Nytibia reminded him, strangely, of both Imeda (whose pre-war vision — treason both personal and political notwithstanding — he was still somewhat in love with) and Conchita (with whom he lately wished he'd stayed and never gone on the road).

When the crowd dispersed (one more automotive anointing, perfunctory and unconvincing, and people drifted away), Noam and Nytibia stood on the nearly deserted main street of Calvary. Nytibia told Noam she worked at the Peace Corps Training Center. She also told Noam of The Brothers of Jesus (she called it a "religious study group") in the town. Noam was interested. She invited him to come to a meeting with her.

After a few days of street-preaching and car-anointing in Calvary, Noam attended a meeting of The Brothers of Jesus with Nytibia. Noam and Nytibia talked with a few of the leaders at the meeting, and the leaders were impressed with Noam. Nominally, he could have been considered a competitor — seeking converts from a small pool of potentials — but Noam was selling only momentary salvation: a little oil on the hood, a lesson shouted out, and he'd move on, perhaps leaving behind a few confused, unsatisfied, quivering souls who'd make willing chaylens in short order. Besides, Noam had a charm which, in some unspecified way at some indeterminate time, the brighter (and this isn't saying much) leaders thought might be useful. Noam and Nytibia were invited back the following week.

To Nytibia's surprise, they were both included in the storefront services. Noam waddled to his seat in a folding chair, wondering where Nytibia had gone. She reappeared among the dowdy women at the periphery, and came down the aisle during the call-and-response. She squeezed her way down Noam's aisle, and knelt in front of Noam. She pulled his wobbly little wiener from his pants and sucked him dry.

As he came, he saw a kaleidoscope of fractured visions of a blonde, beatific Imeda, his fat Oregon wife frappe'd in a blue explosion, cute, dark little Conchita moving her wide, red mouth behind a television desk, and of time itself slipping back through a hole in the universe into a frozen, perfect peace.

Nytibia, nearly choking on Noam's desperate seed, had a different sort of vision — clear, rational, strategic. She saw how primitive and stupid were the male leaders of The Brothers of Jesus. She saw how pasty and compliant the women were. But she also saw how powerful they could become.

After the ritual blowjob, she sat with Noam in her anointed car (dust clung to the oily patch on her hood like mold to old cheddar) and told him that they had a future together in The Brothers of Jesus. She said that the group needed a great spiritual leader, and that he was it. Noam swooned and agreed.

From the wingless airplane, Matte Medium observed nearly everything: the preaching, the anointing, the meeting, the service, the cocksucking, the conversing, the conniving, the conspiring. As he was still considered something of a maverick within the agency, his powers were, however, limited. He couldn't do much about Ken Sabe, whom the agency apparently wanted to keep around, like a big pet dog docile enough not to cause trouble but whose bark could scare people off when that was called for. Besides, Matte Medium told himself, "The Goon" hadn't really tried to kill him, personally. He'd just been doing his job, like they were all doing their jobs, like the whole idiot world was probably doing its job. He could have done something about Noam, but he thought the preacher — at least at this point — relatively harmless.

Nytibia Barbosell was another story. She wasn't harmless. But since all Matt Medium had on her was one large hunch, he couldn't act with as much decisiveness as he'd like to. The agency might push him further toward the fringe. It might stop letting him go up in the wingless airplane. But he could at least get Nytibia off the premises. He had her fired from the typing pool. Nytibia learned she'd been dismissed when she drove to work one day in her car still disfigured (to the secular eye) with the greasy scab of Noam's anointing, and found a note on Peace Corps stationery stuck in her electric typewriter.

Nytibia flew into a rage, cursing, scattering papers and shattering coffee cups, hurling letter openers, threatening the other women.

"Stretcher" Barr cowered astonished behind the water cooler, steadying the tilting, bubbling blue jug that, she more or less rightly assumed, was her only real protection.

"I know goddamned well what the fuck is going on here! I know exactly what this fucking place is!" Nytibia screeched, her eyes bulging, her gums almost curling back to the roots of her teeth. "I have copies! I have my own files! I will destroy this heathen empire!" she screamed. MP's in mirrored chrome helmets came in and threw her bodily off the premises. Nytibia rolled over in the dust outside the high, barbed fence. As she rose, and watched the tailored buttocks of the MPs walking away, she also saw Matt Medium, arms folded across his chest, standing in the distance.

"I don't know who you are, but I know what you are! You are the Devil. You are trying to keep me from my destiny! But I will rise up and destroy you! My destiny is stronger than any of you!"

Nytibia hurled herself behind the steering wheel of her 1955 Ford Victoria hardtop, and gunned the car onto the highway. Fishtailing, she laid rubber nearly all the way back to the city limit of Calvary, Idaho.

The King Is Dead, Long Live the Queen

Gradually, Noam lost his outdoor audience in Calvary. People didn't exactly know that he was high [Or loaded, stoned, ripped, wiped, bombed, blasted, wasted. *Quack*], but they felt that something had gone wrong with the nice — if eccentric — pudgy little fellow who'd drifted into town a couple of years before. But as the citizenry-at-large of Calvary drifted away from his elocutions, members of The Brothers of Jesus gravitated to them.

Then Noam discovered drugs. Or, rather, Noam discovered the generosity of Nytibia, who seemed to be a walking illicit pharmacy. Under her tutelage (which consisted mostly of, "Aw, c'mon, honey, can't we both have a little fun?"), he smoked pot (which made him feel lightheaded, giddy and hungry for the twenty-nine-cent "fried pies" in wax paper envelopes they sold at the local Piggly-Wiggly in Calvary), ate magic mushrooms (which allowed him, after wrenching vomiting, to imagine a whole weekend's worth of 1930s movies that, in his impoverished childhood, he'd missed), sucked up into his nose a little bit of the white powder Nytibia carried around in an antique gold cigarette case in her patent leather purse (which allowed him, for a couple of hours, to keep up with the undulations of Nytibia's carrot-tufted body in bed) and, once, even let Nytibia jab him in the crook of his arm with a syringe filled with heroin diluted in spring water (which allowed him to do absolutely nothing for a couple of hours without feeling anxious or guilty about it).

This isn't bad, Noam thought. A little bit of heaven

right here on earth. Certain of the contraband energized his street preaching (which, increasingly, incorporated the dogma of The Brothers of Jesus at the expense of specific references to the biblical Jesus and any scriptural quotations pertaining thereto). It also encouraged him to feel loose, friendly, talkative, and mentorly in The Brothers of Jesus's storefront, among its members.

Over time, Noam honed his preferences in drugs. After the first poke and doze, he rejected the needle, although Nytibia continued to chip smack. Although he found that cocaine didn't agree with his own metabolism or idea of how to pace a day, he found that The Brothers of Jesus's members rather liked it; Noam started passing around short snorts from the packet Nytibia hid in the springs under the front seat of her Ford Victoria hardtop. (When Nytibia found out, she threw a screeching fit, screaming at Noam just how hard it would be to get more shipped up from friends in Los Angeles; Noam said calm down, in the long run the cocaine would do them more good indebting The Brothers of Jesus's members to them.) What Noam found he liked for casual, daily use was simply a little marijuana. [Goofy bush, pot, weed, hemp, mary jane, bong. *Quack.*]

For the big occasions, however, for meditation before major sermons to the leaders, Noam turned to the mushrooms. Over the same time during which he fared and trued his personal preferences, Noam began to advocate to The Brothers of Jesus's leaders the use of natural psychedelics. Noam Sain told his de facto followers that natural psychedelics had taught him in an instant, "Why the Pyramids were built, why Rome fell, why Auschwitz, why the H-bomb, and, personally, why the balloon bomb." Noam Sain told them, "On a mass scale, if people were able to break free from the deadlocks of history, then the whole of history itself, from the Pyramids to my arrival in Calvary, would become just a couple of footnotes in time."

One day, higher than a kite, he put it to the leaders: Minister Noam Sain must be made unequivocal, omni-

potent leader of The Brothers of Jesus, over all other leaders, over all members, over, perhaps, even the Jesus they
pretended to worship. "If this seems like totalitarianism to
you, then I say that totalitarianism is merely premature
holism," Noam said, adding that totalitarianism would be
necessary to protect The Brothers of Jesus from what Noam
had decided — under the influence of one exotic toxin or
another — was the an imminent and unavoidable nuclear
war.

The Brothers of Jesus, Noam said, would henceforth
have to devote itself to the building of a massive bunker
beneath the small mountain whose apron commenced some
two miles north-northeast of the rickety screen door on
the storefront. Members of The Brothers of Jesus who balked
in the slightest at a command to psychedelicize themselves,
who hesitated a second to submit to his complete and unquestioned authority, would be denied space in the mountain bunker. Anyone who openly resisted his authority,
Noam decreed, would be exiled into the evil secular world.

In much the same way that the absolute leader of an
entire near-equatorial nation goes by the rank of Colonel
even though he's the commander-in-chief of a bristling
little army whose corps is generously stuffed with generals,
Noam went by the rank of Bishop. (Nytibia, with no title,
was the de facto second-in-command.) Noam ran The
Brothers of Jesus like a field marshal, controlling its members, individually and en masse, through the disbursement
and withholding of psychedelics. (Nytibia controlled a
considerable chunk of Noam's control, albeit indirectly,
through the opening, kinking, and reopening of the wholesale, as it were, channel of drugs through her connection in
Los Angeles.

At times, Noam wanted desperately to unleash the
powers of illicit brain chemistry among the members and
Nytibia would say, "Sorry, dear, there's no shipment due
until a week from Wednesday." Sometimes Noam would
say that he thought the members should be cut off for a

while, and Nytibia, lying back on the bed, picking her teeth with a syringe needle, would say, "Honey, it's piling up and you wouldn't want it to spoil on the shelf, would you?" Sometimes they agreed.

Most of the members of The Brothers of Jesus had little money, personally. But what they had, they pooled, and lived austerely from it. That is, until Noam assumed control. Members who had parents or savings accounts or husbands or brothers earning on the outside were urged to write home (first and safest choice), phone home (second and merely tolerable choice) or go home (last resort) to request some extra cash. Noam gave what he raked in to Nytibia, who socked some away in The Brothers of Jesus's vault (a little safe ordered by catalog from a firm in Salt Lake City), bought provisions by sending low-level members into Calvary to buy the cheapest food the Piggly-Wiggly had to offer, and spent the rest on Los Angeles drugs.

There was no money to be made, however, in re-dealing the drugs outside The Brothers of Jesus's confines; in terms of intoxicants, Calvary was a flinty, straightforward town whose residents preferred abstinence, hard liquor in straight shots, or six-packs of beer hauled around under the seats of pickup trucks, to rarer forms of consciousness-alterers. Besides, the residents of Calvary were by and large law-and-order folk, who would have turned in any peddler of narcotics as soon as they saw money and powder/weed/capsules change hands. And who might have dispensed rough justice on the spot.

So The Brothers of Jesus stole a couple of primitive computers from the agency. [Because, speaking computerwise, these were primitive times. *Quack.*] The theft wasn't difficult. The Brothers of Jesus stole them from a peripheral warehouse inside the barbed wire, where security was thinnest. The agency didn't miss them — as it didn't miss a lot of materiel that was lost, misplaced, filched by employees, or ruined by blowing sand — for months. On the other hand, The Brothers of Jesus had no hope of fencing the machines. So they got high and played with them.

A couple of The Brothers of Jesus were runaway graduate students in fledgling university departments of computer science, so they quickly figured out how to operate the machines. A little rewiring, a spare part here and there, a bootleg printed circuit, and some other electronic razzle-dazzle, and — The Brothers of Jesus discovered — the machines could actually be used to construct fairly sophisticated programs.

Gradually, most of the leaders of The Brothers of Jesus — its corpulent Bishop included — learned how to do more than simply toggle the machines on and off. Bishop Noam Sain took to programming especially well; he learned Fortran IV in a single day, a couple of other languages in a week, and soon loved to pull up a chair in the back room of the storefront, plant his puckered little rear end on it, and peer smiling over the shoulders of the bright former graduate students as they played the keyboards like castanets and the screens on the monitors flickered like meteor showers in a swamp green sky.

The most salient product of all The Brothers of Jesus's frantic computing was a program which would, in theory, predict the end of the world. The program was thought by the programmers within The Brothers of Jesus to be able to, in the words of one of them, "project a model of the consciousness of humanity" forward to a date derived from the Mayan calendar (in spite of its name, The Brothers of Jesus, under Noam, was nothing if not historically ecumenical), the equivalent of the year 2024 A.D. The imparting of the what, how, and why of this date to the members of The Brothers of Jesus, Noam and his programmers believed, would take the place of drugs. It would, to invoke Noam's phrase, "electro-psychedelicize" them. Then, The Brothers of Jesus could go about the business of "electro-psychedelicizing" the entire human race.

Once humanity — or a goodly part of it (or, being realistic, Noam thought, maybe a couple of hundred thousand people not previously members of The Brothers of Jesus) — was properly transformed, he and The Brothers of Jesus could go on to the second phase: a program that would actually find God, and speak to him, ask him to hasten the date of doom, or to extend it, or, if that seemed best to everyone concerned, leave it exactly the same. Noam and the elite within The Brothers of Jesus promised each other that they would bust their asses to get it done. They settled for a name for their project: "Time Wave Zero." Nice sound to it, thought Noam, especially if — no, *when* — it works.

However euphonious its name, "Time Wave Zero's" cataclysmic ambition was to stop time, at least cybernetically. For that, Noam figured, The Brothers of Jesus would have to come up with some women programmers — recruit them, grow them, something. Noam thought women programmers essential because their sensual femaleness was inherently anti-linear. Their very natures allowed them to slip in and out of time — emotionally now, intellectually if properly trained. If that ability could somehow be harnessed to the keyboard, The Brothers of Jesus would truly be in the eternity business. One day, Noam announced to the gathered members of The Brothers of Jesus, "A particular focus of my work is the enlightenment of women."

Those enlightened women, Noam decreed, would no longer be allowed to indulge in oral sex (or, more accurately, indulge their men in oral sex, except during services in the storefront). Furthermore, Noam decreed, ritual fellation could take place in the storefront only if he, as Bishop, observed and consecrated the act. The reason Noam had to be present (Noam felt it necessary to give reasons, once in a while, behind his decrees) was that male orgasm during fellatio not only altered the perception (on the part of the fellatee, of course) of the body in time, but actually altered the body's physical presence in time. Who else but the Bishop — a veteran of two mysterious displacements in the temporal flow — was so eminently qualified to see if the bodies of the fellator and — playing the longshot — fellatee changed in any way during the act.

"What about cunnilingus?" some members (a few suddenly plucky women and a couple of quizzical men) asked. So Noam gave a sermon on the subject.

"Dear Brothers of Jesus," he said to the gathered faithful, "my message to you today is of the most supreme spiritual significance. In the life of this holy fellowship, There are few concerns closer to the heart of our Lord than the love that can exist — that does exist, that must exist! — between the glorious men and women who are his chosen children. Basking in the light of true knowledge of the Lord's ways, we of The Brothers of Jesus have righteously disavowed the outside world's satanic conventions of marriage. We know there is a holier way!

"Our holier way follows the Lord's path in the mysterious sea of time. Our way delves not only to the heart of the bond between the Lord's chosen men and woman who have seen his wisdom and have been called to the furtherest rim of The Great High Desert in order to secede from the outside world and better serve the Lord, but it penetrates to the core of the Lord's ecstasy itself.

"The man has seed, does he not?"

(The congregation, scooching around in their folding chairs, answered in small waves of assenting grunts.)

"And the release of the man's seed into the woman is a holy act, is it not?"

(More amens, but sounding only tentatively convinced.)

"But when the man's seed is released into the woman's lower realm, where it mingles with her eggs, and causes flesh to produce but more flesh, bone to produce but more bone, blood to produce but more blood, holiness is tempered. There have been those among the Elevated Masters who have even said that holiness, in seed release into the lower female, is mitigated, canceled, struck down!

"Why is holiness thus compromised?

(Noam allowed the question to sink in.)

"Because the Lord is timeless. He came before Time, he created Time, He wants his chosen children to be able to conquer Time. He wants us to be holy by being able to exist — even for a moment or two — outside the Time that ends in death. He wants to rescue us from the Time-bound sin of our own creation and elevate us, moment by moment, meditation by meditation, act of love by act of love, into the timeless. But, in the act of love, should the man's seed meet the woman's egg and create, in an instant, more flesh, bone and blood, time in the human sense, vulgar time, time of the flesh, one-dimensional time streams helplessly forward, like a muddy rivulet running down a weathered hill. The flesh of both the man and the woman goes dumbly forward, into another sin that will create another being who will have to be rescued by the Lord from the mad river of human time.

"But when the seed of the man enters the mouth of the woman, enters that holy orifice by which she speaks the word of the Lord, there is no such impurity. The man is transported at the moment of his release into the woman's most holy orifice into the realm of the timeless. Every man-Brother has felt that moment. Your Bishop has seen to it. Your Bishop continues to feel that moment, not only in his own holy acts, but in observing yours. You, gentle children of the Lord, have seen to that.

"Ah, but the woman, what does the woman feel? The woman swallows the life of the man in that timeless moment, and thereby takes possession of his timelessness herself. For the woman, there is no greater reward.

"But some have asked your Bishop — and I say and have always said, be not afraid to ask! — if there is another moment of timelessness for the woman, one in which the man places his most holy orifice upon her mundane cavity and causes the woman to feel a moment of being lost in time. But, dear children of the Brothers of Jesus, this moment is counterfeit, an illusion, a mere instant of divergence in the secular river of time.

"Only the man, not the woman, can release.

"Only the man, not the woman, can direct his seed away from flesh creating but flesh, bone creating but bone, and blood creating but blood.

"Only the man, not the woman, can cross, can swim upstream, can even redirect the secular river of time.

"Only the man can thus please the Lord who watches over The Brothers of Jesus.

"But, dear children, it is only the woman who can receive the man, who can welcome him with her mouth, who can call him into this service to the Lord. It is only the woman who can feel the full magnificence of the man as he creates a moment outside of time in the service of the Lord.

"And, it is only the woman who has been given by the Lord the ability to take the fluid representation of that moment into her own body through her most holy orifice. It is only the woman who can receive it, digest it, and convert it into her own flesh.

"Perhaps, in the infinite wisdom of the Lord, there is reserved for the woman, and not the man, an ultimate moment outside of time when all of the seed of the man's timelessness that she has taken within herself will transport her physical body once and for all beyond the bounds of time. Even I, your Bishop, do not know if that will be the case. I await the Lord's message to me. I await a sign.

"So, dear children of The Brothers of Jesus, as I perform my holy duties as Bishop, as I observe you in your holy couplings manifested in the proper circumstances within the sacred commandments of our fellowship, I await a sign. I await the transference of your physical bodies beyond the bounds of Time.

"If it happens — and I believe our Lord wants it to happen — I will see it! Yes, I will see it, and I will proclaim it to all the world! I will proclaim how the holy men and women of The Brothers of Jesus have joined our Lord in conquering time!

"Go, and await with me. The Lord is with you, holy Brothers of Jesus.

"But do not go away from our fellowship. One step outside this holy ground, one word outside The Brothers of Jesus, one false thought that shows itself to our Lord or his representative on Earth, your Bishop, and you are cast into the secular river of time whose only outcome is in the lake of death.

"Amen!"

Short, but effective, thought Noam, stepping from behind the cheap, mahogany-veneer lectern that served as the storefront pulpit.

What a crock of shit, thought Nytibia, sitting in a rearmost folding chair, filing her nails.

A tweedy, diminutive, mustachioed art historian, Rose Madder (the first name was an old southern — specifically Robeson County — family eccentricity) lived in a bed-sitting room in London. He supported himself by forging and selling fake John Singer Sargent paintings. He didn't do very well by this trade as, at that time, there was a limited market for Sargent. Madder lived frugally, and he also lived in fear. He was on the lam from certain people in the United States.

This is why Rose Madder fled:

In 1954, he was living in a furnished room in Washington, D.C.. He was at that time an "independent scholar" (meaning, an art historian who couldn't get himself a university teaching job) at work on a dual biography of Dieric Maender and John Singer Sargent. The premise of Madder's unusual dual biography was that there was a previously unknown but exquisitely subtle, barely perceptible connection between the two painters. It was Madder's ambition to have his dissertation prove this highly improbable connection, to have the dissertation published by a legitimate art-book house, and to have professors eventually say that "Madder has caused us to rethink the entire field of comparative biography."

Madder did much of his research in the National Archives and in the Library of Congress. In the latter, he came upon indirect evidence of a baffling American appearance of a Dieric Maender painting. The evidence indicated that the picture was once owned by the American religious visionary [I'd say kook, but have it your way. *Quack*], William Halliwell.

More astounding, Madder had the very painting in his possession. He came about it by stealing it from the National Gallery of Art, where it hung (donated anonymously by a soldier just home from occupied Germany) in the guise of a painting which was painted, according to its label, by an unknown artist, presumed French or Belgian, somewhere around 1930. The roughly two-foot by three-foot painting was by and large abstract, although, to the initiated viewer, a small area, a kind of gutter, across the bottom, revealed traces of human feet, shod in the manner of fifteenth-century Flanders, and a few folds of gold-encrusted robe, reportedly worn by high-ranking clerics of the time.

The painting had hung in a rather neglected and under-attended gallery, devoted to early European modernism in the low countries, within the museum. Madder noticed it one day on a stroll he took through the museum to clear his head of the throbbing with which serious research pained him. Something about it — he could never say exactly what — attracted him. Perhaps the color: an overall silvery grey that modulated into dirty, but not unappealing browns, at the periphery. Perhaps the paint application: delicate palette-knifing, as though a particularly sensitive plasterer had been trying to cover a crack in an historically landmarked wall. Perhaps the proportions: comfortingly placid and horizontal, on a small scale, as reassuring as the silhouette of an old briefcase. Whatever the case, Madder stared at the painting long enough to realize it might be the missing Maender his research indicated might exist.

That night, in its absence, Madder found the painting strangely addictive. The picture called to him like the ghost of an old lover in a B-movie. He returned to it (neglecting his research) the next day, and again the day after that, and again and again, every day for a week, basking in the reaffirmation it offered that the Maender-Sargent connection was no figment of his imagination. The painting told Madder he was a genius.

Madder decided he had to have the painting with him, at least while he completed his book. Later, most likely, he'd find a way to return it. But, for the moment, he concentrated on finding a way to remove it from the National Gallery.

He came to the gallery near closing time, wearing a bulky, baggy herringbone coat with a homemade, over-sized pouch on each side of the lining. On one side — in the pouch open only at the top, like a conventional pocket — he carried two collapsible umbrellas which looked deceptively like the uncollapsible English variety, a thin sheet of tinny steel, and a metal coaster. The two umbrellas were of wildly different colors, one a bright red, the other a dull green. The dull green one had a wooden handle which had been perforated, drilled out, filled with molten lead, allowed to cool, and then resealed. In the other — which opened completely on the top and along one edge by means of snaps — he carried a linen bag and a conspicuously large guidebook, *The Wonderful Museums of Our Nation's Capital*. Madder made a show of checking the collapsed red umbrella, asking three or four unnecessary questions about the number of his checking tab, whether or not a tip was required, and how soon before the museum closed did the coat check counter shut down.

In a momentarily unpatrolled section of hallway between two galleries, Madder placed the metal sheet on the
floor and propped the uncollapsed (or, rather, re-extended)
dull green umbrella over it, its heavy handle leaning against
the wall and its tip resting on the coaster on the floor. Then
he hurried to the gallery where his beloved Maender was
hanging. When (as Madder had test-timed it at home, on
his bathroom's museum-like tile floor) the coaster, under
the pressure of the leaning umbrella, gradually slid outward from the base of the wall, causing the weighted handle
of the umbrella to crash with a tenor clang upon the metal
plate, the nearest guard to him, and the handful of guards
nearest, in turn, to that guard, rushed in the direction of
the noise, Madder sprang for the painting.

In a second, he covered it with the linen bag. In a few
more, he'd unsnapped his right-side pouch and slipped the
guidebook out and the painting in. In a few more after
that he was walking — rapidly, but pseudononchalantly —
back toward the coat check counter and the exit. He carried the guidebook, open and flapping, with the hand on
the side of his jacket where the painting was stashed. He
leaned against the coat check counter and made an equal
show of retrieving his red umbrella and of holding open
the guidebook. Madder's hope was that anyone who noticed him would notice, not the strangely rigid right-hand
side of his jacket, but rather the open and flapping guidebook. His ancillary hope was that anyone who remembered him in the museum on the day of the falling-um-
brella incident and the day the minor abstraction was stolen would remember him checking and retrieving a bright
red umbrella.

Madder walked out of the National Gallery of Art the
de facto owner of the Dieric Maender painting. He kept
the painting and worked on it — fussing with Q-Tips and
solvents — in his room. Trying to repaint the painting into
some approximation of what (he imagined) it must have
been like when it last left Maender's easel, drove Madder

to a state of frustration and near-madness. But the picture defied him at every turn; each morning, no matter what Madder had accomplished with his little brushes and paints the previous night, the painting would be exactly the same as when he first saw it on the wall of the National Gallery of Art.

Of course, Madder was never completely unsuspected. The National Gallery tended him a polite phone call, asking him to drop in, should he be pleased to, and advise them on how to handle a somewhat indelicate matter involving the disappearance of a minor work of art that was, nevertheless, part of the nation's cultural patrimony. Madder did drop in, twitched his thin moustache, pretended to be interested, as a patriotic American, in the problem, told a foolproof (in his own estimation) story indicating (if that was what they wanted to draw from it) that he couldn't have possibly been involved, managed, however, to convince everyone in the room that he most certainly was the perpetrator, and left.

The FBI surveilled him. It surreptitiously entered Madder's room, looking for the stolen abstraction. But all the agents could find was an old-looking religious painting, depicting Jesus Christ, his mother, and a few oddly dressed rich folks and a cleric of its era, resting on a desk easel, being restored. Cleaning and retouching, the invaders concluded, was what Madder did to support himself.

When Madder — who was fearful and obsessive enough to close a hair seal between his front door and its frame each morning he left for the National Gallery or the Library of Congress or the National Archives — discovered his premises had been violated, he packed up and left for England. Rose Madder took the religious painting — in his uninspected baggage — with him to London. But when he opened his full-sized bag (after living out of a small satchel for a couple of weeks in a hotel) in his modest bedsitting room, it had been transformed (once again) into a geometric abstraction.

London being the capital of a foreign country, the agency took over the surveillance of Madder. But they were more interested in Madder's secondary interest (merely off-handedly footnoted in the FBI reports) in early aviation (especially the experimental flights of Serge Protector over Calvary, Idaho, early in the century) and high-altitude flying (especially some hand-written notes, obviously transcribing second-hand descriptions, concerning Matt Medium's flights in the "wingless" aircraft over the same town in Idaho).

The agency, too, stealthily broke into Madder's quarters. It saw the painting he'd stolen from the National Gallery in the United States but, even though it had reverted to its circa-1930 configuration, didn't recognize it as the work noted on the National Gallery's theft report to the FBI (the bureau occasionally paid a price for so jealously guarding the particulars of its files.) It also saw the "Sargents" that Madder was producing for income. Admirable, but nothing criminal as far as they were concerned (the agency couldn't tell a Sargent from a soup can, so it had no idea the works were attempting to counterfeit anything). Instead of arresting Madder (which they had no legal power to do, but which they could have easily pulled off on sheer bluster and intimidation), the agency recruited him, and began to contrive a way to plant him in Idaho.

★ ★ ★ ★ ★

Almost as soon as Noam had pronounced himself Bishop and started slipping off to the storefront to witness the bouts of ritual cocksucking, Nytibia Barbosell started telling nearly everyone she could buttonhole in The Brothers of Jesus that it was she, not Noam, who had the meta-physical ears of such exotic and (until recently, among the

Brothers, unfamiliar) Elevated Masters of the Ages as El
Malya, Master Shine-o-Light and Oromantis. She also possessed, she assured them, open "tunnels" to such familiar
departed (or, for all anybody knew, undeparted) souls as
the Archangel Michael, Shakespeare, Buddha, Pope John
XXIII, and Jesus Christ himself.

When Noam Sain objected to her self-aggrandizing
mysticism, she said to him, "All you have to do is take the
title and lead; the followers will follow." In other words:
If you don't like the competition, act like a real Bishop
instead of whining to me. When he objected that this sort
of jockeying between them would harm the spiritual integrity of The Brothers of Jesus, she said to him, "The blood
of Christ is money; this is a business." In other words: Since
when has this flea-bitten congregation of frumps and failed
lumberjacks had any spiritual integrity? Survival is the first
order of business here. When he reminded her that she was
his white-robed amanuensis in the salvation of The Brothers of Jesus, she said to him, "I'm not somebody's savior;
this is a business." Noam gave up the argument. He thought
Nytibia's delusions would somehow run their course.

They didn't. In fact, she upped the ante. Nytibia claimed
that she, and not the Pope, was the true Vicar of Christ and
the leader of the Catholic Church in absentia. She said
that if The Brothers of Jesus would follow her teachings,
they would eventually — and not that far down the line —
inherit the Vatican. Then she said that the women in The
Brothers of Jesus were no longer required to fellate the
men. *Au contraire,* the men would henceforth be required
to perform cunnilingus on the women at intervals to be
decided by her, forthwith. And she wouldn't need to watch.

Her campaign worked. The women bought cunnilin-
gus; the men bought the possibility of coming into all the
Vatican's goodies. Who knew: maybe there'd be beatified
computers in those Roman vaults. On December 4, 1967,
Nytibia Barbosell informed the former Bishop of The
Brothers of Jesus, Noam Sain, that he had twenty-four hours

to clean out his pulpit and be gone over the horizon of Calvary. The word around the storefront, dorm and tunnel was: so sayeth Nytibia, and so goeth Noam.

The dust hadn't yet settled on Noam's exile, when Nytibia began to issue a flurry of theological decrees of her own. She decreed that Hell is movement, and that Heaven is an immovable anchor in time and space. The Brothers of Jesus henceforth believed that pretending to move is one way of defeating movement; acting is the best form of pretending. The Brothers of Jesus henceforth believed that preachers are actors, and that while actors may not exactly lie, what they do is not really telling the truth, either. The Brothers of Jesus believed that spies (like Matt Medium flying overhead; Nytibia didn't miss too many tricks) are, in a disturbing way, superior to preachers because preachers and actors know nothing beyond the not-truth that they're telling. Spies do know something beyond it. What they know is a secret (that they're spies, if nothing else) that they're not telling.

One prescient male member of The Brothers of Jesus (they weren't all stupid) said to another smart one, *soto voce,* "She's obviously a good actress or a psychotic, and she's probably a fake. But she sure is a spellbinder." You're right, the other one thought. They both knew that from Nytibia's own teaching: Though facts are often false, spells are always real.

The Last of the Moccasins

Besides my boots and jeans and the T-shirt I was wearing, all I had when I went over the wall were a coat, a flashlight, and a Buck knife. And I was lucky to have them, considering how fast I made my getaway from The Brothers of Jesus.

I lived out in the wild, in an arc beyond the town, beyond the last outlying shack, beyond the agency base for eight days. It felt like an eternity. And my surviving it was just about a miracle, considering what I knew — or, more accurately, didn't know — about the great outdoors. My father may have raised the world's greatest hothouse jock, but I was still Gym Boy, not Daniel Boone. My father trained me to be tough for sports, but he didn't teach me anything about being tough against nature. In fact, he really didn't teach me anything at all about how to be a man. I needed civilization, such as civilization was in Calvary.

Sure, the reason I left The Brothers of Jesus was that I was scared of them — in a dull and creepy kind of way. But I was outright scared shitless of being in the wild by myself. I'm big and strong and fast and mean when I want to be, but I'm very afraid of the dark, afraid of animals, afraid of little bugs and things that I can't see that crawl around on the ground and under it. But for about a week, at least, I did pretty well by making it up as I went along.

Water I got from dew runoff and a few puddles. At first, I just drank from my hands and licked my fingers, but then I found a discarded plastic bag blowing through the brush and used it to collect the moisture. I cracked a rock in half on another rock to make a kind of hand shovel, and dug a little sleeping pit with it. Some brush in the bottom, and the coat over the top of me, and I could sleep in fits through the night. Sometimes, I swear, there were cold noses with hot breath poking in under the coat to see if I was worth eating. I was too terrified to move. I would have panicked if I ever felt teeth on my jeans, but I never did.

Food was harder to come by than water. I chased a couple of rabbits and tried to hit 'em with stones, but came up empty-handed. Eventually, I got a bird — wounded it, and then had to whack its head on a rock to kill it — but it took so long, and its death was so grisly that even during a couple of days when I was practically starving, I couldn't bring myself to hunt any more birds.

What I did do, ultimately, was to break into my parents' house. It wasn't too difficult. I'm surprisingly — well, maybe not surprisingly — fluid in movement and light on my feet, and efficient in the dark as long as it's indoors. I knew the house well — if not perfectly — from memory. And, face it, my father, for all his athleticism, was never what you'd call sensitive. He never rose above being an agency goon. He slept like a fucking rock.

Mom was different, at least when I was a kid. She just loved me and hugged me and patted me on the head and then just let my father have his way with me. She never had more children; maybe she just didn't want to produce more gymnasium fodder for my father. For whatever reason, she gradually lost her wake-and-warn instincts as a mother. She remained asleep in her room, my father in his, and I had my run of the goddamned house for a couple of hours.

The cash take, as I remember, was $236.40 from stashes in sock drawers and in the proverbial cookie jar mom thought was a clever ruse because it was so obvious. Little did she foresee that when she was finally burgled, it'd be her own goddamned son, who knew the secrets. I also picked up a couple of tarps from the tool cabinet in the mud room, an axe, a five-gallon gas can with barely a half-

gallon sloshing in the bottom, and a ratty blanket that
smelled like dog shit. We never had a dog when I was a kid.
Now, I guessed, they had a dog.

Actually, I froze in my tracks when I smelled the blanket: Maybe the goddamned dog was a watchdog and my
ass was up a creek!, I thought. It turned out they didn't
have one, or if they did it slept as deeply as my father. So I
made a stop at the fridge on the way out. I put the blanket
around my shoulders and spread it, with my hip and one
arm, to keep too much light from coming out of the fridge.
But I probably didn't need to worry that much. Nobody
in that house moved besides me.

A couple of days later, early in the morning as soon as
the stores opened, I walked into downtown Calvary, carrying my ill-gotten gains. A couple of hundred bucks could
go a long way in Idaho in 1976.

First thing, I bought a razor and some brushless shaving creme and shaved in the Mobil station restroom. A guy
my size can scare people into calling the police just by
showing up with stubble. Then I went back to the drug-
store for a bunch of toiletries: soap, shampoo, deodorant,
toilet paper, toothbrush, toothpaste, dental floss, fingernail
kit, Vaseline, and some antiseptic.

My stomach was still empty — the last thing I'd eaten
was the last half of a sandwich my mother'd made for my
father's lunch the next day (or so I surmised). I was nervous, fidgety, weak from no food, but too jumpy to start off
my mission with a cup of strong black coffee, which was
what I really wanted.

The sales clerk at Keller's Hardware & Outdoor Supplies didn't recognize me as my father's prodigal kid, which
was how I'd hoped it'd work out if I came in very early,
before all that local hobnobbing and asking after people's
relatives started. So I calmed down, and methodically
bought — checking for price and quality like a real citizen
with nothing to hide — a pup tent, sleeping bag, parka,
two pairs of off-brand jeans, two flannel shirts, a six-pack

of hiking socks, some flashlight batteries, and a big canvas duffel to put everything in. I could have used a Coleman stove, but I didn't have enough money.

I walked out of Calvary in the opposite direction of The Brothers of Jesus's storefront and that fake Peace Corps Training center where my father worked for the agency. I wanted to be, to put it mildly — on the opposite side of town — out past the high school. I walked for maybe, I don't know, two hours. (Actually, yes, I do know. I've walked the distance since then, many times, and the average time it took me was about two hours and ten minutes. I figure I was walking about twelve-minute miles, so I must have gotten about ten miles out of town. Actually, there's no need to estimate; I've measured the distance precisely on the Beemer's odometer, and it's always ten-point-six, ten-point-seven. I don't know why I prefer to estimate, even when I know the right goddamned number. Must have something to do with a fear of the truth).

I came to a place I just liked for some reason (it was close to the road, you could see everybody, a little nestled in some miniature hills, dry, domed where I thought of bedding down and probably well-drained, and with just a bit of tree and bush cover) and turned off the road.

I ended up homesteading it, after a fashion. I didn't know whether it was private land, government land, land open to the public, or, perhaps, simply unclaimed land. I cleared an area maybe ten yards square, set up my pup tent, and took a nap. When I woke up, I ate some more of my parents' food, and found a good place to store my stuff (including the tent, rolled up, so nobody could tell from the road that anybody was living there). Then I left again for town.

At a gas station just before town, I saw a farmer about my father's age, maybe a little younger, filling his pickup truck with gas. I walked up to talk to him. He squinted and smiled and said I looked familiar. Instead of trying to bullshit him, and saying I was just drifting through or something, I just let him look at me until he satisfied himself he couldn't really place the resemblance. We kind of got along, if that's what you can call it. He hired me to do some day labor on his farm.

It turned out he needed me for three weeks, and let me bunk there most of the time. He paid me a hundred bucks when I left, and told me I'd done five hundred dollars worth of good. I said to him if he felt he owed me something, he should tell the same thing to his friends. I ended up getting a lot of work from the farmer's friends, and made a real fistful of money — enough, at least, to buy a walk-in tent, that Coleman stove, and an old Harley off a skinny young kid who'd broken his leg on it, was scared to death of the thing, and wanted it out of his sight.

I had to time my trips in and out of Calvary so that I didn't meet anybody from The Brothers of Jesus. Not that anybody in it had ever threatened me directly; I was probably too big and strong for that, and they didn't seem to have guns around. (But who knows what kind of arms they had squirreled away?) Still, I thought I couldn't be too careful with them. And then, of course, there were my mother and father. I didn't want to meet up with either of them.

So I gave myself a real bad short haircut. The last time they saw me, or, I figured, the last time, they saw a picture of me, I had hair down to my shoulders. And I let my beard start to grow. Except for some muttonchop sideburns in my ABA days, I'd always been clean-shaven. On the days I wasn't working for some farmer or rancher, my object was to get into town, get my provisions, and get the hell back out to my tent.

Eventually, people did notice me out there by the highway. A few cars and pickups slowed down to get a look at this burly guy puttering around a big blue tent. But they did no more — in just a few cases — than stop. Couples and families with a couple of kids stared at me through their car windows and then moved on. Funny, they were in rolling cages, and I was out free, but they thought I was the animal in the zoo and they were the ones at liberty. Fine, I thought, as long as they just drove away. For all the angry things I could say about Calvary and its inhabitants, I have to admit they do tend to leave a person alone.

I lived that way for a long time, minding my own business (save for the businesses of the people I worked for), and having other people mind theirs. The Brothers of Jesus did whatever they did, and I did what I did. Actually, I know a lot about "whatever they did," but that's not for here.

My father was either so caught up in his work for the agency that he never heard about the six-foot-five guy living near the highway a few miles outside of town, or he heard about the guy and dismissed it, or he knew who it was and decided not to venture out to visit me. I don't care which reason it was. The result was the result, as the Werner Erharders say. And I was happy with it.

My big mistake might have been trading up for the Beemer. If I hadn't gotten the really good bike, then I wouldn't have been going to the Calvary High School Games. Actually, my bigger mistake was thinking that money could buy happiness. That was an especially absurd idea to come to a guy who'd blown off a few hundred thousand a year and a pro basketball career to sleep on the floor in a cult, and who had then blown off the cult to live by the side of a road.

But I had started making a lot of money. By that I mean, I was making more money than I needed for my bare upkeep. I mean compared to my upkeep. A few months after I got away from The Brothers of Jesus, I was probably making — pro-rated, you understand — a few thousand a year from farm labor, ranch work, nightclub bouncing and bartending at the few shabby cinderblock roadhouses around here that the stupid local kids tried to convince themselves were discos, a little security work, and some bill collecting that I readily admit was strong-arm stuff.

Well, it was potentially strong-arm. Even farmers and ranchers and local merchants get bad debts and bad debt-ors, and a few of them hired me to just drop around on the people who owed money and to ask them, nicely, if they'd hurry up and pay it back. I never hurt anybody; I just scared a few people by showing up on my Harley, beard grown down to my second plaid-shirt button and my head shaved as close as a convict's, at least a half a foot taller than they were, and reminding them they were a little late on their repayment schedules.

My outgo was minuscule; I could get by on a hundred a month if I had to. So, avoiding the local banks like the plague, I had a big sackful of twenties and fifties buried out back of the tent.

When I saw the BMW — a big ol' RS1000 shaft-drive with a full molded windscreen, modified cafe handlebars, and a flare seat (I didn't have anybody to put on the back, but it looked nice) — sitting out in somebody's front yard with a For Sale sign on it, something just popped into my head and told me it'd be nice to have a shiny new motor-cycle.

Actually, when I got the bike, I already had the Air-stream. That was a gift. A rancher I worked for had bought it with the idea of taking his whole family on extended vacations through the great American northwest. His kids grew into surly teenagers before he could let himself feel that everything on the ranch was well enough taken care of to leave for a month or five weeks. The idea of the four of them locked in constant familial combat inside that hot aluminum bubble didn't seem so attractive. He tried to sell the trailer, but couldn't get his price. His wife lorded it over him for buying the damned thing in the first place, and one of his kids liked to sneak out into it with a six-pack of beer and, one night, a girl. So, one day, quitting time, we were sitting on the back porch; the weather was nice, and the rancher wanted some company. His wife made some iced tea, brought it out, and sat with us. He turned to me in front of her, and asked, "You live in a tent, don't you."

I said yes.

He said, "Ever think of getting something better?"

I said like what, an apartment, in this town?

He said, "No, like that goddamned Airstream trailer that's just sitting around here so's Wyatt, my older, can sneak beer into it, get drunk, and try to snag some cheap pussy."

His wife slammed down her iced tea glass and stormed off. I asked what would he be asking for the trailer.

He thought for a minute and said, "Give the damned thing to you."

I said that he didn't really want to do that. I said he was probably just trying to make a point with his family, sort of cut off his nose to spite his face sort of thing. I said that he should think up a reasonable price and maybe I'd consider it.

He said, "No, I've been thinking about it for a long time. I want to get rid of it clean. I thought about just burning it, but then I'd be left with a lot of melted aluminum and a bunch of ashes on my hands. I thought of pushing it in a river or lake, but I've got too much respect for the land to do something dumb like that. I made up my mind to give it to somebody, but I couldn't think of anybody who deserved it until you came along. Besides, as far as I can tell, you need it. So take it."

So I said yes.

We hitched it right up to his big Dodge pickup and towed it to the site. We had to uncouple it on the shoulder of the highway and then pull it by hand across a little gully to where I wanted it. The rancher took the hitch end and I pushed the butt, but I almost wasn't strong enough to do it. That's when I realized that ever since Africa, I'd been getting not only soft in the head but weak in body, too. I made up my mind to get back into some kind of shape. There was no sentiment, no ceremony, when we were done. He just said, "Enjoy it in peace, kid," and drove off.

With something with rigid walls to live in, and a fast, dependable mode of transportation, I was practically a regular member of the respectable bourgeoisie again. Actually, the Beemer was more than just a way to get around. It was like me: too big, conspicuous. But oddly, with something conspicuous in itself to race around on, I didn't feel so noticeable myself. It was like hanging around with a friend who was as big and hairy as I was so people wouldn't notice me in particular. I started going into Calvary whenever I damned well felt like, saying to myself to hell with my father if I met up with him, to hell with The Brothers of Jesus if I meet up with any of them. As a matter of fact, I thought, to hell with anybody who looked at me cross-eyed.

I started going to the games at the high school. It was spring when I started wheeling around on the bike, so I went to baseball games.

High school baseball games are dull; even if they're exciting, they're dull. The game doesn't really give young guys with throbbing testicles any way to get their ya-ya's out. You swing at a pitch, you hit the ball way over there and some guy chases it while you run around the bases. It's all so indirect, so far away from the other guy you're really trying to smash. If you could hit the thing right back through the pitcher's gut, it'd be another thing. Basketball is O.K. You get to put moves on the guy guarding you, you get to go up over him and dunk it in his face, you get to pick his pocket on defense, and you get to send him into the first row of seats with a hip when you take a rebound away from him. But there's nothing like football for creaming somebody, for making the other guy a doormat. In sports there's always The Other Guy, clearly marked, with a whole different uniform, in different colors, than yours; sports is sanction to obliterate The Other Guy and not feel any guilt about it. I couldn't wait for football season.

The Calvary High School Fighting Christians played their games on Friday nights in the fall. In Calvary, the fall is wonderful. It's colder than most other places at the same time of year, but with none of the crap: no snow yet, very little rain, no low, grey clouds. It's just clear and sharp and amazingly bright. The shadows are like cracks on a full moon. At night, everything turns dark blue — not black, but still blue. The temperature drops even lower. Your breath makes little clouds in the night. Your evaporating sweat steams off your forearms like surf.

The first season, I just watched, quietly. I parked my bike beneath the bleachers — I didn't bother to lock it because after the opening game everyone knew who it belonged to and nobody would have touched it — and sat in the stands with a big Coke and a hotdog. The team stunk, so there wasn't much to cheer about. But the kids were still beautiful in those all-gold outfits with the big purple numbers piped in white. And they smashed into one another like crazy.

The second season was better; they were winning. That's why the incident probably happened.

It happened like this:

The second-to-last game of the regular season, the last home game of it, they'd only been tied once, and hadn't lost. They were playing that same school whose star basketball player, long ago, my father had once almost killed on the court. That school was even better than Calvary — unbeaten, untied, and had kicked the crap out of everybody they'd played. People said that this was the biggest game in the history of Calvary High School, which wasn't, of course, saying all that much. But the point is they were saying it, feeling it, and sitting in the packed stands on a frigid Friday night screaming their tiny little hearts out about it.

Cavalry was losing at the half. I forget what the score was, but they were behind by at least a couple of touchdowns, which meant that if they were going to win the game, they were going to have to transform themselves in the second half. They were going to have to start hitting the other guys real hard.

I got caught up in their desperation. Not that I care all that much about Calvary actually winning the game; no, what I cared about, or suddenly noticed, was that some of that same electricity was in the air, the same kind of buzzing, zapping, tingling all around me that I used to feel when I played basketball there. It's hard to explain, but it was like being in a huge field of sparklers, on the Fourth of July. I was surrounded by one big sizzle. Every breath I took in was prickly with anticipation. All those people were feeling it, so the players were feeling it, so I was feeling it. And I hadn't felt it in a long time.

But there was a worriedness, a slightly sour feeling, a nasty edge to the desperation in the atmosphere, too. These poor, dumb, helmeted golden angels, trotting back onto the field after some stupid speech in the locker room by their potbellied, sandpaper-voiced coach, looked a little lost. Their tight, pimpled faces glistened with greasy sweat. Their pale eyes looked hollow, like robins' eggshells above the crescents of black anti-glare greasepaint beneath them.

I saw the quarterback coming out of the gymnasium at the end of the field. He was trailing the team, which was clacking its cleats on asphalt as it made its way back toward the glowing grass. I could tell he was thinking, meditating even. I could tell he was spiraling downward inside, toward imagining defeat.

And then I saw something: a thin border of firelight around the profile of his golden uniform, like the tiniest-gauge red thread laid perfectly around his silhouette. It flickered. And I knew he had it. I knew he had the ability that I'd once had. If he could feel the heat, just for a millisecond, he could disappear, he could jump time, he could transcend this whole earthly plane. He might even win 'em the goddamned game.

I must have knocked over a couple of people when I

scrambled down out of the stands, because I heard some swear words behind me. And I must have violated some groundskeeper's rule or other because a couple of security guards started to run alongside me. But I just kept going and no one wanted to tackle me or pull a gun and arrest me.

The golden team parted before me like the Red Sea. The coach turned and stared, holding his clipboard limp at his side. I embraced the quarterback. I hugged the shit out of him. I put my big hands up on his helmet, palms over the earholes. I looked right into his wide, scared eyes. I could feel his frightened, warm breath in my face. I pulled him toward me, so close that my lips touched his cold face mask.

"You can do it!" I yelled. "You can stop the whole goddamned universe if you want to! You can find the crack in time and slip through it! You can defy time! You can, you can!"

Some kid on the team, from the safety of the back of the pack, said, "Who's he, some kind of fag?"

"Yeah," said somebody else, "a fag."

Then there was a chorus, which grew quickly louder, of words like "fag," "creep," "crazy asshole," and "screwball." Then I heard "How'd he get down here?" Get 'im outta here," "Get the cops," and "Where's security?" A hand fell on my shoulder. I turned, quite calmly, to look at it, and saw that the back of it was covered in liver spots, its wrist was manacled by a big metal wristwatch and band, and that it protruded from the sleeve of a policeman's jacket.

"I don't want any trouble," I said.

"I think you've already made some for yourself," the cop said, smiling with satisfaction. His other hand rested on the handle of his holstered gun. He tilted his head back in the direction of the stands, gesturing (I understood immediately) for me to listen. The crowd was taunting me, shouting insults, and laughing.

I broke and ran, heading for the back of the bleachers. A few of the Calvary players started after me but, I could see peripherally, were held back by the raised arm of their coach, clipboard in lofty hand. The cop, however, chased me, as did several civilians who poured out of the stands.

"That's the highway hermit!" somebody yelled.

"Get his ass!" somebody else said.

"Hell, let him go!" still somebody else said.

I cracked my head on a bleacher beam when I got to the bike, but I got the Beemer backed out onto the asphalt in plenty of time to straddle it before the crowd caught up. Some Coke ice somebody threw from the top hit my face. I throttled the bike. A little blood from the cut on my head coursed down my cheek and leached into my beard. I could taste it. Then I shot forward on the Beemer.

I almost lost the bike taking the left out onto the highway. The Beemer did a little fishtail "S" with me tilting at about forty-five degrees, but the rear wheel stayed with the road.

"Wheeeee-ha!" yelled somebody back in the stands. They hadn't forgiven me, but in an instant the whole event had been transformed for them into a lark, part of the Friday night fun. At least that was how it seemed to me, speeding away like a bat out of hell, running away and scared again for the second or third or fourth time in my life — I don't really know — which is a disgrace for a man my size. Anyway, I never looked back or went back to check it out. My enemies weren't the people in the crowd back there. My enemy, if I had one, was myself. I decided enough was enough: I would stay out on the highway and subdue him.

The next day, I started building the track.

Twenty Questions, Nineteen Answers

XXXXXXXXXXXXXXXXXXXXXXXXXXXXXXXXXXXXXXX

XXXXXXXXXXXXXXXXXXXXXXXXXXXXXXXXXXXXXXX

XXXXXXXXXXXXXXXXXXXXXXXXXXXXXXXXXXXXXXX

XXXXXXXXXXXXXXXXXXXXXXXXXXXXXXXXXXXXXXX

XXXXXXXXXXXXXXXXXXXXXXXXXXXXXXXXXXXXXXX

XXXXXXXXXXXXXXXXXXXXXXXXXXXXXXXXXXXXXXX
XXXXXXXXXXXXXXXXXXXXXXXXXXXXXXXXXXXXXXX
XXXXXXXXXXXXXXXXXXXXXXXXXXXXXXXXXXXXXXX
XXXXXXXXXXXXXXXXXXXXXXXXXXXXXXXXXXXXXXX
XXXXXXXXXXXXXXXXXXXXXXXXXXXXXXXXXXXXXXX
XXXXXXXXXXXXXXXXXXXXXXXXXXXXXXXXXXXXXXX
XXXXXXXXXXXXXXXXXXXXXXXXXXXXXXXXXXXXXXX

Quack quack quack. Quackity-quack. Quack. Oh Jesus, this again. Don't I ever learn? All right, take a breath, a deep breath. Breathe deep. Breathe deep, the gathering gloom. Inhale, exhale. That's it: in, out, one, two, three, pause. Be calm. Act normal. It's coming now: the calming calm. The calm before the norm. Speak normally now. Now, speak the norm. Norman Now. That's it, Mr. Now, now that you're here, in the here and now. Feet on the ground. Head held high. The giggle has landed. Don't laugh; laughing hurts. One small strepp for mankind. Pro-ceed. Hut! Hut! Column, ho! *Quack.* Breathe. Again. Breathe. Ahhh. That's it.

★ ★ ★ ★ ★

Billy, Billy, Billy.
Judy, Judy, Judy.
What the *fuck* is going on?
Where to begin, Billy?

Yours is a difficult job, yes, I understand, tying all this shit together. Look at what you've got: an old Flemish Primitive painting that comes and goes, sometimes as realism, sometimes as abstraction; a 19th century religious wacko (probably a redundant term, I'll concede); a brilliant immigrant boy who thinks with his dick; some dumb town in some godforsaken part of southern Idaho that's apparently too flat to be a ski resort and not rich enough to have a Mormon temple, named after the dirgiest site in Christendom; a pudgy little Southern preacher (with that punny name — is the dude *Black*, or what? No, he couldn't be; they'd have hung his ass in Oklahoma first time he came through, pinching housewives' butts) who seems to wind his evangelical way through the whole history of the late 20th century; the inimitable ol' Axis Sally herself; an ambitious Chicana secretary with a one-footed dad; a sort of Seven Brides for Seven Brothers cult that ends up being run by the Wicked Witch of the West with henna'd hair and a bumblebee Ford convertible; a couple of scientist-spies, or spy-scientists; vague allusions to the CIA (like they could actually *sue* you or something if you blew their cover); one precipitously retired professional jock and borderline head case who lives alone in an Airstream, rides an RS1000, and broods about his dad; and a lot of mucking about with the dimension of time, as if "disappearing" for a millisecond or two is the central miracle of consciousness that explains the ripped cheesecloth fabric of memory that everybody's life — right up to the moving-at-the-speed-of-light razor's edge of NOW — really is.

It's too much, Billy babe. You're simply trying to do too goddamned much. You're raising more questions than can possibly be answered. Want a list? Why not? This book is already full of fucking lists. It might as well include one of mine.

O.K., Billy: Take a piece of lined notebook paper. Number it one to thirty down the left-hand margin. Fold it vertically in the middle. Call the left-hand side "Column A," the right-hand side "Column B." And in the upper-right-hand corner, write "Page One." And better have a full tablet. Just kidding, amigo. Anyway, here we go.

First, I haven't got the tiniest clue about the house where William Halliwell first claps eyes on that fateful painting. I have to tell you, I'm not particularly entranced by a house in the middle of the upstate New York woods that seems like the dressed facade of Tara teleported from the back lot of M-G-M. Why is it there, out in the middle of the woods? Who built it? Why is it empty when Halliwell happens upon it? You should've dropped us a clue, Billy. Lord knows you've got clues to spare.

The painting itself is a whole other deal, but I find myself no more than superficially amused by the idea of a Northern Renaissance panel painting that pops up here, there, and everywhere in various guises: in Flanders in 1465, in upstate New York in 1815, in Calvary, Idaho, in 1911, in Germany from 1940 to 1945, in Calvary again in 1946, in Washington, D.C. in 1954, a quick trip to Old Blighty, and back in Calvary in the late 1970s. And that's just so far. Who knows what the hell, you've got in store? Well, all right, I know, but let's pretend.

And how the hell could William Halliwell tell instantly that what he saw was a painting? You, an over-educated rube from Robeson County, North Carolina, can't tell a painting instantly, and Bernard Fucking Berenson himself couldn't tell a painting instantly under those circumstances. Even he'd have needed a couple of seconds. So how can this gawky duckling from the infancy of America, steeped in the awe of God, spot a painting instantly? That one really grates on me, Billy, it does.

Furthermore, this turkey Halliwell derives from an austere, no-graven-image, Protestant tight-assedness. He, of all people, wouldn't have gone in for iconographic delectation in the face of this thing. My guess is that he'd have torched the picture, house with it, and galloped back to yell and scream to his elders that he'd just done battle with Satan himself and won. Of course, you have him having done just about that when he wakes up and sees the painting a second time. But isn't that late in the game for Willie Halliwell to be fleeing from scary omens?

And why can't you fill us in a little more on exactly how Serge falls under the spell of William Halliwell, which, in your typically convoluted plotting, he has to in order to fall in with the splinter group that ends up in Calvary, which he has to do in order to become — taking your word for it — a spy of some kind. Of course, there are those lost years of Serge — travelling the world, wandering in the desert for all I know, meeting up with Annie Besant, getting the Sikorsky into crates and shipped to the States. They scream for an explanation.

And you can't (well, of course you can, but it ain't advisable) cop out with rhetorical smoke about for whom, and about what, Serge Protector becomes a spy. It had to be for some mighty visionary folks with a wiggy cause for him to have ended up in Idaho in 1911, flying a Sikorsky DL-117 for The Brothers of Jesus. Or is he spying *on* The Brothers of Jesus? If so, for whom? Can't you just tell us right out, right away, or is this some of that convenient, teasy, clue-dropping they do in English mysteries?

Those are a few *hors d'oeuvres* in the lacunae department. Now for some heavier stuff. Pure and simple, Billy, I don't get Noam. Not just his race (I know, I know, the odds are overwhelming he's a cracker.) He's a radio preacher, so he should be either a totally demented Jesus freak who really believes all that crap he sends out over the airwaves, or he should be a goddamned snake oil salesman, in it for the power or the ego trip or the bucks. One or t'other, make up your mind, is my recommendation. The way you got it, Noam pops back and forth. Sometimes he preaches from something resembling conviction; at other times, he's just a second-rate smart operator. And occasionally, he merely seems lost.

Then, after wandering back from his brush with death (to understate the case) in Oregon, Noam is suddenly a kind of prototype New Ager. While I can understand (hell, I'm the Embodiment — or the Disembodiment — of Understanding) how being eardrum-to-eardrum to a bomb blast could have altered his metaphysical outlook, the Mitsubishi floater doesn't seem quite adequate to blow Noam that dramatically right out of Gantryhood and right into the Elevated Masters of the Ages. That seems more like Nytibia's territory. Why didn't you have *her* introduce Noam to Master Shine-o-Light (sounds like a new brand of flashlight battery from the 1940s) and Oromantis (a killer cookie?) and the rest of that crew. Incidentally, that treads a little close to my turf. But I'm trying not to be territorial, for the time being.

Let's see…. Ah! This space-time continuum bit in his television sermon: Noam is a little under-educated to begin with, and, after nearly buying the farm in Oregon, he would have been too shaken to have earned himself an autodidact's doctorate in quantum physics, wouldn't he? Where did he learn all that stuff?

And just what, I have to ask, does Noam *want*? Noam is the fat man of a thousand faces. Supposedly he wants Imeda, but that's hard to believe. Even porcine, horny Noam wouldn't have fallen so heavily for a spun-glass blonde with a hairline that begins on the crown of her head. Not when his preacher's mojo, however wobbly, still worked. Besides, she's a Nazi-in-waiting. The same goes for Nytibia, who seems, if anything, worse than Imeda. And Noam gets that furtive, back-seat handjob from Conchita (albeit, technically speaking, in the front seat), but I suppose that doesn't register on Noam's Dial of Deeper Needs.

Noam's stepkids are almost invisible. They seem to make an appearance simply in order to get blown away. And I suppose that leaving Pasadena in 1940 and getting bombed (you know what I mean) on the Oregon coast in 1945 allowed Noam just about enough time to get his ass, and his 1934 Ford on rationed tires, up to the Pacific Northwest, find a mate (the area wasn't exactly famous for its fast women, you know, especially during the war), and land a convenient congregation in the duck state. Still, a pretty tall order for a such a short stack, if you ask me.

But I'm supposed to be asking you the questions, not supplying answers. So: Where did Noam find the nameless mother of his stepchildren? The woman dies a horrible, if quick, death. I think she deserves at least a name and a trace of personal history. If I were your editor, I'd certainly think so.

Regarding the balloon bomb and its origin: I registered a small complaint at the time, but, impressed with that tour de force section on the various odds of particular events taking place, I allowed you to get on with your story. But it's been bothering me more and more. Since the whole idea is partly my fault, I can't come down too hard on you about it. So I'll just ask this: Might not you have found a more credible method of getting rid of The Second Mrs. Sain?

No, you couldn't have, could you? If you did, you couldn't have Noam doing his shirt-ripping number on television and, worse, there wouldn't be any special significance to Noam's surviving a second explosion at Matt Medium's mansion. Ah, Billy babe, what a tangled web you weave!

But you have to do some thinking about the sensation of extreme heat that Noam and Robo both experience just before they slip through one of those cracks in time. Robo's are plausible; they arise during intensely competitive athletic contests. The go with the territory of jockdom, you might say. But Noam's hyperthermia sprouts up, very conveniently, in two instances, just before he's about to be vaporized. I suppose you intend the sensation to be a heightened version of the tingle practically everybody (I hear tell) feels a split-second before the telephone or doorbell rings. The two experiences of inner heat — they have roughly the same consequences, but are they the same thing?

Let's get on to Ken Sabe, who just might be my favorite character. In fact, I like him enough that I wish you hadn't been quite so relentless in turning him into a heavy. I know where you're going with him, so my plea is uttered that much more plaintively. When we met him — a big, powerful, physically aggressive but actually quite naive young hunk — he's a very sympathetic character, at least to my hardened little heart. Poor kid — a magnificent physical specimen with equally wondrous athletic talents, stuck out there in the boondocks at precisely the wrong moment in American history. He's like a large, energetic dog who wants to serve a master and love a family but doesn't know how to do anything except knock over the porcelain tea set with his out-of-control tail.

People certainly don't treat him fairly. The agency, for example, is either selling him a bill of goods about what's going on at Matt Medium's ol' Agape Lodge, or cold-bloodedly ordering him to assassinate a colleague, along with a bunch of other folks who, while not exactly innocent, are certainly bystanders to the main event. Then, when the agency reels him back to Calvary, it reduces him to a veritable janitor, with no way to redeem himself except — at least in Ken Sabe's own eyes — creating a better version of his failed self in his son. The agency is probably compelled to screw him over. But why can't you treat him a little better? Don't you like him?

Let me rephrase that. I know you don't like him, and I know why you don't like him. Your whole story — and all the stories within this story — have a subtext about time and paternity. Paternity is time, since paternity — God's in creating the universe, Dieric Maender's in painting the painting that turns up all over the place, Serge Protector's in fathering Ken Sabe, Ken Sabe's in inseminating the egg that turned out to be Robo, Ken Sabe's grotesque attempt to re-father Robo post-partum, and Robo's abortive (no pun) metaphorical attempt at it that night with the Calvary High School football player — is what keeps things moving along, the phenomenon allows events of any kind to take place, the quality that allows a world to exist in the first place.

Of course, women (and the female side of me) are going to object strenuously to the implication that maternity is nothing but the ether of the universe, the ground of being and not the figuration of it. But that's a metaphysical problem, probably too big a mushball for you to try to correct this far down the narrative road.

The point is, Billy, ol' pal, I'm hip to your leitmotif. And I'm also cognizant of your own personal history — Robeson County and mom, sexual orientation (or should I say indecision?) during your university years, and your choosing a profession that is (you fear) one of the paternalistically paler human imitations of the Big Bang (that of "creating" useless, made-up stories with mere words). So I know perfectly well what you've got against Ken Sabe and why you want him to end up a goon. But can't you cut him a little slack? He seems too much like an engagingly clumsy colt at seventeen to turn into such a flaming schmuck a few years later. Is that what the fight game does to a body, beside play four-wall handball with its brain? And even if it is, Ken Sabe still has the decency to try, however misguidedly, to impart to Robo the moral bearings that he himself had somehow lost. Give the guy a break.

I also doubt that the agency — as you insist on adumbrating it — would entertain such myriad cross-purposes for Matt Medium. It sets him up in a big house on Orange Grove Boulevard, surrounds him with a baroque coterie that includes techno-nerds from the Institute, a rabidly anti-communist Congressmen who dabbles in Satanism, a few rank-and-file Satanists themselves, a science fiction writer and some unfortunate knocked-up woman who's always weeping or bleeding or both, and, apparently, tenders him a big budget and a one-signature check-writing clearance.

So what's his mission? Getting the inside skinny on the nascent John Birch Society? Nipping Scientology in the bud? Entrapping devil worshippers? Or is Matt Medium — as I suspect is the case — after bigger game, namely the how-to of time slippage? If so, why does he approach it from the Noam Sain angle? Noam's only experience, at that juncture, is to have fluked himself out of being blown up in Oregon.

O.K., O.K., the real story in Oregon wasn't Noam, but the airplane and the bomb. The airplane couldn't have made it across the Pacific if the supposition of the existence of ether, on the part of some mighty unorthodox Axis aeronautical engineers, weren't spot on. I'll concede that Noam's ex-wife, Imeda Jinsokt, a. k. a. Axis Sally, might well have flogged to the authorities in the Reich a vague, imprecise belief in the existence of ether, but I doubt those theories out of her mouth would have carried any clout with *der Führer*, Goering or Goering's lieutenants. Tackling the ether issue — rolling up his sleeves and getting down to brass tacks in his basement on Orange Grove Boulevard, instead of coyly interrogating Noam in the parlor — would have, on the other hand, taken Matt Medium back to the trail of Serge Protector, who was, after all, part of the Cleveland experiment that Matt Medium is trying to recreate in Pasadena.

Cut to Conchita. Now she's a quick study, ain't she? In practically the blink of an I, the little lady goes from a pious, dutiful daughter, to an opportunistic whacker-offer, to a de facto television exec, to a self-help tycoon.

And fill me in (I like that one) on The Brothers of Jesus's tunnels. Almost six feet high, running under one building to another, and then a second one started in what you deem the opposite direction. Such a major feat of ad hoc engineering! With no mention of how in hell The Brothers of Jesus manage to slip shipments of the requisite materials — shovels, picks, gunny sacks, four-by-four's and two-by-twelve's for buttressing — under the noses of Calvary's ordinary citizens. Or are secret subterranean honeycombs the norm in this piously cozy little burg? And what about the earth removal? Haven't you ever seen a prison break movie? The big problem isn't stealing soup spoons to dig with from the mess hall; the big problem isn't making a trap door and sneaking a couple of guys out of roll call to dig. The big problem is stashing the dirt from the excavation. A couple of hundred willing chaylens working for much less than scale are certainly a big help, but they couldn't have eaten the goddamned dirt. What are they doing with it?

Do you expect me (moving right along…) to believe that Robo can have kept himself sequestered incognito from his father, however untalented a spook his father was, for the duration? In a metropolis the size of Calvary, word of his being in town would have eventually leaked out to Ken Sabe. What he would have done with the info is up to you, but personally, I think he would have made some effort to revisit the fruit of his loins. To scold the musclebound fuckup for blowing his B-ball career, most likely, or, failing that, just to satisfy his curiosity.

In between those poles, of course, lies the agency. I doubt whether the agency would have hesitated to ask Ken Sabe to suborn his own son to get a line on The Brothers of Jesus, and I doubt whether, if asked, he would have refused.

And now poor, benighted Robo. Doesn't the mature Robo — the recluse Robo who's taken flight from his father and The Brothers of Jesus, the eccentric Robo who's been hooted away from the Calvary High School football game for embracing the quarterback — know that his schtick of impressing high school girls with his big Beemer is over with? They think he's a homo. Why is he persisting — at least when we first met him? Doesn't he know his sex appeal has gone right down the toilet when he tries (or so everyone in the stands thinks) to soul-kiss the quarterback through his facemask?

And hey, man, *everybody* in broadcasting videotaped basketball games, even in Idaho even in the late sixties or early seventies. There's no excuse for Robo's little disappearing act not to have been captured on VHS by some sports slummer with a handi-cam. How come you don't dig out the cassettes and show 'em to Robo? How come you leave the poor bastard visually unenlightened about his own past?

Finally, here are some random queries that seem a little picayune to bundle up in topical paragraphs. Consider them loose ends (but, of course, not *all* the loose ends):

★ If Dieric Maender's painting of Cardinal Oeups subsequently turns up again and again (in spite of its having been abandoned in a Flemish hayloft), why isn't it mentioned in some published provenance? Surely, some connoisseur along the way would have noted in writing its existence.

★ What, exactly, are those schoolkid contests in Nevada that earn Serge Protector all that early attention?

★ Why do the good people of the state of California invite an out-of-state Elkhart lad to attend their most prestigious university?

★ Do you realize that William Halliwell would have been ninety-four years old in the year that he might have met Serge Protector and, if he had, pronounced emphatically the date of the impending end of the world? (I imagine him looking like one of those phony photographs of the allegedly still-living Hitler in a tabloid weekly at the Piggly-Wiggly checkout counter.)

★ Where does Serge Protector recruit enough ground support crew members from The Brothers of Jesus — in Calvary, Idaho, in 1911 fer chrissake — to allow him to get a giant Sikorsky DL-117 off the ground? One grease monkey for horseless carriages and two board-pounders wouldn't have cut it.

★ If Noam passes through Calvary on his first wandering in the wilderness, from Louisiana to Los Angeles, why doesn't he seem to recognize it on his second?

★ Do you really think the Japanese send that balloon bomb to Oregon because they think California is too well-protected, or because they don't want to kill American-born Japanese who might eventually be won over to their side? We're talking end-game here, Pancho.

★ What happens to all the pointed ends of the shards from the balloon bomb that are partially embedded in Noam, and in transit to the other side of his body, when he manages to disappear? (Think back, Billy, to that old grammar school riddle asking at which point in space does a bowel movement by the Invisible Man become visible.)

★ How does Ken Sabe's boxing nickname segue so easily into his legal name, especially given his employment with the agency?

★ Why would even such a cheapskate station as KCCT-TV run a film of a boxing match at least two years old, when they could get any amount of more recent — not to mention local — fight footage to broadcast?

★ What do all those people at Matt Medium's mansion do while a few are watching the fights on television? Does Matt Medium throw a sort of Satan's open house each week?

★ Given everything he's seen and been through, why is Noam shocked to see Conchita come to the door late at night with a cigarette in her hand?

★ Doesn't the National Gallery of Art, even circa 1954, have their paintings wired to an alarm?

★ What do all those people in The Brothers of Jesus do for their livings, especially in a tightly knit, suspicious burg like Calvary (which strikes me, quite frankly, as the economic hub of practically nowhere)?

★ Who leads The Brothers of Jesus for all those years between the demise of Serge Protector (one has to assume that he kicked off sometime soon after World War II) and the arrival of Noam?

★ ★ ★ ★ ★

Now I realize that, in a certain very crucial sense, all of the foregoing is picayune in the extreme. My complaints concern lapses of fact, logic, or common sense — all of which might have some real consequence if you, Billy, were writing a piece of nonfiction, or a naturalistic novel of the Dreiserian variety, or even a good old-fashioned whodunit in which an array of seemingly (I'd write that *seemingly*) accurate, consistent, and necessarily connected facts and descriptions skim the reader quickly over narrative surface — like, say, a water-skier on a lake — in order to deliver him or her to the weeded shore of a satisfying conclusion.

But you ain't, Billy. You be writin' a semi-fantasy, a meditation on the illegitimacy of the power of words — conjured up out of no more than the squiggles of typography on a page, or a temporal linkage of uttered minigrunts — to create pictures in people's brains that have no basis (I'd write that *no basis*) in either physical or historical reality. So, what the fuck difference does it make to you what inconsistencies I spot?

Worse: Since I am in my ghostly essence Every Story Ever Told and Every Story Hereafter Tellable, all at once, all rolled into one incomprehensibly global megastory which leaves out nothing (I'd write that *nothing*), my very existence, right now, as an audible voice in your consciousness's inner ear, is a deliberate inconsistency. We covered that in the beginning, didn't we?

Point is, inconsistency is the name of the game. Inconsistency — holes in the chronology, ages that don't add up, mysterious or unbelievable motives, dialogue that real people just wouldn't say under any circumstance except, perhaps, under threat of having their toenails pulled out with red-hot tongs, crude rhetorical blankets of simplicity thrown over events dependent on a thousand crucial details — is exactly what drives any narrative forward. Or, in your case, pushes it in several different directions. The very fact that I'm lurking here, in the interstices of your words, Billy, owes itself to the inconsistency called incompleteness. (Like I said, we covered this earlier.) So I'm a hypocrite: I pillory you for committing in a relatively minor manner the very crime — leaving things out or unconsidered — that breathes life into me. Bit of a shit I am, huh?

Ah, but wait. There's a surrebuttal. Otherwise, I wouldn't be running my mouth (so to speak). You knew that, didn't you? Here it is: You need me in my pre-manifested form — the ground of possible perfection, of Complete Completeness — against which to align your peculiar figurations: characters, passions, thoughts, events, coincidences, consequences. Otherwise, your story'll just go spinning off into nowhere. So, in effect, I'm giving you my hypocrisy as a present. I'm making you gifts of my rants about picking up the measuring stick of quotidian reality at least once in a while and stacking your material up against it.

If, for instance, you don't at least wonder why you haven't indicated precisely and unequivocally whether Noam Sain is a black man or a white man (yes, I know: the narrative incongruities arising out of Noam Sain as a black man outnumber those concomitant to his being white about a thousand to one; but still...), then Noam has no resonance, no fixedness, no being firmly situated in the history of our times (well, your times).

That's why I perform this ugly service for you. Do you think I descend from the realm of, as I called it before, Complete Completeness, just for the fun of acting like a goddamned bun-in-the-back, wizened old senior composition teacher, with thick ankles, a pointer, and a Speigel catalogue sale dress? No, I do it to sharpen your skills, to force you, if I can, to be more convincing (I'd write that *convincing*), even in this openly hallucinatory tale.

Oh, that's right, I forgot. It isn't a fantasy to you. It's

reality extended somewhat in the direction of implausibility in order to get at deeper truths. That's what they all say. But it just could be laziness, Mr. Lockjaw. It just could be that you can't paint with words like Dieric Maender could with oil; you can't render those tiny highlights on the metallic gold threads in the cardinal's robe. You could have a palette loaded with Winsor Newton's whole inventory, a two-hair sable brush, and an entire century in which to daub and you still couldn't nail a detail like the threads in the cardinal's robe because not only can't you paint (metaphorically speaking) well enough, but because you can't *see* well enough.

So get back to work, Billy, my boy. And try to stay focused.

You know I'm always here if you need help.

Quack.

Moving Up in the Next World

At the time of the re-election of Ronald Reagan as the fortieth President of the United States, The Brothers of Jesus still occupied only a small storefront on the main street, and a nearby dormitory building within the town of Calvary. (Before the cult managed to occupy the storefront, it had been a laundromat; before the dormitory building had found its purpose with The Brothers of Jesus, it had been a feed-and-grain warehouse.) The Brothers of Jesus used the storefront as both a recruiting office and a temple. Inside, at the rear of the storefront, a trap door lead to a tunnel which ran several miles underground to The Brothers of Jesus's ranch. The ranch had been purchased surreptitiously, one parcel of land at a time, in the years since Noam Sain was run off as Bishop,.

A wooden, one-story, split-level ranch house (accessible by both tunnel and dirt road), painted a sky blue (including its flagstone half-basement's exterior), stood at the entrance to the ranch. Seen from certain angles, such as that from a car passing a couple of hundred yards away on the highway between the house and the foothills, the house was practically invisible. The ranch behind the blue house sprawled for nearly 12,000 acres.

A newer tunnel led from beneath the ranch house, under the highway, toward the foothills and mountains. At the end of the tunnel, under one of the foothills, was a large, concrete-lined bunker. In the bunker, The Brothers of Jesus operated the second-largest genealogical library in the world.

Computers — older models putatively purged and then dumped by the agency's alleged Peace Corps Training Center, which had then been salvaged, resuscitated, reconditioned and updated by hacker members of The Brothers of Jesus — housed the library's information. The information was used (according to semi-truthful, internally distributed cult manifestos) to enlarge the "Word." The Word was based on a topological concept which had, in turn, arisen from the programmers' experience in trying to construct an infinitely orderable database for the library. The Brothers of Jesus's programmers had discovered that the body of genealogical information resembled what in topology is called a "simply connected form" — one which, without being disassembled, can be contracted into a sphere. To a topologist, a sphere is a two-dimensional form existing in a three-dimensional universe.

One of topology's more intriguing propositions, the "Poincaré Conjecture," posits that if the so-called "two-sphere" is the only simply-connected ultimate form in our quotidian, three-dimensional, spatial universe, then in a hypothetical four-dimensional universe, the only simply connected ultimate form would be something you might call a "three-sphere." In a five-dimensional universe, it would be a "four-sphere," and so on, to infinity.

Similarly, but in reverse direction — posited The Brothers of Jesus's programmers — a two-dimensional genealogical database would require a three-dimensional Word (the Word being the primary cause of the universe). If The Brothers of Jesus's programmers thought that if they could order their database along an additional axis in an additional dimension, then the dimensions of the Word would also increase by one. If the database were infinitely orderable, then the Word would possess a number of dimensions equal to infinity plus one.

"How holy!" the programmers exclaimed (to one another).

The Brothers of Jesus also believed that, with the Second Coming, dead human beings would be united with their previously riven souls, if those souls were not already in the clutches of Satan (The Brothers of Jesus's theology retained a primitive, demonological touch). The Second Coming, they believed, would not only solve the mind/body problem for the fortunate saved, but the religion/espionage problem as well. The Brothers of Jesus was of the opinion that the religion/espionage problem, although obviously subcategorical to the mind/body conundrum, might be more important. At any rate, the cultists believed that saved and spiritually reconstituted human beings would themselves become gods (of a sort) and physically travel to other planets to save the souls of lost creatures of other races.

The information in the genealogical library boasted, however, a more immediately practical aspect. It was used to blackmail members of The Brothers of Jesus into remaining with the cult, into contributing more and more money to it, and into pressuring family and friends, as well, into giving.

The Brothers of Jesus believed, of course, that it was the only true church, that all other churches or religions were wrong and, in being wrong (by professing errant belief) rather than being merely ignorant (by professing ignorance), were worse than simply useless. All other churches (in the broad sense) were outright enemies. (Of course every church in the world — ancient or born yesterday, huge or minuscule, gentle or thuggish, cloudy or specific — believes some concentrated or diluted version of this, express or implied.)

By Reagan's second inauguration, The Brothers of Jesus had dropped almost all its anti-permissiveness rules, except that against unsanctioned oral sex on storefront premises. Nytibia, in fact, began, in her sermons, to build a case against the overregulation — especially by government agencies — of human conduct — especially that which pursued pleasure. (Members of The Brothers of Jesus, of course, were still subject to extreme regulation of their conduct by their church; they accepted it because they considered themselves, in the spiritual wars imminent in America, to be soldiers and not civilians.)

Accordingly, and with few expressed qualms of conscience, The Brothers of Jesus went into the business of selling cocaine in small, wholesale lots to neophyte street dealers in the Pacific Northwest. Business got so good so fast that Nytibia Barbosell's old friends in Los Angeles couldn't keep her supplied. So, to feed this new and lucrative outlet, Colombian producers' shippers themselves added an additional, arduous series of legs to their usual Columbia-Carolinas air routes. To accommodate the pilots, The Brothers of Jesus built a landing strip on the ranch. But many planes never made it, crashing instead in the Rockies. One pilot, one night, had to put his Helio down — with the aid of a serendipitously heavy headwind — on Robo's running track. Robo heard the roar and, fearing The Brothers of Jesus had finally come to assassinate him, huddled on the floor of his Airstream until, a few hours later, a second roar carried his imagined assailants away.

There were, however, occasional defections from The Brothers of Jesus. After the embarrassment of Robo's sudden departure, the escapees were hunted and usually quickly found, either wandering the cult's vast ranch or trying to become inconspicuous on the streets of Calvary. Upon capture, they were killed. The members of The Brothers of Jesus assigned to commit the murders rationalized their conduct partially on the same grounds they cited (within the compound) to justify their dope dealing. But even indirect involvement in murder (not everybody pulled a trigger or wielded a knife or tightened a rope) felt different, more severe; it left one queasier. So Nytibia told the members that they were actually performing a service for the victims, namely preventing them from losing their eternal souls to Satan. And in the bargain, Nytibia said, they were returning to these lost people their chances — however slight — of becoming interplanetary gods.

On 12,000 acres of wilderness, bodies were quite easy to dispose of.

★ ★ ★ ★ ★

In November, 1986, shortly after the American midterm Congressional elections, and right at the peak of the buying frenzy in the international art market, the collection of the estate of Rose Madder went under the gavel at Christie's auction house in London. The pristine condition of the John Singer Sargent paintings in particular — as "if freshly painted this morning," one newspaper critic wrote — was astonishing. Those pictures brought in a record 4.6 million pounds sterling. Even an unattributed minor geometric abstraction from (one guessed) the mid-1930s that America's National Gallery of Art seemed to have forgotten it ever owned was sold, to an unnamed bidder phoning in from across the Atlantic, way out west in Idaho.

Attention, Crass

The elderly, but still fully marbled, retired preacher Noam Sain resided in comfortable isolation on an eighty-acre, fully fenced ranch inland in far northern California, less than one hundred miles south of the spot in Oregon where he'd been nearly killed by a Japanese balloon bomb forty-one years earlier. Noam Sain had not been seen in public by a member of The Brothers of Jesus, or anyone else for that matter, for a long, long time.

He lived well, from the profits accrued from having written, all told, 592 published works, including 52 non-fiction books selling some 32 million copies, and 26 science-fiction novels selling some 33 million copies altogether, [There'll be a quiz, kids. *Quack.*]

At his ranch, Noam Sain continued to write prolifically. He'd acquired an ability to dictate constantly, while doing almost anything, including copulating with prostitutes who were Jeeped onto his ranch by an "editorial assistant" and deposited in his big, redwood bedroom; and he was practically umbilically attached to every electronic writing device imaginable. Fax, modem, desktop, notebook, printer: Noam spewed into them all, all day, and most of the night.

He'd kicked hard drugs, but had acquired, along with a good part of the nation, a multiple-cup-a-day espresso habit. Noam possessed inordinate amounts of energy. He also chain-smoked. Nevertheless, his elocution was quicker, crisper, sharper than it had been during his preaching days. But he'd somehow acquired a slight East Indian accent, probably from reading too much Krishnamurti. [How's *that* work? *Quack.*]

From his ranch, Noam Sain tried to spy on The Brothers of Jesus. Here's how he did it:

Since Robo's defection (Noam had found out), the cult had been trying to recruit semi-famous jocks (although not nearly as semi-famous as Robo) to replace him. Noam tried to interdict the recruiting by recruiting the jocks himself, before they were recruited by The Brothers of Jesus, train them to be recruited with their fingers crossed, so to speak, by the cult, and then to report, somehow, back to him.

Noam would don a disguise — a simple prop shop grey beard and a pair of sunglasses were sufficient — and fly coach (less conspicuous) to Los Angeles to conduct seminars, under an assumed name, in "The Ultimate Personal Trainer: How You Can Defeat Your Mortal Enemy, Time" in a rented meeting room at the Sportsman's Lodge hotel on Ventura Boulevard in Sherman Oaks. By special arrangement with the management (that is, the payment of a large fee), the meeting room could be fitted out on the occasion of each seminar with a set that rendered it an exact duplicate (if you didn't count a smaller floor plan) of the interior of The Brothers of Jesus's storefront temple in Calvary, Idaho.

To attract as large an audience as possible, Noam's seminars were held under the aegis of "The Amazing Memoranda Mental Maintenance Program." [It pays to stay in touch with old friends. *Quack.*] Originally intended to help students doing poorly in high school and college, Conchita Memoranda's system had been predicated on the belief that true "mental information" was not obtainable through the mundane five senses alone, that it had to be absorbed by "spiritual osmosis" as well. But, as under-achieving high-schoolers (their desperate parents paid attention to the brochures; the college kids ignored them) proved to be a limited market, Conchita shifted her entrepreneurial sights to hungry salesmen and frustrated middle managers.

At the time of Noam's importuning, Conchita was holding her own, but barely that. Three decades older, wiser, greyer, greedier, Conchita thought her mental maintenance program — by now ossified into a litany of self-help cliches, boot-camp rote memorization, and a light glaze of the supernatural — could use a little new juice. Why not some good, old-fashioned, inbred, cult perversion from a harridan's computer-driven circus of fellators and cunnilinguists [Fellow Tories! Cunning linguists! It pays to keep in touch with the enemies of old friends. *Quack.*] sequestered in underground cement in a forlorn patch of Idaho? She told good ol' Noam she'd see what she could do.

"Mr. Matt Medium," the agency man said to the audience, "has, as you know, given generously of himself before — to his country, and to our organization in particular. And, as most of you also know, he has, over the last several years, amassed a tremendous personal fortune in the fields of avionics and propulsion systems. But Matt — I feel I can call him Matt — has never hesitated to put his energy, his insight, his technical skills and — most uncommonly — his material assets at the service of his country and this agency.

"Well, he's at it again. [Polite, and somewhat nervous, laughter.] Matt has got it in his head that a little something called the "Z-zero particle" is absolutely essential to our national security. The trouble is, the very government — our government — whose fat he's trying to pull from the fire, thinks the Z-zero particle is a bit of a longshot in terms of the money — people in Washington like to call it "funding" — it would require to build the accelerator necessary to find the elusive little buggers.

"Now, Matt is here at the Training Center to talk to us today about — what is it you're here today to talk to us about Matt?"

"The big picture," said Matt Medium, seated to his introducer's side, impeccably dressed in a dark blue double-breasted pinstripe suit, subtly iridescent maroon necktie, and plain, but elegant, capped-toe Italian black leather shoes with the thinnest soles this side of the hospital chapel in an anorexia ward.

"Ah, yes, the big picture. Well then, without further adieu, Mr. Matt Medium." [Polite and somewhat nervous applause.]

Outside, a high wind blew dust and sand across the paint jobs of the shiny, jujube-colored cars huddled in the ad hoc parking lot. A powerful gust hurled a blast of air-borne dirt against the corrugated metal wall of the build-ing in which Matt Medium was now rising, now striding confidently, toward the podium. It sounded like a drum roll.

"Good afternoon. [Behind the podium, shuffling, with the dexterity of a card shark, of a few sheets of paper. In front of the podium, chino-encased buns shifting on metal chairs, nervous positioning of feet beneath the chairs, several coughs.]

"Matter in the universe is balanced by something called, for lack of a more precise term, anti-matter. [Pause.]

"Although currently accepted theory says there should be a nice, tidy fifty-fifty balance of matter and anti-matter in the universe, that is not, unfortunately, the case. The universe, gentlemen, is made up of as much as 99% anti-matter. And it's getting worse. Anti-matter, or 'nothingness,' as the philosophers among us would have it, is expanding more rapidly than anything else — or should I say than nothing else — in the universe. Nothing is devouring everything in its path.

"How did we arrive at this sorry pass? Some people say it was the Democrats. [Laughter — still insincere, but throatier and not so nervous as before.] A few people say it was the Republicans. [No laughter.] Not the case. This problem predates even the first term of the late Honorable Earl Dillingham, the first and last Congressman I ever voted for." [A smattering of applause.]

"The expanding universe, and its also-expanding nothingness was created in one sub-instant by what we now call the "Big Bang." Now, how did a Big Bang produce, out of absolutely nothing — no matter, no anti-matter, no space, no time — a great big universe, and an irregular one at that?

"First, there *was* a Big Bang. The evenness of background radiation beyond even the most distant galaxies detected by astronomers tells us that. That radiation is the smoking gun, so to speak, of the Big Bang. We know that radiation comes from the Big Bang precisely because it is so even — it was zapped out in all directions in perfect, encompassing symmetry in the Big Bang.

"Nevertheless, there's a problem. The evenness of background radiation is contradicted by the configuration of the universe itself, by the fact that the universe even *has* a configuration in the first place. If the Big Bang was an instant, even, and symmetrical event, then why isn't its spawn, the universe, one consistent and undifferentiated thing? Why aren't we all just medium grey specks floating in a thick stew of medium grey specks against a background of medium grey specks, that all look exactly like us? Well, it beats the hell out of me, Sarge — I'm not the regular crew chief around here." [Faint, scattered bits of laughter.]

"I do, however, know this: If the universe, upon creating, had been one consistent and undifferentiated thing, it would have needed some intrusion of irregularity in order to exist for more than the instant that it took for the Big Bang to occur. All those zillions and zillions of medium grey specks would have hovered in an unimaginably thick concentration, about .00000000001 centimetre from a point I'll call Space Zero, for about .00000000001 seconds. Then they would have collapsed right back into that infinitely dense point in the middle of a space that didn't even exist yet.

"And that would have been it for the universe."

"No gaseous nebulae. No whirling stars. No cooling blobs. No primeval soups. No lightning bolts. No amino acids. No organisms. No flora and fauna. No fishies crawling ashore. No warm blood. No mammals standing up. No opposable thumbs. No frontal lobes. No Neanderthals sparking flints. No Cro-Magnons smelting bronze. No fur togas. No domestic animals. No family farms. No huge pyramids. No cuneiform. No birth of reason. No imperial legions. No illuminated manuscripts. No madonna-and-childs. No sun kings. No revolutions. No steam engines. No manifest destiny. No powered flight. No wars to end wars. No Pax Americanas. No cold wars. And of course, my friends, no agency." [Very nervous laughter.]

"Fortunately, the universe was irregular enough to last. It's made up of clusters of matter, rather than an even distribution of matter. And that's why we're all here today, in this lovely building, in this lovely part of the United States of America." [Very unsure laughter.]

"But the universe also contains, I must caution you, clusters of anti-matter. The alternating empty-filled configuration of the universe resembles a sponge-in-negative. The material stuff in a sponge is like the holes in the universe; holes in the sponge are like the material stuff in the universe. With qualification: Even the stuff in the universe is made up of mostly empty space, which means that there are, ultimately, holes within holes within holes within holes, all the way down to the tiniest little part of the universe in existence, something called the Z-zero particle.

"Now, although the universe is, of necessity, irregularly configured, there is, nevertheless, a kind of overall structure to what might be called the 'filled' areas of the universe. Galaxies are clustered in clusters. The clustered galaxies are clustered in superclusters. The superclusters are clustered in supercluster complexes. But one li'l ol' cluster can be as large as one billion light years in one direction, a hundred fifty million in another and contain as much as ten percent of the matter in the entire universe. Obviously, not a lot of clusters are as big as that. But that particular cluster is so big that it's just about impossible for anything — even a beam of light — to travel across it. That means not only is this cluster so big it's hard to imagine, but it's so big that even the proposition that it's imaginable by somebody, somewhere, violates the laws of physics. Consciousnesses capable of imagination are, after all, nothing but electrical impulses which are essentially particles of light travelling very, very short distances. Attempting to hold this vast cluster in your imagination means, metaphorically, sending an electrical impulse of consciousness out across a distance it cannot possibly traverse. But I digress.

"How did this sponginess, this clumpiness, this clusteredness, if you will, arise out of the total regularity and uniformity that must have existed immediately after the Big Bang? We don't know. But we do know that there had to be some kind of Original Fly in the Ointment. A gap, a slip, a pin prick, an impurity.

"But there are also huge areas of nothingness — presumably great seas of anti-matter — in the universe, that are as much as one hundred million light years wide. There are a lot more of them — superclusters of nothing, let us say — than there are superclusters of something. Moreover, there are zillions of smaller pockets of nothingness interspersed within the clusters of something. Based on our calculations of the amount of matter — the amount of something — in the universe, there's just too damned much anti-matter.

"So we have two Original Flies: first, the little buzzer that caused enough irregularity in the immediate result of the Big Bang to allow a configured — as opposed to an undifferentiated — universe to exist, and (therefore) to exist for longer than a micromininanosecond; and second, the apparently fecund flyer who's out there in the great beyond breeding all that anti-matter."

"Whatever the proportion of something-to-nothing it's filled with, the universe is still expanding from the force of the Big Bang. And in its continuing expansion, the universe is gaining more and more of everything, including more nothingness. In fact, as I have indicated, the nothingness is expanding at a far more rapid rate than the somethingness. Eventually, the nothingness will devour everything else.

"The universe, however, may be nearing the end of its expansion. If it's not exactly showing signs of slowing down, it's at least showing signs of showing signs. Faint creaks and groans here and there. Wobbles at the edges. Wheezing in the firmament.

"What does that mean — cosmological stasis and job security for everyone? [A few muted chuckles.] No. If the universe ceases to expand, it won't just come to a halt and remain the same size forever. It won't manage to balance itself on a perfect point of stasis. So, what will it do? The universe will, of course, start to contract — just like Sisyphus's stone, once it's been rolled to the top of the hill, will then start to roll back down the side of the hill. The reason the universe will start to contract — if there is indeed enough matter, enough somethingness in it to halt expansion in the first place — is that the same density of matter will prove sufficient to cause it to contract.

"There is, in fact, a supergalaxy in one of those clusters that we call The Great Attractor. It's pulling everything in our celestial neighborhood, including the Milky Way, and our sun and our planet and our government and our agency and our training center toward it. As the universe contracts, the contracting matter in it will become surrounded by more and more nothingness. This contraction and surrounding will go on and on and on, until all the matter in the universe will have contracted to a pinpoint.

"And guess what? If this pinpoint further contracts — as there's every reason to believe it will — to a point of infinite density, then we will have once again the conditions for a Big Bang — a Big Bang Two. Or, for all we know, a Big Bang Seven Hundred Million Nine Hundred Eighty-Six Thousand Four Hundred Twenty-Two.

"We can, however, find out whether we're faced, in the ultimate contraction of the universe, with the end of everything once and for all, or the re-beginning of an end-less cycle. Nothing in the universe is absolutely secret. The fingerprints of the culprit who set things in motion are there. We just have to get out the dusting kit, go around the house from room to room, take out each and every piece of the family china, and look for them. In this case, the cups and saucers and plates and platters and gravy boats on which are smeared the fingerprints of whatever or who-ever caused this whole expanding-contracting circus of matter and anti-matter to come into being in the first place, are the aforementioned Z-zero particles.

"But the way we find the Z-zero particles in the uni-verse is not, as you have probably guessed, by strolling lei-surely through the kitchen and dining room and opening conveniently placed china cabinets containing conveniently shelved china.

"No, we'll have to build an accelerator. We'll have to fire it up and get those bigger particles — the china cabi-net particles, you might call them — racing around the accelerator on a collision course. When they collide, the doors will pop open, the china plates will fall out, and then we can dust for prints.

"If the prints reveal that this is Big Bang number ump-teen, then we'll know we're in an infinite, cyclical process. We'll know that this contraction-expansion thing goes on not only forever, but a forever of forevers — which is, I personally suspect, the case. We will, in an abstract sense, have found God.

"And why would we — an agency allegedly driven by cold, hard logic, of a government allegedly driven by some-thing approaching reason — want to find God? Well, ask yourself a couple of questions.

"First, could not God be considered the ultimate weapon? Dr. Oppenheimer thought the first test explosion at the tower in Alamagordo had opened the bathroom door on the Old Guy taking a dump, so to speak. Except he put it a little more poetically than that. Well, we had God on our side for a while. It would be nice to see if we could get him to re-enlist.

"And second, if we don't do it — if this agency, if the government of the United States of America, doesn't do it — somebody else might do it. Somebody who — by the freakish luck of having started with blind faith and prayer and having been lead by blind faith and prayer to a point at which they don't need a cheap accelerator, an expensive accelerator, an accelerator of any kind — might take that final step to enlightenment. And who might that be? Well, think about it for a second. It'd be somebody stumbling onto the secret by accident, wouldn't it? But it'd also be somebody with a lot of brainpower, somebody with a lot of computer capability, somebody with a bunch of hackers with little else to do, and somebody who's always noodling around with the possibility of finding God — wouldn't it?

"Who do we know who's a bit like that? Well [leaning out, over the podium, gripping the sides of the lectern with white knuckles as conspicuous and as surrounded by red skin as pimples], we — all of us here — know that we know somebody not just a bit like that, but a lot like that. And we don't know just one, but tens, perhaps hundreds, maybe even thousands. [Pause for effect.]

"The Brothers of Jesus, that's who! [Another pause for further effect.] Think about the consequences to the security of the United States of America of The Brothers of Jesus finding — absolutely, once and for all — the hiding place of God. Think about it. [A full minute's pause for maximum effect. One cough.]

"Thank you very much."

[An explosion of thunderous applause.]

The Penny Plummets

Ken Sabe was the first presumed voluntary defector in the agency's history. He was certainly old enough to retire, but he submitted no papers. He was old enough — on the actuarial charts — to die of natural causes and not raise any suspicions, but he was known to be in excellent shape for a man his age. Ken Sabe's disappearance — which is the only event, even if it was an event in the negative, anybody knows took place for sure — was, by all indications, of his own volition.

At the time of his vanishing, the silver-haired, slightly stooped Ken Sabe resided in a split-level, flagstone-and-aluminum-siding ranch house with a half-basement, on a one-third acre lot, at 117 Delano Circle, a residential street in a small housing development just within the boundaries of the town of Calvary. If the house had been a cheaper, smaller model and had been painted sky blue, it would have been identical to the one standing near the entrance of the ranch owned by The Brothers of Jesus. The development was, in fact, a moderately successful investment enterprise of the group. The Brothers of Jesus had, through a financial intermediary which disguised the capital source, constructed a clot of austere but cheery, efficient but homey, economical but not tacky single-story homes on a street (which The Brothers of Jesus built and the town maintained) whose path, seen from the air, resembled a keyhole. Delano Circle exited a two-lane, crown-surface, county highway at an abrupt and, given the absence of other streets and other clots of houses, surprising right angle.

Someone driving at speed along the highway could have missed the lonely pole in the high, dry grass hoisting a white-on-ultramarine street sign. No ceremonial gates, nor even regulation curbs announced the intersection. Any automobile knowing or careful enough to make the turn onto Delano Circle from the county highway would arrive at the street's bulbous conclusion fairly quickly. Only three houses on each side occupied the street's stem and only four gathered around the asphalt circle at its end.

The street itself was curbless, and the land alongside it had been built up with trucked-in earth, so the lawns ran uphill from a shallow, gravel-speckled gutter, to the small, cement front porches of the houses. The effect of the incline — insofar as that kind of effect was considered in a little pimple of a development like this — was supposed to be one of bourgeois well-being, of having been lifted up a little from farming the hardscrabble earth of southern Idaho, of being able to survey the terrain instead of merely mining it. Not that The Brothers of Jesus indulged in such subconscious commercial subtleties; they just furnished the money. The developer thought up the embellishments. Whatever the topographical garnish failed to accomplish, the rainwater drained nicely.

Ken Sabe and Cynthia lived in the third house (counting clockwise on approach) on the cul-de-sac. They'd lived in it only a little over two years, since Ken Sabe had finally consented to sell the property on which Robo had grown up. Cynthia had wanted to sell it all along, ever since Robo left to play in the ABA, but her husband had insisted on holding on to the big back yard with the home-built gymnasium. She didn't know exactly what he did in the outbuilding (Ken Sabe spent hours in it, after dark, in the dark) but, she knew, it couldn't be good for him. The longer he was in it, the more morose he got, lumbering back into the house muttering about bombs, blue explosions, fat preachers and how somebody a mile overhead in an airplane with no wings could probably even see him going to the toilet.

The smaller house, with a horizontal band of flagstone facing outside, and soft carpeting, lots of homey maple furniture inside, and Ken's dusted-off high school basketball trophies poised as shelved knick-knacks inside, seemed to steady him. He came home from the agency (Cynthia had stopped working) with satchels full of paperwork, indulged himself with a small glass of domestic burgundy, and spent quiet evenings at the circular dining room table, under a plastic version of a Tiffany swag lamp, working, or at least thinking and moving a pencil.

There were a few instances, however, in which Cynthia was given grounds for pause. She heard — with the acuteness of listening a mother who has been robbed of her child can develop — the returning Ken Sabe make a left-hand turn onto Delano Circle instead of a right. He was nothing if not punctual, arriving home within the same five-minute window night in and night out ("If they want patriotic overtime from me, they can make me a patriotic general with a general's salary," he'd say to her). He always drove down the highway within the same five-miles-per-hour bracket (fifteen miles per hour over whatever posted speed limit), so she knew, when she heard the tires crackle on the granite chips sprinkled by traffic across the intersection, that he'd driven an equal distance in either direction.

The odd thing (unknown to Cynthia) was that the smaller version of their house, the one that stood sentry beside the entrance to The Brothers of Jesus's ranch, was, almost to the tenth of a mile, the same distance — in the opposite direction — from their home as the agency's training camp. An odder thing (also unknown to Cynthia) was that, in yet a third direction, the chain-link fence that protected the construction site of Matt Medium's nascent (and hardly off the drawing board) "cheap" accelerator, lay at equal remove from the Sabe-Barr household.

★ ★ ★ ★ ★

Robo's homemade running track was a little more than a quarter of the length of the international-regulation oval (recently resurfaced in an exotic, electric blue synthetic compound made in Belgium, in a factory on the site of — but nobody knew it, not even the factory's chemists, owners and bankers — the ancient, temporary atelier-in-a-barn of the painter Dieric Maender) at Calvary High School. The Fighting Christians' track was, however, but a tiny, tiny fraction of the length (nearly fifteen miles) of the oval ditch being cut into the hard, ungiving ground of an enormous tract of land adjacent to the agency's training compound.

The ditch was shallow; a man could stand in it and his head and shoulders would clear the ground plane. Some men — helmeted workers — did, day after day. But they were gone now; construction had shut down. Beside the ditch were piled lengths of metal tube, larger in diameter and longer in section than sewer pipe, and special waterproof and dustproof containers, resembling outsized picnic coolers, containing some of the exotic electronic equipment necessary in the building of a particle accelerator. The tubes and the boxes were all made of — or at least coated with — a foggily silver metal. In the cold grey dawn on the morning of Ken Sabe's disappearance, they rendered the construction site a kind of ghost cemetery with spectral corpses, coffins and mourners. Flowers — or at least occasional moments of primary color — were provided by the dusty yellow bulldozers and backhoes with dried red mud (they'd dug after it rained; in fact, they preferred to dig after it rained) caked in their giant, chevron-treaded tires, standing silently to the side of the symmetrical scar in the earth.

The chainlink fence ran for tens of miles, in double file, around the perimeter of the construction site. The outer fence was ten feet tall and topped with a jagged, continuous curlicue of razor wire. The inner barrier, twenty feet further inside the boundary (so that an intruder who'd managed to clear the ten-footer, would have to drop to the ground, before attacking the problem of the second), was also garnished with razored metal spirals. And it was lethally electrified. Matt Medium's pet project could rest in the high desert, suspended and unattended, for as long as it had to.

The initial go-ahead had come from the agency: short of total financing, but with a substantial down payment. Then there had been a small problem with Matt Medium: unauthorized — or at least overlong as against what agency policy allowed — flights in the "Shakey J." The aircraft was by now antique and, officially, inoperable. But nobody else could fly it as well — perhaps nobody else could fly it at all — as Matt Medium. So the agency was a bit loose, even sentimental, about Matt Medium taking it up. But he'd been abusing the informality, staying aloft for hours, circling directly over The Brothers of Jesus's storefront, gatehouse and ranch. And he'd been peering down on Ken Sabe's new house as well as keeping tabs on the old one, the one with the big back yard and home-built gymnasium. He'd been wasting gas and not filing reports. There was a limit to what a consultant, a high rider (outside the overt chain of command within the covert agency) such as Matt Medium had become, could get away with. Somebody had to slap his wrist, at a minimum. So they put a six months' hold on construction financing, and grounded the "Shakey J." Matt Medium was, therefore, not airborne on the evening of Ken Sabe's disappearance.

★ ★ ★ ★ ★

"Look, Stretcher, baby," Ken Sabe was saying to Cynthia Barr one night a week before he disappeared. They were sitting at the circular maple dining room table, under the warm yellow glow (a color not unlike a lightened version of the bulldozers' custard) of the swag lamp. "I'm not crazy. I've figured it out. They didn't want me to figure it out — I was always supposed to be just a goon, some muscle with, perhaps, an I.Q. of two above the plant life of their workaday hit men. I wasn't one of their fancy boys like Matt Medium, up there in his own fucking airplane — aw, Jesus, hon, I'm sorry for the language, I won't do it again — in his own airplane, looking down at me do everything from eating my breakfast to plumping my pillow at night. I wasn't like him with his own big fat science projects to try to make the clock run backwards.

"But I've figured it out anyway, in spite of them. It's all about looking and seeing and believing and betraying.

"Hon, *Jesus* was a defector. Jesus was a defector from the Jews. Jesus was a kind of traitor. But he wasn't a traitor to God. No, he defected from the Jews in order to spy on all of mankind for God. God needed spies.

"Sounds crazy, doesn't it? But it isn't — if you figure that if God needed to send a walking, talking, breathing, flesh-and-blood man down to earth to carry out a plan of salvation that he, being omnipotent, could have done just as easily from heaven with a snap of his fingers, or whatever it is that God uses to snap. If he needed an ordinary man to carry out his plan, then he could have needed — he probably did need — an ordinary man to get information for him. He needed a spy. Jesus was a spy. And in order to do the good work of his holy spying, he had to defect from the Jews, who didn't go in for that kind of stuff. Their God — the wrong God, of course — liked to argue and command, rant and rage and get revenge, but he didn't like to spy.

"Then there's Judas, who defected from Jesus in order to spy for the Romans, maybe the Jews, too, maybe just the

Jews. I don't know that specifically, but it doesn't matter. What I do know is that Judas had to do it. He had to defect from Jesus and spy on him in order to make Jesus mortal again, in order to get the clock running right again.

"There's nothing worse than time not going in the one direction it's supposed to be going in. You get chaos, you get absolute meaninglessness, which is worse, far worse, than any of the tragedies you think the world has to offer. What you get is no world at all.

"And that's what the agency wants. That's what the late Congressman Earl Dillingham and all his devil-worshipping friends wanted. That's what Matt Medium and those of them that are left still want. They want chaos. They want time out of control. They want no world at all. They hate the world because they know that just its mere existence means that there's more good around than evil. So they know that the only way they can call the complete evil they want into being is to destroy the entire world. Can you imagine that, Stretch, baby, no world at *all!*

"But I figured it out even though they didn't want me to. I started figuring there was something funny when the agency sent me to blow up Matt Medium's mansion — yes, Stretch, hon, I did do things like that for the agency; I was no angel, I never told you I was an angel. And then he turned up working for the agency right here in Calvary!

"I started thinking about what they gave me to do it with, that stuff that made a big, blue-white explosion that was different than all the other kinds of explosions the agency said I was going to deal with. It was like a surgical explosion, like an excavation more than anything else. It did something funny, like it collapsed things in on themselves, at least at the core of the explosion, rather than blasting them outward. It made holes in time that a person was thrown into. It didn't explode people, it collapsed them into points of disappearance; it hurled them back through time to when there was no time, and extinguished them. That's worse than killing, hon, that's erasing, that's extermination with no trace left. That's killing a person's whole history along with the person.

"Maybe it had rays of some kind. Maybe it was stuff left over from the atomic bomb. Maybe some of it got onto me, maybe the rays penetrated me. Maybe that's why our Robo turned out the way he did, the reason he had the strange talents he had. It wasn't my goddamned training him — sorry, hon, the language, I know — it wasn't my training him. I know that now. All that was a joke. Maybe the agency wanted me to believe I was doing something, so that I wouldn't know. Oh, hon, Robo could have been an experiment!

"The Brothers know about this, too, hon, The Brothers of Jesus. Oh, I know what you think of them, and I think some of that, too. The weird sex and the drugs, I know about that. But they're up against the agency, Stretch; they're up against Matt Medium and you and me and all of science and everything that's making chaos in the world. They do some bad things, but they have to do bad things because they're trying to stop the world from ending. I mean that, hon: The world could honestly end.

"But I've figured it out, hon, and they haven't figured out yet that I have. Now I need to get out. I need to disappear, too, but just for a while. Just until I can make it right. With you and Robo and Lord Jesus. You understand, don't you, hon?"

Cynthia "Stretcher" Barr said she understood, but she didn't. She didn't understand anything anymore. The nice, stately church in Calvary where she'd met her husband had been closed down, boarded up like an abandoned hardware store, for fifteen years. There was even a for sale sign — chipped and faded from prolonged exposure to the wind, sun and snow — in front of the tall, piously elegant front entrance. The big squalling infant to whom she gave birth and the incredible physical specimen and athlete he became had vanished from her life. For all she knew, her son was dead, or had been captured and enslaved by villagers in Africa, which was the last place she'd ever heard from him. The agency where she'd typed all those years had been revealed to her not as a bastion of defense of God and country, but as a strange, almost autonomous government unto itself. And her loving, loyal, faithful husband — at least she had never had reason to doubt those qualities in him — now sat ranting at her and exposing himself to her as a professional killer with an obscene streak of apostasy.

Nevertheless, she listened and said nothing. She tried to be sympathetic, calming, while she hoped this would all blow over. After all, hadn't she recovered from her little bout of defection: being gulled by her desire for a more immediate form of salvation into going to a storefront meeting of The Brothers of Jesus and ending up on her knees, between rows of folding chairs, sucking and salivating on the penis of a man she'd never so much as said hello to until then, and swallowing the seed of a stranger?

No, she hadn't fully recovered, nor had she fully repented. She needed to make further amends to her husband. So she listened to Ken Sabe and promised him she'd do whatever he told her to do when the time came.

"...Hon," he was saying, "The Brothers of Jesus have built the most incredible computer memory bank of genealogical records in the history of mankind, and it's entirely encoded in a system which, because it's built on a matrix of what they call 'no knowledge' encryption — it's too difficult to explain to you, hon, because I hardly understand it myself. And I've been working on it out in the gym for a long time. All I know is that 'no knowledge' prevents a potential intruder, a spy, from entering the system with partial knowledge and forcing his vettor to reveal, inadvertently, further information just by his asking the necessary questions he has to ask to determine whether the intruder is indeed a spy — is almost foolproof. Are you listening, hon?"

Of course, she was listening, but only to the sound of his deep voice, and not to the perfectly ridiculous words he was saying.

"Notice that I said 'almost' foolproof, hon. It's not because there's a flaw in their thinking. The Brothers of Jesus believes that everything has a numerical pattern, that no part can be divulged to anyone without giving the whole enterprise away. The Brothers of Jesus believes in sevens. The Brothers of Jesus's own mathematicians and the agency's both believe that seven shuffles, for example, is the minimum necessary to get, for practical purposes, a random mix of playing cards. The Brothers of Jesus believes that ultimately, however, all random number generators will fall into patterns of seven, and that these patterns mean that the universe of matter and space is finite and that the patterns will then repeat themselves into serial time so that the universe of time and space will go on indefinitely. But in going on in patterns of seven, it will only repeat itself endlessly. It will not truly exist, but only be a shadow, a ghost of one of its seven former incarnations. The world will, in short, have ended, only we just won't know it.

"Now I, hon, think differently. I believe that, on the other hand, a true random number generator is possible. I think that if you take any number as X, divide it by the product of two prime numbers, take the remainder as X and repeat the process, it will generate random numbers infinitely. That means there is no pattern of seven. It means that the world is contingent. And it means that it would be possible, by applying this knowledge in ways that you or I can't quite imagine — but the agency sure as hell can — to spin out an infinite number of universes, each of them as real, more or less, as the next.

"The point is this, hon: The agency knows about the records and, worse, Matt Medium knows about the records. And while Matt has been flying around up there in that strange airplane, using some kind of weird thing he calls the 'ether lens' to try to see right through the mountain into The Brothers of Jesus's genealogical vaults, the agency has been sending every little number, every little electrical impulse that Matt Medium can sense and they can measure, through some kind of giant number cruncher. And I know what they're doing. They think that if they can find some kind of numerical pattern to all this, that if they can find a reversal of time in certain people connected by blood — and I have a hunch they're talking about paternity, not maternity — that they'll be able to find out how to throw the whole world into chaos. The agency just wants to know so that they will be the first and only ones to know, so that they can keep time reversal from being used against America. Maybe that's all they really want; maybe they're innocent.

"But Matt Medium is different. He wants to know for other reasons that I think are connected with his so-called 'cheap' accelerator that, for some insane reason, the agency is actually letting him build out there in the desert. And I think that Matt has some idea that I, because I'm the father of Robo — wherever he is, God bless him — that I'm some kind of laboratory sample for him to experiment with.

"I think he's plotting to kidnap me, hon. I think he's going to make a move on me real soon, and he's going to do it with the agency's help. He's slowly been building a case that I'm some kind of traitor, that I've been giving secrets away. That's why he flies over our house all the time. You can't see him, he's up there so damned high, but I can see him. And I know he's really up there. And I think he's coming to get me.

"But I know a few things he doesn't know. I know a few things that The Brothers of Jesus knows that he doesn't know. Hon, are you listening?"

Cynthia replied, "All I know is that you're about to ask me to do something that I won't really want to do. But you know, Ken, dearest darling, I'll do it. So just tell me what it is. You don't have to tell me why. You don't have to do all this explaining."

Ken Sabe leaned across the table, took his wife's small white hand in his two giant reddened paws and looked into her eyes. He was crying.

"I know something about Robo. It took me a long time to figure out, but I know it now. But I don't know what to do about it. That is, I won't know what to do about it until I can do this: take what I know about Robo into the genealogical vaults in The Brothers of Jesus's mountain, and run them through their computer. Then I will know for sure; then I will know enough to stop Matt Medium from bringing complete evil unto the world."

Cynthia thought: I ought to be astonished; I ought to be horrified at what's happened to my husband's mind. But I'm not. I am, oddly, perfectly cool and calm and ready to help him. But first, just for my own peace of mind, I must ask him: "Is Robo alive?"

"Yes, hon, I think he is."

"Are you going to bring him back to us?"

"I'm going to try."

"How are you going to get into The Brothers of Jesus's mountain?"

"I have been talking to someone inside, against regulations. He's said they'll allow me in to do what I have to do, provided I share what I find with them."

"Can you trust The Brothers of Jesus?"

"I have no other choice."

"Will you come back to me?"

"If I am able to come back at all, I'll come back to you. You know that, hon."

"Yes, I guess I do."

★ ★ ★ ★ ★

Even by springtime Calvary standards, the night was unusually pleasant. The higher sky was black and crystal clear, so that the ancient idea of the cosmos as a dark dome with pinholes punched in it by the needle of God so that his bright and holy light might shine like diamonds through it seemed the aptest description. The lower stratum of the sky, the one that Ken Sabe and Stretcher Barr walked pseudononchalantly in, across the cement apron from their side door to their newish car, a grey-green four-wheel drive prettification of a Jeep, was stirred by a slight, balmy breeze. The air was dry, as usual, but the perfume of high desert flowers hung in it like bait on thousands of invisible hooked lines.

Cynthia "Stretcher" Barr wore a simple, swaying skirt, a dark blue turtle neck, whitish Fair Isle sweater, and a pair of practical, but nevertheless slightly dressy, low-heeled shoes. She was hatless, purseless, but held a set of car keys, ringed to a can of Mace, in her right hand. Ken Sabe was garbed entirely in dark blue: jeans, canvas-and-suede light hiking boots, turtleneck identical to Cynthia's save for its much larger size, dyed leather bomber jacket, thin knit gloves, and sized, not plastic-banded wool New York Yankee baseball cap with the white insignia covered by three short strips of black electrical tape. Ken Sabe carried a small canvas duffel — also dark blue — in his left hand.

Cynthia unlocked and opened the driver's side door — an action which also, electronically, opened the passenger's side door — and got in. Ken Sabe tossed his duffel into the back seat and settled quickly into his seat. The click of their safety belts' being fastened was simultaneous within nanoseconds.

Ken Sabe had decided to split the surveillance difference. If he had skulked to the car and gotten in without igniting the dome light a half-hour, or so, ahead of Cynthia, he could have concealed himself from the agency watchers he knew had been stationed around his cul-de-sac for a couple of months now. But Cynthia's driving out for a solo errand at night would have attracted just as much attention from their shadows as this openly dual departure. If he walked openly, slowly and upright to the car, he figured, the surveillance personnel might notice Cynthia's perky getup more and ignore, to an extent, his swat team couture. Cynthia, at his behest, lighted the dome light once the doors had been closed and checked her lipstick in the visor's backside mirror. They were hardly being surreptitious.

Cynthia backed the 4WD smoothly onto Delano Circle, stopped dutifully at the highway intersection, and made a neat, cautious right turn. She left the highway after a couple of miles for another county road that drifted up into the lowest foothills. It was curvier than the highway, offered better views and more enjoyable driving; there was nothing unusual in anyone's taking it into Calvary on a circuitous, nonstop pleasure drive on a night like this, except that the road looped the town and then entered from the other end, near the high school, closer to town but not that far from the point on the main highway where a live-in Airstream trailer was parked by the side of the road. Cynthia had seen it once, asked Ken Sabe who lived there, and had been told "some trapper, who's got about as much chance of catching anything with fur on it living out there as I have of being made director of the agency."

They passed the high school. Ken Sabe thought the bleachers in dim, backlight silhouette looked like multiple gallows. He said so to Cynthia. She said he was morbid. She said she was nervous enough about what she was doing and asked him not to talk anymore.

He obeyed her, except to utter, a few minutes later, one word: "Here."

When he said the word, Cynthia moved the 4WD into the right lane, levering her blinker on even though, as far as she could tell, there wasn't another vehicle — except for a parked car or two — in town that night. She put the gearbox into neutral and coasted, slowing. Their car was going about fifteen miles per hour in a dark patch between streetlights when Ken Sabe, in one quick, fluid motion that would have been astounding in its grace, silence and efficiency to anyone but Cynthia, rolled himself over the seatback into the rear compartment of the car. As Ken landed, and crouched below sill level, Cynthia reached into the foot well on the passenger side and brought two dark pillows, which had been taped and tied together, to an upright position in the passenger seat. The small pillow on top wore a Yankee cap.

The car rolled into the glare of streetlights, along the section of downtown curb that had been ridiculously furnished with parking meters (anyone driving into Calvary, even during what there were of rush hours, could always find at least ten free slots). She was directly in front of Keller's Hardware & Outdoor Supplies, then the single motion picture palace oddly named The Cossack, then the laundromat that had replaced the one taken over by The Brothers of Jesus, which was further down the street, unilluminated.

As Cynthia's vehicle left the last edge of motionless shower of light from the streetlamps, and cruised into darkness, the right rear door of the car opened and closed almost instantaneously, with hardly a sound. Cynthia and her pillow-husband continued on down the highway to the point were the town's architecture gave out entirely. Then she made a serene, leisurely U-turn, and drove slowly back through Calvary in the other direction, talking somewhat animatedly — so the surveillance later reported — to what appeared to be her husband. But Ken Sabe, a man with a six-foot-five frame and huge hands, had several minutes earlier been able to roll like an indigo tumbleweed into one of Calvary's few alleys, and disappear, as far as the agency ever knew, forever.

It's Beginning to Look a Lot Like the End

The Brothers of Jesus's computer patch into the pictures sent back by the extra-terrestrial Hubble telescope was, for all intents and purposes, as good as the agency's. And the data interpretations were almost as good, too. A rock on the surface of Mars was called "Dutch Shoe" by an agency drone, and "bent Midas Muffler" by a religious fellatee under the Idaho mountain. When the satellite lenses swung around to peer into deep space, the man strapped to an agency screen said, "We're going to see right back to the beginning of time, you know that, don't you?"

And the subterranean bearded man in denim overalls said (roughly simultaneously), "We run these suckers through Time Wave Zero and we're home free, no one can touch us." Both gave only the smallest thought to the remote possibility that the rocks not only looked like "something," but were "something" too, beside rocks.

Nytibia Barbosell, of course, had her own suite of excavated rooms in The Brothers of Jesus's labyrinth, from which, increasingly, she seldom emerged. When she did, she wore her ceremonial Bishop's hooded cloak, and it was almost impossible for anybody to see her face clearly. Rumors circulated underground that a cancer was ravaging her looks.

Nytibia also had her own outsized and overpowered computer, with her own feed from the Hubble. Nevertheless, she demanded, as Bishop, that "reports" in the form of color photocopies of still pictures taken from screens in the outer chambers be brought to her personally. When they were, she said to the young chaylen who brought it, "I yem so fairy heppy to be served in the nem uf our Lord." The chaylen noticed the change in the Bishop's accent. When he'd heard her address The Gathered Body of The Brothers of Jesus at services, her elocution was tinged (as far as his uneducated ear could tell) with a bit of German. But what he noticed more — a thousand times more — was her unhooded face in that unlighted room, caught in the monitor's glow. She looked to be at least one hundred years old.

★ ★ ★ ★ ★

"Benny The Jaw" Spumante was living a miserable life, cooped up in a small apartment, on Sullivan Street, in SoHo, on the fourth floor of a building with an Italians-only "dominoes and social club" in the rear of the ground floor. The ground floor's storefront contained a laundromat which was, except for the absence of a sign reading, DON'T TALK. THIS PLACE IS BUGGED, the exact duplicate of The Brothers of Jesus's original headquarters in Calvary, Utah.

"Benny the Jaw" stayed dressed, twenty-four hours a day, in one of three pairs of identical, dark blue polka dot pyjamas. When two pairs became dirty — that is, when the aroma of quarts of cheap, noxiously sweet-scented aftershave with which "Benny the Jaw" rinsed himself in lieu of taking showers wore off — an assistant appointed by the executive committee of the dominoes club retrieved them from the apartment, personally washed them (permanent press, no bleach, double ration of fabric softener) and returned them to "Benny the Jaw," who, though grateful, said nothing.

Wearing his pyjamas, sitting in a tattered, overstuffed, floral-patterned armchair the color of raw liver and French mustard, "Benny the Jaw" passed the days cuddling, and gazing upon, his memorabilia, which included:

Several rolled black-and-yellow prizefight posters advertising — in the small type near the bottom reserved for the depths of the undercard — the heavyweight bouts of Ken Sabe; a creased glossy photograph of a toothily smiling Imeda Jinsokt, in a soft, white booth of a wartime Berlin nightclub, her arm around Reichsminister Oeups, who looked, for all his regalia, decidedly nonplussed; a highly detailed, very accurate (although derived from bootlegged plans) plastic model of an aircraft known in the vernacular (by some people) as the "Shakey J"; a bible with a white plastic cover whose edges rolled partially over the pages, imprinted in peeling gold letters, "Gift of the Noam Sain Ministry, Pasadena, California"; four red-wine-stained pamphlets from "The Amazing Memoranda Mental Maintenance System"; a videotape (though "Benny the Jaw" possessed no radio, let alone a television set, let alone a VCR) of "The ABA's Greatest Bloopers and Blunders (featuring never-before-seen footage of that 'Where Is He Now' Man we all knew simply as 'Robo'!)"; a form letter, soliciting donations, from one Nytibia Barbosell, Bishop, The Brothers of Jesus, Calvary, Idaho; an uncracked hardbound copy of Rose Madder's dual biography of Dieric Maender and John Singer Sargent (*"Penetrating, authoritative, and unusually readable* — Matt Medium, independent scholar," it said on the back of the dustjacket); another plastic airplane model, this one of a Sikorsky DL-117; a "commemorative" William Halliwell wall calendar for the current year, with the dates of each "Great Disappointment" noted in the appropriate box; and an autographed, hardbound first edition (there was only one edition) of Billy Lockjaw's first novel, *Route 12, through Whistletune.*

Despite his comfortable chair and fond possessions, "Benny The Jaw" was afraid for his life. He was convinced he would be assassinated — if he ever left his apartment alone for the street, even for a moment — either by The

Brothers of Jesus, the agency, Ken Sabe, or a Nazi who would say, mockingly, with the voice of Axis Sally as she set off the strange, blue explosion that would blow him in the opposite direction of Heaven, "How's that for action, boxing fans?"

"Benny The Jaw" prayed, and wept, incessantly.

Then, one morning, he said to the assistant from the dominoes club who was bringing him two pairs of neatly washed and folded pyjamas, "I godda get da fuck outta here."

The assistant said, "But Benny, you never go nowhere. You're all tore up inside about goin' out. You sure you can handle it? A short walk to Washington Square, maybe. I'll check with the guys. I think we can manage that."

"No," "Benny The Jaw" said. "I mean I really godda go. For good. Da time has come. I wancha do me a favor."

"Anything," the assistant said, like a gofer in a film noir, not meaning it.

"I wancha go up ta Grand Central an' get me an open ticket from New York to as close as you can fuggin' get to a place called Calvary, Idaho."

"Calvary? Idaho?"

"Yeah, like with Jesus."

"By fuckin' train?"

"Benny the Jaw" turned his reddened eyes toward the model of the "Shakey J." "Damn right. Flying's too fuggin' risky."

"A fuckin' train ticket, to some fuckin' shithole town in Idaho?"

"Don' laugh, just do it. And you don' hafta tell anybody downstairs about it. Special favor. Dere's a hunnert in it for ya."

The assistant bought the ticket, took the two fifties, and told anyway.

★ ★ ★ ★ ★

Noam Sain was living with Conchita Memoranda in the newly built "Wayfarers' Inn," one of The Brothers of Jesus's more recent real estate enterprises, just outside the borders (and minimal building codes) of Calvary, Idaho. The luxury-class motel [If having your own Dr. Pepper vending machine in your room is your idea of luxury. *Quack.*] was actually turning a nice profit, thanks to the confluence of chaylen wannabes (toting power-of-attorney forms, ready to be signed), mid-level cocaine wholesalers, and various overt and covert federal employees, all needing temporary lodging. Noam did not, however, live in the same room with Conchita. "The Amazing Memoranda Mental Maintenance System Foundation, Inc." had leased an entire floor — 32 rooms — to house Noam (with his laptop, modem, fax, cell phone and tangerine crate of floppy discs, at one end of the U-shaped hall), Conchita (at the other), and their chaylen pseudo-wannabe hunks, four to a room, in between.

That Conchita occasionally — no, frequently — entertained overnight one or more of their undercover-to-be athletes quickly ceased to bother Noam. Occasionally — no, frequently — he thought about Conchita's precious handjob, thirty years ago, in the chiaroscuro'd confines of his old Ford, on Roubidoux Street, while Señor Memoranda's gangrenous foot prevented him from falling into anything but fitful sleep. The memory no longer prompted a full erection from Noam. Actually, nothing did anymore. His testicles had metaphorically ascended to his brain where, bile replacing semen as their chief export, Noam's only hard-on had to do with The Brothers of Jesus. And Nytibia.

It could be and yet it couldn't be. Nytibia and Imeda, Imeda and Nytibia. They didn't look alike, they didn't talk alike, and — if the billions of bytes in the tangerine crate held any truth among them — the trajectories of their lives had never crossed other than, unsimultaneously, through him. Yet the three greatest horrors of his life (not counting, of course, the trauma of that night at Matt Medium's mansion) — being deserted, having his family slaughtered in Oregon, and then, in an ignominious domestic coup, being deposed as Bishop of The Brothers of Jesus — seemed to have a certain (how should he say it to himself?) moral symmetry.

[Oh *tell* them, Billy! About the sympathy aroused by a stinky old lady plucked from the bowels of bombed-out Berlin, about ex-Nazis and the agency's overriding sense of utilitarianism, about what dermatological surgeons, even back in the '60s, could accomplish at Walter Reed Army Hospital after hours, in the burn ward, about what the feds would have given — and gave they did! — to get their hands on Time Wave Zero, not to mention a couple of hundred pounds of pure, uncut nose candy. Oh, tell, do! *Quack.*]

★ ★ ★ ★ ★

While Noam sat in his room computing, while Conchita lay in hers copulating, while their jocky trainees roamed the halls of the Wayfarers' Inn waiting for their final, prove-it-or-lose-it assignment in the rigorous curriculum of "The Amazing Memoranda Mental Maintenance System," The Brothers of Jesus began the retreat into the now almost completed community of bunkers under the mountain. The Gathered Body of The Brothers of Jesus (those who lived in the dormitories and, then, under the mountain) had summoned The Greater Body of The Brothers of Jesus (supporters — often relatives — who still lived in the outside world, but who gave, and prayed) to witness the result of William Halliwell's prophecies, as interpreted by Time Wave Zero, projected forward to the date picked from the Mayan calendar by the departed (and uncredited)

Noam Sain, and filtered through the most recent readings from the Hubble telescope. In other words, more or less the end of the world.

There were cars backed up for miles on the highway leading to the gate. The various police agencies, not knowing what to make of the procession, but not wanting to incite something they couldn't handle, sent a few men to lay down flares and direct traffic. But the serpentine was orderly, even passive, even trancelike, and the armed men in uniform had very little to do. At the end of only two days, all the cars belonging to members of The Greater Body of The Brothers of Jesus were parked in neat, parallel crescent rows just inside the locked fence. And the people in them had all been swallowed up by the landscape.

With nothing but silence and wind to police, the authorities went home.

A Man's Got to Due

I am flying down the highway.

This is my last chance to make it right. This is my last chance to explain it to you. This is my last chance to explain it to myself. I'll have to talk pretty damned fast. No guarantees. I could lose the bike at any moment.

They've always called me Robo. All right, I am Robo. If that's all the name they're going to give me, then that's what I'll take. I'm big enough to face my fate, and smart enough to face my history. Robo's all right with me. I don't need to be anybody else but Robo. I am big Robo, solid Robo, fearsome Robo, weird Robo. I am Robo curled up in his trailer all day, seeing no one, no one seeing him, Robo out on his little homemade track in the middle of the night because he just can't take being alone all night as well as all day, because he can't take being strange and stupid any longer; I am Robo running his absurd hundred yard dashes, trying to make his harder, older body move through space the way it used to.

Did I tell you I did a goddamned nine-one the other night? Legit, too, maybe even faster, because my incomparable neuromuscular system hesitated just a tick before I clicked the stopwatch button. I felt good. Little beads of sweat like cool moons clung to my tanned-brown flesh. Yeah, I think it was probably more like nine-fucking-flat.

So, I am Robo the magnificent, and there's a lesson for everybody in me: If you're going to try to slowly change somebody from a human being into a veritable robot, you might as well do a good, complete job of it, right? You might as well make a real impressive specimen, and not an imitation of some clumsy, overgrown oaf you could find any day on the streets of Calvary, Idaho, or in the halls of Calvary High School, for that matter. And, lo, I am that miracle model. I am that which they made.

Are you surprised? Did you think my father made me? Did you think all that ridiculous training from a crude, lumbering, failed jock who didn't really know beans about fining and faring and truing the human body (forget "mind" for the moment) is what made me? No, oh no no no. *They* made me, and they did a goddamned good job of it. Am I not strong? Am I not fast? Am I not blessed with silky co-ordination and the reflexes of a lizard's tongue? Am I not one big sonofabitch in the bargain?

And do I not have a little of the poet's touch? Yes, I do. And that is the problem, for *them*. They forgot to take out my soul, which would have prevented the growth of the poet inside me. Oh, I admit "poet" is an overstatement. On a scale of real poets, the ones they forgot to teach me about in that crummy college, I probably sound merely like a bleat-ing, wounded bear. But for all my shortcomings (Ha!), for all the strands of lovingly developed purple muscle fastened to my bones, I know that I feel — inside, in my soul — as intensely as any real poet. I know that something is beat-ing, almost bursting, within my chest. And I know that I must find the words to tell it all.

A fine time to start — hurtling down the highway (a poetic way of putting it, no?) at about a hundred and twenty miles an hour on this ratty old RS1000. The ma-chine is roaring like hell beneath me; it sounds like it has no muffler at all. It sounds like a neverending explosion, an interminable, eternal bomb. Maybe it'll throw a rod. For all I know, smoke is pouring out behind me, and I'm about to blow the goddamned engine. I don't know, because I can't see anything in the mirrors. It's night. Deep into the night, creeping back toward dawn. But still as black as grief.

Out here, night is solid and thick; you feel like you're

frozen in ebony ice. But I'm moving through it, going like hell, in fact. The air all around me is as still as a boulder, but the bike cutting through it makes a wind that's like needles shooting into my cheeks, which are rippling in the wind like pennants. The asphalt road streaks by underneath the motorcycle's chrome carriage, lighted by the half-moon, like a mad, speckled river.

It's peculiarly soothing. I think maybe I'd like to jump off the bike, jump in for a swim. But I'm not quite that mad. I'd hit that grinding wheel of a road and my skin would fly all over this desert like a scattered flock of bloody pink crows. Still, part of me says the road is an illusion. It's there and it's not at the same time. If I think it's there in all its concrete vengeance, then it can't be moving so fast beneath me. Nothing moving that fast beneath me can be there, there, there, and there all at once. But if it's not there, if the sliding grey is really something sliding and grey, then what holds me up, what allows the bike its traction? I can compound the feeling by closing my eyes. (Don't worry, I'll pick a straight stretch of road.) One's coming up.

There: eyes closed. *One, two, three, four* — where is my mind? Is it actually moving at speed across this patch of earth — *nine, ten, eleven*? Or is my mind the reality, the reliable, fixed, and stationary point through, by, and around which this intolerable world passes at speed? *Nineteen, twenty* —

Open. I can see the darkness again, as opposed to thinking it. Yes, of course, I could have been killed. While I was huddled sightless within my own mind, a cement wall could have materialized across the highway and the bike and I could have rammed it full on, at speed. I would have felt — what — a slamming pinprick of collision?

And then nothing, most likely. Stillness, nothing. The point is, I would have felt like I'd been annihilated — while still enclosed within a stationary mind — by an inexplicable wall presented to me by the world as it sped by. But if my eyes were open, and I braked, or swerved, or lost the bike because I saw the wall, then the world is real and I'm just a poor, ignorant, pitiful, ruined body speeding through it on my way to nowhere.

What the fuck is the difference, you ask? All the difference in the world.

Nowhere is where it feels like I'm going — fast, down, and deep into this ungodly cold. The cold cuts through my scruffy leather jacket in flapping sheets of freeze. My hands are numb on the grips. If something did happen, if something did appear in the road, I probably couldn't even uncurl my fingers in time to lock the brakes. But I don't let up on the gas.

I can't hear a goddamned thing other than the engine. Can anyone else hear the bike? Is there even anyone out here to hear the bike? I can see a couple of sparkling dots on the horizon, another halfway up a foothill — probably a dwelling of some sort, probably a miner or rancher who's fast asleep now and sees this landscape mostly in the glorious, symphonic daylight when every fence post and every pebble is a jewel with sharp shadows underneath to set it sharply and gloriously into the golden surround.

Fancy talk, huh? Fancy talk from a will-o'-the-wisp mesomorph careening through the night on a Beemer on its last legs, tearing the hell out of a dying engine just to get down the black road to nowhere as fast as he fucking can. You betchum, Red Ryder. Where else have I got to go? Where else can I take my big useless body with its primitive soul and its half-formed mind? What else to do with it? It has no purpose, probably never did, even to them that made it. It was a just one of those for-the-hell-of-it, let's see if it works things. Pure research, or pure faith, one of the two — if there's a difference.

Christ almighty, its cold. Let's see if we can kick up the speed a notch and make it a little bit colder. The speedometer says a hundred and thirty-one, but that's just the average between the wild ends of the wiggle of the needle. It snaps over to a hundred and forty once in a while. Like there. But the speedometer isn't any more reliable than anything else I'm telling you. You read it where you want to read it; you pick the instant on the oscillation you want and say yes, that's the truth, right there, and everything else is just chaos, noise, irrelevance, panic.

Let's say I want it to be hundred and forty; maybe you want it to be a hundred and twenty. For a split second now and then, we're both right. Then we're both wrong again.

The cold hurts now. And I'm a man used to living with pain. My father caused most of it. My father, Ken Sabe. Hell of a name, ain't it?. He made it up. He told us some illiterate trainer back in his fighting days gave it to him. He never told us the real one, however. The man was a deliberate stranger to his own family. Who knows what his real name is? Who knows out of the end of whose dick he came? *¿Quien sabe?* Ha!

So he's my father. But he's not the one who made me who I am. So what did he do for me? It's what he didn't do for me. He never pulled me out of the pit they dug. He never gave me back my soul. He never loved me. Maybe that sounds trite. But not to me, not right now, not with me trying to get to nowhere as fast as I fucking can without this bike shaking apart right under me. Not with the scream of these frantic cylinders in my ears, not with no one nearer to me than five miles. Not with anyone ever nearer to me, really, than a thousand miles.

Ken Sabe, my father — heavyweight stooge, agency goon, and now, I gather (I have my sources) loose-cannon double spook on the run — saw to all that. Yeah, I think he's a double, that is if he knows what he's doing at all. But he may not. He may have mirrors in his head by now, and think that every reflection on any of them is the real thing, the real ordered world, the authority to whom he should report. He always needed an authority. At first it was his coach, then it was that guinea gangster in New York, and his seconds. Then it was the agency. He deluded himself into thinking he was training me when all the time he was training himself.

He bought the line that he was raising a super son in his own self-aggrandized image. The big guy with the big hands in the little school, who beat the shit — in the metaphor of organized competition, of course — out of anybody he cared to, thought he could raise his own coagulated semen to the same dubiously wonderful level through the application of his own devotion to physical pain. He was trying so hard to set up a regimen for me that he probably didn't have time to think, in any proper sense. To him, I was just the meat that fleshed out his mission.

Tires on a rusty, rickety contraption he built in the back yard — what a fucking joke. A corrugated metal gym building right at home — the ugliest goddamned thing you ever saw. Some borrowed scientists popping over from the agency on their lunch hours or after work, spouting biofeedback theories and drinking my poor, innocent mother's homemade iced tea. And him believing all that complicated psychological shit they told him about his son's beleaguered synapses. He thought he was building a super human being in me, but he was just slowly unmasking himself as the unquestioning drone he always was, losing whatever humanity he had in pointless graphs, charts, schedules, weighings and timings all centered on me. He became my clock, my scale, my stopwatch. Not a father, just a monitor. An idiot to start with, he became a heartless idiot.

Now, confused and panicked, he's a headless idiot as well. The irony of it is that the agency never really needed him for this dirty work. If he'd had the capacity to think, he could have figured it out. The agency could have just as well boarded me out to the scientists, raised me inside the fence. Maybe not. What would they have done with mom? Taking me outright would have sent her around the bend. The wonder is that living with Ken Sabe didn't do it sooner.

So why didn't I tell you all this before? Simply because I didn't know this before. I didn't know anything before. I knew nothing. Up to the time my father went AWOL — or whatever they call it in the agency — I didn't know he was a double. I didn't know that up until the time he was a double, he was a dupe of the agency who did the dirty work of turning his own son into a robot with a cheerful guilelessness. I didn't know that The Brothers of Jesus wanted him. I didn't know that he'd be quite stupid enough to go.

Now that I know all that, I can't hide anymore. I can't stay out there by the side of the highway in the Airstream and run hundred-yard dashes in the middle of the night so that, maybe, I can at last lose this terrible body that my father, and the agency, foisted on me. I can't disappear forever; I can only do it in flashes that always land me back on earth.

Whatever my father did to me, I simply kept on moving. When in doubt, move — that's always been it with me. On the court — in that awful split second of doubt when you know that either the points will come from the flow of your magical hands, or that the points will be taken from you by, say, a momentary mispositioning of one or two fingers — I always chose to move. I moved quickly, decisively, with my whole body. And I moved into the tangle of bodies, not away from it. I sought human density, not isolation. You might say I sought companionship, but that's probably a stretch.

The thing is, I moved toward the heat. And lo and behold, sometimes I found it, sometimes I hit a flash point. Then I was gone for a millisecond or two, and popped up somewhere else, just far enough away from the web of limbs to drop the ball into the basket. I always moved toward the heat, and not the cold.

Christ, it's getting even colder. More speed, Jeeves. It looks like this old kraut hog can't give any more. I'm top-ending it now, trying to take more than the old bike can give. The bike has limits. I have limits. They must have built in some limitations. They must have put in some checks so that, whatever else I did, I wouldn't move so fast I'd anni-hilate myself. They must have built me so that I'd always be around. We'll just keep the needle leaning way over to the right, and see what happens.

You think I'm crazy, don't you? You wonder how I can be so certain of some great, profound pattern, and yet so hazy on the details. How can I be so sure that something beside mom-and-dad fucking created me, yet still be unable to point to a single screw or wire on my whole magnificent frame? I'm like one of those quiet maniacs you read about in the newspapers who kills a dozen people and then says voices inside his head — voices he says are certainly not his own — ordered him to do it. You think I'm like that. You think that living alone inside an aluminum hull all these years has cut me off from reality. But I can tell you that it has only connected me with reality. And I am a better, if unhappier, man for it.

★ ★ ★ ★ ★

Up ahead, there it is. On the left, where the mountains break and you can get a peek at the horizon again. A little grey light. Look closer. The grey breaks apart — into a transparent, climbing curtain of blue that blends upward into the black ceiling sprinkled with stars, and, underneath, a thin snake of fire hugging the earth. Soon, in minutes, the snake will win, and the sky will turn honey at the horizon. Night is over. But not the cold.

The cold ends only in forgiveness.

I must forgive him, for believing he could give me a body that would survive this pit of mortality, for not wanting to believe that those who said they'd help him do it only wanted a human machine, not a son.

He's coming to The Brothers of Jesus, I know it.

He's lost me, he's lost mom, he's lost the agency. Where else has he got to go but to them? He'll try to show them about time, show them that he understands that salvation means turning it around. But he doesn't really have anything to give them except empty mechanics and a guilty soul. But I can show them. I can be his evidence. I can give my body back to him and let him offer it to them. Maybe I can even forgive them, too.

The race, for good ol' Robo, is over.

But — *Jesus motherfucking Christ* — I'm losing the goddamned bike!

An ice patch, maybe. Perhaps just a little bit of water in a dip. The rear tire, old and bald, leans into the moisture and cannot hold its edge. I feel my buttocks sink, the handlebars rise.

Pushing down on the grips, I turn the front wheel to the left, slightly, in the direction of my impending slide, hoping the better tread at the front will catch on drier pavement, hoping that I can stay close enough to forty-five degrees to claw my way back to speed. The danger is that I'll make speed, but be unable to change course again. The toe of my right boot kisses the rushing road; the highway grinds like a lathe, and in an instant the road is through to my skin. Blood and gravel.

But the front wheel has caught. I have traction. I stomp on the pegs and lurch forward, shoulders almost directly over the headlight, trailing a burning, bloody toe. The rear wheel exits the edge of the water patch, and the bike whips like a casting rod — upright, too far, fishtailing, back to a rightward lean, fishtailing the other way, and then upright again. Course corrected, safe.

No, not really. I am across the left lane, the dotted line in the middle of the road a Rubicon only a few feet, but forever nevertheless, behind me. I am headed for the ditch, still doing at least a hundred. I leave the pavement, barrel in a split second through the gravelly shoulder, and plant the front wheel in the culvert beyond.

The powers of disappearance have apparently abandoned me. I am shackled, this go-round, to the unbroken continuum of time. I must endure the moment full. My arms both break at the elbow, but the impact still practically tears my shoulders from my torso. The seat is a catapult, and sends me high and helpless and flailing into the desert night. The bike cartwheels below, shedding fenders and saddlebags like a mad dancer. It hits the ground, skids through the scrimpy brush, and settles to a stop before I do. I have further to go, and more to consider, before I return to earth.

Sky and ground alternate like repeated lecture slides, one, then the other, then the first again. The sky stays more or less the same — blackish blue, with a dusting of stars, and an orange fringe whose location changes from left to right and back again each time around — but the ground changes. A grey-green featureless carpet, then shadowed, furrowed, rutted, rocked, it comes nearer every revolution.

Then I land on my back on the ground, peculiarly painlessly, and in a funny, picturesque position: legs spread, arms outstretched, head on a rock as if I'd been tucked into bed and it lay on a pillow. Except that the spinning motion of my body has slammed me down on the stone as if by a giant holding me by the heels, and the rock has invaded my head. I think it's halfway buried in my skull. I can feel something warm cascading down my shoulders beneath the motorcycle jacket. If I move my head the slightest, I hear the crackling of eggshells.

Intelligence must reside in the frontal lobes, after all, because they're all I've got left and I am still aware of the partial moon overhead — a bit less than half — at about ten o'clock. I know what it is, the moon, and I know how I got here.

I still know where I came from and what I was trying to do. Fuck, I gave it a shot. That's all a father could ask.

Then I know nothing, truly nothing at all.

Hey, Y'all, and Farewell

Billy Lockjaw sits — in a motel room off the highway leading to Calvary. He is, however, closer to the site of Robo's demise than to the town. He has written in the past of his now.

Outside, the wet black parking apron, herring-boned with the yellow lines designating individual parking slots, is crowded with police cars, marked and unmarked. The more garish local vehicles, festooned with painted words and candy-machine complexes of cab-top lights, belong to the cowboy-shirted town and county authorities who are investigating the grisly death, up the road apiece, of a large man who was riding a motorcycle and crashed in the middle of the night.

No signs of another motorcycle or car involved (the deputies are telling each other), no identification on the corpse, no worried phone calls from a next of kin saying that the rider hadn't returned home last night. The only thing they have to go on — and it isn't much — is a track timer's stopwatch found in a pocket of the motorcyclist's blood-caked leather jacket.

The more austere vehicles — blue-silver vans and se-dans without any signage — are federal property, transpor-tation for conspicuously inconspicuously grey-suited agents concerned with intelligence-gathering and drug enforce-ment. Although the vehicles are spotless, with uncluttered interiors, atop their hoods and beneath their carriages lie (uneasily, pivoting and rolling on the ground in the gentle breezes) white styrofoam coffee cups leaking small amounts of cold, tan, coffee-cum-nondairy-creamer. The agents prefer to talk to each other (about just what sort of bomb it was that has caved in the network of bunkers constructed under a nearby mountain by a religious group called The Brothers of Jesus, long known by them to be supported with the proceeds of a cocaine trade) outside the confines of rented quarters that they never quite believe have been successfully debugged.

Noam Sain never cared whether or not the motel's rooms were debugged. Once his surreptitious hunks had infiltrated The Brothers of Jesus (no great feat; in the last weeks prior to the retreat into the mountain, The Brothers of Jesus would talk to anybody who could sign a check and promise to shovel), and Conchita had started the drive back to Los Angeles to elevate her marketing from hotel seminars to television-direct, Noam checked out of The Wayfarer's Inn and into something cheaper. His money was finally running short.

But lost wealth is of no concern to the minister anymore. Noam is dead on his bed, with his laptop on his belly. "Heart attack" will be the preliminary judgment of the agency junior who will, in a few days, brave the odor, break down the door, and discover the fat blue cadaver.

But Billy is alive. Billy, no longer the writer writing, rests in the present of his then, reading slowly aloud what he has written. In Calvary, where he has come (Billy has told himself) to see this thing — the dope, the feds, the agency, The Brothers of Jesus, and the origin of his own fragile consciousness — through to the end, he has found himself no closer to the truth of it all than he was when he sequestered himself inside a small, ascetic white wooden frame house in Mylar, North Carolina. In fact, he realizes, exhausted, he may be further away.

Although Billy is adamant (to himself; and would be to us were he able to speak directly) that he has written every word of his story, he admits (to himself, and, indi-rectly — by the course of his wandering narrative — to us) that he has not been able to control it fully.

Billy would rather Robo had lived, to have had him released from exile, happily rehabilitated and reconciled with his father, and, perhaps, reincarnated in the rubble of The Brothers of Jesus's bunkers beneath the mountain (collapsed, possibly, by a bomb brought through the gate by Ken Sabe).

Billy would also rather that Nytibia Barbosell had not survived the disaster, that Noam Sain's part in the destruction of The Brothers of Jesus been made clearer, that Matt Medium's whereabouts at the time of Robo's death had been known (and that, for that matter, of the "Shakey J," oddly not in its hangar that night), and that somebody had perceived early on the full implications of Conchita Memoranda's mind control system.

He even wishes he had been kinder to "Benny The Jaw" Spumante. (Benny sits slumped in the row of seats in one of the federal vans, handcuffed, with a scruffy raincoat draped over his lap and wrists — his apprehension a small-change consolation prize to the agents in the motel parking lot.)

But, alas, Billy's story got away from him. Billy sits quite still — perhaps actually paralyzed — with his failures. He nods his head slightly, sleepily, over what he has written. And he feels (or is it that he hears?) a faint noise at the back of his head. It sounds vaguely like eggshells cracking.

★ ★ ★ ★ ★

A long haul, but I'm done with 'em now, all of 'em.

I'm pooped. You wouldn't think a guy (or a gal, or a force, a spirit, a blast from the past) like me could tire out, would you? But, hell, Billy did, and Noam did, and even indefatigable Robo did, and they're no more prone to the depletion of energy than I am.

Surprise? It shouldn't be. It ain't easy, chumleys, being the ontological court of last resort, the final, finger-leaky dike between this eschatological page and dreary nothing. Sometimes I don't know why I do it.

Maybe there's just nothing better to do. When I don't do my duty — when I cease for even a proton's twitch to serve as the connecting tissue among all the particles of all the souls who, without me, would be lost to history, when I cease to allow the words from the tortured Billys to flow through me — the universe actually stops. Or it disappears. As it will now, in a second, when I finally bow out.

But be not afraid, chumleys. Another universe, with just a few minor variations in detail, will immediately replace it. Watch.

Quack!